Jeanne Whitmee bega[...]ss. After her marriage and a period spent as a teacher of speech and drama, she achieved a lifelong ambition to become a professional writer. She worked for some years as a freelance writer for popular women's magazines, writing short stories, serials and, at one time, a weekly column. To date she has published more than thirty novels under various pseudonyms.

Jeanne Whitmee has two married daughters and four grandchildren and now lives with her husband in Cambridgeshire.

Eve's Daughter

Jeanne Whitmee

WARNER BOOKS

With grateful thanks to James Bain
of Granada Television
for technical advice.

A *Warner* Book

First published in Great Britain in 1998
by Judy Piatkus (Publishers) Ltd
This edition published by Warner Books 1999

A catalogue record for this book
is available from the British Library.

ISBN 0 7515 2568 5

Typeset by Hewer Text Limited, Edinburgh
Printed and bound in Great Britain by
Mackays of Chatham plc, Chatham, Kent

Warner Books
A Division of
Little, Brown and Company (UK)
Brettenham House
Lancaster Place
London WC2E 7EN

Chapter One

Northampton, September 1941
'Got room for a little 'un, Mrs Kenning?'

Eve snapped off the hall light as she opened the street door and stepped out on to the pavement, the better to see who her visitor was. Alf Barnes, the local billeting officer, stood outside, accompanied by another figure that was barely more than a shadow in the half light.

'What do you mean, Mr Barnes? Who've you got there?' She peered through the gathering autumn dusk at the girl half hidden by the billeting officer's bulk. She looked hardly more than a schoolgirl. Surely they weren't still evacuating kids from London? But as Eve's eyes accustomed themselves to the gloom she saw that the slender, fair-haired girl was older than she'd first thought: in her late-teens perhaps.

'This is Mrs Tyler,' Alf said. 'Just up from Portsmouth to work at Samson's along with a dozen other lasses recruited into munitions. Minute I clapped eyes on her I thought of you – working there too and being on your own, like.' He looked at Eve hopefully, his head on one side. 'Well, what do you say then?'

Mrs Tyler! Eve's eyes widened. So this girl was married? Jack and Eve Kenning had moved into the little terraced house at 17 Brook's Lane when they'd married just eighteen months before the war broke out in '39. But ever since Jack had joined up Eve had lived here alone. A lame excuse rose to her lips. In spite of her loneliness she felt oddly reluctant to share her home with this young

1

woman. Then she noticed how dog-tired the girl looked and immediately felt ashamed of her selfishness.

'Of course she can stay,' she said, guilt making her over-effusive. 'Come on in.'

'Just the ticket!' Alf beamed. 'I knew you'd say that.' He heaved the girl's suitcase in through the door before Eve had a chance to change her mind, clearly relieved at placing another of his charges. 'Right. Well, I'll leave you to get to know each other then,' he said, stepping backwards. 'Watch that blackout now, Mrs Kenning. G'night, ladies.'

In the narrow hall Eve closed the door carefully before switching the light back on. The blackout precautions had become an automatic routine after two years. In the dim light from the forty-watt bulb the two women regarded one another. The girl had shoulder-length blonde hair and she wore a red coat, cut in the fashionable military style. It had fancy buttons and a tie belt, but it was travel-creased and the material was rubbed and cheap-looking.

Eve held out her hand. 'I'm Eve Kenning,' she said with a smile.

'Sally Tyler.' The girl smiled hesitantly. 'I hope it's all right,' she spoke with a West Country burr, 'having me dumped on you like this? If it's not, just say.'

'Of course it's all right. Come through, I was just making some supper. You look as though you could do with a sit down and a nice hot cup of tea.'

'Well, I won't say no. Seems ages since we left Pompey this morning.'

The living-kitchen at the back of number 17 was small but warm and cosy. There were two fireside chairs with wooden arms, one on either side of the range, a dresser and a scrubbed-top table, now covered by the red chenille cloth Jack's mother had given them. A half-glazed door led to the back yard with its wash house and lavatory and another concealed the narrow flight of stairs that led to the two bedrooms on the upper floor. Sally looked admiringly at the brightly patterned rug that lay in front of the glowing range, and the willow-patterned china on the dresser shelves.

'You've got it really nice,' she remarked, taking off her coat. 'Warm too. It's parky outside.'

'Nights are drawing in now,' Eve said. 'Soon be winter, worse luck.' She turned from the sink where she had been slicing cooked potatoes. 'We moved in here after we got married,' she said. 'Jack and me had been engaged five years. We saved up all that time for a place of our own.'

'It's yours then? Not rented?' Sally said, impressed.

Eve nodded. 'Sometimes I wish we hadn't waited so long. We only had eighteen months together before he got called up.'

'In the army, is he?' the girl asked.

'Yes. King's Royal Rifles. But he was wounded and taken prisoner at Dunkirk.'

'Oh, I'm sorry.'

'At least he's alive.' Eve set the frying pan on the range and bent to stir the fire. 'Corned beef and fried potatoes all right?' she asked.

Sally nodded eagerly. 'Sounds smashing, thanks.'

'For four months I thought he'd been killed,' Eve explained. 'Hearing he'd been taken prisoner was the best news I've ever had.' She smiled ruefully. 'Funny, isn't it – hearing your husband's behind bars being a cause for celebration?'

'That's war for you.' Sally shuddered visibly. 'My David's in the navy. He's on H.M.S. *Stamford*. My mum didn't want us to get married so we just went and did it. We never even had a honeymoon, never mind a home of our own.'

'When was that?'

3

'Six months ago. The day after my twentieth birthday. Mum hasn't forgiven me, hasn't spoken to me since. After Dave joined his ship I was going to join up, the WRNS or something. But Dave wanted me to go for something safe. He suggested the Land Army.' She laughed, wrinkling her nose. 'I'm too much of a town girl to fancy the country life though, I didn't fancy the idea of freezing cow sheds at five in the morning, so I volunteered for munitions instead.'

'And you've come all this way? You'll miss your family, I expect.'

Sally pulled a face. 'Reckon Mum won't miss me,' she said ruefully.

Eve's heart went out to the girl. Since Jack's capture she had been grateful for the support of her family. 'Never mind,' she said. 'At least you'll be safe here in Northampton. So far we haven't had any bombing to speak of. All we make here is boots, apart from Samson's going over to aircraft parts.' She grinned. 'I doubt if old Hitler's heard about that yet. I reckon they must have taken over Samson's factory because it's three miles out of town.' She shook her head. 'God help those poor souls in London. They've taken a real pasting these past twelve months.'

'Portsmouth was no picnic either,' Sally said. 'It'll make a nice change not to hear that siren going all the time.'

'We do get air-raid warnings,' Eve told her. 'The Gerry planes fly right over here some nights, droves of them. But they don't often drop any bombs, apart from the odd stray one. Saving them for better targets, I reckon. So you're going to work at Samson's?' she said, changing the subject. 'I work there too – in the canteen. As I said, it's a way out of town but there's a bus that picks us up from the market place. I think you'll find they're a good bunch of girls.'

She felt slightly hypocritical as she said this. Many of the women she knew at the factory, married ones included, went out dancing or drinking on Saturday evenings. Some of them brazenly had affairs with servicemen they picked up in the pubs or dance halls. Since the war had started morals seemed to have gone right out of the window. Eve was no prude but she wanted nothing to do with that kind of behaviour. The only man she would ever love was stranded in a prisoner-of-war camp somewhere in Germany. So, although she was friendly with her workmates, she kept herself to herself in her free time. Not that there wasn't always plenty to do. As well as the shopping and keeping the house nice for when her husband came home, she visited her family and Jack's mother as regularly as her shiftwork allowed.

'You haven't got any kids then?' Sally asked suddenly.

Eve shook her head, her straying thoughts jerked abruptly back to the present. 'Kids? No. Jack and I always planned to have a big family, four at least, but I never fell. Doctor says I probably never will.' She glanced sideways at the other girl. 'Something not quite right – you know – inside.'

'Oh yeah?' Sally took a packet of Woodbines out of her handbag and lit one, blowing the smoke ceilingwards. 'Probably just as well though, eh, what with the war and everything? I think that was mostly why Mum didn't want me to get married. She thought I'd be daft enough to saddle myself with a baby right away. We're not ignorant now though, not like when she was a girl. She had to marry my dad, see? 'Cause she had me on the way.' She drew hard on her cigarette, inhaling the smoke. 'She and Dad never really got on. Always rowing, till he walked out and left her with four of us to bring up on her own. I suppose she saw me heading for the same. But

David and I were careful. I'm not sure I want any kids anyway. Still, you never know. After the war I might feel different.'

Eve tipped the potatoes into the smoking frying pan and shook them vigorously. 'Depends how long it goes on for,' she said. 'We've been at war for two years now and it seems things are only getting worse. No sign of it ending. Even if I could have some kind of treatment it might be too late by then for Jack and me. I'm already twenty-nine, you see. And if anything were to happen to him . . .' She bit back the unspeakable thought. Glancing at the girl, she felt a sudden stab of irritation at the casual way she lay sprawled in Jack's chair, smoking her cigarette. 'You can lay the table if you want to make yourself useful,' she said sharply. 'Cloth and cutlery's in the dresser drawer.'

'What? Oh, okay.' Sally got up and looked around. 'Got an ashtray, have you?' She sensed disapproval in the way Eve silently took an ashtray out of the dresser cupboard. It had a picture of a seagull on it and bore the inscription 'A Present From Hunstanton'.

'Just one thing, Sally,' Eve said as she handed it to her. 'you won't smoke in the bedroom, will you? It makes the curtains and everything smell so stale.'

'Okay, if you say so.' As Sally laid the table she watched out of the corner of her eye as Eve sliced the corned beef thinly, dividing it with meticulous fairness between the two plates. Twenty-nine, she said she was, yet in Sally's opinion she might as well have been fifty. She wore her brown hair rolled tightly round a ribbon in the dowdy style they called the 'victory roll.' The shapeless tweed skirt and home-knitted jumper did nothing for her figure and the round face with its homely features was innocent of make-up. Not so much as a dash of lipstick. Her eyes were nice though, Sally decided. Large, dark brown and clear, set off by finely arched eyebrows. Sally's

6

glance shifted to the dresser where a photograph of a young man in uniform held pride of place. That must be her Jack. He too had plain, unremarkable features which were not enhanced by the severe army haircut. He stood rigidly to attention, tunic buttons neatly fastened, his eyes screwed up against the sunlight as he smiled stiffly into the camera. Not a patch on her Dave, Sally told herself with satisfaction.

Eve bustled around the room, tweaking at a corner of the tablecloth and smoothing a wrinkle with her hand. She took a chromium-plated cruet set and a jar of chutney out of the dresser cupboard and placed them squarely in the centre of the table. Then she turned back to the range to attend to the pan of frying potatoes. Sally pulled a wry face. She hoped her new landlady wasn't going to turn out to be the pernickety sort.

'Well, are you ready then?' Eve seemed to have regained her good humour as she placed the two steaming plates on the table. 'Sit down and tuck in, then we'll see about making you up a bed.'

As the months passed and autumn turned to winter the two women settled down together. But the relationship was not without its difficulties. Sally's cavalier attitude to life often drove the more fastidious Eve to distraction. The girl was careless and untidy, leaving discarded clothes lying all over her room where the bed was often left unmade for days at a time, and her cigarette ash seemed to get everywhere. But she had a warm, fun-loving nature and soon found that she could jolly Eve out of her irritation by making her laugh.

For Sally's part, she tried her hardest to persuade Eve to relax and enjoy herself more, encouraging her to listen to popular dance music on the wireless. She managed to coax her to be more adventurous with her appearance, too. She discovered that, once released from its tight roll, Eve's hair was abundant and shiny and urged her to make the most of it, telling her she looked just like Ingrid Bergman. It was Sally who wheedled Eve into accompanying her to the cinema where they saw *Gone With The Wind* and *For Whom The Bell Tolls*, and occasionally they would go to a variety show at the New Theatre.

In return Eve taught a reluctant Sally how to darn her stockings neatly and wash her woollies so that they didn't shrink; how to clean her room and keep it tidy, and eke out the meagre meat ration with vegetables to make a tasty, filling meal.

That Christmas Sally was invited to spend the holiday at Eve's parents' house where they were joined by Eve's sister, Rose, her husband, Ted, and their two children. Jack's mother and her widowed sister completed the party, all of them crowding into Albert and Freda Harrison's semi-detached villa at Kingsthorpe. Eve's father Albert worked on the railway as a ticket collector. He was a keen gardener and kept chickens and rabbits at the bottom of his neat garden where he grew all the family's vegetables.

Sally's eyes almost popped out of her head at the spread that Freda produced on Christmas Day, roast chicken and all the trimmings, while at tea there was home-made bread and crisp white celery followed by a rich fruit cake, made, Freda told them proudly, with four whole new-laid eggs from their own chickens and the dried fruit she had been saving up 'specially all year.

After tea they played charades at which Sally proved a real star turn, keeping everyone, especially Rose's children, in stitches with her uninhibited antics. But later, when Eve and her sister went off to the kitchen to wash up, Rose carefully closed the door on the merriment in the living room, her face grave and meaningful.

8

'I think you should have a word with that young lodger of yours, Eve,' she said, her mouth pursed disapprovingly.

Eve paused in the act of drying one of her mother's best plates. 'Sally, you mean?'

'Of course. Who else?'

'Why?'

'I'd have thought that was obvious! All that dancing and kicking her legs up in the air.'

Eve chuckled. 'It was only a bit of fun.'

'Fun, you call it? Showing everything she'd got. You could see her knickers! With Ted and Dad looking on too. Brazen, I call it!'

Eve shook her head. 'Come off it, Rose. It's Christmas.'

'That's not all though,' her sister said darkly. 'You do know she's getting herself talked about, don't you?'

'No. What for? Who's talking?'

Rose raised her eyebrows. 'Only half the town. I can't think why you haven't heard.' She plunged her hands into the soapy water. 'You don't always work the same shifts as her, do you?'

'No. But what's that got to do . . . ?'

Rose silenced her with a look. 'So you don't know what she gets up to when you're not there? Who she's *entertaining*?' She emphasised the word with a nod.

'I don't know what you're talking about. Anyway, she's a grown woman, Rose. I can't tell her what to do.'

There had always been rivalry between the sisters. Eve envied her sister her two beautiful children and, although she would never admit it, resented the fact that Rose still had her husband at home. Ted had failed his medical on the grounds of his flat feet. Rose, on the other hand, would never have confessed that deep down she grudged Eve her freedom and independence.

'Maybe you can't tell her what to do, but you can get rid of her before you are tarred with the same brush,' Rose said bluntly.

Eve put down her tea towel and faced her sister. 'Just what are you saying? Why don't you come to the point, Rose?'

'She's married, right?'

'Yes, of course she is.'

'To a sailor. Poor devil, risking his life out there on the sea, while his wife . . .'

'While she *what*, Rose? For heaven's sake, spit it out if you're going to. If not, shut up!'

Rose coloured. 'No call to speak to me like that, our Eve.' She drew in her breath. 'She's seeing someone else if you really need me to tell you.'

Eve's mouth dropped open. 'I don't believe you.'

'All right. If you can't believe your own sister, just ask anyone. It's common knowledge! It isn't as if she bothers making a secret of it.'

'Who is it? Who's she seeing?'

Rose bridled. 'How should *I* know? What do you think I am, a gossip monger? All I know is she's been seen with this man.' She sniffed. 'Hanging on his arm and making an exhibition of herself. Disgraceful if you ask me.'

Eve was shaking her head. 'But have you actually *seen* her with him?'

'Well, no, not personally,' Rose admitted reluctantly. 'But plenty of people have – going into *your* house too! I told you – she's brazen, doesn't care who knows. What about those silk stocking she wears? And that lipstick and stuff that no one else can get for love nor money? Didn't it ever occur to you to wonder where they came from?'

Eve tried to hide her unease. She herself was wearing pure silk stockings given to her as a Christmas present that morning by Sally. She'd been quite shocked when she opened the package, knowing they must have cost far more than the cheap little charm bracelet she'd bought for Sally. 'Someone at work gets them from a cousin in Australia,' she said. 'She sends parcels over and lets the girls at work buy them . . .' She broke off as she caught sight of the scornful expression on her sister's face.

'That what she told you, is it? I'd have a sharp word with that young woman if I was you,' Rose advised. 'And quick! Ask her to tell you the truth about where she gets these luxuries and, more to the point, what she has to do for them! Mud sticks, you know. You wouldn't like your Jack to get to hear that you're sharing his house with a tart, would you?'

'*Rose!*'

'They'll be pointing the finger at you next.' Rose sniffed as she looked her sister up and down. 'She's already influenced you, if you ask me.'

'What do you mean?' Eve demanded hotly.

'Your hair for a start. Who are you trying to look like – Veronica Lake? I never saw you wearing powder and lipstick before either.'

'Don't be so old-fashioned, Rose. Everyone wears make-up nowadays.'

She sniffed dismissively. 'Oh, well, it's up to you, Eve. Suit yourself, but don't say I didn't warn you. I'm only thinking of you.' She swished the cloth around the bowl as though washing her hands of the whole affair. 'I've said my piece so I'll say no more,' she said with an ominous toss of her head.

As they walked home that night Sally was in high spirits. 'Your mum and dad are smashing,' she said. 'And your sister's kids. And what about that feast your mum put on? I swear I won't need to eat again till New Year! And wasn't it a laugh, playing charades? I've always wanted to

11

go on the stage, you know. Some people think I've got a natural talent for dancing. Ever since I can remember I've wanted to learn to dance properly. But there was never any money in our house for lessons.' She took a few steps and twirled ahead of Eve. 'Look at that. Reckon I could do just as well as some of them on the pictures. What d'you think?' She began to shake her hips and sing, ' "*He's the boogie woogie bugle boy from Company B . . .*" ' jiving ahead till Eve was forced to tell her to keep her voice down.

'Shhh! It's late. You'll wake the whole neighbourhood,' she admonished. But Sally only laughed.

'So what? It's Christmas.'

Ever since they'd left her parents' house Eve had been racking her brains to think of some tactful way of broaching the subject of her sister's accusations. It was awkward. In spite of the girl's sloppy, devil-may-care ways she liked Sally and didn't want to quarrel with her. Supposing it was all just a rumour? Rose had always been a terrible gossip. Eve decided to wait till they were indoors.

While she made cocoa in the kitchen Sally fiddled with the wireless, trying to find some dance music.

'Before the war I used to like Radio Luxembourg,' she said, lighting a cigarette. 'They used to play all the latest . . .'

'*Sally*! Turn it off, will you? I want to talk to you.'

Startled by Eve's urgent tone, Sally turned the knob and the room was suddenly plunged into silence. She faced Eve, grinning impudently. 'Okay then, baby. Shoot!' she said in her Mae West voice.

'Is it true you've been going out with someone?' Eve asked quietly. She looked hard at the other girl. 'I want the truth, please.'

Sally hesitated, the grin melting from her face, then

with a defiant toss of her head she said, 'Okay, I have been seeing someone. His name's Eddie Wilson. So what?'

Eve's heart sank. She knew Eddie Wilson very well. He had a grocer's shop in Albemarle Street and a stall on the market. The general opinion was that he was a questionable character, into all kinds of shady deals including the black market. He'd managed to get the contract for supplying groceries to the canteen at Samson's and often arrived with little under-the-counter 'extras' which he sold on the quiet to some of the employees there. And his reputation with women was common knowledge. 'Oh, Sally,' said Eve.

'*Oh, Sally*!' the other girl mimicked. 'Come on, Eve. It's nothing to get upset about,' she protested. 'Eddie's a laugh. He knows how to treat a girl.' She sighed and slumped into a chair. 'I get fed up, never having any fun, and the service blokes never have any cash.'

'Do you think you're being fair to Dave?'

Sally looked up, her eyes defensive. 'I'm not the only one by a long chalk. What Dave don't know can't hurt him. Besides, how can I tell what he gets up to, on leave in them foreign places? Either way it's got nothing to do with him and me. It's the war.'

'Why did you lie to me, about the stockings and make-up and things? You got them from him, didn't you? From Eddie Wilson?'

'All right, yes. I didn't tell you 'cause I knew what you'd be like if I did,' Sally said, pouting truculently. 'And I was right, wasn't I? You're proving that now!'

Eve sighed and sat down. 'Sally, can't you see, you're playing with fire? Everyone knows Eddie Wilson. He's as crooked as a corkscrew.'

'He's not!' A look of uncertainty flitted momentarily across Sally's face, but she quickly recovered her defiant expression. 'It's all a fuss about nothing. It's only a bit of fun,' she said sulkily.

'Is it?' Eve looked at her. 'You do know he's married?'

Sally stubbed out her cigarette, avoiding Eve's eyes. 'Well, yes, but they're separated – he's told me.'

Something about Sally's sudden discomfort alarmed Eve. Remembering something Rose had hinted at, she asked, 'Have you been bringing him back here, when I've been on nights? Have you been taking him upstairs, Sally?' When the girl avoided her eyes she reached out and took her by the shoulders, shaking her gently. '*Tell me!* It's my house. I've a right to know what's going on in it.'

'Oh, all *right*!' Sally's eyes met hers defiantly. 'Yes, if you must know. But it's my room. I pay you for it, don't I? Surely I can bring a friend back . . .' Suddenly her boldness dissolved and her eyes filled with tears. 'I can't help it, Evie. I miss being *loved*. I miss being kissed and cuddled and, all right, I miss the *sex*. Oh, don't look at me like that,' she said as Eve turned away. 'It's not something to be ashamed of. It's natural. It's what you get married for. And you miss it too if you're honest.'

Eve looked away, her colour rising as she remembered the restless, yearning nights she often spent.

Sally went on, 'Eddie's passionate and exciting.'

'And *unfaithful*!' Eve broke in. 'He isn't separated, Sally. If he told you that then he's lying. He's just taking advantage of your loneliness – using you. He's got a wife and three children. They live in a posh house at Kingsley Park. To him you're just a bit on the side, and not the first he's had. Not by a long way. You'll get hurt if you don't stop.'

'I won't! I'm not daft. I know what I'm doing, Eve.'

'How can you say that? You're the talk of the place. It seems I'm about the only person who didn't know.'

'Who told you anyway?' Sally asked, subdued.

'It doesn't matter. Just be warned, I don't want to see you get hurt.'

14

'Just say if you want me to go . . .'

'I *don't*! Of course I don't, Sally. I like having you here. I just want you to be sensible, that's all.'

It was three months later that Eve heard the news. It was quite by chance that she happened to have the wireless on. She'd been on night shift and after sleeping fitfully all morning she'd got up to do some ironing. As she worked away in the kitchen she switched on to listen to *Music While You Work*. Suddenly the programme was interrupted by a news bulletin. A British convoy on its way to Murmansk had been attacked by German planes. One of the Royal Navy escort ships, *H.M.S. Stamford*, had been sunk at sea. There were no reported survivors.

H.M.S. *Stamford* . . . That was Dave Tyler's ship! Eve put down the iron and pushed the rest of the clothes back into the basket. She looked at the clock. Sally was on early shift. She would be home in half an hour. There would be an official notification, of course, but she must try to prepare the girl for what was to come. What did one say? Eve filled the kettle and set it on the range.

They sat on either side of the fire drinking tea and talking until it was time for Eve to go to work. Sally had taken the news badly. When Eve had told her that H.M.S. *Stamford* had been sunk with all hands she had turned so deathly pale Eve had thought she was going to faint. She had refused to eat anything but sat looking stunned as Eve vainly tried to reassure her, reminding her of the weeks she had mistakenly believed her Jack was dead.

'Think of the confusion in all that bombing,' she said. 'Some of them are sure to have been picked up. You have to hang on to that hope, Sally. Dave will be all right, I'm sure of it.'

But Sally shook her head slowly from side to side,

Tears rolled down her cheeks as she sat twisting her handkerchief between white-knuckled fingers and moaning softly. 'It's because of me. It's my punishment,' she said over and over. 'It's because of what I did.'

'Of course it isn't.' Eve did her best to comfort the distraught girl, assuring her that nothing could be further from the truth. She stayed with Sally for as long as she could, glancing anxiously at the clock as the minutes ticked by until at last she knew that she would have to run all the way to the market place if she was to catch the factory bus. 'I don't like leaving you,' she said as she pulled on her coat. 'Shall I go and fetch Mum to come and sleep here with you?'

'No. You go or you'll miss the bus,' Sally urged. 'I'd rather be on my own. I've got a lot of thinking to do. Don't worry about me.'

When Eve got home next morning she found Sally standing at the kitchen window, her eyes blank as she stared out into the yard. She wore her coat over her nightdress and the hand that hung limply by her side clutched a slip of paper. Eve prised it from the stiff fingers and quickly scanned the impersonal printed words of the official War Office telegram informing Mrs Sarah Tyler of her husband Able Seaman David Tyler's death. For a moment they stared wordlessly at each other, then Eve gathered the trembling girl into her arms.

'I'm sorry, love,' she whispered. 'So sorry. Just let go and have a good cry. You'll feel better for it. Believe me, I know how you feel.'

'No! No, you *don't*!' Sally pulled abruptly away. 'You can't possibly. How *can* you? You don't know the half of it.' She turned away, her hands to her head. 'I'm in trouble, Eve. Terrible trouble. This has just about finished everything. It's like some horrible cruel kind of justice.'

She stared into Eve's shocked, uncomprehending eyes. 'Haven't you guessed? *I'm expecting*! Yes, it's Eddie's. I finished with him like you said, soon after Christmas, and then a few weeks later I found out.'

Eve gasped and caught her lower lip between her teeth. Now she understood what Sally had meant when she'd spoken of 'justice' and 'punishment'. 'No, I hadn't guessed. How far gone are you?' she whispered. 'Will he – will Eddie help?'

'He might have if you hadn't made me finish with him!' Sally turned on her angrily. 'Oh, why did you have to interfere? I went to see him at the shop last week and told him I was having a baby. But he said we'd been finished for weeks and it could be anybody's. He's not interested! I even threatened to tell his wife, but he just – just laughed at me – said to go ahead if I wanted my eyes scratched out.' The words caught in Sally's throat. 'God knows what I'm going to do now.'

'You're better off without him,' Eve told her. 'I know you don't think so at the moment but you are, really.'

'It's all right *you* saying that!' Sally slumped into a chair and covered her face with her hands. 'I've tried everything I could think of. I've had pills off some woman at work. I've drunk gin till I was sick, sat in hot baths till I looked like a lobster, but nothing will shift it. I was just beginning to think that perhaps Dave would understand and forgive me. I know I could have got round him somehow, he's always been such a soft touch. I'd even started a letter to him. But now – now he'll never read it, and I'm stuck with all this on my own. Oh, God, Eve, I can't believe this is happening to me! What am I going to *do*?'

Suddenly Eve was very calm. An idea was beginning to form in her mind. An idea so daring, so outrageous that she hardly dared allow it to take shape. 'Don't worry, Sally,' she said. 'Everything will be all right. I'll help you.'

'What can *you* do?' Sally wailed. 'It's me who's got to carry a kid I don't want and put up with all the nasty things people will say! It's me who's got to go through it all. It would have been bad enough trying to face Dave. But now I'm all alone.' She sobbed into her handkerchief. 'I can just hear my mum saying: *I told you so.* I'll be just like her, struggling for years to bring it up on my own. Old before my time, never having any fun.' She dabbed at her swollen eyes. 'My life is over, Evie.'

'Not necessarily.' Eve swallowed hard. 'Look, I'll take care of you. And when the baby's born, I'll – Jack and me, we'll adopt it. If you'll let us.' She knelt in front of Sally and took both of the cold trembling hands in hers. She looked into the other girl's eyes, trying to convey strength, striving to conceal the ferocious longing in her heart. 'What do you say, Sally?' She held her breath. 'It's the answer, isn't it? It would be ideal for you. And I won't let you down, I promise.'

The months passed slowly. As the spring of 1943 blossomed there were nightly air-raid warnings. On the nights that they were both at home Eve and Sally got up when the siren went, but they didn't go to the communal shelter at the end of the street. Sally said the smell in there made her feel sick. So instead they made themselves as comfortable as possible with cushions under the sturdy table in the kitchen, listening anxiously as the German bombers droned overhead on their way to drop their lethal burdens on less fortunate Midland cities. Occasionally a damaged plane, limping to safety, would jettison its bombs at random, but for the most part the town suffered little damage.

But the nightly tension and lack of sleep took its toll on nerves and constitutions, especially Sally's. As her pregnancy progressed she looked pale and gaunt, became edgy and listless. Eve did her best to take care of her, feeding her plenty of vegetables from her father's garden, queuing for fish and off-ration offal at the butcher's to supply the iron the girl needed; making sure she took her cod liver oil and received the oranges allowed to expectant mothers. She even managed to persuade her to give up the Woodbines she was so addicted to. Her solicitousness did not go unnoticed by Rose who was critical and scathing.

'I don't know why you make such a fuss of her,' she said, sanctimoniously. 'Knitting all those baby things for her and fussing round like some old hen. She's only got what she asked for. I warned you about her long ago, Eve. She's bad through and through, that one. You should have chucked her out when you had the chance.' When Eve made no reply she went on, 'She doesn't know how lucky she is. Most people would have put her out on the street for getting you a bad name like that.'

'How has she got *me* a bad name?' Eve challenged. 'Unlike you, some people have human feelings, Rose. Sally made a mistake that lots of women have made since this war started, but what would you know about that? This war hasn't touched you at all. You don't know you're born. Sally's lost her husband. Surely that's punishment enough to satisfy even your nasty vindictive nature?'

Rose bridled. 'Well, *really*! I'll say this, our Eve. Since that girl has been in your house you've had a tongue on you like a viper!'

'And high time too, if you ask me,' she retaliated. 'I put up with your bossiness when we were kids but I'm not standing for it any longer. Go and nag poor old Ted if you want someone to bully. He would have been better off fighting the Germans, if you ask me!'

Stunned into speechlessness Rose retreated and Eve

wondered what her sister would say if she knew that Eve was about to adopt Sally's baby. But she felt strong enough to meet that challenge when it came. Now she had something to work for. She was going to have the longed-for child after all. When Jack came home they would start life afresh as a real family.

The only person in whom Eve had confided her intention to adopt Sally's baby was her mother. To begin with Freda had had misgivings.

'It's all very well, love. I know you both want a family. But shouldn't Jack have a say in it?' she asked.

'I've written to him,' Eve told her. 'We had discussed adopting a baby before he went away, when the doctor said we couldn't have any of our own. I'm sure he'll be pleased, Mum.'

Freda sighed. 'Well, I hope you're right.'

'I'm just worried about Sally,' Eve confided. 'She looks so poorly. She hardly eats enough to keep a kitten alive and you know how much sleep we've all lost with the raids.'

Freda's face brightened. 'I know – why don't you take her down to Hunstanton to stay with Auntie Kate for a few days?' she suggested. 'The sea air would do her the world of good and they don't seem to have been troubled much with raids there.'

Freda's sister Kate had a boarding house in the little Norfolk seaside town. A short visit was arranged for July when Sally would have stopped working and Eve was due for a week's holiday. They travelled down by train on Saturday, 17 July.

Although Eve's Aunt Kate made them welcome and comfortable the holiday was not a success. The weather was bad. All week a strong wind blew off the North Sea and it rained almost every day. Sally, her pregnancy now well advanced, complained of tiredness and discomfort. Her clothes were too tight and she hated the way she looked. She had constant indigestion and insisted that the baby was 'kicking her to ribbons'.

'I can't wait till it's over, Evie,' she said. 'You're not missing much, not being able to have kids, believe me. It's nine months of sheer bloody hell. No feller's worth going through all this for. I don't care who he is!'

It was while they were sitting on the cliffs one afternoon, sheltering from the wind in one of the covered seats, that Eve broached a subject that had been troubling her.

'Sally, what are you planning to do afterwards? When you've had the baby, I mean?'

Sally turned to look at her. 'Do? Go back to work, I suppose. They're always wanting people at Samson's.'

Eve bit her lip. 'Stay on, you mean? With me?'

'Yes. Why?'

Eve tried to hide her dismay. 'Oh, nothing. I just thought you might want to go back to your mum's now that Dave . . .'

'You want me to go, don't you?' Sally challenged her. 'You want the baby but you don't want me, that it? All this fuss you've been making – it's not for me, is it? It's all for the kid.'

'No! I want you both to be healthy,' Eve sighed. 'I just thought it might make things awkward, you staying on.'

Sally laughed. 'Oh, I get it! You're scared I might change my mind, aren't you? Well, you can rest assured, Evie. All I want is to be free of the little horror.' She patted her bulging stomach. 'Once I've got rid of this, it's all yours, believe me. I can't wait to get on with my life again.'

Sally's baby was born exactly six weeks later, early in September. They were in the middle of an air raid when her pains began. Eve went at once for the midwife in the next street, only to find that she was out on another case. Leaving a message with the woman's husband, she

21

returned to the house to find Sally kneeling on the hearth rug, doubled up with the contractions, which were strong and very regular. Although everyone said that first babies always took their time it was clear that this was one baby that would wait for no one.

Eve stared at her helplessly for a moment, then made a decision. 'I'm going for Mum,' she said. 'I'll go on my bike. Stay under the table. You'll be safe there. I'll be back as soon as I can.'

But Sally reached out and grabbed at her hand, refusing to let go. 'Don't leave me here alone. What if you get killed?' she said hysterically. 'I'm going to die, I know I am. If the kid doesn't kill me a bloody bomb will. Don't leave me, Evie. I don't want to die alone!'

'You're not going to die and neither am I.' Kneeling on the floor Eve wiped the girl's damp brow with her handkerchief. 'You'll be all right till I get back. You'll have to be. There's nothing else for it, Sally. I must get help. Mum was with Rose when she had both of hers. She'll know what to do. I haven't got a clue.' From the doorway she looked back anxiously at Sally whose face was contorted with another pain. 'Hang on,' she said, trying not to show how afraid she was. 'I'll be as quick as I can, I promise.'

Luckily it was a fine, moonlit night and Eve pedalled as fast as she could to Kingsthorpe. Freda rose to the occasion quickly, running round the house and gathering up the things she'd need: her sharpest scissors and a reel of strong white thread; clean white towels and the big bottle of Dettol she always kept in the bathroom cabinet for emergencies. Bundling everything into her bicycle basket, she joined her daughter on the ride back to Brook's Lane.

When they arrived it was clear that there was no time to be lost. Sally was well into the second stage of labour. The birth was imminent. Freda turned to Eve who hovered anxiously. 'Stir up that fire and make sure the kettle's boiling,' she commanded as she rolled up her sleeves and scrubbed her hands at the sink. 'Then get the baby clothes and put them on the clothes horse to air.'

Luckily Freda's authoritative presence had the required calming effect on Sally who stopped writhing and groaning and did as she was told. Freda sterilised the scissors with boiling water from the kettle and laid her improvised instruments out on a spotless towel.

'Now, young lady,' she said sternly, 'just do as I say and we'll soon get that baby born.'

Half an hour later she delivered Sally of a seven-and-a-half-pound baby girl just as the 'all clear' sounded and a breathless midwife arrived on the doorstep.

The four women sat in the hot little kitchen drinking tea. Eve felt light-headed. It was over. At last the baby was here. *Her baby*. She had never seen a baby born before and she was still reeling from the excitement and the miracle of it all. They had moved Sally into a chair, a cushion at her back and her feet raised on a stool. She looked pale and tired but infinitely relieved as she sipped her tea. The baby, bathed by the midwife, lay on a pillow in a drawer taken hurriedly from the dresser. Wrapped in the shawl Eve had knitted for her, she made contented little kissing noises and gazed with wide blue eyes at the ceiling. She had a halo of soft golden hair and was so incredibly beautiful that Eve was completely mesmerised by her. It was fate. As though it had all been planned, she told herself. Sally coming here, the baby being born in Eve's own house, attended by Eve's mother, herself present at the birth. This child was as close as possible to being her own. It was as if it was meant to be.

'What are you going to call her, Mrs Tyler?' the midwife asked.

Sally looked at Eve over the rim of her teacup. 'Carol,' she said decisively. 'I want to call her Carol. Carol Louise.'

'That's nice.' The midwife put her empty cup on the table and rose briskly. 'Now I think we should get you up to bed, dear. A good sleep is what you need, and with a bit of luck Gerry will allow you to have it for once. I'll pop in in the morning,' she said briskly. 'To see to you and get you started on your feeding routine.'

Freda glanced at Eve, a frown between her brows. When Sally was in bed and the midwife had gone she made another pot of tea and she and Eve sat drinking it together.

'What's going to happen now?' her mother asked.

Eve looked up. 'Sally will go back to work when she's well enough. I'm giving in my notice right away.'

'What about in the meantime?'

Eve looked nonplussed. 'I'll be at work and Sally will be here.'

'With the baby?'

'Of course.' She looked at her mother. 'Well, what else could we have done?'

Freda shrugged. 'When babies are given up for adoption they're usually taken from the mother right away.'

'Yes.' Eve frowned. 'But we know that I'm having the baby so it's different in our case. I'll be having the baby in my room right from tonight. We agreed. It's only for the next couple of weeks that Sally will see to her in the daytime.' She laughed. 'If you're afraid she'll change her mind and want to keep it, you couldn't be more wrong, Mum,' she said. 'Sally can't wait to start making a new life for herself.'

Freda looked doubtful. 'Well, I hope you're right . . .'

Eve worked out her notice with undisguised impatience. At the end of each shift she hurried home from the factory, eager to take the baby over from Sally. Little

Carol was a joy, slipping into the four-hourly feeding routine without any trouble and sleeping placidly in between. When Eve was on a daytime shift the baby slept in her room and she rose in the night to give Carol her bottle and change her. Nights broken by feeds as well as occasional air raids often made it hard to get up in the mornings in time to catch the bus. But Eve didn't mind. Holding the baby in her arms made it all worthwhile and she counted the days till she could have baby Carol all to herself.

Completing Eve's happiness was the fact that she had at last received a letter from Jack. Mail from the prison camps, which came through the Red Cross, was irregular. Often it was lost on the way and always the letters were heavily censored. But Eve was able to glean from the unpencilled sentences that he was delighted that they were to be the parents of an adopted baby. He said that he was well, apart from the wound in his leg which sometimes gave him trouble, and that he was counting the days until he could be home with her again.

'I can't! I can't do it, Evie!'

'What do you mean?' Eve stared uncomprehendingly at Sally.

'I can't let you have Carol. I know I promised, but it's no good.'

The words simply refused to be absorbed. Eve could not believe she was hearing them. 'I don't know what you mean . . . you can't let me have her?' she said dully. 'We agreed. You said . . .'

'I know, but that was before.' Tears welled up and spilled down Sally's cheeks. 'I didn't know I'd feel like this. I can't give her up. She's my baby and I want to keep her. I *have* to keep her, Evie.'

Eve shook her head disbelievingly. Her mouth was so

25

dry that she had to clear her throat before speaking. 'But – I've given up my job and everything. I've made so many plans. I've even written to tell Jack. How can you do this to me, Sally? You don't want her. You never have. And now that you're on your own . . .'

'But that's *it*! Don't you see? Dave's gone. Mum's not interested any more. Carol's *mine*. She's all I've got, Evie. How can I just give her away? I want to bring her up and give her the chances I never had. Maybe she'll be a dancer. A film star even.'

Anger swelled in Eve's breast. An anger such as she had never known; so frightening that her heart drummed wildly against her ribs and her legs shook so much she had to put out a hand to steady herself. She wanted to hit Sally, to scream and shout – to turn her into the street there and then. But natural common sense came to her rescue. Reason told her that if Sally went she would take Carol with her and Eve would never see either of them again. Somehow she must stay calm and persuade the girl to be sensible. She realised now that this was what her mother had tried to warn her about. She swallowed hard and took a deep breath.

'Look, Sally, you're a bit hysterical. You're still feeling low,' she said slowly. 'Once you're back at work with the other girls you'll feel different.' An alarming thought occurred to her. 'You are still going back to work?'

'Yes. I've got to. I must save as much money as I can from now on.' Sally reached out one hand to touch Eve's. 'She's going to have the best I can get for her, my Carol.' She looked at Eve apologetically. 'You'll still have her all the time I'm working, Evie,' she said. 'It'll be almost as if she was yours.'

Eve swallowed her resentment. 'Yes, for the time being.'

'Maybe we could even still live together after the war – share her?' Sally said hopefully.

'Jack will be home. How can we? There won't be room.' Eve sighed. 'He'll be so disappointed when he knows.'

'Look, I'm sorry, Evie,' Sally said. 'Really sorry. I never knew I'd feel like this. If you'd ever had a baby of your own, you'd understand. She's mine. She's part of me.'

But in spite of Sally's newfound maternal feelings she still allowed the baby to sleep in Eve's room and took little interest in doing the chores connected with motherhood, complaining she was too tired when she got home from work whereas Eve had all day.

As baby Carol grew and developed, Sally enjoyed playing with her and walking out with her in the pram at weekends. Very occasionally she bathed her and put her to bed, but when the baby was fretful or needed changing she soon became bored and handed her back to Eve.

With the arrival of the US Air Force Sally's social life took on a new dimension. As soon as she heard about the Saturday night dances held at the USAF base she decided to go. On Saturday evenings, the moment she had had her tea, she would say goodbye to Eve and Carol and set off for the market square, decked out in all her finery, to wait with the other girls for the American transport that would pick them up. After her first visit she arrived home at two a.m., waking Eve up to let her in because she had forgotten her key and prattling on excitedly about all that had happened as they sat drinking cocoa in the kitchen.

'You should see what there was to eat, Evie!' she said, her eyes alight. 'Ice cream and ham and chicken . . . fruit piled up to the ceiling . . . and as much booze as you could drink. And they're ever so smart and good-looking. You should hear them talk!' She giggled. 'Just like on the pictures. And the band!' She rolled ecstatic eyes to the ceiling. 'Just as good as Glenn Miller. I never stopped dancing all night. It was smashing!'

Eve nodded sleepily. It was only after she had gone back to bed and lay waiting for Carol to wake for her early feed that the first positive thought she'd had for weeks occurred to her. If Sally began to have a really good time, if she met a new man, she might think again about letting Eve adopt Carol. Maybe she should encourage her in this new social life.

In Eve's care baby Carol thrived. She grew bonnier and prettier as the weeks passed, quickly growing out of the clothes that Eve had made for her so that her spare moments were occupied with knitting and sewing. At Christmas they went once more to Eve's parents' for the day where Carol was the centre of attention. Much to Rose's resentment, Freda remarked that she had never seen a more contented child. Once again Rose could not resist having her say on the subject of Sally when she and Eve were alone in the kitchen after tea.

'I see she's started smoking again,' she said with a sniff. 'Lucky Strikes this time. Freebees, I shouldn't wonder. Stinking things! And the length of her *skirts*!' she exclaimed. 'I mean, I know we're supposed to be patriotic and save material but that skirt of hers goes way beyond patriotism. It's the absolute limit! You want to watch it, our Eve,' she warned. 'This time next year she'll be making another of her little *mistakes*. You must be mad, giving up a good wage and sitting at home with her child while she goes gadding off! I've seen her with all those other brazen hussies, climbing into the lorries the Yanks send for them on a Saturday night. And what goes on at that American base hardly bears thinking about. She's as bad as they are. No better than a bunch of . . .'

'*Rose!*' Freda had overheard the conversation and

stood in the kitchen doorway, her face stern. 'That's quite enough! I won't have gossip like that in my house and well you know it. As long as Sally's a guest here you'll treat her with respect.' But when a disgruntled Rose had gone upstairs to see to her children, Freda closed the door and looked searchingly at her younger daughter.

'When is the adoption going through?' she asked.

'Oh, soon.' Eve bit her lip, averting her eyes. She hadn't mentioned Sally's change of heart to her mother, ever hopeful that the girl would reconsider. But her daughter's strained appearance had not escaped Freda's notice.

'You look worn out. Are you having bad nights with the baby?' she pressed.

'She's been a bit fretful with her teeth starting to come,' Eve admitted. 'But apart from that she sleeps through the night now.' She edged towards the door. 'I think we'd better be off home now, Mum. Time Carol was tucked up for the night. Oh, and I'd be glad if you'd keep the adoption to yourself for the time being.'

Freda frowned at her suspiciously. 'There's nothing wrong, is there?'

Eve shook her head. 'Oh, no. It's just, you know what Rose is like. She can't keep anything to herself and I'd rather it wasn't common knowledge till everything's legal.'

Eve had just finished hanging out some washing in the yard two weeks later when she heard someone knocking on the street door. Putting the clothes basket down on the kitchen table, she went to answer it. A man in naval officer's uniform stood on the pavement outside, his back towards her. When she opened the door he turned, taking off his hat.

'Mrs Tyler?'

Eve shook her head. 'No. She's at work. She won't be home until this evening. Can I give her a message?'

The man hesitated. 'Are you a relative, Mrs – er . . . ?'

'Kenning. No, I suppose you could call me her landlady.'

'But you're friends?'

'Yes.'

He smiled. 'Perhaps I should introduce myself? Lieutenant James Dobson. I'm a Royal Navy padre. May we have a little talk, Mrs Kenning? Inside, perhaps?'

Eve ushered the man through to the kitchen, apologising for the mess. 'I've been washing and I haven't had time to tidy up yet.' She swept a pile of clean nappies from a chair into the empty basket. 'Please sit down. I've just made a cup of tea. Would you like one?'

'Thank you.'

When the business of pouring was done with the man looked at Eve. 'I'll come back later to see Mrs Tyler myself, of course, but I wonder if you would be kind enough to prepare her for what I have to tell her?'

Eve's mouth was suddenly dry. 'Of course. If I can help in any way . . .'

'You will know, of course, that Able Seaman Tyler was reported dead when his ship, H.M.S. *Stamford*, went down off Murmansk last year?'

'Yes.'

'It was thought at the time there had been no survivors, but it seems that three of the crew managed to get into a boat. They must have drifted for a long time, but they were eventually picked up by a Norwegian fishing boat. Of the three survivors one was already dead and another unfortunately died soon afterwards. But the third, Able Seaman Tyler, recovered. For a long time he was very seriously ill, too ill to be moved, but he was flown back to England yesterday and is undergoing further treatment in the Royal Naval Hospital in Portsmouth, which is where I've come from today.'

'I see.' Eve was stunned. 'Is he badly hurt. Will he be . . . ?'

'Disabled?' The man shook his head. 'Not disabled, though he is badly scarred. When he was picked up he was suffering from exposure and severe dehydration due to malnutrition and burns. He has undergone skin grafts which have been fairly successful and is due to have further surgery. However, the mental suffering affected him far more than his physical injuries. He'd had a very harrowing time as you may imagine. But with time and care he should make a full recovery. What he needs most now is to see his wife and start making positive plans for his future.'

'So – you want me to break the news to Sally?'

'If you could, Mrs Kenning. Even though it's good news it's going to come as a shock to her. I'll come and fill in the details for her later and give her what support I can, but the news will come better from a friend initially, I'm sure.'

For the rest of the day Eve went about her routine abstractedly. Deep inside her a tiny seed of fresh hope was beginning to germinate. Now that Dave was alive, Sally would surely agree to give Carol up. He was still ill. The news that she had been unfaithful to him, given birth to another man's child, would be a further blow. For Eve to adopt the baby was the obvious answer for them all. Sally would have her husband back, Eve would have Carol after all and Dave would recover, none the wiser. Her excitement mounted as she waited for the hands of the clock to creep round to six o'clock.

Sally's first reaction was one of disbelief. 'Dave – still alive? There must be some mistake. Why didn't I hear about it before? Someone's having us on, Evie.'

'Of course they're not! Who would play a joke like that? It's true, Sally. This man who came – he was a

31

padre; a naval officer. He's come all the way from Portsmouth to talk to you and he's really nice. He wouldn't tell lies or get it wrong.'

'They got it wrong before, didn't they? Why not again?'

'I don't know. Look, he's coming back later to talk to you. He'll tell you all the details, so you'd better have your tea and freshen up. I've lit a fire in the front room. You can see him in there privately.' Sally seemed not to have heard her as she sat staring into space. Eve seethed with impatience as she looked at her, sitting slumped and white-faced in the chair. 'Oh, come *on*, Sally. Aren't you happy? Don't you realise what this means? Your Dave is alive after all!'

Sally looked up and caught her breath suddenly. 'I can't take it in, Evie,' she said, her hand over her mouth. 'I can't think straight. I feel all swimmy and faint.'

Eve fetched a glass of water from the sink and pressed it into Sally's trembling hands. 'Here, drink this. You'll feel better when the shock has worn off and you've had something to eat. I think they want you to go down there and see him,' she said. 'Seems he's been asking for you. The padre says he needs you – needs to get back to normal again.'

Sally nodded, her teeth chattering slightly. 'Yes. I'll have to ask for some time off.'

Later that evening Eve waited impatiently as Sally and Lieutenant Dobson were closeted together in the front room. She had taken them in a tray of tea and biscuits but that seemed like ages ago. What could they possibly have to talk about all this time? she asked herself as she listened to the low hum of their voices.

She bathed and fed Carol and put her to bed, and had just come downstairs when she heard the street door close. A moment later Sally appeared in the kitchen doorway, her face pale.

'I've agreed I'll go down to Portsmouth tomorrow,' she said, slumping into a chair. 'I had to say I'd go, Evie, but I don't want to and I told him so.' She looked up, her eyes dark with fear. 'I'm scared.'

'You'll be all right. As soon as you see Dave – soon as you're back together again.'

'I *won't*.' Sally got up and moved to the mantelpiece where she'd left her cigarettes. She lit one and inhaled the smoke deeply. 'I've been trying to make the padre understand,' she said. 'I told him everything, Evie, about meeting Eddie and having Carol. But he just said it's happened to lots of wives and that the best thing I could do is to be honest and get it all out in the open.'

'But there's no *need*,' Eve argued. 'Dave doesn't have to know about the baby. It's all right for padres to preach at you about these things but Dave's been very ill. He doesn't need a shock like that. You know I'll take Carol off your hands. Then you can make a fresh start with your husband.'

'I'm not giving Carol up, though. I told you that,' Sally said stubbornly. 'Anyway, it's not that. If you want the truth, I don't want Dave back. Not like that. I can't face seeing him all scarred and twisted. Nothing can ever be the same.' She shuddered. 'I've seen some of those pilots who've come back after crashes. I can't do it, Evie. It's no use asking me. I just *can't*.'

Eve stared at her for a moment, at a loss for words. 'I think you should at least go down and see him like you promised you would,' she said at last. 'Surely you owe him that much after all he's been through?'

'I suppose so.' Sally stubbed out her cigarette. 'I'll tell him about Carol then he'll see that I'm not just leaving him because of the way he looks. That'll let him down lightly, won't it?'

Her selfishness and insensitivity left Eve speechless.

Surely when she saw Dave, pity alone would persuade her not to desert him? But then again, maybe not. 'We'd better have an early night,' Eve said with a sigh. 'If you've a long journey to face tomorrow.'

At dawn Carol woke, snuffling with the beginnings of a cold, and Eve took her into bed with her, as much for her own comfort as the baby's.

Sally returned from work the following day at lunchtime in a strange mood. She ate the meal that Eve had prepared then went upstairs to pack an overnight bag. The coming trip and her prospective reunion with Dave seemed to have made her tense and edgy. She went out, saying she needed to do some last-minute shopping, and at four-thirty returned and went back upstairs. When she came down she was dressed in her outdoor clothes, the red coat and a pair of high-heeled shoes, hopelessly inadequate for the freezing weather. She was also carrying Carol.

Alarmed, Eve jumped up from the table. 'What are you doing with her?'

'What does it look like?'

'You're not taking her with you?'

'Yes, I am.'

'All the way down to Portsmouth? But it's dark and freezing cold outside. You're not taking her all that way on a train at this time of night!'

'I don't see how else I'm going to get her there.'

Eve's heart was pounding so hard she felt dizzy. 'Shouldn't you break the news that you've got a baby to Dave first? Besides, you've got nowhere to stay.'

'Yes, I have. The padre mentioned some sort of hostel for wives near the hospital. He gave me the address.'

'*No!*' Eve moved across the room and positioned herself between Sally and the door. 'You're not taking her. I won't let you. She's not fit. She's got a cold.'

Sally pushed her aside. 'Get out of my way. She's going with me and you can't stop us.' She picked up her holdall and elbowed her way past Eve and through the door.

'No! Sally, *Sally*! Please listen to me. Wait!' But the sound of the street door slamming told her that Sally had gone, taking with her everything that had made Eve's life worth living.

She felt numb with shock, thinking of the long journey ahead of them. Carol had been restless all day, her nose stuffy. Eve wouldn't be surprised if the child was running a temperature. What effect would a long cold train journey have on her? Racked with anxiety, she pictured the worst possible scenario. The cold turning to bronchitis and then – *pneumonia*. Babies died of pneumonia! The terrible part was that there was nothing more she could do. Carol was Sally's child and the law said she could do whatever she wished with her. But how would Sally cope alone with a baby? She'd hardly ever changed a nappy, let alone washed one. She hadn't even fed the child except during those first two weeks when she breast fed her.

Eve saw her future spread bleakly before her, as lonely and featureless as a desert without the little girl who had been the centre of her universe for the past five months. She lowered her head on to her arms as fresh tears streamed down her cheeks.

The first wailing note of the air-raid siren brought her head up sharply, its ominous moan filling her heart with a new, more urgent dread. It was three weeks since there had been a raid. Everyone had been glad of the respite though no one felt secure. There was always the chance that they might be the next target – and everyone knew that the very worst place to be during a raid was the railway station. Railways were a favourite target and the lines were all too clearly visible from the air.

Jumping up from the table, Eve grabbed her coat from

35

behind the door and pulled it on. Snatching up her torch from the dresser, she ran out of the street door without bothering to secure it behind her. It was freezing hard and the first few flakes of snow danced in the beam of her torch. Carrying a bag and a baby, Sally could not have got far, especially on those ridiculous high heels. The ground underfoot was treacherously slippery too.

The quickest way to the station was down to the end of the street, across the main road and over the old railway footbridge. Eve guessed that Sally would have chosen that route. She ran, oblivious to the frosty pavement and the distant droning of enemy aircraft, trying to ignore the stitch in her side which snatched her breath away.

At she reached the footbridge her heart leaped with relief as she saw Sally silhouetted against the sky. She shouted to the shadowy figure and ran on to the bridge. Sally turned angrily to face her as she caught up.

'Why can't you leave me alone, damn you?'

'Don't be stupid! There's a raid on. Didn't you hear the siren?' Eve shouted. 'Chances are there won't be any more trains tonight anyway.' When Sally turned and began to walk on, she called, 'Wait! Just till tomorrow, Sally. At least leave Carol with me if you must go tonight.'

The other girl turned. 'You'd do anything to stop me, wouldn't you? You're like some jealous old maid, trying to get my baby off me. You're obsessed. Well, I'm her mother and you're not having her!'

Eve was angry now; really angry. Her heart was thudding and a mist danced before her eyes. '*Mother?* You're not a mother! You wouldn't know where to start. I'm the one who's loved and cared for her since she was born. All you've ever bothered about is going out and having a good time. You don't give a damn for poor Dave either. You're a selfish bitch! Give Carol to me.'

She made a grab for the shawl-wrapped baby but Sally

turned quickly and began to run. Eve ran too. The well-worn stone of the bridge with its glazing of frost was like glass under her and she grasped at the low stone parapet as her feet slid helplessly beneath her. Catching up with Sally, she pulled the baby from her arms but the other girl reached out and snatched at the child. Carol let out a yell and Eve shouted angrily, hitting out at Sally's arm.

'Let her go! You're *hurting* her, you bitch!' When the other girl refused to let go she lashed out again, striking Sally across the head, blinded by the fury that had taken possession of her.

Afterwards she could not remember in what sequence it all happened. Sally's hold on the baby relaxed and she staggered backwards under the impact of the blow, her arms flailing wildly and her feet slipping on the icy stone. For a split second she struggled to regain her balance, then her hip struck the parapet and before Eve's horrified gaze she toppled backwards over it and vanished from sight. There was a shrill scream, then, from somewhere far below, a sickening thud.

Eve stared disbelievingly at the empty ground where Sally had stood defying her just a moment ago. Only her holdall and one red high-heeled shoe were left. But before Eve had time to absorb the full implication of what had happened the first of the bombs screamed down, hitting the ground with a report that shook the bridge under her feet and left her ears singing. She ran as fast as she could, clutching the screaming baby close to her. She was halfway home when another bomb fell, this time terrifyingly close. Trembling violently, she crouched in a doorway, bending forward to protect the child with her own body as shattered glass and masonry fell all around her.

Taking advantage of the interval that followed, she emerged and stumbled on until she reached Brook's Lane.

Inside the house she closed the door and rushed for the security of the kitchen table, huddling beneath it with Carol held tightly in her arms, her eyes closed as she concentrated on survival, refusing to allow herself any other thoughts.

It seemed an age before the 'all clear' sounded. When it did Eve crawled stiffly out from under the table and for the first time unwrapped Carol to examine her. The baby's little face was smeared with grime and her shawl was tattered and dirty, but to Eve's relief the child seemed unhurt. Looking at the clock, she realised that it was well past time for her feed. She unzipped Sally's holdall, rummaging inside to see if she had packed a bottle. Finding nothing, she shook her head. It was typical of Sally to overlook the fact that the child would need feeding on the journey. There was only one nappy in the bag too. Eve clicked her tongue disparagingly.

Then, with a sudden chilling shock, she remembered that Sally was almost certainly dead. And that she, Eve Kenning, was responsible. The hazy recollection of what had happened on the bridge came back to her now with horrifying clarity. It was like the worst kind of nightmare. The kind from which there was no waking.

Putting the baby down in one of the armchairs, she stood up slowly and looked at herself in the mirror over the mantel shelf. Her own face was grimy and her hair wildly awry. Her clothes were covered in dust and there was a thin trickle of blood drying on her forehead from a cut she had been unaware of. But apart from that she looked no different. She had just caused the death of another human being and yet the eyes looking back at her were the same eyes she had always known.

Carol began to whimper and she dragged her mind back to the child's immediate needs. She stirred the fire into a bright blaze, took off her soiled clothing and washed off the dirt, blood and grime at the sink. Then, as she went about the reassuring routine of making up Carol's feed, she told herself over and over that what had happened had been an accident. She hadn't meant to harm Sally. Her main concern had been for the baby. But it was impossible to erase the guilt and horror of the terrifying, all-consuming fury she had felt in those few critical minutes.

'*But I didn't want her dead!*' she muttered to herself, her teeth beginning to chatter with delayed shock. '*Oh dear God, I never meant to hurt her – never wanted her to die!*' But the feeling of guilt refused to go away. She had prayed for a miracle that would make Carol hers to keep. How could she have imagined that her prayer would be answered in this horrific way?

She dragged out the baby bath. The normality of bathing the child and changing her into clean clothes helped to calm her, but as she held Carol on her lap in front of the fire, watching her take her bottle with wide blue eyes gazing trustingly up, Eve's conscience accused her. This child is motherless, she reproached herself. And it's all because of me, because of what I did tonight. Panic seized her. Suppose there were witnesses? Suppose someone had seen what happened? What if she were arrested – charged and convicted of murder? Murderers paid with their lives. Even a conviction for manslaughter would put her behind bars for years. With her gone, Carol would have no one at all. She would grow up in an orphanage! And Jack – poor Jack – would come home after all he had been through to an empty, cheerless home. Three lives would be shattered and it would all have been for nothing.

If only everything comes out all right, I'll devote the rest of her life to making it up to Carol, she promised herself fervently. I'll do everything that Sally would have

wanted for her. If I get through this, everything I have –
everything I do from today on – will be for Carol.

It was just after eight next morning when a loud knocking
on the door wakened Eve from the fitful sleep she had
fallen into in the chair by the fire. Starting to her feet, she
went to answer it, fully expecting a grave-faced policeman
to be waiting.

Instead her mother stood on the doorstep. She looked
drained, her normally florid face grey with exhaustion.
Eve started with alarm.

'*Mum!* Come in, you look awful. Is something wrong?'

'I'm afraid there is.' Freda followed her daughter
through to the kitchen. 'Eve – where's Sally? Is she here,
upstairs? Or is she at work?'

'Why do you want to know?' Eve's mouth was dry as
she stared at her mother.

'Just tell me, is she here?' Freda repeated.

'No.' Eve bit her lip hard to stop its trembling. 'She's
gone to Portsmouth.'

Freda's eyes widened. '*Portsmouth?*'

'Yes. We – she had news of her husband – yesterday.
He was found alive, drifting in a boat weeks after his ship
sank. She went to see him in the hospital.'

Freda groaned. 'Oh my God! What time was this?'

Eve moistened her dry lips. 'About half-past four.'

'Just before the raid.' Freda sighed and sat down at the
table. 'Eve, love, sit down. It's bad news, I'm afraid. A
bomb hit the railway just down the line from the station
in last night's raid.'

Eve's eyes widened with fear. 'Oh! *Dad!*'

'He's all right.' Freda reached out a reassuring hand.
'It's not your dad. He'd just come off duty when the siren
went. He was on his way home when the first bomb fell.
When the second one dropped the explosion almost lifted

him off his feet and he knew the station must have caught it, so he went back to see if there was anything he could do.'

'Was – was anyone killed?' Eve whispered.

'There were some casualties, but not from the railway staff.' Freda touched Eve's hand. 'The old footbridge was completely demolished, though. Everyone had to work hard to clear the rubble because the London train was due. Your dad helped.' She pressed the cold hand under hers. 'They found a body under the wreckage, Eve. There was nothing anyone could do. She was dead when they got her out.' Freda swallowed hard and pressed her handkerchief to her lips. 'It wasn't – wasn't possible to identify her. She was too badly injured. But your dad felt sure he recognised the red coat. He thinks it was Sally, love.' Freda paused. 'And I'm afraid it looks as if he's right. She must have been on her way to the station, taking the short cut across the old bridge, when the bomb fell.'

Too stunned and confused for words, Eve swallowed hard and tried to take it all in. Her mother was talking on, about notifying the police, Sally's mother, about the official things that must be done, but all Eve could think of was that no one could prove now that she was responsible for Sally's death. Perhaps it was not the fall – not her blow that had killed her, but the bomb?

The overwhelming sense of relief brought tears to Eve's eyes. No one would ever know now what had happened on the bridge last night. It felt like a sign, a kind of reprieve.

Chapter Two

September 1950
Carol sat at the piano, practising her scales. Her allotted hour was almost up and her chubby little fingers were cold and stiff. She longed to stop but the thumping of the piano shut out the sound of her parents' arguing in the next room.

As usual she was the subject of their disagreement and Carol hated it. Finally, unable to continue with the stumbling scales any longer, she stopped, closed her eyes and put her hands over her ears. If only they'd let her *choose* what she wanted to do. If only Mummy wasn't always trying to turn her into something special – drumming into her what her cousins were doing, making her feel guilty. Daddy understood, but Mummy would never listen to him. Even through her hands she could still hear their muffled voices going on and on. She slid down from the piano stool and let herself quietly out of the room, escaping across the hall to the sanctuary of her bedroom where she could indulge in her favourite fantasy where she was a beautiful princess imprisoned in a tower, waiting for a handsome prince to come and rescue her.

Jack Kenning had returned home from the prison camp in poor physical shape. The neglected wound in his leg had never healed properly and after his repatriation he spent many weeks in hospital having a series of painful operations that nevertheless left him partially disabled. Unable to resume his work in the building trade, he and

Eve had bought a little newsagent's shop in Clarence Street with living accommodation above. Due to the post-war housing shortage the little terraced house in Brook's Lane had made a good price and, together with Jack's army gratuity, they had raised enough money to put down a sizeable deposit on the business.

The flat was far more spacious and convenient than number 17 Brook's Lane. There was a bathroom, a sitting room and dining room as well as two bedrooms and a kitchen. There was even a small garden at the back with a patch of grass where Carol could play safely with her dolls' pram and tricycle.

Eve was delighted with the business. She enjoyed the work even though it was hard and the hours were long. Taking delivery of the morning papers and marking them all up for the boys to take out meant getting up at the crack of dawn, but at least Jack didn't have to turn out in all weathers or do any heavy work.

When he had first come home for good in August 1945, Carol had been almost three. At first she had been shy and slightly afraid of the tall dark man with the gaunt face and shuffling walk, and not a little jealous of all the attention her mummy gave him. But as his health improved and his gaunt features softened, she soon learned to accept and trust him. Jack was patient and gentle with the child and before long he was rewarded by her smiles. Soon she was sitting on his knee while he told her stories, and by the end of that year was following him everywhere and calling him Daddy as though she had known him all her short life. But right from the first, Jack had disagreed with the indulgent way Eve was bringing up their adoptive daughter.

'You're stifling her, love,' he'd warned. 'You never let her out of your sight. You won't even let your mum baby-sit with her. It's all very well now, but you'll suffer for it later and so will she. I know how you feel after waiting so long for a kiddie, but a child needs to be able to stand on its own feet. And she needs discipline as well as love.'

Eve disregarded his warning and the first time Jack smacked Carol's legs when she'd run out of the side gate into the road, she flew at him in fury.

'Don't you *dare* hit my child!' she shouted, gathering Carol up in her arms. 'Look, you've made her cry!'

'She's going to be my child too,' he reminded her gently. 'Should I have just stood there and let her run in front of a car? Is that what you would have done? Look, Eve, as long as I'm her father I'll teach her what's right and wrong. As well as what's safe and what's dangerous.'

Eve seethed with resentment. She knew all about danger. Hadn't she protected Carol that night when the bombs were falling, used her own body as a shield? But no one knew she'd been out with the child on that fateful evening. She couldn't tell Jack about that, or the real reason why she trusted no one else with Carol. No one must ever know the secret of what had happened on the night Sally died.

Eve had tried her best to forget that night. She had done her best to expunge every trace of Sally from her mind too, going back to her old nondescript hairstyle and drab way of dressing, throwing away the lipstick and powder the girl had encouraged her to wear. As far as she was concerned that part of her life was over and done with. Long ago she had made herself believe that fate had stepped in where Carol was concerned. The child was always meant to be hers. Sally would not have been a good mother. Yet try as she would, her guilt at what she had done that night would not go away. She tried to justify it, burying it under a mountain of rationalisation. She told herself that if it hadn't been for her Carol would never have been born. Sally had tried hard to get rid of her unwanted pregnancy. Chances were she would have succeeded eventually, left to her own devices, and probably killed herself into the bargain. And when all was said and done, Sally had died like thousands of others in an air raid. Eve had been there when Carol needed her. And she would always be here, come what may, to give her the best and bring out the best in her, whatever Jack said or did.

When the time came for Carol to start school the wrench of parting with her was almost physical for Eve, and the dancing lessons she had vaguely promised were firmly dismissed. It was bad enough parting with her child for hours every day at school. Miss Frencham, the piano teacher, came to the house so that seemed like a good compromise. Music should be the first of Carol's accomplishments.

To Eve's disappointment, marriage and her post-war relationship with Jack was not the same as it had been before he went away. The romance of their first year together, the ardour and passion she had dreamed of, had somehow never been rekindled. To begin with there was Jack's illness. Apart from his leg wound he still often wakened in a cold sweat at night, dreaming of the hell of battle and the prison camp; of comrades who had died. He would have liked to talk to her about it but Eve refused to let him dwell on it.

'It's over now,' she would tell him firmly. 'You've got to put it all behind you. We have our future to think of now. Ours and Carol's.'

The legal business of adopting the child had gone through during that first year after the war ended. It had been straightforward. As a war orphan, cared for from birth by Eve, the powers-that-be had accepted her and Jack as the obvious choice for adoptive parents. In the year following Jack's return a date was set for the official court hearing. But the week before the hearing was to take place something disturbing happened. That afternoon haunted Eve for months afterwards and added a new fear to the guilt that stalked her constantly.

It was a Saturday in April 1946 and she was alone in the shop that afternoon. She had persuaded Jack to go to the football match with Rose's husband, Ted. He didn't get out much and had seemed a bit down that week. Eve thought the outing would do him good. Carol was upstairs, having her afternoon nap, and Eve was arranging packets of cigarettes on the shelves behind the counter, her back to the door, when she heard the shop bell tinkle. When she turned round her heart turned over. A man stood facing her. He was dressed respectably enough in civilian clothes, a light grey gaberdine macintosh unbuttoned over a dark suit. But one side of his face was terribly distorted, the skin white and tightly stretched with what everyone had come to recognise since the war as burn scarring.

'Yes? Can I help you?' Eve asked, trying not to let her voice echo her dismay.

He smiled as though to reassure her. 'Mrs Kenning?'

Her eyes widened in surprise. 'Yes, but . . . ?'

'I'm Dave Tyler.' He offered her a gloved hand across the counter. 'I went to your old address and the lady there told me you'd moved here. My wife Sally lodged with you at the end of the war. Before – before she was killed.'

'Yes. Yes, that's right.' Eve clutched at the edge of the counter to steady herself. She felt the blood drain from her face and the strength go out of her legs. She was sure he must be able to hear the pounding of her heart.

'She wrote to me about how well she got on with you and how kind you and your family were,' the man went on. 'I was too ill to attend the funeral, but I wanted to come and thank you for helping her. It can't have been easy for her, thinking I was a goner all those months.'

'No.' Eve licked her dry lips. 'It was good of you to come all this way.' She paused. The man seemed to be waiting for her to say something else. 'Can I get you something?' she offered. 'A cup of tea?'

'Thanks. I wouldn't say no.' He looked pleased. 'It'd be nice to talk to someone who knew Sally. We hadn't been married long, you know. Only a few weeks really.'

Eve took him through to the small room at the rear of the shop where she would brew up tea or coffee when they were too busy to take a break upstairs. There were two chairs and a table squeezed in among the piled up stock. 'I hope you don't mind if I don't take you up to the flat,' she said, 'only I'm on my own this afternoon?'

'This is fine.' He made himself at home at the table, taking out a roll-up kit and making himself a cigarette while Eve put the kettle on and took mugs, milk and sugar from the cupboard.

'Sally's mum chucked her out when we got married,' he said. 'I went to see her but she wouldn't talk to me. Said Sally'd still be alive if it wasn't for me.'

'That's very unfair.' The shop bell went and Eve escaped into the shop to serve a customer. Coming back, she sat down opposite Dave, wondering how long her ordeal was going to last. She poured tea and passed the sugar bowl, watching as he spooned sugar into the tea and stirred. Something told her that he had not come all this way simply to pass the time of day. He looked up and met her eyes.

'I'll be straight with you, Mrs Kenning,' he said. 'I got this letter when I was in the hospital. It was from someone living here in Northampton. It wasn't signed but it said that Sal had had a baby.'

Eve gasped. 'I can't think who would write to you with . . .'

'Is it true?' He was leaning forward urgently.

47

'Yes. It's true,' she said reluctantly.

'You see, the letter didn't say when. Didn't give any dates or anything, and I wonder . . .'

'*Oh!*' Eve's heart sank. 'Oh, I see.' She bit her lip, avoiding his eyes. 'I'm sorry. I'm afraid . . .'

'It wasn't mine? Is that what you're trying to tell me?'

'I know she never meant to let you down,' Eve said, her heart contracting at the pain she saw etched on his damaged face. 'She was so lonely, missing you. The whole affair hurt her a lot. It was very hard for her. I know she thought an awful lot of you.' She felt ashamed as she heard herself mouthing the trite clichés.

He was shaking his head slowly. 'You're sure?' He looked at her hopefully. 'I mean, that the baby couldn't have been mine?'

'I'm afraid so. Look, I can show you the birth certificate, if you like.' Eve rummaged nervously in her handbag and produced Carol's birth certificate, which she always kept with her, spreading it on the table between them. 'There's the date, you see.' She pointed. 'September the sixth, 1942. That was just a year after she came to stay with me.'

But Dave was looking at the place where the father's name should be inserted, staring hard at the shameful word *unknown*. He looked up at her. 'Who was he?' he asked grimly. 'Do you know?'

Eve shook her head. 'I know that when Sally heard you were alive she meant to tell you about the baby and ask you to forgive her. She wanted so much to be with you again. She was on her way to see you in the hospital that night when . . . when . . .'

'What happened to the baby?'

Eve swallowed hard. 'I've brought her up right from the first. My husband and I are – we've adopted her.'

'She's here now?'

48

In the pit of Eve's stomach there was a cold feeling. Was it possible that at this late stage this man could do something to stop the legal adoption going through? Just a few days from the hearing? Panic rose in her throat. She looked at him appealingly. 'We love her very much, Mr Tyler. She's the whole world to us. We can't have any of our own, you see.'

He nodded. 'Sally was lucky to have known someone like you, Mrs Kenning. I'm very grateful to you for making her last year happy and I'm sure you've looked after Sal's little girl up just as she would have wanted.' He took a deep breath. 'There's just one thing – one favour I'd like to ask?'

Eve steeled herself. 'Yes?'

'Could I – would you mind if I just – saw her?'

Eve wished Jack were here. He would have known what to do. She looked apprehensively at the man. 'I don't know. Is that wise?'

'It can't do any harm, surely?' He lifted his shoulders helplessly. 'It's just that she's all that's left of Sal and I – I . . .'

She saw his face begin to crumple and nodded. 'I'll go and get her. She should be awake by now. If you wouldn't mind just keeping an eye on the shop for a minute?'

Eve trembled as she lifted the sleepy toddler from the cot and carried her downstairs. Dave Tyler stared at Carol for a long moment. He made no attempt to take her from Eve or to touch her, sensing that his disfigured face would frighten her. 'She's lovely,' he said huskily. 'The image of Sal. Same big blue eyes and fair hair.' He nodded to Eve. 'Thanks for letting me see her, Mrs Kenning. It means a lot.'

Racked with pity and guilt, Eve opened her handbag again and produced a snapshot of Carol taken the previous summer. 'Would you like to have this?' she said. 'Just as a little keepsake?'

He took it and looked at it briefly before slipping it into his pocket. 'Thanks. And thanks for being so under-standing, Mrs Kenning.'

She followed him through to the shop. At the door he turned and took a last look at the baby. Eve had sat Carol on the counter where she was playing with a display card for Rowntree's chocolate. Nodding to her, he let himself out and Eve watched as he passed the shop window. It was only then that she began to wonder who could have been spiteful enough to write to this man who had suffered so much. And just who or what that person had hoped to achieve.

As well as the trouble Jack had with his leg, he still suffered from time to time from a stomach complaint he'd picked up in the camp. The doctor had warned him that there might always be recurrences of it. Sometimes a sudden bout of pain and sickness would confine him to bed and Eve would have to manage the shop, Carol and the house on her own for a few days. On these occasions Rose would sometimes help out, though Eve did not ask her unless she was hard-pressed. The relationship between the sisters did not improve as time went on.

Although she was grateful to have Jack home again and tried not to resent the fact that he was a mere shadow of the man who had gone away, she could not fight off the irrational feeling that she was being punished for what she had done. In her obsessive attempt to make amends, she concentrated all her hopes and ambitions on Carol. But when Jack began to feel that Eve's ambition to foster every spark of talent in Carol was becoming a fixation, he decided to step in.

'Look, love, she's just an ordinary little girl,' he argued. 'Let her enjoy her childhood. Just be glad that she won't have her life blighted by war as we did.'

'I *do* want her to enjoy her childhood,' Eve protested. 'But I want to give her every chance. She deserves it. If she's got any talent then we must encourage it.'

'Then let her stop those damned piano lessons for a start,' Jack begged. 'The poor little scrap hates them and it's plain to anyone that she's got no musical talent. Surely even you have to admit that? Thump thump thump! It's enough to drive anyone barmy!'

Unable to deny it, Eve bit her lip. She had to concede that Jack had a point. Carol had been having lessons for ages and seemed to be making no progress at all. Only last week when Rose had come to help in the shop she had been boasting about how clever her children were. Michael was thirteen now and top of his form at the grammar school and Elizabeth had just started at the girls' high school. Carol's end-of-term school reports made frustrating reading and Eve despaired of her ever matching up to her cousins' academic prowess. The main complaint was that she seemed prone to inattention. Her teacher complained that she was forever staring out of the window. Then there were all those fairy stories she was forever making up in her head, shut up in her room, talking to herself! Eve sighed. She'd never pass her elevenplus at this rate. And now the music had proved a non-starter too.

Reading her thoughts, Jack went on, 'If only you didn't push her so hard. You expect too much. Have you any idea what it's like, having other kids' successes rammed down your throat from morning till night? Being made to feel guilty about something you've no control over?'

Eve bridled. 'I don't do that!' she said indignantly.

51

'Yes, you do! You don't want to let Rose keep needling you. Think of Carol's feelings once in a while.'

'How can you *say* a thing like that to me?' Eve demanded, her face scarlet. 'Everything I do is for that child!'

'Is it, Eve? *Is it?*' Something in the way Jack looked at her made her turn away guiltily. 'Sometimes it seems to me it's more for you.' He touched her arm. 'I know you want her to do well, love,' he said. 'We both want that. But it's no use making the kiddie's life a misery, is it?'

Eve turned to him and to his dismay he saw that she was crying. 'I want the best for her,' she said brokenly. 'I want her to be happy, that's all. I want her to have a good, successful life.'

'And so she will – if you let her!' He took out his handkerchief and dabbed at her cheeks awkwardly. 'Come on, love. Look on the bright side. Carol's a real picture. She's going to be a little smasher when she grows up. She's bright too. She might not be clever in the way Rose's kids are but she's got all her chairs at home, all right. She'll turn out fine, you'll see. And if not – well, some likely young feller-me-lad is going to whisk her off to the altar by the time she's twenty anyway, so why worry?'

But turning out 'just fine' or being 'whisked off to the altar' as some kind of consolation prize wasn't good enough for Eve. Maybe it was time to let Carol start dancing classes. It was true enough what Jack had said about her looks. She smiled to herself. At least that was one area where she scored over Rose. Carol was losing her chubby baby look now that she had turned eight, promising to grow up tall and slender. She was unquestionably pretty with her corn silk hair and wide blue eyes. She made Rose's Elizabeth, with her blunt features and stocky legs, look lumpy and plain by comparison. Eve implied as much to Rose a few days later, but her sister merely reminded her caustically that, being adopted, Carol owed nothing of her good looks to either Jack or herself.

'You'll need to watch her in a few years' time,' Rose said darkly. 'Let's hope she doesn't take after her real mother. Bad right through, that one was.'

'Don't talk like that!' Eve snapped. 'Poor Sally was just a kid. She was lonely, vulnerable and insecure.'

'Oh, is that what you call it?' Rose said scathingly. 'By the way, have you told Carol about her yet? Does she know she's adopted?'

'No, we haven't, and I'll thank you to keep your voice down, Rose,' Eve said sharply. 'We'll tell her when the time's right. When we feel she's ready.'

'Well, if you want my advice, you'll do it before someone else is kind enough to do it for you!' Rose warned.

'Thanks. When I want your advice, I'll ask for it.'

'Okay. Have it your way.' Rose gave her a look that spoke volumes and pulled her mouth into the familiar *Don't say I didn't warn you* look.

It was a few weeks later that Eve was asked to display the poster. A boy came into the shop just as she was about to close for the night and asked her if she would pin it up in a prominent position.

She rather took exception to the request for a 'prominent position'. Taking the rolled-up poster from the boy, she looked at it doubtfully. 'I haven't got a lot of room for posters,' she said. 'What's it for anyway?'

'A Christmas concert,' he said. He was a tall, good-looking boy of about fifteen with wavy dark hair and brown eyes. He unrolled the poster carefully and pointed to the colourful lettering.

Kitty Manson's School of Dancing and Dramatic Art
proudly presents
CHRISTMAS CRACKERS
Songs, dances and sketches with a festive theme
At the Town Hall from December 7th to 9th inclusive
Matinee performance on Saturday

Eve stared at the poster. 'Who's Kitty Manson when she's at home?' she asked.

The boy grinned. 'She's my mother actually. We came up here from London during the war. She used to be a professional dancer and actress.'

'And now she's started this school?'

'She started it five years ago,' he told her. 'When we were left on our own she had to do something to earn a living so she started the school. I help too,' he added. 'I play the piano for the dancing classes sometimes after school.'

The boy had an air of disarming confidence. He had none of the gawky shyness usually associated with teenagers and he spoke with the kind of accent that Rose would have referred to as 'la-di-dah'. She would have pronounced him cheeky and written him off as toffee-nosed. But, for all his outspokenness, Eve found him likeable.

'Where is it then, this school?' she asked.

'Chine Way. Opposite Midsummer Meadow. Do you know it?'

Eve did know it. She was impressed. The houses in Chine Way, with their view of the willow-fringed river and the sweeping expanse of green locally known as The Meadow, were large and spacious. This Kitty Manson must be doing well if she could afford to live there.

The boy was still talking. 'My mother supplies dancing troupes for the local pantomimes,' he said proudly. 'Kitty

Manson's *Dancing Babes*. Perhaps you've heard of them?'

Eve nodded. Now that he mentioned it she dimly remembered seeing some such name on the programme at the New Theatre when she took Carol to see *Jack and the Beanstalk* last year.

'Right,' she said. 'I'll put your poster up. Do I get a complimentary ticket to the show for doing it?'

The boy grinned. 'Why not?' He delved into his pocket and produced two. 'These are for the matinee. Hope you enjoy the show, Mrs Kenning. Thanks.'

Eve took Carol to see *Christmas Crackers*, leaving Jack looking after the shop. She was impressed by the standard of the children and young people who performed. There was nothing amateurish about the show. It was slickly produced, the costumes attractive and the material fresh. No one, not even the youngest child, faltered. To Eve's eyes it was even better than some of the touring shows she'd seen at the theatre. If she were to let Carol take dancing lessons, if she were to entrust her daughter to anyone's care, then perhaps this was a suitable place to send her. By the time the first half had come to an end and the lights went up for the interval, her mind was made up. She glanced at her daughter.

'Are you enjoying it?'

Carol nodded enthusiastically. 'It's lovely.'

'Do you want an ice cream?'

'Yes, please.'

As Eve queued for the ice cream she wondered if Carol might fit in to Kitty Manson's set-up. She reminded herself that Jack had said the child should not be pushed, and recognised that she must approach the question diplomatically. Back in her seat she watched speculatively as Carol tucked into the ice cream.

'It must be fun for those children up there on the stage, eh?'

Carol glanced up at her. 'Yes. I like those little ballet dresses. The ones with the frilly knickers to match.'

'You like dancing, don't you? You're always twirling round to the music on the wireless.'

'Mmm.'

'So – how would you like to learn to do it properly?'

'Where?'

Carol looked up at her and Eve searched the child's face for signs of genuine enthusiasm. She shrank from the thought of another failure like the piano lessons.'

'Who would teach me?' Carol asked.

'This lady. Mrs Manson.' Eve pointed to the programme.

Carol scraped the bottom of the ice cream carton thoughtfully and slid the last spoonful into her mouth before replying. 'If I went to dancing classes, would you let me give up piano?' she asked.

'If you really don't like it, yes.'

'And would I have one of those dresses with the frilly knickers?'

'Of course. If that's what you have to wear.'

Carol nodded. 'All right then.'

Once Christmas with its frenetic rush was over, Eve looked up the address of Kitty Manson's school in the telephone book and rang to make an appointment. But when she arrived at number 22 Chine Way the following afternoon she was a little disappointed. It was at the end of the road nearest the cattle market. The wrong end. Down here the houses were less grand and not so well-kept. She noticed as she stood waiting to be admitted that the paint on the front door was chipped and the brass knocker could have done with a good polish. But she told herself that a woman who ran a school of dancing and dramatic art could not be expected to spend all day cleaning and polishing.

A grim-looking woman in a print overall opened the door and, when Eve said she had an appointment, ushered her grudgingly into a small sunlit room with red patterned curtains and a red rug on the wood block floor.

'I'll tell Mrs Manson you're here,' she said, looking Eve up and down. 'She's taking a class at the moment.'

As she waited Eve could hear from somewhere above the sound of a piano and rhythmically pounding feet; a loud female voice was shouting instructions. Presently the noise stopped and the sound of girlish voices and hurrying feet could be heard in the hall outside. A few minutes later the door opened and a head came round it.

'*Hello!* I'm so sorry to keep you waiting. Do let me introduce myself – I'm Kitty Manson.' The woman stepped forward, holding out her hand.

Slightly taken aback, Eve stood up and shook the soft white hand Kitty offered. She had the reddest hair Eve had ever seen. She wore red tap shoes fastened with big bows and a brightly coloured tunic over black tights. She had hastily flung a thick red cardigan over this ensemble, pushing the sleeves up to her elbows. 'Do excuse the garb,' she said with a giggle. 'I've just finished taking a class and it doesn't do to get cold. Now – let's see, you're Mrs Kenning, aren't you? Shall we sit down and make ourselves comfy?'

Eve sat on the chair Kitty Manson indicated at a small table near the window. 'I was wondering if you had any vacancies?' she began. 'My daughter Carol is eight . . .'

Kitty smiled and nodded. 'A good age to begin. In what branch of the performing arts is she interested?'

'Well . . .' Eve cleared her throat. 'She's – er – very graceful,' she said. 'Always dancing to the wireless. You know, twirling round on her toes and that. And she loved your show, *Christmas Crackers.*'

57

'She has expressed a wish to come to the school, I take it?'

'Oh, yes!'

'Good. So many mothers push their daughters into it, you know. For all the worst reasons. You should see some of the poor little wretches I've had to deal with in the past. Not an ounce of talent and hating every minute of it, poor lambs. This is why I now audition children for a place at the school.'

'Audition?' This was something Eve hadn't bargained for. After all, if she were willing to pay for lessons . . .

'Well, I don't know,' she said doubtfully. 'Carol's a bit shy. She may not take kindly to a test. She hasn't had any actual dancing lessons before, you see.'

Kitty smiled and waved one hand. 'Don't worry, Mrs Kenning. It isn't the ordeal it might sound. I have my own ways of sniffing out a child's suitability and potential. Bring her along next Saturday morning at ten and I'll soon tell you if you have a little performer on your hands.' She got up and went to a desk in the corner where she took out a leaflet. 'Meantime, take my prospectus home and discuss it with your husband.' She peered at Eve. 'You – er – do have a husband?'

'Oh, yes.'

'I'm glad. So many mothers struggling to bring up families on their own since the war. Tragic. Fathers are so important to a child's development and upbringing.' She raised her pencilled eyebrows. '*Some* fathers, that is!'

'Your son tells me you are alone,' Eve said conversationally. 'A widow?'

'Alone, yes. A widow, no,' Kitty said. 'My husband was with ENSA all through the war. He played the trumpet with a dance band. I'd have gone too but I had my son Steven to bring up. When it was over, Al – my husband – chose to abscond with an exotic dancer from Wigan.'

'*Oh!*' Acutely embarrassed Eve felt herself blush. 'I'm so sorry,' she mumbled.

'My dear, *don't* be. It was the best thing he ever did for me! Well, actually it was the *only* thing he ever did for me! I just hope it keeps fine for him. I mean, a dancer I could have understood. But an *exotic dancer*! And from *Wigan*! She used a snake in her act. A python, I understand.' To Eve's astonishment she began to laugh, shaking like a jelly till tears made mascara trickle in dark streaks down her cheeks. 'Oh dear what *will* you think of me?' she spluttered, her face pink. 'You'd have to have met him to see the funny side. But, believe me, it's good riddance.'

'Oh.' Eve cleared her throat. 'I see.'

'Yes. Since it's been just me and Stevie, the school has gone from strength to strength,' Kitty told her. 'Whereas the last I heard of him, he and this woman had given up working the clubs. Seems her snake died. A happy release for the poor thing, if you ask me!' She began to laugh again. 'They're running an old people's home now – in Bognor! My dear, I *ask* you!'

Kitty herself showed Eve out and she walked back towards the town centre in something of a daze. After meeting the amazingly frank and affable Kitty Manson, she was beginning to wonder if she was doing the right thing. It wasn't in the least what she'd expected. She'd imagined it would be a matter of booking a course of lessons, not this audition thing. On the other hand, strange though the woman was, she obviously knew what she was doing, at least as far as dancing was concerned. And Jack would think it sensible to see if Carol had any aptitude before wasting any more money.

'Have you seen how much it costs to send her to this

dancing school place?' Jack held out the prospectus, a look of outrage on his face.

'That's for full-time,' Eve pointed out. 'Six lessons a week in all the different branches – singing, dancing and acting. I thought just one dancing lesson a week to start with, after school. Anyway, Mrs Manson's suggested that I take Carol for an audition on Saturday. If she's not suited to it, Mrs Manson will say so.'

'Huh! Is that what she told you?' Jack scoffed. 'She's having you on. Think she's going to turn away good money? Never! She'll kid you on that Carol is the next Gertrude Lawrence for money like this.'

'She won't,' Eve said firmly. 'She's an odd sort of woman, I grant you, but I believe she's absolutely straight.'

And to her own surprise, she found she actually meant it.

Carol's audition took place in the large room on the first floor at Chine Way, the room she would later learn to call 'the studio'. Eve took her along at the appointed time on Saturday morning and, at Kitty's request, left her there, arranging to pick her up later.

Carol looked apprehensively round the large empty room with its barre fixed along one wall and the mirror at the far end, a curtain half drawn across it. In one corner stood an upright piano with a record player perched on top. To begin with she felt rather in awe of the colourful lady introduced to her as Mrs Manson, but the moment her mother had left, the woman seemed to change. Smiling conspiratorially, Kitty pulled up two of the chairs at the end of the room and invited Carol to sit down with her.

'Right. Let's get to know one another, shall we? I'm Kitty Manson and you're Carol, right?' She nodded, but

Kitty shook her head. 'I want you to answer me, Carol. With your *voice*, darling, understand? I want to hear what you sound like. Now, tell me about yourself?' Smiling expectantly, she cocked her head on one side. Her dark eyes were bright and beady and she had the same perky air about her as the robin that came each morning to be fed at Carol's bird table.

Warming to her new friend, she said, 'My name is Carol Louise Kenning and I'm eight years old.'

'*Good!*' Kitty laughed delightedly as though she had said something wonderfully witty. 'Now then, tell me what you like doing when you're not at school?'

Carol thought carefully. 'I like playing – with my dolls and my tricycle, only I'm getting too big for that now. I might get a two-wheel bike for Christmas.' She paused, then added, 'And sometimes I have a friend to tea.'

'Yes, what else?'

'I like reading stories and – pretending.'

'What do you pretend?'

Carol shrugged. 'All sorts of things.'

'Tell me about your favourite pretend?'

Carol hesitated. She had never told anyone about the princess before and she was afraid of being laughed at, but there was something compelling about the bright eyes that were looking at her. 'I like – pretending I'm a – a princess,' she whispered.

Kitty clapped her hands. 'How lovely! What's the princess's name?'

'Crystal,' Carol said, encouraged. 'She's Princess Crystal. She's locked up in the castle and she's got a wicked stepmother who's cruel to her and makes her play scales on the piano all day long. But the prince is going to come and rescue her soon.'

'How exciting! I bet you love pretending that. Now tell me what you *don't* like doing?' Kitty asked surprisingly.

Carol did not hesitate on this one. 'Practising the piano,' she said. 'I hate that.'

'Fancy that! Just like Princess Crystal. So you don't like music?'

'Oh, I like music, but scales aren't real music. They're boring, and anyway I can't do it.'

'I see.' Kitty got up from her chair and switched on the record player. 'I think we've sat still long enough,' she said. 'I want you to listen to this.' She lowered the needle on to the record. 'I'm going to have a little dance to it and you can join in if you want to. There's no one here but you and me, so you needn't be shy.'

Carol watched in astonishment as Kitty began to dance to the jaunty strains of *Music, Music, Music*. She had seemed a bit odd to Carol at first with her strange clothes and colourful make-up, but the moment the music started she was transformed, kicking her shapely legs in the air, tapping and twirling unselfconsciously. She was quite unlike any other grown-up Carol had ever met. Once her initial surprise was over she began to enjoy the spectacle. Mrs Manson was very good at dancing, she decided admiringly, as she watched the bright red hair bouncing and the twinkling feet tapping out the infectious rhythm.

'Come on, join in,' Kitty sang out, beckoning to her invitingly. 'Don't be shy. I can tell you want to.'

Carol got up and began to try to copy Kitty's movements, wiggling her diminutive hips and shoulders and kicking out with her feet in an attempt to produce the fascinating tapping sounds the teacher made. When the record came to an end she was quite sorry.

Kitty collapsed, laughing, on to her chair. 'Ooh! *Wasn't* that fun? Did you enjoy it?'

Carol nodded, her eyes bright and her cheeks pink.

Kitty closed her eyes and breathed deeply for a moment, then suddenly she opened her eyes and looked at Carol. 'Tell you what, if I put another record on, will you dance for me on your own? Just making it up as you go along?' Again Carol nodded and Kitty wagged a finger at her. 'You've forgotten what I told you about answering with your voice, haven't you?'

Carol bit her lip. 'Sorry,' she said. 'Yes, I'd like to dance – please.'

Kitty laughed and patted her cheek. 'That's better!'

She put another record on and a moment later some very different music drifted across the room. The dreamy, romantic theme from Tchaikovsky's *Romeo and Juliet*. 'You can be Princess Crystal if you like,' Kitty told her. 'Close your eyes and pretend. Then, this time, let your pretend turn into a dance.'

Carol slipped off her shoes and ran to the centre of the floor. In her imagination she was wearing a white gauzy dress with silver threads that floated around her as she moved. Her long hair was bound up in braids and tied with golden ribbons like the princess in her fairytale book and on her feet she wore tiny satin slippers. Through half-closed eyes she could see the cold stone of the tower walls and glimpse the silver of blue sky through the latticed window. Lost in the fantasy she danced, drifting and pirouetting, rising on her toes, her arms outstretched and her head thrown back, then sinking gracefully to the floor. When the music stopped she opened her eyes and looked uncertainly across the room at the teacher. Had she been silly and babyish? Would Mrs Manson laugh and call her a silly goose just as Daddy had when he'd caught her dancing to the wireless?

But Kitty wasn't laughing. 'I enjoyed that,' she said, getting up. 'Thank you, Carol. Now, would you like to come downstairs and have some lemonade and biscuits?'

Carol started to nod and then she remembered. 'Thank you. I'd like that very much,' she said carefully.

Kitty nodded her approval and held out her hand. 'Come along then. You've worked very hard.'

All the way home Carol chattered excitedly about her meeting with Kitty Manson, but Eve hardly heard. She was busy with her own thoughts. When she had called to take Carol home, Kitty Manson had left the child drinking her lemonade and slipped into the hall to speak to Eve privately.

'I'd be delighted to take Carol, Mrs Kenning' she said. 'She's a graceful child, just as you said. But more than that, she has a remarkably well-developed imagination and, I believe, a natural talent for acting which deserves encouragement. I'd like to enrol her for dancing and drama classes, if you're agreeable?'

Eve's cheeks were flushed with excitement. Jack would have to take her seriously now. Hadn't she always said that Carol was gifted? Hadn't she always promised to nurture her talent?

'I'll have to talk to my husband about it, of course,' she said.

Kitty nodded. 'Naturally. The new term has already started, so if you wish her to begin straight away I could give you a small reduction on this term,' she offered. 'Let me know when you've had time to talk it over.'

Walking home with Carol prattling beside her, Eve remembered that Christmas nine years ago during the war when Sally had kept them all entertained with her uninhibited inventiveness at charades. Now it was clear that Carol had inherited that talent. Whatever happened, whatever *anyone* – including Jack – said, Carol must be enrolled at Kitty Manson's. She looked down at the child skipping happily beside her.

'Would you like to go to the dancing classes then?' she asked.

Carol nodded and then, remembering Kitty's instruction, quickly said, 'Oh, yes, *please*, Mummy.' Adding for good measure, 'More than anything in the world!'

'Kitty Manson? You don't mean that awful woman with the dyed red hair and the green eyelids? I've seen her on The Meadow with those kids on summer afternoons, encouraging them to make exhibitions of themselves! Flitting about, waving bits of net. I'm surprised you want your Carol having anything to do with the likes of her!'

As usual it was Rose, trying to put a damper on Eve's enthusiasm with her forthright opinions as they washed up in their mother's kitchen after Sunday tea.

Eve swallowed her annoyance. 'She's a very nice person as it happens,' she said. 'An ex-professional.'

Rose laughed knowingly. 'Oh, yes? An ex-professional *what*?'

Ignoring the barb, Eve went on, 'Carol has come on wonderfully well in the six months since she's been at the school. Anyone can see how her deportment has improved. She holds herself so well. And you should see her dance.'

Rose grunted disapprovingly. 'And where's all that going to get her?' she asked. 'She'll only start getting big ideas about herself. And you surely don't want her to go on the stage, do you? An immoral lot, they are, by all accounts. Mrs Jennings at the end of our street lets out her spare room to some of the turns who come to the New. She says she could write a book about some of the goings on!' Rose pulled down the corners of her mouth. 'and I mean, she's already got that *streak* in her.'

'What *streak*, Rose?' Eve's face was scarlet with fury. 'What are you hinting at?'

'Keep your hair on! You know what I mean. Face it, Eve, you'll have to keep a tight rein on her in a few years' time. I mean, you have to admit that her mother wasn't exactly an angel, was she? None too bright either. Couldn't have been to get herself into trouble with the first man who dangled a pair of nylons under her nose! You can't make a silk purse out of a sow's ear, you know.'

'A *sow's ear* now, is she?' Eve bridled. 'Well, when it comes to animals, your Elizabeth is more like a carthorse than a girl! At least Carol is pretty and feminine!'

'*Eve – Rose!* For goodness' sake!' Freda Harris opened the kitchen door and admonished her daughters sternly. 'We can hear you in the sitting room, yelling at each other. I'd have thought that women of your age would've stopped all this silly squabbling by now! You're no better than when you were kids!'

The three children had been sent to play. In the front room Michael, who was almost fourteen, was reading the *Hotspur* and trying to distance himself from the girlish banter of his sister and cousin. They never could get together without quarrelling and this afternoon was no exception. Carol had been dancing, showing them the latest steps she had learned at her classes.

'You're a show-off!' Elizabeth accused.

'I'm not!'

'Yes, you are. My mum says so. Just because you go to that silly dancing school, you think you're somebody.'

'I don't then!'

'Yes, you do. Prancing about like a lot of soppy kids. It'll get you nowhere. Mum says!'

'When I'm thirteen I'm going to be in the pantomime and wear a frilly frock – *and* get paid for it. So *there*,' Carol said. 'I'm going to be in the *Dancing Babes*. Mrs Manson says I can.'

Elizabeth's face turned crimson as she reached out to tug a handful of Carol's hair. 'You're a rotten little *swank*! You've got nothing to brag about. You're just a *brat*. Mum says so. Auntie Eve isn't even your real mum. Mum says *she* was a slut!'

'*Liz!*' Michael sprang to his feet. 'You're not supposed to say that. You know you're not. I'm going to tell Dad.' He headed for the door, but his sister got there before him.

'If you do, I'll *kill* you!' Elizabeth flew at him, clawing at his face and kicking his shins, until the door opened and Jack and Ted rushed in to separate the fighting children.

In the midst of the uproar, Carol ran out of the room and up the stairs to lock herself in the bathroom. What had Elizabeth meant? she asked herself as she stood trembling, her back against the door. How could it be true that mummy wasn't her real mummy? Yet for Michael to be so shocked with his sister there must be some truth in what she said. She felt a big lump in her throat and her eyes stung with tears, but she hastily swallowed them when someone startled her, tapping on the bathroom door.

'Carol? It's Daddy. Are you all right, lovie?'

'Y-yes.'

Jack twisted the handle. 'Will you open the door for me, please?'

After a moment's hesitation Carol turned and unlocked it. Jack held out his arms to her. 'Don't cry. It's all right, lovie. Really it is.'

She clung to him. 'Is it true what Liz said?' she whispered. 'Is it true that Mummy isn't my real mummy?'

Jack closed the bathroom door and turned the key again, then, sitting down on the cork-topped stool, he took Carol's hands and pulled her towards him. Taking out his handkerchief, he dried her tears.

'Listen, Mummy and I love you very much,' he said.

'Every bit as much as Auntie Rose and Uncle Ted love Liz and Mike. Mummy was there at the moment you were born and she's looked after you every single day of your life since.'

'But Liz said . . .'

'Your real mum was killed in the war, like lots of other mums, when you were very, very little,' he went on. 'Some of those children who lost their mummies and dads had to go and live in children's homes and never had a family or a proper home again. You were lucky.' He kissed her forehead. 'And *we* were lucky too – so lucky. We couldn't have any little babies of our own, you see, and when we knew we could have you for our very own, we were so happy.' He held her hands between both of his and looked into her eyes. 'You're very special to us, Carol. You always will be. Our precious only child. I want you to remember that, always.'

Reassured, she nodded. 'Yes, Daddy. But why did Elizabeth say my real mum was a slut?' She looked up at him. 'What is a slut, Daddy?'

Jack winced. 'It's a nasty word. One that nice people don't use,' he said. 'Elizabeth lost her temper. Sometimes people let their tongues run away with them and say spiteful things that they shouldn't. They don't mean to hurt. Not really. You'll forgive her, won't you?'

Carol frowned and shook her head and Jack pulled her close and cupped her face in his hands.

'Listen, lovie. We've got so *much*, the three of us. Because of that, because we're all so *sure* that we belong together, it doesn't matter what anyone says. It's like a great thick wall, all round us, keeping us safe. Like – like an air-raid shelter, if you like. Right?'

She began to smile. 'An air-raid shelter? Like the one at the end of the street that they pulled down?'

'Yes. Only no one can ever pull ours down.' Jack

laughed and tickled her. 'All the bombs and all the bullets they fire can't get us, eh?' He picked her up and stood her on the stool. 'Come on, I'll give you a piggy-back downstairs again. You haven't had one of those for ages, have you?'

'How could she? Oh, Mum, *how could she*?'

Eve was in floods of tears. Rose and her family had departed under a cloud with Ted muttering dark threats to his errant daughter. Now Freda was trying to placate her younger daughter in the privacy of the kitchen.

'It was only a childish quarrel between kids,' she said, trying to take some of the heat out of the situation.

'But how could Rose have been stupid enough to discuss it in front of them?' Eve demanded. 'She might have known one of them would come out with it sooner or later. I wouldn't be surprised if she *meant* this to happen.'

'Oh, I'm sure she didn't. Not really.' Freda sighed. 'Maybe she thought you'd already told Carol she's adopted?' she ventured. 'To tell you the truth, I'm a little surprised myself that you've waited this long.'

'It was *my* decision when I told her, Mum, not Rose's,' Eve said. 'I was going to do it at the right moment, when the time was right. Now she's gone and spoilt it all. God only *knows* what damage she's done!' She gasped and fumbled for her handkerchief. 'Honestly Mum, there are times when I really *hate* Rose. She's always had this nasty, bitchy, jealous streak!'

She burst into noisy tears again and Freda took her arm, easing her gently on to a chair and reaching for the kettle. 'Sit down, love. I'll make us all a nice cup of tea,' she said soothingly. 'You just have your cry out. It'll do you good.'

Freda had been concerned about Eve for some weeks now. She was touchy and over emotional; uncharacteristically temperamental. There were other suspicious signs too. She had that *look* about her. To begin with she had discounted her motherly instincts. After all, Eve was close to thirty-nine now. It was unlikely – and yet . . .

'Eve,' she ventured, 'I've been meaning to ask you, love. You are all right, aren't you?'

Eve stopped snuffling into her handkerchief and looked up at her mother. 'What do you mean – all right?'

'It's just that you've been so emotional lately. Getting yourself worked up over the least little thing. Not worried about anything, are you? Not doing too much?' Eve looked away and Freda peered closely at her daughter. 'Tell you the truth, love, in any other woman I'd have had my suspicions.'

'Suspicions?'

Freda looked her in the eye. 'That you were expecting.'

Eve bit her lip and her cheeks coloured. 'I can't be, can I?'

Freda smiled ruefully. 'Don't ask me, girl. You know better than I do.'

Eve twisted her handkerchief between tense fingers. 'I have missed – several times now. But I thought perhaps it was my age . . .'

'How many times?' Freda asked.

'Well – you know what I'm like. Never all that regular.'

'You must have some idea.'

Eve paused. 'Three. Or . . .'

'Or what?'

'Might even be four.'

'Right!' Freda took a deep breath. 'That settles it. You and I are off to see the doctor tomorrow. You can't afford to play around with your health, my girl. Not when you're having your first baby at your age!'

The doctor confirmed Eve's pregnancy the following afternoon and she floated home on a cloud of wonder and

70

disbelief. She'd meant to keep the news to herself until later that evening, after the shop closed, but once home she found it impossible to contain herself. The moment the shop was empty of customers she broke her surprising news to Jack. To begin with he was as disbelieving as she had been, but the moment Eve had convinced him, he became anxious and solicitous.

'Right, that's it,' he said firmly. 'No more getting up at five to do the papers. And no more standing all day long in the shop. From now on you'll be putting your feet up.'

Eve laughed, blushing like a girl. 'Oh, Jack! Doctor Philips says I'm as fit as a flea. My blood pressure is fine and he doesn't see any reason why I shouldn't sail through the pregnancy. There's no need to fuss, honestly.'

'You're not *his* wife though, are you?' Jack said. 'And you're not about to present him with *his* first child! You can let me decide what's best for you, and I say that from now on you're taking it easy. I'm a lot better than I was.' He grinned. 'Well, I must be, mustn't I?'

She laughed, her cheeks pink and her eyes dancing with excitement. She looked young and pretty again, just as she'd looked when he'd first met her. Suddenly he was overwhelmed with emotion and felt his throat tighten. 'Oh, Evie, love!' He hugged her. 'December, you say? Oh, I can't *wait*. You know, I still can't take it in. A baby! Just when we'd given up hope of having one of our own! This will be the most wonderful Christmas present you've ever given me!'

Carol ran silently through the stockroom on her sandalled feet. She'd been playing in the garden, but the friend who'd come round to play with her after school had gone home. She'd been about to go upstairs to the flat and turn into Princess Crystal who'd just escaped from her tower down the silken ladder and run away into the enchanted forest. She was looking forward to getting to the bit where she met the seven dwarfs.

She had one foot on the bottom stair when she heard her parents' voices in the shop. At first she couldn't make out what they were talking about and normally she wouldn't have been curious, but something about her father's excited tones made her pause to listen.

'December, you say? Oh, I can't wait! You know, I still can't take it in. A baby. Just when we'd given up hope of ever having one of our own! This will be the most wonderful Christmas present you've ever given me, Evie!'

For a moment Carol stood, transfixed, then she ran upstairs and shut herself in her room. None of it was true then? Everything he'd said to her – every word of it was lies. He'd said they couldn't have any babies of their own and that because of that she was special. Now it seemed they were going to have another baby. *One of our own.* The words echoed painfully in her head till she put her hands over her ears and shut her eyes tightly. She wasn't their real little girl; wasn't going to be their *precious only child* any more. A new baby was coming to take her place. When it came, what would happen to her?

In spite of Doctor Philips's optimistic prognosis, Eve's pregnancy was not all plain sailing. After the mid-term month was up she began to suffer problems. She suffered from violent indigestion, her ankles swelled and her blood pressure began to see-saw alarmingly. The doctor threatened that if she didn't take things very quietly he would have to send her into hospital for the remainder of her time. She did not need much encouragement to rest. As her weight increased she tired very easily.

Jack worried constantly about her, and, because the worry and the extra work made him tired too, his temper was sometimes short. Once when Carol's tap-dancing

72

practice in the room directly above the shop irritated him, he ran upstairs and admonished her.

'For heaven's sake, child, stop that stamping,' he shouted.

'I wasn't stamping. I was practising my dance for the concert,' she protested indignantly, but Jack was in no mood for arguments.

'Don't answer back. Do as you're told,' he snapped. 'You know your mother's not well. She's trying to get some rest. You're old enough now to know when to keep quiet.'

No one had actually told Carol that there was to be a baby. They thought she was too young to understand. She resented this. Even if she hadn't overheard their conversation that day it was obvious from her mother's expanding tummy that she was having a baby. Other children's mothers at school had appeared in the same condition and she had learned that that was the reason. All anyone had ever said to her was that Mummy wasn't well. It felt like a conspiracy – as though they were trying to shut her out. No one seemed to have time for her any more. They were grumpy and distant. Sometimes she wondered if they wished she wasn't here at all. In bed at night she lay awake, thinking with dread about those children's homes Daddy had mentioned. Would they send her to one of those once this new baby arrived? They might if she was naughty and upset them enough. As a result she became withdrawn and anxious, and now, at her father's obvious anger, she dissolved into tears.

'S-sorry, Daddy,' she said, hanging her head.

At once Jack regretted his outburst. Stepping forward, he pulled the weeping child into his arms. 'Oh, don't cry, duckie,' he said awkwardly. 'I didn't mean to snap at you. It's just that this is a difficult time for Mummy – for all of us really.' Taking out his handkerchief, he dried her tears.

'Maybe it's time you knew. You might be surprised at this but you're going to have a little brother or sister. Won't that be exciting?'

'Y-yes.'

'There's something else I've been meaning to tell you. Because it's so difficult, picking you up from Mrs Manson's now that the evenings are drawing in, we're going to have to stop your classes for a while.'

Carol's eyes widened as she stared at him disbelievingly. 'But – I'm in the Christmas concert. I *have* to go.'

Jack shook his head. 'It can't be helped, sweetheart. We can't let you walk home on your own in the dark.'

'I don't mind.'

'No. You're too young. I'm too busy with the shop to come for you and Mummy's legs are poorly.' His face was stern and serious. 'You're a big girl now, Carol. Big enough to know that we all have to make sacrifices sometimes.' He patted her drooping shoulder. 'It's not the end of the world. You'll be able to start again in the new year when the nights get lighter.'

When Kitty Manson arrived in the shop two days later Jack was taken aback. It was the first time he had encountered the formidable Kitty first hand.

'Mr Kenning? We haven't met before but I'm Kitty Manson.' She stood at the counter, her bright eyes challenging him. She wore an emerald green coat with a broad leopardskin collar and her red hair was wildly windswept.

'What can I do for you, Mrs Manson?'

'I know this might not be the ideal time or place, Mr Kenning, but we're both busy people and it is important that we have a word.'

'About Carol?'

'Yes. The child is devastated that you're stopping her

classes,' Kitty said reproachfully. 'She's doing so well. It really would be a pity to make her give up now.'

'I've told her it isn't permanent,' he said.

'But she's worked so hard, rehearsing for the Christmas concert, and she loves it so much.' Kitty rested her arms on the counter and leaned forward earnestly. Jack's nostrils received the full impact of *Chypre*, the exotic perfume she always wore when she was at her most determined. 'Your daughter has real talent, Mr Kenning,' she told him. 'So, if it's really just a matter of someone to see her home, my son will be happy to oblige. He's sixteen and a very capable boy. Would that help to change your mind?'

'Well, I suppose that would be all right,' Jack said.

'*Wonderful!*' Kitty's eyes lit up like twin beacons. 'You won't regret it, I promise. And we will be seeing you and your wife at the concert, I take it? Naturally I'll send round some tickets.'

'Well, we'll come if we can,' he said doubtfully. 'My wife is expecting a baby next month, you see, so we can't make any firm plans at the moment.'

'I see.' Kitty looked at him thoughtfully for a long moment. A *baby*! That explained a lot. She beamed at him again. 'Congratulations! And do come along if you can.'

The Christmas concert was wonderful. Carol adored every minute. She was in two musical numbers. In one she did a little solo dance dressed as a swan and in the other took part in a musical sketch, singing a whole verse all on her own. She'd been dreadfully nervous before the curtain went up, but Steven, who was playing the piano, winked up at her encouragingly before she began. When she saw his face smiling encouragingly at her, she felt confident and secure.

Carol and Steven had become good friends since he'd

been walking her home after rehearsals. Steven was sixteen, almost grown up, yet he never treated her like a baby. He was a kind boy. Not rough and rude like the big boys at school who were always pushing the little ones out of the way. He made her feel safe. He never laughed at her for being scared of the dark and understood that she was nervous of performing for the first time in front of lots of people.

'It's okay to be afraid,' he told her reassuringly. 'Everyone is. I'll tell you a secret: every time you're afraid and you still go ahead and do it, it's like killing a dragon. It means that's something you'll never have to be scared of it again.'

Mummy and Daddy hadn't come to the concert. She'd known they wouldn't be there because Mummy had gone into hospital late the previous night and as soon as the shop had closed Daddy had rushed off to be with her, dropping Carol off at Granny's on the way. Granny would have come to see her in the show, but at the last minute she'd said she was going to the hospital too.

At first Carol had been miserably disappointed that none of them would be there to see her, but once she was dressed in her costume and made up she forgot her disappointment. The butterflies in her tummy, the lights and the applause, sent everything else spinning away out of her head. She enjoyed every minute. And now Steven was seeing her home, the stars were shining, there was a big yellow moon in the sky and there were two more performances of the concert to look forward to. Carol walked on air.

'You did really well,' he said, looking down at her. 'Did you enjoy your first show?'

'Oh, *yes*!' Carol said dreamily. 'It was lovely!' She was thinking of Marianne Timmins, the big girl who'd taken a leading part in the show. Marianne was fourteen and already in Kitty Manson's *Dancing Babes* troupe. She had been in almost every number. As well as being pretty, she had a beautiful voice and could dance like an angel. Carol wanted to be just like her when she grew up. She confided this to Steven as they walked together. He laughed.

'You're going to be much better than Marianne,' he said loftily. 'You can act as well. When you take a part, you really *turn into* the person you're playing. I've been watching you at drama class. You can cry real tears. That takes talent. Ask Kitty.'

Carol was thrilled. Her feet hardly touched the ground all the way home. At Granny's, Grandpa was waiting to give her supper and see her to bed. Upstairs in the spare room she undressed quickly and slipped into bed. Putting out the light, she closed her eyes tightly and was immediately in the fantasy world that belonged to Princess Crystal. But now at long last Crystal's prince had come. He was tall and strong and handsome and *very* kind. And his face was just like Steven's.

Wendy Ann Kenning was born at five a.m. on 19 December 1952 after a protracted and complicated labour. She lived for just twenty minutes.

Jack and Freda sat helplessly in the bare waiting room all night, trying to support each other through the anxious hours, and when at last the sister called them into her office to break the news, Jack wept in his mother-in-law's arms.

But the nightmare was far from over. The doctors weren't satisfied that Eve was recovering as she should and kept her in hospital for almost three weeks following her confinement. Once home she sank into the grim depths of depression. It seemed that nothing could cheer her. Each day dawned grey and oppressive and she went through the motions of caring for home, husband and child like an automaton. At night she sank into a deep oblivion from which nothing could wake her.

Jack was exhausted: up at five every morning to see to the papers, then working unaided in the shop all day. Most days he went upstairs after closing the shop to find Eve sitting staring into space, the beds unmade and the sink full of dirty dishes. He felt as though he were living with a cold, uncaring stranger. She seemed oblivious to his exhaustion and his own considerable grief at the loss of their child. She seemed not to care about the neglected flat and to have quite forgotten the needs of the daughter who had once filled her life.

Among the other obsessions Eve developed during this time was a violent aversion to her sister. She could not bear to have Rose anywhere near her, so Jack's mother and Freda took it in turns to help him in the shop for as many hours as they could spare. Each of the older women was concerned about their respective offspring but both could sympathise with the stress Jack was under. None too strong since the war and still suffering from his recurring stomach complaint, they feared that he might crack under the strain, and the two mothers did what they could to take some of the pressure off him.

In all of this Carol became little more than an added duty to the adults in her life. She had spent the Christmas holidays at her grandmother's house, returning to Clarence Street in time to go back to school in January. After that her father and grandmothers saw to her immediate needs. She was fed and supplied with clean clothes but her emotional needs were overlooked. It was Freda who misguidedly suggested that she might be packed off to stay with Rose at weekends so as to take as much pressure as possible off her overstretched father.

Rose helped out with a poor grace. Deeply resentful of her sister's rejection, she frequently expressed the opinion that Eve was squeezing every last ounce of drama out of her predicament and putting on her family too much. She was scathing about her sister's depression too.

'All in her mind, if you ask me,' she complained to her mother one Friday evening when Freda dropped Carol off for the weekend. 'It's months now since she lost the baby. And it isn't as if it lived long enough for her to get attached to it. We all feel down when we've had a baby. After I'd had our Elizabeth I could've cried buckets if anyone as much as looked sideways at me. But no one danced attendance on *me*. I just had to get on with it.'

'I'm sure I gave you all the support you needed,' Freda told her daughter sharply. 'Eve was getting on to be a mother for the first time. She wanted that baby so much. It's terrible for her to have lost it. You might try to have a bit more sympathy, Rose.' She lowered her voice. 'And don't let Carol hear you going on about her mother. The poor child's having a difficult enough time of it as it is.'

'Huh! *She's* having a difficult time, I like that!' Rose snorted indignantly. 'You don't know what that child's like, Mum. Last weekend she kicked my Elizabeth really hard on the shin. Bruised her quite badly. She's getting to be a nasty spiteful little girl, is Carol. If you ask me it's a good thing she *hasn't* got a baby sister. God knows what she'd have been like with it, jealous little madam!'

'It's been hard for her too,' Freda put in. But Rose wasn't listening.

'It's nothing but squabble and pick on our Elizabeth from the minute she comes in that door. It's sending me up the pole.'

'I'm sure she doesn't mean it . . .' Freda began, but Rose was in full flow.

'There's Michael can't get peace for his homework, and Ted – he's going to put his foot down soon, easy-going as he is. I'll tell you this, Mum, if I have much more of it I'm going round there myself to tell Eve straight, depression or no depression. It's high time she pulled herself together and started thinking about what she's doing to the rest of her family.'

But straight talking was not the solution to Eve's problem. Since the baby's death she had sunk into her own private hell from which there seemed no escape. She could not get Sally out of her mind, haunted by guilt for what she had done that night on the old railway bridge. Deep in the darkest recesses of her troubled mind she was convinced that she was being punished for causing Sally's death. All the signs were there: the torture she had suffered in labour; the baby's death; her family, none of whom understood her anguish. But, worst of all, the silent reproach of Sally's own child.

Carol was growing more and more like her mother as the years passed. The large violet-blue eyes seemed to accuse her until she could hardly bear to meet them. If only she could confide in someone, confess to what she had done. But to do that would be to alienate and isolate herself even more.

Sometimes she was tempted to blurt it all out – go to the police and admit to Sally's manslaughter. Often in her despair she longed for the peace and solitude of a prison cell. But before that would come the trial, the judgment, the conviction; the ultimate condemnation. And she knew she would never find the strength to face that.

As for Carol, her world seemed to have fallen apart. The happy indulged childhood she had known seemed to have ended abruptly on the night her baby sister was born and died. Her parents no longer had time for her, and in some strange way that she couldn't define, she felt guilty, as though it were her fault.

Her grandmothers each tried in their own way to

console her but her parents' rejection was plain to see. Weekdays were bad enough, coming home from school to a harassed father and a mother who seemed to be living in another world. But the weekends spent with Aunt Rose and her family were becoming a nightmare. Carol felt increasing dread as each Friday approached.

The only chink of light in her bleak little life was the time spent at Kitty Manson's classes. Mondays and Thursdays became the highlights of her week, a series of stepping stones in a deluge of despondency. All her suppressed energy went into her dancing and her pent-up emotion found release in the weekly drama classes, which, without her really noticing, gradually began to take the place of her fairytale fantasies.

Carol's unhappiness did not escape Kitty's notice. In the weeks following Christmas she had watched as the child grew more and more withdrawn and nervy. She knew about the baby, of course, and guessed that the family must be going through a difficult and traumatic time, but when one Monday evening she noticed bruises on Carol's arms and legs, she was seriously concerned. Fearing that any attempt to question Carol directly would be construed as interference, she asked Steven to find out what he could when he walked the child home.

Carol adored Steven. Although he was almost grown-up he was still close enough to her own age to understand how she felt without judging her or thinking she was being silly, and she felt she could talk to him.

'How did you get those bruises, Carrie?' he asked as they walked home to Clarence Street the following Monday evening.

'I – fell.'

'How did you do that?'

'I have to go and stay with my cousins at weekends.'

'Don't you like them?'

81

Carol shrugged. 'Mike's all right, it's Elizabeth . . . Yesterday she made me climb the apple tree in their garden, then she shook the branch till I fell out.' She lifted her fringe to show a darkening contusion on her forehead. 'I did this too.'

Steven stopped walking to inspect the bruise by the light of a street lamp. 'That looks nasty. What did your auntie say? I bet she was mad.'

'I – I didn't tell. Elizabeth said she'd do something worse to me if I did. She's always saying that Mummy doesn't want me.' Her lip trembled as she decided to disclose the devastating statement her cousin had made the previous day. 'She says Mum wishes I'd died instead of the baby.'

Steven pulled a face. 'Your cousin sounds like a nasty piece of work to me. But she's just trying to make you angry, can't you see that?' He took her hand and squeezed it hard. 'Tell you what – I bet *she's* the one who's jealous really.'

Carol shook her head. She walked beside him in silence for a moment. 'It might be true though, what she said.' She paused before voicing her worst fear. 'I'm not their real little girl, you see. That's what Liz means.'

He grinned down at her. 'You look real enough to me.'

'No!' She shook her head impatiently. 'I'm not real like Liz and Mike are real.' She glanced up at him to see if he had grasped her meaning and what effect the information was having. 'My mummy and daddy – they didn't . . .' she frowned. 'They didn't *born* me.'

'Oh, I see!' Steven looked unsurprised. 'You mean, you're adopted?'

She nodded. 'My real mum got killed in an air raid when I was a baby.'

'Okay, so they adopted you. But you have to want a kid very badly to adopt it, so they must have been very keen.

And after all, you've been theirs more than eight years, haven't you? No one stops loving their kid just like that.'

Carol digested this piece of logic. 'I suppose not,' she said slowly. She looked up at him. 'It's just that since Mummy came out of hospital, she's been so different. Sometimes when she looks at me it's as though she wishes she'd got the baby instead of me.'

' 'Course she doesn't. Sometimes grown-ups get all tied up in other things. I expect your mum and dad have just got a lot on their minds.' He considered for a moment, then came up with an idea. 'Hey, tell you what. Would you like me to ask Kitty if you can stay with us at weekends for a while?' he suggested. 'Just till your mum's better.'

Her eyes danced as she looked up at him. 'Oh, Steven! Do you think she'd let me?'

He grinned. ' 'Course she will.' He squeezed her hand warmly. 'Try and cheer up, Carrie. Just be 'specially nice and make sure your mum and dad know you're still around and that you need them. Maybe they just need reminding of how much they like you.' He grinned at her. 'It'll all get sorted out in the end. Don't worry, kid.'

'I'll try not to.'

'That's the girl. Just think, three more years and you'll be old enough to be a *Dancing Babe*. You've got that to look forward to.'

Feeling infinitely better, Carol looked up at him adoringly. 'Steven – will – will you be my best friend, please?'

He blushed and was glad of the fading light. ' 'Course I will, *silly*.'

Chapter Three

December 1956

Backstage at the Opera House the atmosphere was electric as curtain-up time drew near on the first night of *Dick Whittington*.

As Carol waited in the dressing room with the other girls she could hear the musicians beginning to tune their instruments in the band room next door. She took a last surreptitious peep at herself in the mirror and saw a small, piquant face alight with excitement. Her skin was flushed under the greasepaint and her lashes were spiky with mascara. At the inner corner of each blue-shadowed eyelid was a red dot, designed to accentuate the brilliance of her eyes. Kitty had been in earlier and made up all twelve of her *Dancing Babes*.

The twelve Babes were divided into 'girls' and 'boys', and grouped into six pairs. For the opening scene the 'girls' were dressed in little gingham dresses, pink or blue, with white tap shoes and sun bonnets. The 'boys' wore tight shorts of the same material with a bib and straps, white shirts and matching gingham stocking caps. Carol preferred the girls' costumes and was secretly glad she'd been chosen to be one of them.

Because she was one of the lightest in the troupe she'd been chosen at the very first rehearsal to take part in the flying ballet. Five other Babes had been chosen with her, among them Carol's special friend, Janet. They'd collapsed with giggles when they'd first been introduced to the ungainly harnesses they would be required to wear under their feathered bird costumes, and after a week of rehearsals they'd both been sore from the chafing of the straps as they were hauled aloft on their wires. But Carol didn't mind. It was a wonderful feeling, soaring out above the stage during the transformation scene, the highlight of the production. Hovering there in the tableau that ended the first half of the show, her 'wings' outstretched and her toes pointed, Carol felt important and special. Tonight was the first night of the panto; the culmination of weeks of rehearsals. At last she was a real professional. At the end of each of the four weeks that the panto would run she would be paid four whole pounds. It was a start. One foot on the professional ladder.

The call boy banged on the dressing room door, making the girls jump with his raucous cry of, '*Overture and beginners, please!*'

Janet gave a little squeak and clutched Carol. 'Ooh! That's *us*. We're on.' And the twelve girls spilled excitedly out into the corridor, feet clattering in their tap shoes as they climbed the short flight of stairs to the stage to take up their places.

The five years that Carol had been at Kitty Manson's school had passed quickly. Kitty's invitation for her to stay at Chine Way at weekends instead of with her cousins had been a life saver. Carol had never been into the Mansons' living quarters previously. On first passing through the door at the back of the hall and down the basement stairs she'd found herself embraced by the cosy intimate world that was the Mansons' home.

She was fascinated by the large living room-cum-kitchen with its Aga and cluttered kitchen table. She soon learned that this room was the centre of Kitty's world. The school was run from here. The large oblong table, which doubled as her desk, was never cleared. Letters, books and forms mingled happily with gramophone records, sheet music and swatches of material. At mealtimes one end would be cleared and laid with a cloth so that they could eat.

As well as the table there was an upright piano where Steven did his practice; a radiogram, a television set and, over by the back window, the treadle sewing machine Kitty used to make most of the costumes for the shows she put on. Comfort was provided by a sagging three-piece suite covered in faded cretonne, and the walls were adorned with dozens of playbills and photographs.

'I like to have them where I can see them, dear,' Kitty explained. 'Never had any use for dusty photograph albums that never see the light of day.'

The framed photographs fascinated Carol. Here was a pictorial record of Kitty Manson's career, from a study of her in fairy costume taken at the age of six, progressing through adolescence – Kitty in concert party pierrette costume then, later, in a daring costume glittering with sequins as a variety *soubrette*. There were glamorous grown-up portraits; happy, smiling groups of summer show companies; Kitty playing in musical comedy; in revue sketches, gesturing extravagantly, and others dazzlingly attired as Principal Boy. But what fascinated Carol most of all was the portrait of Kitty as Eliza Doolittle in Shaw's *Pygmalion*, complete with grime-streaked face, battered straw hat and basket of flowers.

'I always said that would make a good musical,' she said wistfully. 'And now they've done it. What I wouldn't have given to have played Eliza in that!' She smiled at Carol. 'Maybe one of these days you'll do it!'

The winter after her mother had lost the baby Carol learned how to play Scrabble and Monopoly. She and Steven would spend long rainy Saturday afternoons at the clear end of the table, while Kitty sat, either at the other end wearing her glasses and sighing over her sadly neglected paperwork, or working away at the sewing machine. They were as companionable and easy together as any family.

When spring came Steven took her over to The Meadow where he introduced her to the delights of flying a kite. Carol loved it. Running hard into the wind to get the kite into the air, the tug of the string in her hand, almost made her feel as if she were flying too. They would come home laughing, cheeks pink and hair ruffled by the blustery March winds, ravenous for their tea.

On Saturday evenings they watched the television when there would usually be a variety show and sometimes a play. TV was a great novelty to Carol as the Kenning household hadn't yet caught up with this innovation. Kitty had bought the set initially in order to see the Coronation of the new Queen in '52. But there was a much more practical reason behind her investment. It was necessary to keep up with the changing tastes in entertainment, she pointed out. It would never do to fall behind the times. Besides, many of the variety theatres and some of the small repertory theatres too were closing now that folks could get their entertainment at home.

'It'll mean that standards will rise,' Kitty prophesied. 'Once people have been used to having London shows and the cream of entertainment in their own living rooms, they're not going to pay to see some tatty number ten touring company at the local Hippodrome.' She was soon to be proved devastatingly right.

As the year advanced Eve gradually began to emerge from her black depression and Carol's weekend stays at Kitty's ceased. She missed them more than she could say. Life at home seemed a poor substitute. The shop was open for most of the weekend, which kept Jack and Eve busy, so she was left very much to her own devices. But by that time both Kitty and Steven regarded her as a member of their family and she often sneaked off to join them, knowing that there was always a welcome for her at Chine Way. Kitty's kitchen was a haven, a gloriously cluttered place where no one fussed if you dropped crumbs or spilled your drink. Carol frequently took refuge there from her mother's tense scolding.

Carol had known for some time that she had no real talent for dancing. She had managed to pass all her exams, both ballet and tap, but mainly because she knew that Eve would have tolerated nothing less. Dancing was fun and it was all right for now. She enjoyed her classes at Kitty's. But what she secretly yearned for was to study acting in more depth. She nursed hopes of applying for a place at one of the major drama schools when she left school.

Eve thought differently. Her ambition for Carol to pursue a career on the musical stage had become an obsession and each time the subject came up she was adamant.

'After all the years you've studied dancing?' she'd say, scandalised. 'Why change now? You'll never make a name for yourself in straight acting. One of the ballet schools maybe, once you're done with your "O" levels. We'll have to see how hard you work between now and then.'

Even when Carol was chosen out of a dozen other girls to take the part of a schoolgirl in a play at the local Rep, and received acclaim in the press for her performance, her mother wasn't convinced. To Eve there was only one kind of theatrical career that brought the kind of lifestyle she visualised for her daughter, and that was the glitz and glamour of the musical stage. Nothing else would do.

Steven was absent from Carol's life for almost two years doing his National Service. Afterwards he stayed away, studying in London at the Guildhall School of Music. Carol looked forward eagerly to the occasions when he came home. He was due back for Christmas and had promised that if possible he would make it in time for the first night of the panto. Now, as the full chorus stood grouped on the stage, waiting in breathless anticipation for the curtain to rise, Carol wondered if he had managed to make it and if he might actually be sitting out there already in the audience.

Her family would certainly be there; her parents with both grandmothers and Grandpa too. The thought of Eve's presence and critical eyes on her made Carol extra nervous.

Suddenly her attention was attracted by a movement in the wings and she saw Kitty standing there. She had changed into an evening gown of electric blue satin, embroidered with silver sequins. Her red hair was piled high and long diamante earrings dangled from her ears. The sight of the familiar flamboyant figure waving and holding up her thumbs was reassuring.

'Good luck, my darlings!' she called. Then, specially to Carol, she mouthed the words '*Steven is home*' and gestured that he was sitting out in front. Carol's tummy lurched and she nodded excitedly to show that she had understood. He was there then. He had kept his promise! Then the orchestra struck up the first notes of the opening chorus and the curtain began to rise. The age-old story of Dick Whittington was about to unfold.

In the front row of the dress circle Eve's heart was bumping anxiously. Carol must do well. But she would, of course. She could outshine all the others if only she would put her mind to it, of that Eve was sure. She was developing into quite a pretty girl and of course she was talented. Anyone could see that. If only she would push herself more. This was her first professional appearance.

It was the first step on the ladder to stardom, she told herself. *Sally's daughter must be brilliantly successful.* And she, Eve, must make sure it all happened. It was the only way she could make sense of the terrible thing she had caused to happen.

Sitting next to his wife in their dress circle seats, Jack could feel the tension emanating from her like an electrical current. Eve's obsession for Carol to make an outstanding career on the musical stage worried him greatly. She was making life unnecessarily hard, not only for herself and for him but more importantly for their daughter. So he had been pleased and relieved when, with the end of rationing in 1954, Eve had had the idea of expanding the business to include a small grocery section.

The little shop had been doing well since the end of sweet rationing and Jack could see that stocking groceries could really set them on their feet. Grateful that Eve had found a diversion, something other than Carol in which to become absorbed, he'd agreed enthusiastically to the scheme, adding the suggestion that his wife should take over that side of the business and run it herself.

For Eve's part, if she could have foreseen that it was to be this new branching out of their business that would bring Eddie Wilson back into her life, she would have thought twice about the venture.

Since the end of the war Eddie had gone from strength to strength. He now owned a wholesale cash and carry warehouse on the outskirts of town and supplied many of the small corner shops. Unknown to Eve, Jack had arranged for him to call and Eddie's sudden appearance in the shop one afternoon was a shock to her. Meeting the man again after all these years brought her face to face once more with a past that seemed inescapable.

He hadn't changed very much. The slicked back dark hair was now touched with grey but his moustache was as dark and pencil-thin as ever. His strangely light grey eyes glinted as he faced Eve across the counter.

'Afternoon, Mrs Kenning.' He removed his trilby hat and held it against his chest. 'Long time, no see, eh?'

Eve felt the warm colour rise to her hairline. 'I'm sorry. My husband is out this afternoon.'

'That's okay. He said I was to ask for you anyway,' Eddie said with his impudent grin. He unzipped the briefcase he carried. 'I've brought a list of everything I can supply,' he told her. 'You won't find a better deal anywhere else in town, and if you don't have transport I can arrange delivery at a small extra charge.'

'I see. Well, if you'd like to leave your list, I'll look at it later.'

Eddie leaned one elbow on the counter and smiled at her engagingly. 'No need to be so formal. How about a nice cosy cuppa out the back while you have a quick look-see? You could give me an order right away. No time like the present, is there?'

'I don't know. We've got alterations to make to the shop first,' Eve hedged. 'Nothing's really settled yet and . . .'

'You're looking *remarkably* well, Eve.' He leaned closer and she wondered why she suddenly felt threatened. 'Come on, love, get the kettle on.' He winked. 'I bet you were just going to anyway.'

In the back room Eve made the tea, keeping an eye on the shop as she did so. Eddie looked perfectly relaxed, his feet in their handmade shoes resting on an empty packing case as he nonchalantly lit a cigarette with his gold-plated lighter.

'Seems a long time since you worked in the canteen at Samson's, I daresay?' he remarked, flicking ash onto the floor.

'Yes, it does. Shall I have a look at that list then?' Eve pushed the mug of tea towards him across the table.

'No hurry. You can look through it at your leisure,' he said. 'My phone number's on there. Give me a ring when you want to place an order. Or just come round the warehouse and pick up what you want. That's what most people do.'

Eve frowned. 'Then why did you . . . ?'

'Sally Tyler used to lodge with you, didn't she?' he said suddenly. 'When you lived in Brook's Lane.' He examined his fingernails. 'Nice girl, Sally. A good sport. I was really sorry to hear she'd bought it when that bomb dropped on the station.'

'I daresay,' Eve said dryly, feeling her cheeks colour again. 'It was very sad.' She got up and began to busy herself, peering into the shop in the desperate hope that a customer would come in and bring the uncomfortable conversation to an end.

'She had a kid, didn't she?'

'Yes.' Eve kept her back towards him. Of course he knew Sally had had a baby. Why was he asking all these questions about her? He'd shown precious little interest when she went to him for help.

'Little girl, so I heard?'

'Did you?' Eve turned to him. 'If you've finished your tea . . . And as you say there's no hurry to place an order, I shall have to ask you to leave now,' she said. 'There's only me in the shop this afternoon and I really haven't . . .'

'What happened to it – her?'

Eve shook her head. 'What?'

'The kid.' He lifted one shoulder. 'Just as a matter of interest.'

'I've no idea.'

'Really?' He raised an eyebrow. 'Relatives take her? An orphanage?'

'Possibly. Now if you wouldn't mind . . .' The shop bell tinkled and Eve turned gratefully towards the shop, only to see Carol skipping through, her fair hair flying and her schoolbag bouncing on her back.

'Mummy, we played hockey and I – oh!' She stopped as she saw that her mother was not alone.

Eddie got slowly to his feet, his slate-grey eyes glinting as he looked from mother to daughter and back again. 'Well now, what have we here? Hello, little lady. What's your name?'

Carol stood shyly in the doorway, looking hesitantly at Eve. 'Carol,' she said. 'Carol Louise.'

'And how old might you be then, Carol Louise?'

'I'm nearly twelve.'

'Nearly *twelve*, eh?' Eddie looked at Eve. 'Lost no time starting a family after hubby came home, eh? Invalided out, was he?' He winked knowingly and reached out to finger Carol's flaxen hair. 'Not much like your mum, are you, duck?'

'Nip up and see if your dad's got the kettle on, will you, Carol?' Eve said, giving her a gentle push towards the door. 'You'll be wanting your tea.' When the child had gone she stared at Eddie coldly. 'I don't think we'll be interested in buying our supplies from you, Mr Wilson,' she said. 'But if we change our minds I'll let you know.'

He shrugged, the rebuff glancing off his smooth exterior. 'Suit yourself. You know where I am if you need anything.' In the doorway he turned. 'Must be nice to have a daughter. All my kids are boys – far as I know, if you follow me?' He chuckled. 'Well, been nice seeing you again, Eve.' He smiled. 'Been fun catching up with all your news. 'Bye then. Be good!' In the doorway he stopped and looked back. 'I hope you'll change your mind about ordering. Won't find a better deal anywhere. Be nice to do business together – for old times' sake, eh?'

When he'd gone Eve's legs were trembling so much that she had to sit down. As far as she knew no one but she realised that Eddie was Carol's father. And he had disclaimed her. So why should he be interested in the child after all these years? And why had he asked about Sally? What could he possibly have to gain by raking up the past? Carol was hers and Jack's, legally, by adoption. No one could do or say anything to change that.

As it happened in the end they were obliged to deal with Eddie Wilson. Jack pointed out that he was by far the cheapest supplier. He laughed off her dislike of the man, telling her it was all in her mind and there was no black market any more. Anyway, he pointed out, they didn't even have to see him if they didn't want to. But Eve's uneasiness about Eddie remained and she avoided contact with him whenever she could.

The pantomime cast lined up for the final curtain call, the principal boy and girl in their dazzling spangled costumes centre stage, with Monty the cat wearing a tinsel bow. Carol felt a glow of triumph. Everything had gone without a hitch, apart from the breathtaking moment when she'd almost lost one of her shoes in the opening number of the second half. But Janet had assured her that no one else had even noticed.

From her place high above the stage in the flying ballet she had even managed to spot her family, sitting in the front row of the dress circle. And now there was to be a party for the Babes at Kitty's. And Steven would be there! Her tummy churned with excited anticipation.

In the corridor outside the dressing room her parents were waiting for her. Jack hugged her tightly.

'Well done. You were terrific, sweetheart,' he said. 'We really enjoyed the show, didn't we?' He turned to Eve who stood a little apart.

'You nearly lost your shoe during that sailors' hornpipe thing,' she admonished.

'I know.' Carol was devastated that her mother had noticed. 'I didn't let it put me off though. Janet said no one had noticed.'

'How could they not notice?' Eve said sharply. 'It was so careless. You must remember to do the laces up properly. I was so asham . . .' She was stopped by Jack's hand surreptitiously squeezing hers.

'You know what your mother's eyes are like,' he laughed. 'She makes a hawk look half blind. I'm quite *sure* no one else saw a thing wrong.' He hugged her again. 'You were lovely, duckie. Just wonderful. Now, I'm going to drop you and Janet off at Mrs Manson's for the party on the way home so run and get your things.'

'But you're not to stay too long,' Eve put in. 'Dad will come back and pick you up in an hour.'

Carol's face fell. 'Oh, Mum!'

'No arguments now. I want you in bed well before midnight. There's another show to do tomorrow, remember? You don't want to let Mrs Manson down with any more mishaps, do you?' she added meaningfully.

Kitty was waiting at Chine Way to welcome everyone at the front door.

'Darlings, you were a credit to me. The best troupe of Babes I've ever had!'

Everyone knew that she said this every year, but they were gratified just the same. As the girls crowded into the downstairs cloakroom to take off their coats Carol felt her spirits flag. She'd looked forward to this evening for so long. It was only one small slip. Not even that. A near miss. Yet it was enough to incur her mother's displeasure and dampen her spirits. As they peered into the mirror together, Janet nudged her.

'Come on, misery guts. You might smile. What's up?'

'Nothing.'

'It's a party we're going to, you know. Not a funeral.'

'I know. Sorry. It's just that I'm only allowed to stay till eleven.'

'All the more reason to make the most of it then. Well . . . ?' Janet was peering at her.

'Well what?'

'Have you seen him yet?'

'Seen who?'

Janet raised her eyes to the ceiling. 'Come off it. *Steven*, of course. He was there, you know. Out in front at the theatre.'

'How do you know? You've never met him.'

'One of the other girls pointed him out to me. Stalls – three rows back.' She rolled her eyes. 'Tall, dark and handsome! He'll be here tonight, won't he? Aren't you just dying to see him again?'

Carol shrugged with studied nonchalance. 'For all I know he's brought his girlfriend home for Christmas.'

Janet's eyes widened. 'Has he got a girlfriend then?'

'Might have,' Carol said, doing her best to sound unconcerned. She combed her hair carefully, tweaking at her fringe.

Janet was really mystified now. Ever since she'd known Carol she'd talked of no other boy but Steven. It was obvious she'd got a huge crush on him, so why this sudden lack of interest? 'You write to him though, don't you?'

'Yes, but he doesn't tell me everything, does he?' Carol snapped.

Janet regarded her friend for a moment. 'You're not still worrying about your shoe, are you?' She opened her bag and produced a bottle of perfume. 'Here, splash some of this on. I pinched it from Mum's dressing table. It's called *Shalimar*. It's dead romantic.'

'Thanks.' Relenting a little, Carol dabbed some of the

perfume behind each ear, then gave the bottle back to her friend. Janet was six months younger than her, still not quite fourteen. She'd enrolled at Kitty Manson's when she and her parents had moved down from Yorkshire a year ago and she and Carol had taken to each other on sight. Janet was small, dark and vivacious. She'd been dancing since she began ballet classes at five years old, but unlike Carol had no wish to pursue a career in the theatre. In the 'A' form at school and a year ahead of other girls of the same age, Janet was brilliantly clever. Once she had taken her 'A' levels she was hoping for a place at university where she planned to study medicine and follow in her doctor father's footsteps.

'Come on then.' She took Carol's hand. 'Let's go upstairs. If your dad is picking you up at eleven we'd better not waste any more time.' She grinned. 'Besides, I'm dying to meet this stunning Steven of yours.'

Carol saw him as soon as they walked into the studio. He was putting a record on the turntable. He looked taller and broader than she remembered him and it struck her with a small shock that he was suddenly no longer a boy, but very much a man. As he lowered the needle on to the record the strains of *Fly Me To The Moon* filled the room and Janet gave an ecstatic sigh.

'Oh, listen. It's my favourite!'

Steven saw them and walked across, a smile on his face. 'Carrie! You were terrific, specially the imitation of the budgie!'

Janet giggled and Carol blushed scarlet. Two years ago she would have thumped Steven and enjoyed the joke. But now suddenly he seemed like an adult stranger of twenty-two – laughing at her, still a fourteen-year-old child.

'It's those costumes,' she muttered. 'They have to be like that to hide the . . .'

'I'm only pulling your leg, stupid! Aren't you going to introduce me to your friend?'

Abashed at forgetting her manners, Carol made the hasty introduction, but when he'd exchanged a few polite words with Janet he held out his hand to Carol. 'Come on then. Come and dance.'

He led her on to the floor and for a few bars she concentrated on the steps of the slow foxtrot, her eyes downcast.

'You okay?' he asked.

She nodded. 'Fine, thanks.'

'I thought you were very good in the panto, honestly. It was a successful show.'

'Thanks.'

'It's wonderful to be home, Carrie. And to see you.'

She blushed again, slightly ashamed of her own churlishness. 'It's good to see you too, Steven.'

When they reached the doorway he stopped dancing and drew her out on to the landing. 'Come and sit down,' he said, leading her to the top of the stairs and pulling her down beside him. 'Now – tell me about it?'

'About what?'

'Is everything all right?'

'Fine.' She looked at him properly for the first time, wishing she knew why she felt so shy with him. It must be because he'd had so much more experience of life than she had; the army and college. She was still a silly little schoolgirl making stumbling mistakes, she told herself despondently.

'Come on, Carrie. It can't be as bad as all that, surely?' He squeezed her hand. 'We're still friends, aren't we? You can tell me.'

She sighed. 'It was so exciting, being in my first professional show,' she said. 'But then I had to go and spoil it, didn't I?'

He frowned. 'Spoil it? How?'

'Oh, come on. You must have noticed.'

'No. Everything you did looked perfect to me.'

She turned to look at him, searching his eyes for signs that he might be patronising her. 'You must have seen? It was in the opening number of the second half.'

'That hornpipe number?'

'Yes. My shoe nearly came off. I had to shove it back on again.'

He laughed. 'Is that all? Anyone'd think you'd taken a nose dive into the orchestra pit. I didn't notice a thing.'

'Mum did.'

'I see. So that's what this is all about.' He slipped an arm around her shoulders and hugged her. 'Things still tough at home, Carrie?'

She shrugged. 'Mum still nags a bit. Well, a lot really. I don't think I'll ever be good enough for her.'

'As long as you're good enough for *you*, Carrie. That's all that really matters.'

She nodded. 'Trouble is, I don't *know* what's good enough. I don't know what I *want* or where I'm going any more.' She looked at him. 'Not like you do.'

'Very few of us are ever really sure,' he told her. 'Even I have my doubts. But you will know some day, Carrie. You will.'

She shook her head. He sounded disappointingly like all the other adults she knew. 'We'd better not sit out here,' she said. 'I can only stay at the party till eleven.'

'Right.' He stood up and pulled her to her feet. 'Come and have something to eat then, Cinderella.' He took both her hands and squeezed them. 'Look, I'm going to be home for two whole weeks so we can see each other every day, if you like? Maybe we can kill a few dragons between us, eh?'

She smiled, poorly reassured. Since that first concert

99

when she'd been so scared 'killing dragons' had been an expression they'd used often to describe solving tricky problems. It warmed her to think that he still remembered, and that he actually wanted to spend some of his time with her. Maybe the gap between them wasn't quite so wide after all. She smiled. 'Thanks, Steven. That'd be really nice.'

'I'd never really thought seriously about it, you see. Not till I met Janet. Up till then I suppose I just sort of drifted. Doing what Mum wanted.'

Carol and Steven were sitting by the river, throwing bread to the ducks. It was a bright frosty January afternoon. The sky was a pale azure blue, strewn with ragged whisps of cloud. As they huddled together on the bench, pale lemon sunshine cast long shadows across the grass and Carol watched the naked wands of the willow trees stirring the water, fragmenting their own reflection.

'Janet loves her dancing,' she went on, 'but it's only a hobby with her. No one pushes her because everyone knows she's planning to be a doctor. She's got it all worked out. 'O' levels, then 'A's; university and medical school. Dancing's just to help give her confidence and poise; something to do for physical exercise.'

'Okay. That's fine for her,' Steven said. 'But you mustn't let other people influence you. You have to decide what it is *you* want.'

'Yes. But what *is* that?' She looked at him. 'Ever since I can remember Mum has been telling me that I want to be a dancer.'

He laughed. 'Well, you have been doing it for a long time now.'

She sighed and crumbled the bread in her hand. 'I'm not really all that good, you know,' she said candidly.

'You passed your exams.'

'Only just. I'm not brilliant. Mum wants me to be *the best*. She'll never be satisfied with merely good. She expects me to end up a star. A sort of second Julie Andrews or someone. Nothing less will do. It's quite frightening really because I know I'll never be that good.' She threw the crumbled bread on to the water and watched as the ducks swarmed towards it, churning the water as they squabbled over the scattered pieces. 'It's easier for Janet. She's clever. Confident. Knows exactly where she's going. It's the same with my cousins, Mike and Elizabeth too. Mike's already got his name down for university and Liz is planning to go to teacher training college, whereas I . . .' Her shoulders slumped. 'I'm not much use at school, and I'm going to end up just a ten-a-penny dancer.'

'You can still make a career out of it.'

Carol shook her head. 'But I don't want to, Steven. It wouldn't be the kind of career I want. And certainly not what Mum's got in mind. Kitty has already said that now everyone's got television the standards are getting higher.'

'So, if you had the choice, what would you really like?'

She turned to look at him. 'I want to act. I asked Mum if I could drop the dancing and have extra drama lessons with Kitty, then try for RADA or somewhere when I leave school.'

He looked at her. 'Yes. And . . . ?'

She shrugged. 'What do you think? When I did that week with the Rep she didn't even come and see me. She wants me to apply for a ballet school. I'd never get into one of them. Kitty knows that.'

'Then ask her to have a word with your mother.'

She looked at him. 'Do you think I should?'

'If you want it hard enough it looks as if you're going to have to fight for it, Carrie. It might make life difficult for you, but you'll have to ask yourself if it's worth it.'

101

Steven looked up at the sky. 'Come on, let's walk. The sun's going down and it's getting cold.'

As they walked along the tow path he took her hand, pulling it through his arm, and Carol felt a small glow of happiness. In the two weeks that Steven had been at home her awkward shyness had gradually disappeared. He teased her just as he always had, but there was a new respect in his approach to her now. He treated her almost as though she were the same age as him. She loved him for that.

'What I can't work out,' she said, 'is why Mum is so set on me going on the musical stage? Once when I asked her she said something about my real mother being talented.' She looked at him. 'But it doesn't follow that I'll take after her, does it?'

'There's no other way but to tell your mother what you want. And be positive about it. It's your life after all.' He grinned down at her. 'Take your courage in both hands and kill that dragon.'

She looked up at him ruefully. 'I don't think Mum would like being called a dragon!' They both laughed and the tension lifted. 'I'm going to miss you when you've gone back to London tomorrow, Steven. It's back to school on Monday for me too,' she added dejectedly.

He grinned at her. 'You won't miss me a bit. There'll be some nice young lad knocking on the door before long and you'll be out dancing every night. And in a few years' time I'll come home and find you're an old married lady.'

His words depressed her. She visualised staying for the rest of her life in Clarence Street, or somewhere like it; turning into someone like her mother or Aunt Rose; never getting the chance to find out whether she had any real acting talent or not. Besides, he obviously couldn't see that there never had been – never *would* be – anyone for her but him. Clearly all she would ever be to him was a little sister.

Swallowing her despondency, she made herself laugh. 'Just for that, Steve Manson, you can treat me to the pictures tonight. *Murders in the Rue Morgue* is on at the Savoy – in 3D!'

He gave a theatrical shudder. 'Ugh! What a penance! Okay, you win. But I'll remind you of what I said one of these days, though. Just you see if I don't!'

Eve sat in Kitty's drawing room impatiently peering at her watch from time to time. She wasn't looking forward to the coming interview. On the last night of the pantomime she and Jack had had one of their rare quarrels. And it was all over Carol.

'I'm not saying she hasn't any talent, love,' he'd protested patiently. 'Or that we've been wasting our money. Just that she simply hasn't the ability you seem to think she has. Look, I went to see Mrs Manson myself yesterday afternoon. She more or less confirmed what I thought.'

Eve stared at him, aghast. 'You went to see Mrs Manson, behind my back? Well, if she thinks Carol is such a dud, why has she been taking our money all this time then?'

Jack shook his head. 'She didn't say the girl was a dud. Far from it. Look, I asked her point blank if Carol had this – what is it you're always on about – *star quality*? And she said no, right out. She said that Carol is a competent dancer but that's as far as it goes.' He hesitated, rubbing his chin.

'Well, go on,' Eve had prompted. 'You might as well twist the knife now you've started.'

He'd sighed. 'I'm only telling you for your own good, love. And for Carol's too. Mrs Manson said she was glad to have the chance to speak to me about it because in her view Carol's heart wasn't in it any more.'

103

'*Rubbish!*' Eve's heart had pounded with anguish. 'If she didn't like the classes, she wouldn't go.'

'She goes to please you, Eve,' he'd told her gently. 'She can see how tense you are about it. We all can. I think it's time you let go a little. Let the child do what she wants.'

'And what's that, may I ask?' Eve's voice was shrill with disappointment. 'What does she want to do? Clean floors? Stand behind a counter in Woolworth's? Drive a *fire engine*?'

'What Mrs Manson suggested is that you go and see her. Have a chat. Then maybe you can both talk to Carol together.'

So here she was, sitting in this room with all the thumping feet drumming away overhead, and seething with resentment as she waited for the woman to finish her class. All these years she'd nurtured Carol's talent, only to be told at this late stage that the child's heart wasn't in it! It was quite preposterous. It had taken all Jack's powers of persuasion for her not to go right in and tackle Carol about it there and then, but in the end she had promised to see Kitty Manson first and try to make some sense of it all.

The door opened and Kitty breezed into the room with her usual exuberance. 'Mrs Kenning! I'm so glad you could come. Would you like some tea, or a coffee perhaps? It won't take a minute.'

'No, thank you.' Eve sat up very straight, her handbag clutched tightly on her lap, both hands on the handle as though Kitty were about to snatch it from her. 'I'd like to get right to the point, if you don't mind? My husband tells me you feel Carol has lost interest in her dancing?'

Kitty sank into a chair opposite. 'Not *quite* that. It's more that she's grown out of it. Lots of girls do, you know. But I do think she'd be interested in going on to another branch of theatre.'

Eve drew a deep breath. She might have known. This was a conspiracy. 'Ah – I see. She's been discussing it with you. It's the acting you're talking about, isn't it?'

'Well, she does have a flair for it. I've always known that. I remember telling you so when she first came to me.'

'I'm not paying for her to have any more drama lessons.' Eve's lips were set in a determined line.

Kitty smiled. 'Actually, I did have an idea . . . I could do with some help with the baby classes on Saturday mornings, and perhaps one evening in the week. If Carol could come and give me a hand with those, we could sort out a couple of extra drama classes by way of payment.'

'Out of the question! We don't need charity. Besides, she has her school work.'

'It wouldn't be charity, I assure you. And it would only be for a couple of hours a week. Carol says . . .'

'Oh, I see! You've already *spoken* to her about it?' Eve's face turned red.

'It was only mentioned in passing – as a vague idea.'

Eve got to her feet, still clutching her handbag tightly to her chest. 'You've done all this between you, haven't you? Carol, Jack and you. You've ganged up on me! Well, don't think you're going to walk all over me. The answer is no, Mrs Manson. Definitely no!'

'Mrs Kenning.' Kitty rose to face her and reached out a hand. 'Please, sit down. Can you tell me what it is you have against Carol's taking up straight acting? You never minded her dancing and it isn't so very far removed, so why this prejudice?'

Reluctantly Eve sat down again. She felt suddenly deflated by Kitty's calm manner. Put like that she could see that it must seem odd. 'I do have a special reason,' she began. 'Carol – she's not like other children. At least, she is, but . . .' She broke off, chewing her lip. 'It's not

105

generally known, Mrs Manson, but Carol is adopted. Because of that I've always wanted to do the best for her.'

'Well, naturally. We all want to do the best for our children, but I . . .'

'She didn't come to us from a home or anything like that,' Eve went on. 'I knew her mother. She and I were close friends in fact. We shared a house during the war when our husbands were away.' She sighed. 'Sally was pretty, and talented too. Though of course she never had the chance to develop that talent herself. She told me she'd always wanted to learn to dance, but she came from a poor family and there was never enough money for training. She always said that if she ever had a little girl she'd make sure she had the chances Sally herself never had.'

Kitty was beginning to see. 'Ah. And you're anxious to carry out her wishes?'

'I was there when Carol was born,' Eve was saying, her eyes clouded with reminiscence. 'I cared for her right from birth. She was still only a baby when Sally, her mother, was killed.'

'I'm sorry. Was it . . . ?'

Eve's eyes suddenly focused on Kitty. 'It was in an air raid,' she said quickly. 'So perhaps you can see how much I've always meant – *promised* – to make sure that Carol had the opportunity her mother never had. It's – it's important!'

Kitty frowned. Eve Kenning's ambition for her adopted daughter was more like a fixation. 'But, my dear, we are all individuals,' she said gently. 'Everyone has their own gifts, their own ambitions in life. Perhaps Carol's lie in another direction? Pushing her into dancing against her will could become a burden to her. It might even spoil your relationship with your daughter, and I know you wouldn't want that. Besides, if I'm truly honest, I have to say that I don't really see much future for her in dancing. Not taking today's competition into account, and the way the live variety theatre is in decline.' Kitty reached out to touch Eve's arm. 'Carol would like so much to act. Won't you just give her the chance to prove she can do it? Or even that she can't. That way, at least she won't go through life feeling you prevented her from doing what she wanted.'

Eve sighed. She could hardly argue with the last point. Seeing that hesitation, Kitty seized her chance.

'And the fact that she's willing to work to pay for her own lessons proves how keen she is, doesn't it?'

'Well . . .' Defeated and outnumbered, Eve sighed. 'If everyone is so set on it, I suppose I've got to agree,' she said reluctantly. 'But I just hope no one's going to turn round and blame me when it all goes wrong!'

Carol wrote an ecstatic letter to Steven telling him that his advice had paid off and she was to drop dancing and take drama lessons full time. In the months that followed she wrote to him almost every week, telling him of her progress and how much she enjoyed helping Kitty with the baby classes too. At the end of the following year Kitty entered her for her bronze medal examination for the London Academy. Carol passed in the same month as she had the results of her 'O' levels at school.

Steven replied to her weekly progress reports with long funny letters full of anecdotes. He had left college now and was touring with the orchestra of the Festival Ballet Company, so he didn't get home very often. When Carol heard that the Festival Ballet was to visit the local theatre she was excited. Steven would be at home for a whole week. They'd be able to see each other every single day. She counted the days, crossing them off on her calendar in excited anticipation.

He had written that the company would be moving on Sunday to give the artistes time to settle into their digs before Monday's rehearsal. Steven, of course, would be staying at home with Kitty for the week. As soon as she had had her lunch, Carol hurried round to Chine Way. It was almost a year since she and Steven had seen each other. She had so much to tell him. She couldn't wait.

Kitty's front door was always open and as Carol walked into the hallway Steven was coming down the stairs. He looked taller and even more handsome than she remembered. For a moment she was tongue tied with the sheer joy of seeing him. Then she launched herself at him, throwing herself into his arms.

'Oh, *Steven*! It's so good to see you!'

Laughing and protesting, he held her away from him. 'Hey! Don't strangle me! What a welcome! It's nice to know I've been missed.' It was only then that she noticed he wasn't alone. A tall, graceful girl with long dark hair had followed him down the stairs. He stood aside. 'Carrie, this is Fern Conway. She's a dancer with the ballet company.' He turned to the girl. 'Fern, this is the Carrie you've heard so much about. The closest I've ever had to a little sister.'

The girl made her way down the last few steps and held out a hand to Carol. 'Hello, Carrie. Steven's right. He's told me all about you. I hope we're going to be good friends.'

'My name is *Carol*, actually.' Her face burning, Carol took the hand languidly held out to her and shook it briefly. 'I – I'm pleased to meet you,' she added lamely.

'Well, aren't you coming in?' Steven asked.

She looked at him. He was different somehow. Patronising and artificial. A stranger. Not the Steven she knew at all. 'No.' On impulse she added, 'I only came to – borrow a book.'

'Which book is that? Can I get it for you?'

'It's – it was . . .' Carol searched her mind frantically. 'Stanislavsky. *An Actor Prepares*,' she said. 'Kitty said I should read it.'

He laughed. 'Wow! Method acting, no less! You really are getting down to it.' He turned to Fern. 'Didn't I tell you how seriously she takes everything? She passed her LAMDA bronze medal and got four "O" levels all in one year.'

Fern smiled coolly. 'Congratulations.'

Crimson-faced, Carol nodded. 'Thanks.'

'Wait there and I'll get the book for you.'

Steven disappeared down the basement stairs, leaving the two girls alone in the hall. Carol looked at Fern. The other girl would be in her early-twenties, she guessed. As slender and lissome as a gazelle in her understated white blouse and pencil slim skirt, an air of supreme confidence emanated from her. She regarded Carol with large brown eyes. 'So you study with Steven's mother?' she said conversationally.

'Yes, drama. I used to come to her dancing classes and still help out with the little ones.'

'Really? How nice. But you didn't want to take it up?'

'No.' There was an awkward silence, then Carol asked, 'Have you known Steven long?'

'Since he joined the company. He's a very talented musician.' Fern smiled. 'And a very special person. But then, you already know that, I'm sure.'

'Yes.' Carol blushed and stared at her feet.

Steven emerged, the book in his hand. 'Here you are then. Sure you won't stay to tea, Carrie? Kitty had to slip out for an hour but you know you're always welcome.'

She backed towards the door. 'Can't, thanks,' she muttered. 'Promised to see a friend.'

'But you'll be coming to the show?' he said. 'Come with Kitty. I've given her a couple of tickets for Tuesday night.

You must come. It's *Coppelia*. Fern is playing Swanilda and she's just the most enchanting thing you ever saw.' He slipped an arm round the girl's waist.

Carol nodded, her hand on the door handle and her stiff lips squeezed into a tight little smile. 'Yes, perhaps I will. Well, got to run now. Nice to see you, Steven and – and Fern. I hope you have a good week. Goodbye.'

She ran until she was out of breath, mainly because it wasn't possible to run and cry at the same time. Unable to face going home where her parents would see there was something wrong and ask questions, she made her way to the open spread of green known as The Racecourse and found an isolated bench to sit on, away from the footballing boys and dog walkers.

The words 'little sister' rang mockingly in her ears. Steven had never treated her like a little sister, so why had he made a remark like that? She thought about Fern; picturing the girl's slender grace, the melting brown eyes and elegant high cheekbones. Was Steven in love with her? The thought pierced her heart like a dagger. They'd obviously talked about her too. What had they said? Had Steven shown Fern her letters? Had they had a good laugh at her expense?

Sick with misery, she compared her own appearance with that of the wand-slim ballerina. Since giving up her dancing Carol had put on weight. Puppy fat, her mother called it. She winced, remembering the hated expression. And though for the most part her skin was fine and clear she'd started getting a few spots lately. She put a hand up to her hair, still as blonde, fine and straight as when she was a baby. She still wore it cut in a fringe and hanging to her shoulders, but today she had tied it back in a ponytail, fastening it in place with a little tortoiseshell ring. And she had put on her new dress with its bouffant skirt complete with stiffened petticoats. Getting ready in her room at home she'd thought – actually *believed* – she looked sophisticated. Compared to Fern she must look like an overdressed freak! She pulled the ponytail ring off angrily and shook her hair loose with an impatient toss of her head. That wasn't sophisticated for a start. It just made her look childish and stupid, she told herself. And why for heaven's sake had she had to go and ask for that book. *Stanislavsky*! How stupid and pretentious it must have made her sound. No wonder Steven had laughed. Tears welled up in her eyes. 'I *hate* being sixteen,' she announced to a passing pigeon. No one took you seriously. People thought they could treat you any-old-how. You weren't supposed to have any *feelings* till you were at least twenty!

Picking up the borrowed tome, she set off in the direction of Janet's house in search of sympathy.

'Sixteen is *hell*!' she declared defiantly.

Carol sat beside Kitty in the darkened auditorium and watched with grudging admiration as Fern Conway danced. Taking the part of the mischievous Swanilda in *Coppelia*, she was indeed enchanting. Mimicking the stiff-jointed actions of the automaton whose place she had taken she delighted the audience, and when the curtain came down on the first act their applause confirmed it.

As the lights went up Kitty looked at Carol. 'Isn't she just wonderful?' she said. 'I predict she'll be dancing at Sadler's Wells before very long.'

'She's very good,' Carol conceded unhappily. 'Now perhaps you can see why I wouldn't go on with dancing? I could never compete with anyone as brilliant as Fern. Never in a million years.'

Something about the wistful tone of her remark made Kitty glance at her young companion. Suddenly she saw that the child was almost a woman. And when she spoke of competition she wasn't speaking of dancing alone.

Chapter Four

1959

The little shop in Clarence Street went from strength to strength after Eve opened up the grocery section. Business improved so much that two years later the Kennings enlarged the shop, knocking down the partition wall and taking in the storeroom at the rear. They invested in a deep-freeze cabinet so that they could stock a range of the frozen foods that were becoming so popular, and began to sell ice cream as well as sweets and cigarettes. But as the decade neared its end Jack's health began to deteriorate and he was forced to spend more and more time resting so that much of the running of the shop rested on Eve's shoulders.

Now that Rose had time on her hands, Michael being at university and Elizabeth at college, she was happy to come in most days to help Eve. The sisters worked reasonably well together, though the old rivalry was still there, especially when it came to their respective children. Rose was immensely proud of her son's and daughter's achievements and never lost an opportunity to say so. Although she never actively criticised, she had her own ways of making clear that Carol's theatrical training and ambitions were, in her view, not altogether respectable.

Carol had left school at the end of her 'O' level year to study drama in more depth. Now she worked with Kitty four days of the week, enabling her to take more young pupils, something for which Kitty was grateful. At weekends and on Wednesdays, Rose's day off, she helped her mother in the shop. She was studying hard for her LAMDA silver medal examination and, although it was not what Eve had intended, she had to admit that the girl was totally dedicated and working hard.

Eddie Wilson continued to be a thorn in Eve's side. He persisted in turning up unexpectedly at the shop from time to time, causing her acute discomfort with his sly looks and innuendo. He reminded her of a fox, a sly predator waiting to pounce, though she could not have said why she felt this irrational fear. After all, there was nothing he could do that could possible hurt her. On his visits to the shop he never failed to ask after Carol, something which eventually aroused Rose's curiosity.

'Why is he so interested in your Carol?' she asked one day after he'd left.

Eve shrugged. 'She came in from school one day when he was here,' she said. 'I suppose he was taken with her.' She glanced uneasily at her sister. 'He said he's always wanted a daughter. They've only got boys, apparently.'

Rose sniffed. 'Wouldn't trust that one as far as I could throw him,' she said. 'He's made money, I grant you, but whose face has he ground underfoot to do it? That's what I'd like to know. There's a lot of folks still wondering how he managed to get out of going into the army!' she added pithily.

'As far as I'm concerned he's just a supplier,' Eve said dismissively. 'What he does with his own life is his business.'

It was early one morning, as she was marking up the papers for the delivery boys, that Eddie made his next unheralded appearance. He'd never come this early before and Eve's heart sank as she saw his distinctive pale blue Jaguar draw up outside. She watched apprehensively as he locked the car and sauntered towards the shop, gesturing to her through the window to let him in.

'You won't mind if I carry on marking up, will you?' she said coolly as she returned to her place behind the counter. 'The boys will be here soon.'

'Not a bit, duck. You carry on,' he said, lighting a cigarette.

Eve carried on with her work, but she was acutely conscious of his eyes on her. At last, unable to bear the tension any longer, she said, 'I stocked up the day before yesterday. And I don't think we owe you anything.'

' 'Course you don't. Wish they were all as prompt as your good selves.' He began to walk round the shop, inspecting the shelves and peering into the freezer.

Irritated, Eve looked up. 'Is something wrong, Mr Wilson?'

'No. Far from it. Just wanted a little chat before that sister of yours turns in for work.' He frowned and shook his head. 'Sharp tongue, your Rose. Terrible! Not like you.' He grinned. 'Why do I get the feeling she doesn't like me, I wonder?'

'I've no idea. Look, when the boys have picked up the papers I'll have to go and get some breakfast before opening time, so if there's something you want to say . . .'

'Yeah, yeah.' He leaned across the counter and fixed Eve with his curiously light eyes. 'You know, you've really turned this little business round,' he said. 'Got to take my hat off to you, Eve. You've done wonders.'

'Thanks. But . . .'

'But I can see what hard work it is for you, what with your hubby not being a hundred percent fit and that. So how would you feel about a little proposition?'

'What kind of little proposition?'

'Like selling up to yours truly, for instance?'

'No, thank you, Mr Wilson.' Bristling with annoyance, Eve walked round the counter and put the bags of marked papers by the door, ready for the boys to collect.

'And now, if you've no more to say, I'll have to ask you to excuse . . .'

'Hold your horses! Wait a minute.' Eddie placed himself between her and the door. 'You're not going to turn me down flat before you've heard what I'm offering, surely?'

'I don't have to hear anything. We don't want to sell the shop,' she told him. 'It's our living and our home. And I hope it will be for some time to come.'

'But you don't know what I'm offering.' He took a step towards her. 'Maybe when you do you'll change your mind, or at least want to have another think. Very tempting you'll find it.'

'I don't think so.'

'Shouldn't you talk it over with your husband, Eve?' he asked. 'You'd have enough to buy yourself a nice little bungalow, like the new ones they're building out Moulton way. Bit of country air'd do that hubby of yours the world of good. Now, I daresay he gets a pension. With that and what you'd have left you could live like . . .'

'I said, *no!*' Eve's face was red. 'I've told you. We've built this place up and we like it here. We like the work. Besides, neither of us is old enough to retire.'

He sucked in his breath and shook his head slowly. 'Shouldn't be too hasty, you know, Eve. Your Jack can't help much these days though, can he? And, you know, you're going to kill yourself, working like you do. Up at dawn every morning – working all the hours God sends to make a living.' He looked at her, his head on one side. 'I'm offering you a way out.'

'Well, it's good of you to consider us, but the answer's still no.' Eve pushed past him to the door and slipped off the catch. 'Now, if you don't mind . . .'

He stood where he was. 'That girl of yours, Carol. She's adopted – isn't she?'

115

Eve stared at him, her blood suddenly turning cold. 'What does Carol have to do with this? Who says she's adopted anyway?'

He shook his head. 'Come off it, Eve. Your sister happened to let it drop one day when I was in here. Not that I hadn't already guessed.' He looked at her. 'She's Sally's kid, isn't she?'

Eve's knees were trembling but she thrust out her chin defiantly. 'What if she is? She's legally ours. Has been since she was tiny.'

He nodded. 'Does she know who her mother was?'

'Yes. I've always been honest with her.'

'And her father? Does she know who he is?'

Eve felt her heart lurch in her chest as she looked into the pale eyes. 'As far as Carol is concerned Jack is her father,' she said steadily. 'He's the only father she's ever known. Anyway, it's got nothing to do with you.'

'*Hasn't* it?' He smiled glassily. 'She's mine. But you knew that, didn't you?'

'How can you stand there and say that? When Sally came to you for help you denied her it – said you didn't believe her. So what makes you so sure now? Why claim fatherhood of her after all these years?'

'I'm not claiming anything, Eve. I'm stating a fact. I know Carol's mine all right.' He lit another cigarette, taking his time over the ritual till Eve wanted to scream. As he exhaled he looked up at her. 'I don't think Sally was quite straight with you,' he said. 'That night when she was killed – she was on her way to meet me.'

'*No*! She was on her way to the station – to catch a train to Portsmouth. She was going to see her husband and . . .' Eve trailed off. Could he be telling the truth? If he was there were other, more serious implications.

'Oh, yes.' He took in her stunned look with satisfaction before continuing. 'We picked up again after she'd had

116

the kid. We'd been seeing each other for weeks. She came to see me when she heard that her husband was alive after all. She was in a real panic – said she couldn't go through with having him back, all messed up like that. She'd already told me about the pressure you were putting on her to give the baby up. She didn't know which way to turn. The poor girl was falling apart, so I agreed we'd take the kid and go away somewhere, just the three of us.' He smiled. 'I did think a lot of her, you know. Well, I must have, mustn't I?'

'I don't believe a word of it.' Eve had to clench her fists tightly to control her shaking. 'You're making it all up. You can't prove it and even if you could . . .'

He shrugged. 'I've no intention of trying to prove anything. Just thought you might like to know the facts, Eve, as you're so keen on the *truth*.' He turned towards the door. 'About the business: if you have second thoughts about selling, the offer's still open. It's a good offer – considering. You know where I am.'

He paused, his hand on the door. 'Oh, by the way, maybe you can clear up a little mystery for me.' He turned his piercing, colourless gaze full on her. 'Like I said, Sal was supposed to be bringing the baby with her that night we were going away together. Yet she was alone when they found her under that bridge after the raid. That's something that's always puzzled me. Just for the record, how did you persuade her to leave the kid with you after all, Eve?' There was a breathless pause and her heart seemed to stop as they stared at each other. Then Eddie shrugged.

'Still, just as well you did, eh? Seems young Carol owes her life to you. I'm surprised you don't tell her *that* story. It's one for the grandchildren, that is!' He opened the door. 'Well, cheerio for now then, Eve. Be seeing you. Soon, I hope.'

117

Numb with shock, she watched from the shop window as he went out to the car. As he drove away he waved to her, but her own arm hung as though paralysed by her side.

The events of that fateful night were back with her as vividly as though she were reliving them. She felt again the biting cold, the sting of the driving snow on her face, the treacherous ground under her feet. Once again she felt the fiendish strength of her own emotions as she struggled with Sally in a desperate bid to prevent her taking baby Carol. She saw again with horrifying clarity the look of fear in the other girl's eyes as she slipped and lost her footing; heard her terrified scream as she toppled backwards over the parapet of the bridge.

Eve's hand flew to her mouth to stifle the cry that escaped it. For years she had buried the horror of that night under layers of spurious logic and self-justification, but there was no escaping the stark fact that Sally's death had been her doing. Just as certainly as if she had plunged a knife into her heart. The knowledge of that was a life sentence in itself.

The delivery boys arrived in a flurry of brash, cheerful early-morning banter and set off on bikes wobbling under the weight of the bulging sacks of morning papers. Eve locked the shop door again and slowly climbed the stairs to the flat. In the kitchen she stood at the window, waiting for the kettle to boil, staring out sightlessly over the view of back yards and rooftops as she tried to unravel the convolution of Eddie Wilson's devious mind. Why did he want to buy this shop when he already had a thriving wholesale business and half a dozen other shops, in much better positions than this? There must be a good reason why he wanted it. Eddie Wilson was a shrewd businessman, not given to idle whims. And if she stuck to her guns and refused to sell, what could he do? He couldn't force her. Or could he?

She mulled over his words. Well-chosen words heavily loaded with subtle threat. Did he know more than he was letting on? Had he really arranged to go away with Sally that night? And if so, where had they agreed to meet? Could it have been on that very bridge? Might he actually have been there – standing unseen in the shadows to witness their last desperate struggle? The blood ran cold in her veins as she pictured Carol's reaction if she ever found out; if Jack were to discover that the wife he had dreamed of returning to all those years in the prison camp was a murderer.

Carol enjoyed working with Kitty. The wage she received was little more than pocket money, but she did get her drama classes free of charge. And her mother paid her a little for helping out in the shop, which added to her weekly earnings. Kitty had entered her for the silver medal examination this autumn and with luck she would take her gold next year. After that, who knew? Kitty was in favour of her trying to get some practical experience with a repertory company before applying for a place at drama college, but Carol was content to wait and see how things worked out.

Janet was still at school, studying hard in the sixth form for her 'A' levels. Neither of the girls had much free time and because of her studies, Janet had given up dancing classes. But on Saturday evenings they usually went to the cinema or dancing at the local Palais. Both of them loved rock and roll. They each had a collection of records by Bill Haley and the Comets, Elvis Presley and Tommy Steele. But more recently both girls had become fans of Cliff Richard and Adam Faith.

When they were together their conversation invariably turned to boys. Janet was going out with a studious young man called Geoffrey Cottingham who was in the sixth form at the grammar school. He had a shock of red hair and wore horn-rimmed glasses which made him look older than his nineteen years. In many ways he reminded Carol of her cousin, Michael. Like Janet, Geoffrey was hoping to get into medical school. Sometimes he came with them to the Palais and privately Carol thought him dull and rather boring. But Janet seemed to like him well enough and Carol concluded it was because of all the two of them had in common. She and Steven still kept in touch by letter, though nowadays they hardly ever saw each other, something that Janet found hard to understand.

'Doesn't he *ever* get home nowadays?' she asked. 'I think I'd get fed up with a boyfriend I never saw.'

'The ballet company's still touring,' Carol explained. 'They travel on Sundays so he hardly ever gets a free weekend. Anyway, Steven isn't my boyfriend.'

'No, but you'd like him to be, wouldn't you?' Janet said, with all the frankness of a best friend. 'Is he still going steady with that girl you told me about? What's her name – Fran?'

'Fern? Oh, no, that was over ages ago,' Carol said airily. 'She was only a friend anyway.'

She didn't admit how immensely gratifying she had found the news that the exquisite Fern had left the company. As Kitty had predicted, she had been offered a place in the *corps de ballet* at Sadler's Wells. Neither did she tell Janet that Steven now wrote glowingly about someone called Clarissa who was vaguely concerned with scenic design and costumes.

'Well, I'd start looking round for someone else if I were you,' Janet said. 'I mean, how can you have a romance with someone you never see?'

Carol shrugged noncommittally. Apart from the fact that there was no romance between herself and Steven,

120

the truth was that she had yet to meet anyone who remotely attracted her. All the boys she knew of her own age were spotty and gauche. The clever ones only wanted to show off, talking earnestly about things that were above her head, while the others were football crazy, which she found equally stultifying. But there was one thing they all had in common: the moment you were alone with them they seemed to feel obliged to start pawing you about. No, one letter from Steven was worth a dozen dates with one of them, as she told Janet.

On Carol's seventeenth birthday Jack had presented her with a provisional driving licence and announced that he would teach her to drive.

'If you'd like to earn some extra money you could do deliveries for the shop,' he suggested. 'And go to the cash and carry for us. In exchange you could have the use of the van in your free time.'

Carol was quite excited at the thought, but Eve wasn't so enthusiastic. Every Saturday evening when Carol got ready to go out dancing she couldn't help thinking of Sally; remembering how she would go off to the American air base in her skimpy little dresses, coming home at all hours with her make-up smudged and her eyes glazed. Carol was a grown woman now, almost as old as Sally had been when she was born, and Eve couldn't help worrying.

They were not close. Eve could not bring herself to talk to the girl about adult life, or relationships with the opposite sex. She had absolutely no idea what the girl thought or felt about these things, or how she behaved when she was away from her mother's watchful eye. She fretted about it a great deal. And to make matters worse, Rose had no qualms about airing her own graphic views on the subject.

'I hope you've told that girl what's what,' she said. 'I had a good talk to our Elizabeth before she went off to college. I told her, men are after one thing and one thing only! And once they get it you can say goodbye to any respect they might've had for you. Buy you a meal and a drink and they think they've bought you as well! You want to keep yourself *to* yourself, I told her. And send 'em packing when they start getting frisky ideas. You'll be better thought of for it.' She glanced at Eve whose mouth was tightly buttoned. 'I hope you've done the same with your Carol,' she said. 'You want to remember that girl's background. She's the spittin' image of her mother, you know. And these dances – they're not like the ones we used to go to. Jumping all over the place, doing that rock and roll rubbish, showing their underwear. And that woman she works with can't be too good an influence. I bet she's been a right flighty piece in her time.' She gave her sister a knowing nod. 'I'd keep an eye on young Carol if I were you. You don't want her bringing you a packet of trouble home, do you?'

'Carol's a good girl,' Eve expostulated. 'I haven't had a moment's worry about her.'

'Is that so?' Rose drew in her breath and folded her arms. 'Well, you're luckier than most of the mothers *I* know then! That's all I can say.' She shot her sister a baleful look. 'I only hope you don't have any call to eat your words, our Eve!'

Since Eddie Wilson's early-morning visit Eve had thought a lot about his offer for the shop and its implications. She wondered whether she should mention it to Jack. For all she knew he might actually *like* the idea of selling up and moving. They'd never discussed it. Maybe they should. Eventually, deciding that it would be as well to know how he felt on the subject, she broached it one night after they were in bed.

'Jack, how would you feel about selling the shop and retiring?'

He raised himself on one elbow to look at her in surprise. 'Retire? I'm barely fifty, love. A good fifteen years before I'll be eligible for my State pension and we couldn't live on what I get from the army.'

'We could if we got a good price for the business.'

He frowned. 'What's brought this on? Are you finding it too much, love? Listen, I didn't mention this before, but Doctor Ross reckons I'd benefit from an operation. He called it a colectomy and he reckons it'd put a stop to all the gastric attacks I've been getting. He says the dysentery I kept getting in the camp has caused permanent damage to my inside and that's why it keeps on flaring up. If I were to have this op I'd be fit to help you more.'

Eve felt a rush of love and pity for him. She knew how much it hurt his pride to see her managing the lion's share of the work while he was obliged to stand helplessly by. She also knew that each one of the debilitating attacks weakened him a little more.

'Well, if the doctor really thinks it's going to help then of course you must have it,' she said. 'But you mustn't feel you have to put yourself through it because of me.' She kissed his cheek. 'Selling the shop wasn't just an idea. I didn't tell you but I've had an offer. I said no right off, but I've been thinking since. You've got a right to think about it too.'

'Who's this offer from?' Jack asked – as she had known he would. 'And how much did they offer?'

'It was from Eddie Wilson. I don't know exactly how much because I told him I wasn't interested. But he did say it'd be a good offer.'

Jack linked his hands together behind his head, staring up at the ceiling thoughtfully. 'It might be worth asking him what the offer is,' he said at last. 'But I can't really see it being worth our while selling. We've invested quite a bit in it and it's a good living now. It's our home too.

Besides, if anything were to happen to me it'd be security for you. And we've got Carol to think of too.'

Eve drew a deep breath. 'I've thought of all that,' she said. 'That was why I said no. Not that anything is going to happen to you.'

'You can't be sure,' he said practically. 'Always best to be prepared for the worst even though we hope for the best.' He frowned. 'Seems funny though, Wilson wanting to buy this place. If you can do it tactfully, ask him why he wants the shop and see if you can find out what he'd give us. Then, when we know more, we'll have another think.'

It was the following Saturday evening at the Palais that Carol met Paul. As he sauntered across the floor, his eyes intent on her, Janet giggled and nudged her.

'Hey, get a load of this,' she exclaimed. 'Cliff to a tee! At least, *he* obviously thinks so! And if I'm not very much mistaken he's making a beeline for you.'

The young man in question had dark curly hair with sideburns and a quiff falling over his forehead. He wore a dark shirt and bright red jacket and tie just like the ones Cliff wore on the sleeve of the record Carol had just bought. Standing in front of her, he jerked his head towards the dance floor.

'Dance?'

As it turned out he was a very skilful dancer, whirling her around and surprising her with jive steps she didn't even know she could do. When the music stopped he grinned at her and said, 'Drink?'

She laughed breathlessly. 'I'd love a lemonade. Thanks.'

At the bar he bought her a lemonade and a beer for himself, then nodded towards a table in the far corner. 'Sit down?' he asked in his oddly laconic manner.

When they were seated opposite each other he grinned at her again. 'You dance okay,' he told her. 'Nice and loose. Most girls are all stiff and uptight.'

'I teach dancing,' she told him. 'I've been dancing since I was eight.'

'No kidding? What's your name?'

'Carol.'

'Mine's Paul,' he told her. 'So you teach dancing. Like it?'

'It's all right for now, but I'm studying to be an actress.'

His eyebrows rose. 'An actress, eh? Not many of them round here.'

'I suppose not.' She took a sip of her drink. 'What do you do, Paul?'

'Doing a business course at the Tech. Going into the family business when I'm ready.' As the band started up again he swallowed the last of his drink and looked at her inquiringly. 'Hey, *Chantilly Lace*. How about it?'

It was fun dancing with Paul. He was quick and light on his feet and once she got used to his monosyllabic way of talking Carol began to like him. That morning she had had a letter from Steven. To begin with she'd been excited to learn that the company had a couple of weeks out due to pantomime rehearsals three weeks from now, and he would be coming home. But her excited anticipation was to be short-lived.

I'll be bringing someone with me. I'm twenty-five now and I've been thinking seriously lately that maybe it's time I settled down. And I can't think of anyone I'd rather share my life with than Clarissa, if she'll let me. You'll love her, Carrie. She's so sweet. Beautiful too. As beautiful as Fern, but much more fun. I'm bringing her home to meet Kitty, but I hope you'll be there too. You know how much I've always valued your opinion . . .

When she'd first read the letter she'd wanted to tear it into tiny pieces and burn it. *Valued her opinion?* What a joke! Last time he came home he'd humiliated her, making her look small in front of Fern, just to show off. He was lucky she was still speaking to him after that! When she'd heard that they'd split up she'd looked forward to his next visit so much. It would be just like old times, having him all to herself again. And now he'd be bringing this Clarissa with him and it would be just like last time all over again, only worse, because this time they'd probably be engaged! Hurt and anger brought a huge lump to her throat. He obviously thought she was still eight years old and killing dragons! Well, when he did come home maybe she'd give *him* a shock. Maybe she'd have someone of her own to introduce him to this time. Then she could tell him how much she'd always valued *his* opinion!

When the dance ended Paul asked if he could walk her home. Geoffrey had borrowed his father's car and Janet didn't seem too put out when Carol said she wouldn't be joining them.

'I'll be taking my driving test soon,' she told Paul as they walked. 'My dad is teaching me. He says that once I've passed I can have the use of the van.'

'I can drive already,' Paul said. 'When I join the business Dad'll get me a car of my own. Normally he lets me borrow his but he's using it tonight.'

Carol glanced at him, wondering if he was telling the truth. She suspected that he might be a bit of a line-shooter. Still, he was fun and nice-looking too, as well as being a good dancer. When he reached for her hand she let him take it.

It was quite a long walk home through the frosty late-night streets, though Paul assured her that he didn't mind.

'I don't live all that far from you,' he said casually. 'So it's not much out of my way.'

When they reached Clarence Street and stopped outside the door that led to the flat, Paul looked at her.

'When do I see you again then, Carol?'

She shrugged. 'When do you want to?'

'Next Saturday? I don't get out much in the week.'

'Nor do I. Okay then, next Saturday.'

'Shall I come and pick you up? I might be able to get Dad's car next week.'

'That'd be nice.'

'Right then.' Still holding her hand he drew her towards him. 'Well? Do I get a kiss goodnight?'

'If you like.' She raised her face and felt his arms slip round her. His lips on hers were warm and firm. She closed her eyes and felt her heart beat a little faster. He drew back his head to look at her.

'I like you, Carol. I like you a lot.'

She blushed. 'I – like you too.'

He kissed her again, a little harder this time, then, his hands on her shoulders, stepped back. 'Right then. See you next Saturday. About eight?'

'Okay.'

' 'Night then.'

'Goodnight.' She watched as he walked away, swaggering a little in his red jacket and tight black trousers. When he got to the corner he turned and raised his hand. She waved back, then let herself quietly in. When she reached the top of the stairs Eve called out to her from the bedroom.

'That you, Carol?'

'Yes, Mum.'

'Did you lock up properly?'

'Yes, Mum.'

' 'Night then, love.'

' 'Night, Mum.'

In her room Carol undressed and climbed into bed,

relieved that her mother hadn't asked who'd brought her home. Other mothers didn't seem to mind too much about boys walking their daughters home from dances but Eve was so mistrustful, as though every boy Carol danced with was under suspicion of being a mass-murderer or something.

Switching off the light, she lay in the darkness and thought about Paul. She wasn't absolutely sure he was her type but he was fun. She'd enjoyed dancing with him and he hadn't tried to maul her about like some of the boys who'd walked her home. And he'd kissed her nicely. None of that horrible sloppy stuff. It would be fun to have a steady boyfriend like Janet. It would show Steven too, she thought with drowsy triumph as she fell asleep.

Now that Carol was studying for her silver medal she was having one to one lessons with Kitty. The syllabus for the exam included two set pieces, one from a modern play and one from a classic. Under Kitty's instruction she had read the plays and analysed the characters. Now it was simply a matter of learning the lines and rehearsing the scenes. The examination date was set for Saturday 28 November, and as the time drew closer Carol grew nervous. She spent hours in her room, doing her voice and breathing exercises and lying on her bed repeating her lines over and over.

She had been out with Paul on two Saturdays now, once to the cinema and once to the Palais. In spite of what he had told her he had not so far managed to borrow his father's car, but when she had tried to call off their date for the following Saturday, he had looked disappointed.

'I should be able to get the car next week for sure,' he told her.

'It isn't that, Paul,' she told him. 'It's just that I'll only have a few more days before my exam by then and I'll need all the time I can get to practise.'

'You can overdo it, you know,' he argued. 'I think you should have a break. Tell you what, I'll definitely get Dad's car and I'll take you out to dinner. We'll go to a nice restaurant I know out Kettering way.'

She looked at him doubtfully. 'But won't that be expensive?'

He grinned. 'Dad'll give me a sub. I'll offer to give him a hand on Saturday afternoon. That usually does the trick.'

Eve had had misgivings about this new boyfriend Carol had started going out with. She hadn't minded her accompanying Janet and Geoffrey, acting on the assumption that there was safety in numbers, but she wasn't at all easy about this new boy. So far she'd only caught a glimpse of the young man when he called for Carol on Saturday evenings. Normally at that time she was busy making a meal after Saturday's late closing. She'd seen him from the living-room window as they walked up the street together. In her opinion he looked a bit on the flashy side, but then the young dressed differently nowadays. Clothes for 'best' no longer consisted of a blue serge suit and white shirt. Now it was all drainpipe trousers and velvet collars. And that hair! Flopping all over the place. It made her fingers itch to get at it with her scissors. Jack laughed at her when she expressed these views.

'Every age has its fashions, love,' he said tolerantly. 'Just thank God there's no war on and the kids are free to express themselves. He looks a nice enough lad to me. Why don't you get Carol to ask him to come for his tea next Sunday? Then we can really get a good look at him.'

'Well, all right then.'

Eve had planned to invite Kitty Manson, Steven and his girlfriend round for tea as a little celebration after Carol's exam. She had misgivings about inviting this lad too. After all, he was a comparative stranger and could spoil the atmosphere, but when Eve tentatively suggested to Carol that she might like to include Paul, she seemed quite pleased.

True to his word Paul drove up in his father's car the following Saturday evening. They drove out to the restaurant he had mentioned and Carol enjoyed both drive and meal. They each had scampi and chips followed by enormous ice cream sundaes, and Paul insisted on buying Carol a Babycham to drink with it. In the car on the way home she issued her mother's invitation to come to tea the following week. Paul looked dubious.

'Well, I don't know. Why do they want to meet me, your folks?'

'Because they don't know you. That's just the point,' she told him. 'Mum says that as we've been out together several times, they'd like to know who it is I'm with.'

He shook his head suspiciously. 'Why, though?'

She laughed. 'Why *not*? There'll be other people there too. It's supposed to be a little party after my exam. If you don't come it's going to look as if you've got something to hide.'

He pulled a face. 'Oh, all right then.'

Carol laughed. The Babycham had made her feel light-headed and strangely carefree. Suddenly the exam didn't seem so all-important after all and she was just thinking that Paul had been right to say that she needed a break when he pulled the car over and stopped in a lay-by.

'What's up? Have we run out of petrol?' She giggled. When he reached out and pulled her close she relaxed in his arms and responded to his kisses enthusiastically, but when he began to unfasten the buttons of her dress and breathe heavily into her neck she suddenly grew uneasy.

'No, Paul.' She pushed him away, but he grasped her more firmly.

130

'Oh, come on, Carol. Be a sport.'

She frowned and shook her head. 'No. Stop it. I don't want to.'

'What's the matter? You like me, don't you? You said you did.'

'That doesn't mean I want you to . . .' She gasped as he thrust his hand inside her dress and cupped one breast. '*Stop it!*' She began to struggle wildly till he withdrew his hand and shook his head.

'Okay. *Okay!* Don't blow your top. Just kisses then. You like kissing, eh?'

She calmed down and let him kiss her, but after a few minutes he pushed his tongue against her lips, parting them, and she felt his hand insinuate itself under the hem of her skirt and begin to slide up her thigh. She stiffened and drew back, her hand covering his to prevent its progress.

'Come on, Carol,' he murmured against the corner of her mouth. 'Everyone does this. Just relax. You'll like it.'

But she didn't like it. She thought it was revolting, having someone else's tongue in her mouth and she hated the hot sweaty feel of his hand on her thigh. Suddenly Paul was just like all those other boys. He wasn't fun any more. He was turning out to be disappointingly typical and all she wanted was to go home.

Eventually he gave up. Leaning back against his seat, he lit a cigarette and looked at her over the flame of the match with an exasperated sigh.

'I thought you liked me, Carol,' he said, blowing out a cloud of smoke.

'I did. I do, Paul, but I don't like what you're doing.'

He smiled at her patronisingly. 'You're just a baby really, aren't you?'

'What do you *mean*?' She was close to tears.

'This is what it's all about,' he said patiently. 'Most

131

girls know the score. It's why you go out with a feller. To have fun – smooch, snog. Call it what you want. It's no big deal.'

'It is to me.' Her mind was in a turmoil. Was it wrong to feel this kind of revulsion? Was she abnormal in some way? 'I'm sorry. I can't help it, Paul. Can I go home now, please?'

'*Can I go home now, please?*' he mimicked in a high falsetto voice. 'God! I always thought actresses were supposed to be hot stuff.'

'That's a really stupid thing to say!'

'Oh? That right, is it?' He looked at her pityingly. 'Still, you're not an actress yet, are you? Just playing at being one!' He tossed his half-smoked cigarette out of the window and switched on the engine. 'Blimey! If the blokes at the Tech ever get to hear about this I'll be the laughing stock of the place! Come on then, Baby Bunting. Let's get you home to Mummy and Daddy before Sooty pops up and turns you into a puff of oofle dust!'

They drove back to Clarence Street in silence. When Paul stopped the car outside the shop he turned to her. 'I suppose this means we're through? You won't want me round for the formal once-over with the folks next week now, will you? Not now that you know I'm only a normal bloke and not some kind of plaster saint.'

Carol was about to agree, then she remembered how much she had been looking forward to showing Steven that she had a boyfriend. She bit her lip and said stiffly, 'Of course I still want you to come.'

'You're kidding!' He looked genuinely surprised. 'And you reckon I'll still want to come, do you?'

On a sudden impulse she leaned across and kissed him. 'I'm sorry, Paul,' she said a little breathlessly. 'Sorry that I . . . It's just that I . . . Maybe . . .'

'Oh, Carol.' He pulled her close and kissed her hard.

And this time she reluctantly allowed her lips to part for him. She heard him give a little groan.

'You're so lovely. I wish . . .'

'Got to go now,' She extricated herself from his grasp and felt for the door handle. 'See you next Sunday afternoon. About four, Mum said.' As she stood there on the pavement, watching him drive away, she rubbed the back of her hand across her mouth, erasing the memory of his kiss. She felt a Judas.

The LAMDA examinations were held in a church hall just off Regent Square. Kitty had been quite excited when she saw the name of the examiner.

'Gareth Dean is a very fine classical actor,' she told Carol. 'I heard somewhere that he's taking up directing. There's very little he doesn't know about stagecraft.'

'What's he like?' Carol asked.

'Oh, tall and dark. He has one of those wonderful actor's faces. Sort of ugly-handsome,' Kitty told her. 'I remember seeing him play Othello before the war at Stratford. He was electrifying.'

Carol was there early. Kitty had been tied up with a rehearsal for the Christmas show, but she'd promised to be there when Carol came out. She was shown to the dressing room where several other entrants were waiting nervously. She applied her make-up with meticulous care, knowing she would be marked on her stagecraft too. At least she could get that as perfect as possible. The girl whose turn it was next was twittering anxiously, pacing up and down and muttering her lines over and over. Carol found it irritating and wished she would stop. Remembering Kitty's advice, she closed her eyes, taking deep breaths and emptying her mind in an attempt to calm her nerves.

At last her name was called and she went out into the

corridor leading to the stage. Standing on the stage, shielding her eyes from the brightness of the footlights, she peered out into the auditorium, but she couldn't see the examiner at all. From somewhere out there in the darkness his disembodied voice instructed her to begin whenever she was ready.

The two set pieces went well. As usual she forgot her surroundings once she had begun and lost herself in the characters she was playing. She managed the piece of sight reading without any problems. Then it was time to go down the steps at the side of the stage and talk to the examiner. With some trepidation she approached the table where he sat, halfway down the hall.

'Well done, Miss Kenning,' he said. 'You have given an excellent performance.' He finished marking her card, then smiled up at her over the top of his spectacles. Carol immediately saw that Kitty's description had been right. Gareth Dean was an imposing-looking man. His dark hair was silvered at the temples and his dark, craggy face had an almost mesmeric quality.

'You know, you have a rare gift,' he told her. 'That of sincerity. It's something very precious, worth a great deal in our business. I hope you never lose it.' He looked down at the card. 'I have passed you with honours and hope I shall be here to give you a very good gold medal before too long.' He handed her the card. 'Goodbye, Miss Kenning. And may I wish you good luck?'

Carol stammered her thanks and walked out of the auditorium on a cloud of euphoria. It was over and she had passed! Not only passed but passed with honours, and praise from Gareth Dean!

Kitty, who was waiting outside in the corridor, looked up expectantly.

'I passed!' Her eyes bright, Carol handed her the card. 'Mr Dean was wonderful. He said I had the rare gift of sincerity and he hoped he'd be here to give me a good gold.'

Kitty glanced down the card and hugged her warmly. 'This is marvellous! Well done, darling! Right. Go back and take off your make-up, then we're going out to tea. This calls for a celebration!'

They took a bus back into the town centre and went to The Clipper, a restaurant that had recently opened. It had been decorated to resemble the cabin of an airliner, complete with mock portholes and waitresses dressed as air stewardesses. Carol had never been there before and thought it excitingly cosmopolitan. Over tea and toasted teacakes, she went over every detail of the exam for Kitty, recounting Gareth Dean's every word.

'Fancy him saying that to me,' she said, her eyes starry. 'Only one more exam now and I'll be ready to take a job.'

Kitty looked thoughtful. 'It might be as well to carry on and take your LLAMDA,' she said. 'That would qualify you to teach.'

Carol looked up. 'But I want to act, not teach.'

'You never know what life's going to throw at you, dear,' Kitty warned. 'Look at me for instance. Teaching has been my lifeline.'

Carol said nothing but she was quite sure that life had nothing but good things in store for her. The future lay before her like a shining golden road, just waiting to be trodden.

The moment Eve had the good news about Carol's exam pass, she telephoned her sister Rose.

'Just to let you know that Carol has passed her silver medal,' she said proudly. 'With *honours*! And the examiner was ever so encouraging too. He was a well-known actor and said some really complimentary things to her.'

'Oh? Well, I'm glad of that,' Rose said. 'Maybe she'll have more time to help you out in the shop now that that's over with.'

'She'll be going on to take her gold now,' Eve said. 'There might even be more exams after that. It's not over with by any means.'

'More? Good heavens!' Rose said. 'All that expensive training just to get up on a stage and prance about. If you ask me that Mrs Manson saw you and Jack coming.'

Eve swallowed her anger. Rose knew nothing about it, yet she behaved as though she knew the lot! She had been about to ask her and Ted over to join them at the tea party tomorrow, but now she'd be damned if she would. 'Oh, well, I just thought you'd want to be the first to hear the good news,' she said as coolly as she could. 'After all, you always make sure to let me know right away when it's Michael or Elizabeth. I'll see you on Monday then.'

Carol went to endless trouble over her appearance on Sunday afternoon. She changed into the new dress she'd bought to wear for the exam. It was made of bottle green jersey wool with a fitted bodice and flared skirt; a little scarf of white and gold was knotted at the neck, and she wore her black patent platform shoes with ankle straps. She tried her hair in various ways, but finally decided on a smooth chignon set off by shiny black stud earrings. The effect, she thought as she stepped back to survey herself in the mirror, was very grown-up and sophisticated.

Kitty and Steven arrived on the dot of four, accompanied by a tall girl with a cloud of red hair whom Steven introduced as Clarissa. As Carol shook her hand she eyed her critically, assessing the twinkling green eyes and shapely figure speculatively. She had to admit, somewhat grudgingly, that the girl looked nice; open and friendly and not at all stand-offish. Steven looked happy. He had

136

lost a little weight but Carol decided that it suited him. It gave him a lean, poetic look that she thought romantic. Once all the introductions were over he crossed the room to sit beside her.

'You're looking marvellous, Carrie. Studying hard obviously suits you. Congratulations on getting your silver, by the way. Kitty's told me all about your super marks. She's very proud of you.'

'Thanks.' She lowered her eyes, feeling suddenly shy and awkward. She'd looked forward to seeing him so much. This time she'd intended to be cool and self-assured. To show him how mature she'd become since their last meeting. But somehow the moment she saw Steven she always felt about ten years old again. It was infuriating. 'You look well too,' she told him. 'And I like Clarissa.' She leaned forward to whisper, 'Better than Fern.'

He laughed. 'Rissa has a sense of humour. That was never one of Fern's strong suits. Still, she's doing terribly well with the SWB. Dancing small parts already. Heading for stardom, no doubt.' He patted her arm. 'Like you, eh?'

She coloured. He was humouring her. She shook her head. 'Don't know about that.' Looking up at him she asked quietly, 'Are you and – er – Rissa engaged?'

He shook his head. 'Not officially. At the moment we're playing it by ear. We are together though. You know, sharing digs and all that. We're going to see how it works out.'

Carol was shaken. They were living together! Somehow it hit her harder than if he'd told her they were actually married. A vision of them in bed together suddenly sprang unbidden into her mind and she thrust the unwanted image away in disgust, shocked at herself. She was still searching her mind for something cool and unconcerned to say when the doorbell rang and she suddenly remembered Paul.

'I'll go, Mum.' Jumping to her feet, she ran down the stairs to let him in. He wore his red jacket with a black shirt, white tie and drainpipe trousers. His narrow shoes shone and his hair was glossy with hair cream, sideburns neatly trimmed. He'd clearly gone to a lot of trouble but Carol's heart sank as she remembered her father's slacks and pull-over and Steven's corduroys and open-necked shirt. Paul was going to look as out of place upstairs as a peacock in a hen coop.

'Hello. Come on up,' she said.

He hung back, obviously dreading the coming tea party. 'Look, I've got Dad's car. I've parked it round the back out of the way. I thought we could skip off somewhere. We don't have to stay long, do we?'

'Don't be silly, you're invited to tea,' she said. 'I passed my exam, by the way – with honours.'

He grinned. 'Great!' He leaned forward to kiss her but she stepped back out of reach.

'Not now. Come on. They'll wonder what we're doing. Come and meet everyone.' Taking his hand she led him up the stairs and into the living room where all eyes were turned on them. 'This is Paul,' she announced, then went round the room, introducing him to everyone in turn. Out of the corner of her eye she noted with satisfaction the way Steven looked from Paul to her and back again, and in doing so missed the look in her mother's eyes. It had not escaped Jack's notice though, and seeing the boy's obvious discomfort, he went out of his way to put Paul at his ease.

It was after tea when Eve carried the tray out to the kitchen that she happened to glance out of the window. What she saw stopped the breath in her throat. A car was parked below in the side street. A car she knew only too well. A pale blue Jaguar. Unmistakably Eddie's car. She was still staring down at it in horrified disbelief when Carol came in, carrying the cake stand. Eve spun round.

'Did Paul come in that car?' she demanded, jerking her thumb towards the window.

Carol glanced out of the window. 'Yes, it's his father's.'

Eve felt the blood drain from her face. 'What – what is Paul's second name?' she asked, ashen-faced.

'Wilson. But why? Mum! What's the matter? You look awful.'

Eve grasped the edge of the table as the room began to spin around her. 'Get rid of him!' she said harshly. 'Get him out of here. *Now!*'

'Why?' Carol was alarmed at her mother's obvious distress. What was it about Paul that had upset her so? 'What has he done?' she asked.

'Nothing.' Eve groped for a chair and sat down. 'Nothing yet, I hope. Just – just get him out of here.'

'He did say we might go for a run in the car. I could . . .'

'No!' Eve's hand shot out and grasped hers. 'You're to get rid of him and you're not to see him again. Do you hear me? I absolutely forbid it. You're not to have anything to do with that boy. You're not to go anywhere near him – *ever again.*'

Carol shook her head, her face pale with shock. She had never seen her mother so upset. 'What are you talking about, Mum? There's nothing wrong with Paul. He's . . .'

'I want him out of my house,' Eve hissed between her teeth. 'Now, Carol. *Now!* No more arguing.'

'Not till you tell me why?' She shook off her mother's hand. 'You're being unreasonable. I'll go out with Paul if I want to. There's no reason why I shouldn't.'

'There *is!*' Eve looked as though she might faint. Every vestige of colour had left her face. Even her lips were white. Carol stared at her, completely nonplussed.

'All right then, tell me what it is?' she demanded.

Jack appeared in the doorway. 'You're an awful long time in here. You're not going to wash up now, are . . . ?' He stopped short at the look on his wife's face. 'Eve! What's the matter, love? Are you feeling poorly?'

Carol turned a puzzled face to her father. 'She's telling me I'm not to see Paul again – says I'm to get rid of him. Now! What's going on, Dad?'

Jack shook his head, looking helplessly from one to the other, then he took charge of the situation. 'Go back in there, Carol,' he said. 'Leave it to me. Of course you can't tell the poor chap to go. It's ridiculous.' He pushed her towards the door. 'Tell them your mum isn't feeling too good,' he said quietly. 'Go on now. I'll handle it.'

When the door had closed behind her he turned to Eve. 'What's this all about?' he asked.

She took a deep shuddering breath. 'That boy is – he's Eddie Wilson's son,' she said.

Jack frowned and lifted his shoulders. 'So?'

She opened her mouth to blurt out the truth, but stopped herself just in time. She couldn't tell Jack or anyone else. It was all too complex. The fewer people who knew who Carol's true father was, the better. 'I – I don't want her having anything to do with that family, that's all,' she said.

'That's a bit hard on the lad, isn't it? He can't help who his father is.'

'I won't have it. I won't *have* it, Jack! Do you hear me?'

'All right, all right, love. If you say so.' He was slightly alarmed at his wife's vehemence and obvious distress. 'I'll have a word with Carol, later, when everyone's gone. Come back now and we'll say no more for the time being, eh?'

Eve need not have worried about Paul's presence in the flat. By the time she had composed herself sufficiently to

140

rejoin her guests he had already made an excuse to leave. He had found the Kennings' tea party an ordeal. Even if he'd been insensitive enough not to have picked up on Eve's obvious disapproval, it had been made abundantly clear by the snatch of conversation he had overheard as he passed the half open kitchen door on his way to the bathroom after tea.

By the time he had rejoined the other guests all three Kennings were absent from the room. The four of them spent an awkward five minutes looking at each other in embarrassment and making stilted conversation, then Paul looked at his watch and said suddenly, 'Oh, look at the time. I promised I'd have Dad's car back by six. I'd better go.'

Carol came out of the kitchen in time to see him disappearing down the stairs.

'Paul!' she called. 'Wait.' She followed him down to the car. 'Look, Paul, Mum's not very well. I'll have to stay in with her tonight. Sorry.'

'No need to make weak excuses,' he said with a twist of his lip. 'Didn't take her long to make her mind up about me, did it?'

Carol bit her lip, unable to think of anything to say as they stood beside the car, staring at each other.

'I saw the way she looked at me right from the start,' he said, his face reddening. 'Like I was something nasty stuck to her shoe!'

'You're imagining it . . .'

'I didn't imagine the things she was saying to you in the kitchen though, did I? Telling you to get rid of me. She thinks I'm not good enough for her dear little daughter. That's it, isn't it?'

'You're just being silly.'

'Oh, *silly* now, am I? *Stupid* the other night, now *silly*! Who the hell do you think you are? Well, I won't bother you with my stupidity any more, so you needn't worry.' Scarlet-faced, his eyes burning with humiliation, he got into the car and slammed the door. 'Good*bye*.'

'*Paul!*' Carol tapped on the car window. 'Don't go like that! Please!'

But he revved the engine noisily and pulled away from the kerb with a squeal of tyres that made her jump back out of the way.

As she turned to walk back inside she looked up at the kitchen window and caught her mother looking out. It had been horrible, hurting Paul's feeling like that. All for nothing too. She blushed with shame as she remembered some of the unforgivable things he must have overheard her mother saying. The look of wounded pride on his face clearly told how much it had hurt him and she winced with shame. She'd been forced to hurt his feelings for some obscure reason she didn't even know and she resented it deeply. At that moment she hated her mother. Who was she to judge people she didn't even know? And why should she dictate who Carol could see and who she couldn't? She was grown-up now and could choose her own friends. If she wanted to go out with Paul, then she damned well would!

The following morning Eve left Rose in charge of the shop and set off purposely to pay Eddie Wilson a visit. His office was at the back of the cash and carry premises on the outskirts of town. When she arrived she walked straight thorough the store, knocked on the door and then walked in.

Eddie was having his mid-morning coffee and looked up in surprise when he saw her.

'Eve . . . Mrs Kenning, what can I do for you?'

She came to the point without preamble. 'Did you know that your son has been seeing Carol?'

'Which son? I've got three.'

His expression of faint amusement infuriated her. Her hands clenched and unclenched at her sides and she longed to smack the smug smile off his face. 'Your son Paul,' she said. 'They've been seeing each other for weeks. I only found out who he was yesterday.'

He lifted his shoulders. 'That's a poser and no mistake,' he said coolly.

'You *knew*, didn't you?' Eve advanced on him, her eyes blazing. 'You set it up! You're doing it to . . . to . . .'

'To *what*?' He was on his feet now, the grin on his face replaced by a sudden fury that stopped her in mid-sentence. 'What the hell do you think I've got to gain by setting up a thing like that? Don't you come in here blowing your top at me like that! Sit down, Eve. You're hysterical. Just calm down and be sensible for a minute.'

Shaken by his dictatorial tone, she did as he said and found as she sat down that her legs were trembling and her eyes were filling with tears. 'It was such a shock,' she muttered, fumbling in her handbag for a handkerchief. 'I had to forbid her to see him again, naturally. And I couldn't tell her why, could I? She was so upset and angry. It was *awful*!'

'A coincidence. That's all it was,' he said, lighting a cigarette. 'When you think about it, it was almost bound to happen. This isn't a very big town and they're about the same age. They go dancing.' He spread his hands. 'Not that many places to dance, are there? It was always on the cards that sooner or later they'd meet up.' He leaned towards her across the desk, his face softening. 'Come on now. It's not as bad as all that. I mean, they're not talking about getting married or anything like that, are they?'

'No. But just the same . . .'

He peered at her ashen face. 'Can I get you something – glass of water? Cup of tea?'

Eve pushed her handkerchief back into her handbag, swallowed hard and straightened her back. 'No. No, thank you.'

'So – what were you about to accuse me of?' he asked, leaning back again.

She had been about to accuse him of blackmail, but now she thought better of it. Better to stay on the same side over this. He was utterly ruthless and goodness only knew what he might do if she offended him seriously. Besides, there were still a lot of uncertainties hanging between them. She shook her head. 'Nothing,' she said. 'I'd just like you to promise me that your Paul won't come after Carol again?'

He blew out his cheeks. 'Phew! With the best will in the world I don't see how I can promise that,' he said. 'After all, they're not kids any more, are they? You know how it is. Forbidden fruit and all that. I think you made a bit of a boo-boo, telling her she wasn't to see him again. Probably would have fizzled out before long anyway.' He drew on his cigarette, regarding her with narrowed eyes. 'On the other hand, if you were to take up my offer to buy the shop, you could always move right away from here. That should sort it.'

Eve looked at him for a long moment. He did have a point, but she wouldn't be pushed into making a decision. 'I did speak to Jack about that,' she said slowly. 'And he'd like to know what your offer would be? Not that we're keen to sell,' she added quickly. 'Just as a matter of interest.'

Eddie drew a pad towards him and scribbled something on it, then passed it to her. 'There. How does that appeal to you?'

Eve stared down at the figure written on the pad and tried hard to conceal her astonishment. It was more than three times what they'd paid for the shop. That was nine years ago of course, and they'd ploughed back profits to improve the business over the years. But prices hadn't gone up that much since. Eddie's offer was still more than generous.

She tore the top sheet from the pad and folded it carefully. 'I'll show this to Jack,' she said. 'Of course we'd still have to live. Neither of us is anywhere near retirement age.'

'Nothing to stop you taking on another business,' he said. 'With this kind of money at your disposal, you could go in for something larger.'

'I'm not sure we could manage anything larger.' Eve frowned.

'Smaller then. And have some readies left over to invest. I'd think about it carefully if I were you, Eve,' he advised. 'Could be the best offer you'll ever get.' He watched her for a moment, eyes slightly narrowed, then said, 'Your sister mentioned once that young Carol is training to be an actress. Maybe I can make a contribution . . .'

'*No!*' Eve's head snapped up and she met his eyes unflinchingly. 'Carol is working to pay for her training. She's doing fine. She doesn't need your help.'

His eyebrows rose. 'Perhaps we should ask her what *she* thinks about that?'

The question hovered in the air between them like a suspended sword and Eve's blood froze. She hated the devious way his mind worked, his indirect way of saying things. It made her nervous. 'What would people say – what would Jack think if you started paying Carol's fees?' she asked at last. 'Look, as far as I know, you and I are the only two people who know you're Carol's father and I want it to stay that way. I don't want her upset and confused. It's complicated enough now.'

'I think you're playing with fire, Eve,' he said. 'After

145

all, if those two youngsters were to insist on seeing each other they'd have to be told the truth in the end, wouldn't they?' He looked at her, lips pursed. 'On the other hand, if you were to take up my offer, that situation need never arise.'

'I don't understand. What are you saying?'

He said nothing more. Rising from his chair, he came round the desk and took his coat from a peg behind the door. 'I'm sorry to seem rude but I've got an appointment in five minutes. I'm going to have to ask you to love me and leave me now.' Reluctantly she got up from her chair and he opened the door for her. 'Let me know when you've made up your mind. I'm sorry about the little upset, but no real harm done this time, eh?'

Carol was surprised when she left Kitty's the afternoon following the disastrous tea party and found Steven waiting outside on the pavement.

'Hi, Carrie.'

'Steven! Who are you waiting for – Clarissa?'

'No, I was waiting for you actually.'

She peered round. 'Where's Clarissa?'

'I left her in town, having her hair done. I thought you and I might go for a walk. We could go down to the river.'

Carol shivered. 'It's dark. Cold too.'

'Okay. We could go and have a cup of tea somewhere.'

'Could we go to The Clipper?'

'The Clipper? Is that the *in* place nowadays?' He laughed. 'Fine. I'll treat you to muffins and jam.'

In the closeness of the little booth they tucked into their muffins companionably, knees touching under the table. It was only then that Carol asked, 'Why were you hanging around outside for me? Why didn't you come in?'

'To tell you the truth, I wanted to have a word with you

146

on the quiet,' he said. 'Without Kitty around. Just the two of us.'

'A word? What about?' She buttered her muffin, carefully avoiding his eyes.

'I think you know what about. What happened yesterday afternoon, Carrie? It was obvious there'd been some sort of row. Why did – whatsisname – Paul leave in such a hurry?'

Carol sighed and hunched her shoulders. 'You tell me! Mum went all neurotic and forbade me to see him any more. She went on like something out of a Victorian melodrama. I thought she was going to pass out. It was awful!'

'I see.' He studied her face until she looked up and met his eyes. 'Were you devastated, Carrie? Are you madly keen on him?'

She shook her head. 'No, not really. All the same, it was rotten, having to upset him without really knowing why.'

'Of course. So why do you think she took against him like that?'

'Dad tried to explain to me afterwards. He says it's because Paul is Eddie Wilson's son.'

'Who's Eddie Wilson?'

'He's a wholesale grocer, he supplies the shop. He's an oily little man and I can see why Mum doesn't like him. Apparently he was up to all kinds of shady deals during the war. But it's not really fair to be so hard on Paul just because of who his father is, is it?'

'So, will you go on seeing him anyway?'

'I might.' She looked at him. 'Why?'

Steven stirred his tea thoughtfully. 'To be perfectly honest, I didn't think he was your type.'

'Oh? And what makes you think you know what my type is?' she asked, her cheeks colouring hotly.

He looked at her, his eyes twinkling. 'Oh, come on, Carrie. I've known you an awfully long time.'

Her heart quickened angrily as she saw the corners of his mouth twitch. 'And does that give you the right to laugh at me?' she demanded. 'Does it give you the right to tell me who to like and what to feel?' Her eyes burned as she looked at him. 'I'm not eight years old any more, Steven. This isn't just another dragon to kill. You might think you know all about me, but you don't. You don't know me at all!' She pushed her half-eaten muffin away and snatched up her handbag. 'I'd better go home. Mum'll be wondering where I am.' She stood up, pulling on her gloves. 'And you'd better go and collect your girlfriend from the hairdresser's. Thanks for the tea, Steven. *And* the advice.'

She was standing in the bus queue when he caught up with her a few minutes later. 'Carrie – look, I'm sorry if I upset you,' he said breathlessly. 'I didn't mean to come the heavy big brother.'

'That's all right.' She averted her head so that he wouldn't see the tears on her cheeks. 'You were right anyway. Paul isn't my type. And it must all seem like a great big joke to you. Look, hadn't you better go and get Clarissa? She'll be wondering . . .'

'Rissa will be fine. I wasn't laughing, honestly. Look, Carrie, I . . .'

'Here's the bus.' The red double decker drew alongside the queue, lights blazing, and Carrie began to move, carried forward by the queue. ' 'Bye, Steven,' she said. 'Thanks again for the tea. If I don't see you, I hope you and – and Clarissa have a nice Christmas.'

He watched helplessly as she stepped up on to the platform and was swallowed up by the crowd. He stood back as the bus drew away, a feeling of perplexity inside him. Clearly he'd hurt her deeply, yet he still wasn't really aware what it was all about. All he did know was that, without his realising it, she'd changed. Since the last time he'd seen her she'd become a different person. A woman, with a woman's sensitivity and complex emotions. He pictured the heart-shaped face and smooth blonde hair, her trim dancer's figure and wide violet eyes. Then he remembered the way she'd stood looking down at him in the cafe, eyes flashing as she pulled on her gloves. Something inexplicable about that gesture; the way she'd held her head . . . She was the same Carrie he'd always known, sweetly familiar yet subtly, stunningly, different.

Christmas came. Steven had no more dates to fulfil with the ballet company until the new year but his agent had booked him to record some film music in London. When the hectic rush and bustle of the annual show was over and Kitty closed the school for the Christmas break she travelled up to join him and Clarissa at the hotel where they planned to spend the holiday together.

Seeing Carol's wistful expression as she unfolded her plans to her, Kitty said, 'Tell you what. In the New Year you and I will go up to Town. I'll treat you. If I can, I'll get tickets for *My Fair Lady* at Drury Lane. It'll be a little reward for doing so well with your silver. How does that sound?'

Carol was thrilled. 'Oh, Kitty, that would be super!' But she couldn't help wishing that she and Steven hadn't parted on bad terms. He couldn't help not understanding how she felt over the business with Paul and her mother. She wasn't even sure she understood herself.

At Clarence Street the shop was busy with the Christmas rush. Carol helped out so that Rose could spend more time at home preparing for the family festivities, which were to be celebrated this year at her house.

The day before Christmas Eve Jack received the letter giving him the date of his operation. He was to go into hospital at the end of January. The news gave Eve another opportunity to bring up the subject of Eddie's offer.

'So what do you think?' she asked her husband on the evening he'd received the letter. 'It would be the perfect answer, don't you think?'

But he shook his head. 'We can't think about making plans for the future till we see how this operation goes, can we, love?' he said guardedly. 'It might take me a little while to get on my feet again, but once I'm fit we might not feel like selling. This is getting to be a really good little business, you know. I don't see the sense of starting all over again somewhere else at our age.'

Eve felt trapped. Eddie's solution – the idea of selling up and getting right away – was so seductive. They could all make a fresh start. Carol might make a fuss about having to leave Kitty Manson's, of course, but that couldn't be helped. Better that than having her find out about her doubtful background and the constant risk that she might unwittingly form a relationship with one of her dubious blood relations. It would be the best answer all round. But, frustratingly, Eve couldn't confide these fears to Jack. All she could do was try to persuade him, which was proving more difficult than she'd ever imagined.

The family Christmas at Rose's was, as always, fraught with tension. Freda spent her time trying to keep the peace between her daughters, for whom sharing a kitchen was a minefield, and reassuring Jack's mother, who was anxious about her son's coming operation. Jack, Ted and their father-in-law had the best of it. They spent much of their time at The Crown, their local pub, celebrating Christmas in their own way and keeping out of the way of their womenfolk.

150

Michael and Elizabeth were at home. Michael, who was reading law at university, had grown into a personable young man. He was as quiet and thoughtful as ever and was promising to be better looking than either of his parents. Talking to him, Carol found to her surprise that they had something in common. He shared her taste in pop music. It was the first time she had felt any kind of bond with either of her cousins.

Sadly it was a bond she did not share with Elizabeth. College had done nothing to dampen her volatile domineering character. If anything she had grown even louder and more vociferous than before. Now a large, ungainly twenty year old, she had no interest in music of any kind, stating with something like pride that she was tone deaf. Neither, it seemed, had she any concern for the way she looked. Her large pale face was unadorned with make-up of any kind and she wore her wiry dark hair in an unflatteringly mannish style. Already her upper lip bore the shadow of an incipient moustache. Scorning fashion as only for the 'plebs', she favoured jeans and baggy sweaters.

The old animosity she bore Carol now showed itself in subtler ways. She had an unattractive forceful way of voicing her views and over lunch on Christmas Day, seized the opportunity to make disparaging remarks about her cousin's recent exam success.

'One of the girls at college has a brother whose best friend works in television,' she said. '*He* says there's a snowball's chance in *hell* of making a decent living out of acting.' She pushed a fork laden with turkey into her mouth and looked round the table at her captive audience as she munched. 'I mean, it's all very well passing exams, but when it comes to the real thing – *well*!' She looked across the table at Carol. 'By the way, where are all these medals you've won? I expected to see you wearing them

pinned to your chest on a ribbon like a Russian general!'
She gave a loud whinnying laugh, drawing a reproachful
look from her father.

After lunch Michael invited Carol to hear his latest
Elvis LP on the radiogram in the front room and when
they were alone took the opportunity to apologise for his
sister's behaviour.

'Ignore Liz,' he advised. 'She's always been jealous of
you.' He took the cherished record out of its sleeve and
dusted it carefully with his cuff. 'It's no wonder really, is
it? I mean, with you being so pretty and her so . . .' He
broke off, his cheeks colouring. 'I don't mean to sound
disloyal but she doesn't even *try*, does she? I suppose it's
no wonder she's so bossy when you come to think of it.
Still, I can't help feeling sorry for the class of poor little
devils who get her!' He glanced at Carol shyly. 'I think
you've done really well,' he said. 'I meant to send you a
congratulations card, but somehow I never got round to
it.'

'Thank you, Mike. It's nice to know one member of
your family thinks acting is more than just messing
about,' she said.

'Oh, I do,' he said earnestly. 'It's an art as well as a skill
after all. I can imagine how hard you must have had to
study and – and practise to do so well.' He smiled. 'Carol,
look, I've been thinking. Perhaps we might go out
together over the holidays? We could see a film – maybe
go to a concert or something?'

She looked up at him in surprise and gratitude. 'That
would be lovely, Mike. Thanks. I'd like to.'

Chapter Five

Over the Christmas holidays Carol and Michael went out together several times. They enjoyed one another's company in a purely companionable way and she was happy to have a pleasant diversion to fill the time that Kitty was away. But the friendship of the two young people caused some disquiet between their respective mothers.

'If you ask me they're seeing too much of each other. I've never held with cousins courting,' Rose said as the sisters stood behind the shop counter one morning in mid January.

'They're not courting,' Eve said. 'And anyway, you know as well as I do that they're not really cousins at all. They're not even related.'

Rose's tight-lipped expression intensified. 'All the same . . .' she said enigmatically.

'Just what *is* wrong, Rose?' Eve challenged. 'Why don't you just say what's on your mind? Get it off your chest, come on!'

'All right then. The truth is, I don't want Michael getting involved.'

'With my Carol, you mean?' Eve's face was scarlet with indignation.

'With anyone! He's got a lot of exams to pass. *Real* exams I'm talking about,' Rose said pointedly. 'Michael worked hard to get to Cambridge. I don't want him getting distracted by – by girls.'

'Carol isn't *girls*. Anyway she's got her studies too.'

'Hmm! If you can call them that!'

At which point Jack, who'd been listening with increasing discomfort on the other side of the shop, decided that the conversation was in danger of becoming a quarrel and that it was time to intervene. 'I don't know why you're getting so worked up about it, the pair of you,' he said. 'Michael will be going back to university soon. Why can't you leave the youngsters alone to enjoy themselves?'

But Eve's hackles were well and truly up. She was not ready to let the subject rest. Ignoring Jack's attempt at peace-making she went on, 'You're having a go again, aren't you, Rose? It's because you're afraid Carol will turn out like her mother. That's what you're really getting at, aren't you? Why don't you just come right out and say it?'

'No, I . . .'

'Well, I can tell you now that our Carol has been brought up properly. She wouldn't behave like Sally did. Carol's a good girl and . . .' Her tirade was mercifully interrupted by the sound of the door bell as a customer came into the shop. When she had been served, Rose turned to her sister.

'Look, I didn't mean anything against Carol, Eve,' she said. 'I know you've tried to bring the girl up properly.'

'What do you mean, *tried*?' She glared at her sister. 'Ever since we adopted her you've never stopped sniping with your nasty remarks and hints. You think Carol's not good enough for your boy, don't you? Well, if you want my opinion, I happen to think she's *too* good! And while we're on the subject of upbringing, you want to do something about your Elizabeth. She's as rude and ill-mannered as she's plain. And that's saying something!' Eve walked through to the back of the shop. 'I'm going upstairs to make a start on the dinner,' she told her husband over her shoulder. 'You know where I am if you get busy.'

'All right, love.' He looked across the shop at his sister-in-law's red face. He couldn't help feeling a little sorry for her. He was fairly sure that on this occasion her remarks had been comparatively well-meaning for once. He gave her a sympathetic smile. In response she drew her mouth down at the corners.

'I don't know what brought all that on,' she said innocently. 'I daresay she's touchy because she's worried about your operation.'

Carol had come in through the side door during the exchange between her mother and aunt and had caught the last part of it as she stood with one foot on the bottom stair. *You're afraid Carol will turn out like her mother. Carol has been brought up properly. She wouldn't behave as Sally did.*

When Eve arrived in the kitchen she found Carol standing at the window. She turned as her mother came in.

'You've been arguing with Auntie Rose again, haven't you?'

Eve took a basket of potatoes from the pantry and tipped some into the sink. 'She gets me on the raw,' she said. 'I came up here to get out of her way. Always making snide remarks.'

'It was about me, wasn't it?'

Eve sighed. 'She can never leave anything alone,' she complained. 'She's like a dog with a bone – nag, nag, nag!'

'I know. And I heard what you said.' Carol took a knife from the drawer and began to help peel the potatoes. 'Mum – why is she afraid I might turn out like my real mother? What did she do that was so awful?'

'Nothing, really.' Eve kept her eyes on her work. 'Nothing that need concern you.'

'But I want to know, Mum,' Carol said. 'You never talk to me about her. Dad told me once that you were friends; that you were there when I was born, so you must

155

have known her well. Why have you never talked to me about her? Was there something bad about her? I've got a right to know.'

Eve sighed and turned busily away, putting the pan of potatoes on the stove and drying her hands. 'Nothing bad. Nothing much to know at all. She was from Portsmouth – billeted on me when she came to work at the aircraft factory. She was married to a young sailor who was reported lost at sea. Only it turned out he wasn't. He was rescued after drifting in a boat for days, badly burned.' Eve swallowed. 'By the time she heard about it she'd already – become involved with another man and she'd had you.'

'But she wasn't unfaithful, was she?' Carol said quickly. 'It was only because she thought her husband was dead?'

'Well – I suppose so.' Eve bit her lip. She hadn't meant to gloss over the truth, only to make it sound better. If the girl chose to believe it was like that, then who was she to put her straight, blacken Sally's character?

'She loved you, Carol,' she said. 'I wanted to adopt you right from the start, but once she'd got you she wouldn't let you go. She went back to work after you were born and I stayed at home and looked after you.'

'Why was that?'

'Because Sally needed to earn some money. I still had a husband, even if he was in a prison camp.'

'And then she was killed in an air raid?'

'Yes.' Eve turned away from her daughter's eyes. Taking cutlery from the dresser drawer, she began to lay the table. 'She was going to see her husband in hospital. The bomb fell near the station as she was going across the bridge.' For an instant she remembered Eddie's story about their intended elopement and wondered for the hundredth time if it could possibly have been true. She supposed she'd never know now. In any case that version

156

was not for Carol's ears. She looked up, suddenly aware that the girl had spoken to her. 'Sorry, what did you say?'

'I said, had she left me with you that night?'

'Oh! Yes. That's right.'

'Mum.'

'Yes?'

'You knew her – Sally – well. So you must have known who my father was?'

Eve's mouth suddenly dried. 'No. She – Sally had a lot of boyfriends,' she said. 'After she got the news about her husband she went a bit wild, got herself a reputation.' She lifted her shoulders. 'A lot of girls married young in the war. It was the same with so many of them. She wasn't a bad girl really. It was just the war.'

'So – she never told you – who my father was, I mean?'

'Like I say, as far as I was concerned it could have been anyone.'

Carol winced. 'You mean she didn't *know*?'

'Oh, I'm sure *she* knew,' Eve said quickly. 'She just wasn't telling. I think perhaps he was married and she didn't want to make any trouble for him.'

Carol digested this for a moment, then said, 'Well, I think she was lucky to have a friend like you, Mum. I was lucky too. I still am.' She put her arms round Eve and kissed her cheek. 'Thanks, Mum – to you and Dad – for everything. And Auntie Rose needn't worry about Mike and me. We're only friends.'

'That's what I told her.'

'I think he only took me out to make up for Liz being so bitchy.'

Eve shook her head. 'Huh! As if you'd take any notice of *her*!'

'Anyway, thanks for telling me the truth about Sally,' Carol said.

Eve glanced at the kitchen clock and gave her a little

157

push. 'Good lord, look at the time! There's some cold meat in the pantry. I'll slice it up while you go and give your dad a shout.'

When the girl had gone Eve stood for a moment, listening to her light footsteps on the stairs. *Thanks for telling me the truth.* She felt the burden of her guilt settle on her shoulders again like a yoke of lead. Sometimes she had to think really hard to remember what the truth about herself and Sally really was. Over the years she had retold the story in her mind so many times it had become almost myth-like.

There were nights when she dreamed that Sally wasn't dead at all, that she came back to claim her daughter, threatening to tell the world that Eve had stolen both her child and her life. In the dream a feeling of panic would seize her chest like an iron hand, crushing and squeezing, stopping her breath till she wakened, gasping with the sensation of suffocation. The dream would leave her sweating with terror, dreading to go back to sleep and dream again, yet afraid to stay awake and face the darkness within her. Those were the bad times.

Carol must never know the whole truth. She must never know that Eddie Wilson was her father. If that came out the rest would surely follow and Eve would lose her forever. As she finished preparing the meal she thought about Jack's coming operation. The moment he was well enough she must find some way of persuading him to accept Eddie's offer. They must sell the shop and move. Only when they were miles away from here would she feel truly safe.

Kitty came back from her holiday in London and the school reopened for the spring term. Carol was glad to be back at her work and studies once again. Over coffee on the first morning Kitty told her all about what they had done in the holidays; the shows they had been to, the museums and art galleries they had visited. It was clear from the way she spoke that during the time they had spent together she had grown very fond of Clarissa.

'She has such a sweet nature and she's so good for Steven,' she said. 'They laugh all the time. It's lovely to see him so happy.'

Each word was like a sharp arrow piercing Carol's heart but she didn't allow it to show.

'Rissa has a new job,' Kitty went on. 'She'll be based in London from now on, working in costume design for a film company. They've found a nice little flat in Earl's Court and Steven will go there at weekends whenever he can.' She smiled ruefully. 'Of course it means he won't be coming home much in future, but they've told me I'm welcome to go up and stay with them any time.'

'Steven and I had a row before Christmas,' Carol confided unhappily. 'I wish we could have made it up before he went away.'

'I know, darling.' Kitty smiled. 'He told me about it. He was so sorry he'd hurt you. It's hard for him to see that you're not a little girl any more.' She patted Carol's shoulder. 'He's very fond of you, you know. I think all he really meant was to warn you that that young man wasn't right for you. He just did it rather clumsily.'

'I know. The silly thing is, I wasn't all that keen on Paul anyway. I only invited him that Sunday because I wanted to prove to Steven that I'd grown up.'

'Of course. I understand.' Kitty reached out to touch the girl's hand. Seeing her so vulnerable, so transparent in her hero worship of Steven, made Kitty's heart contract. Young love was the most agonising of all. Opening her bag, she took out an envelope. 'I almost forgot. Look, I promised you a little jaunt. Two tickets for the matinee of *My Fair Lady* for a week next Saturday. And Clarissa says we must go and have tea with her after the show. Won't that be nice?'

Carol was enchanted with the grandeur of Drury Lane Theatre and the show was everything she had ever imagined from the reviews she had read. When the curtain went up on the stunning black and white Ascot set and costumes at the beginning of Act Two, she gasped with delight.

'Oh, Kitty, look! Isn't it wonderful!'

She smiled fondly at Carol's radiant expression and told herself it would have been worth twice the price of the tickets to see so much pleasure on the girl's face.

Afterwards they took the tube to Earl's Court. The flat that Clarissa and Steven were sharing was in a small block quite close to the Underground station. They took the lift up to the fourth floor and Kitty smiled at Carol as she rang the bell.

'Wait till you see the flat. It's charming.'

Clarissa, elegant in an emerald green dress, welcomed them in and took their coats. She had prepared a sumptuous tea: three kinds of sandwiches and hot buttered muffins.

'Steven tells me they're your favourite,' she said, smiling at Carol.

There was chocolate cake, fruit cake and biscuits, all laid out on a trolley pulled up in front of the fire.

'What a spread!' Kitty said with a smile. 'How sweet of you to have gone to so much trouble darling.'

'Not at all. I've been looking forward to it.' Clarissa passed round the sandwiches. 'And I thought it would be cosy having it in front of the fire on such a cold wintry day. Now . . .' she smiled at them as she poured the tea '. . . I want to hear all about the show? I haven't seen it yet, but Steven's promised to take me as soon as we both have an evening off together.'

Carol looked around the room. It was charming as Kitty had said. Quite small, the furniture obviously second-hand, a little shabby even, but comfortably so and obviously chosen with care and love. The phrase 'love nest' sprang into her mind and she cast it out angrily. As she ate her muffin she was reminded of the tea she and Steven had shared that afternoon at The Clipper and had difficulty in swallowing. Later, when she went in search of the bathroom, she saw that the bedroom door was ajar. Standing in the narrow hallway she could see the dressing table and, reflected in its mirror, the double bed that Clarissa shared with Steven. Her mouth filled with bile and she rushed into the bathroom to retch over the toilet bowl. The excitement of her day out, the show . . . everything was spoiled.

The following Monday Carol passed her driving test. Jack was so proud of her, especially as he himself had been her teacher. Eve too was pleased. Jack was due to go into hospital two days later and it helped to take their minds off the coming operation. Carol telephoned Michael to tell him the good news and he insisted on taking her out for the evening to celebrate.

'I'll be gone this time next week,' he told her. 'Why don't we paint the town red? I think we both deserve it.'

He'd booked seats at the Repertory Theatre where the play was Emlyn Williams's *The Corn is Green*. Carol enjoyed it enormously. She had read the play as part of her studies, but had never seen it performed. In the interval Michael nudged her.

'I can just see you in the part of Bessie,' he said with a smile. 'I think you'd do it well.'

Carol smiled back at him. 'What I'd give for the chance!' she said wistfully.

After the show they went to a restaurant for supper.

Carol felt very sophisticated, sitting opposite Michael in the softly lit room with its pink-shaded table lamps. She leaned forward across the table to whisper, 'Isn't it terribly expensive here?'

He grinned. 'You can let me worry about that. Not that I am. I haven't been out anywhere much over the vac.'

'You've taken me out several times.'

'You can hardly say that a couple of visits to the pictures is going to break the bank.' He smiled at her. 'Carol, when I go back, will you write to me?'

She smiled. 'Of course, if you like.'

'Maybe you could even come and visit? I could show you round. Cambridge is very interesting. There are parties – balls and things too.'

'I'd like that.'

'Would you really? I mean, you don't have to be polite. If the idea doesn't appeal, just say. I won't be offended.'

She laughed. 'Mike, I think we've known each other long enough to be able to say what we mean.'

'That's right. All our lives really, haven't we? That's what's so nice about it. I feel I can relax with you. You don't expect . . .' He broke off, shrugging awkwardly. 'Well, you know what I mean.'

'Yes, I do. It isn't easy, getting to know people. You think you know them, then they do or say something to show you how wrong you are.' She paused. 'I don't think Auntie Rose is so keen on our going out together, though.'

Michael shrugged. 'She thinks I should concentrate on my work. But I must have some fun too.'

'I think it's more than that,' Carol told him. 'I think she feels I might be a bad influence on you.'

He laughed uncertainly. 'Come on! You're joking?'

She shook her head. 'It's because I'm adopted. My real mother was married, but not to my father. Auntie Rose is afraid I might turn out to be bad because of that.'

Michael looked angry. 'Of all the utter rubbish! That's like something out of the dark ages! Anyway, I'm over twenty-one and I can do what I like, so you can forget about anything Mum thinks.'

The evening was finished in style with a taxi home. In the dim warmth of the back seat Michael drew her close and kissed her. Carol closed her eyes and relaxed, feeling safe in his arms. She enjoyed the kiss. Michael's mouth was warm and firm and undemanding. She didn't see stars or experience any inner magic, just a feeling of affection and pleasure. When they reached Clarence Street he got out of the car with her and kissed her once more in the doorway.

'You won't forget to write, will you?' he said, looking down at her.

She shook her head. 'No, I won't. I'll miss you, Mike.'

'Will you?' He looked at her earnestly. 'Will you really?'

'Of course.'

He drew her close. 'I'll tell you a secret – ever since we were kids I've been a bit in love with you.'

'Oh, Mike!'

'It's true. Maybe someday . . . well, we'll see. Goodnight then, Carol. I'll write as soon as I get back.' He kissed her once more and let her go, climbing into the cab and waving to her from the window.

As the taxi turned the corner and disappeared from view she puzzled over why her happiness was tinged with an uncomfortable feeling of guilt.

Two days later Jack went into hospital. Eve went with him, seeing him settled into the surgical ward and unpacking his case for him. The operation was to take place next morning and before she left the hospital she saw Mr Franklyn the consultant in his office. He explained to her what Jack's operation entailed.

163

'He'll need rest and a special diet for a while after his recovery,' he said. 'Even after that he'll have to take things very easy. No worries or unnecessary upheavals. He had a very bad time in the prison camp, you know. He probably didn't tell you or anyone else the half of it. Poor diet and bad conditions have caused his stomach to be severely ulcerated and the only course is to remove much of it.' Seeing Eve's stricken expression he reached across to pat her hand reassuringly. 'That sounds frightening, I know, but don't worry, Mrs Kenning. I shall rebuild it for him. It's a comparatively new procedure, but one that has a good success record. Once he's made a full recovery he'll be a new man.'

Eve clutched the strap of her handbag, her knuckles white with tension. 'How – how risky is it?' she asked in a whisper. 'I'd like you to be honest with me, please.'

'Every operation holds its risks,' he said frankly. 'A year or two ago I wouldn't have considered it. But thanks to your care, his constitution and general health have greatly improved. Your husband has every chance of coming through well.'

'Thank you, Doctor.' Eve rose on trembling legs. 'Thank you for being honest with me.'

Carol came home from Kitty's to find her mother had closed the shop early. She was upstairs, sitting in the living room with Freda who was trying to reassure her with comforting words and cups of tea. As Carol reached the top of the stairs her grandmother came out on to the landing carrying the big enamelled teapot. She held a finger to her lips.

'Your mum's a bit upset, love.'

Carol's eyes widened. 'Dad! He's all right?'

'Yes, yes. Nothing to worry about. She saw the doctor who's doing the operation tomorrow. He explained what's going to be done and I think it frightened Eve a

164

bit. I'll freshen this pot. You go in and have a word with her. She needs you. I've told her to take the day off tomorrow. Rose and I will see to the shop.'

'Mum?' Carol went to her mother and put her arms around her. 'Don't worry, Mum. Dad's strong. He'll be all right. Look what he managed to survive during the war.'

Eve held her daughter close and sobbed. 'What would I do without him, Carol? What shall we do if we lose your dad?' What she couldn't reveal was the feeling of foreboding weighing her down like a millstone. She was convinced that all this was part of the punishment she deserved. Jack was suffering on her account – a fact that hurt far more than any physical pain.

'If only I could go through it for him,' she whispered against Carol's shoulder. 'Oh God, I wish I could!'

'But you can't, Mum. Everything will be all right, I know it will.'

Carol slept in her mother's bed that night, something she hadn't done since Jack came home from the war. Neither of them got much sleep. Eve tossed and turned, dry-eyed, all her tears cried out as she stared sightlessly at the ceiling, bleakly wondering how she would survive the coming crisis.

Beside her, Carol slept in snatches, disturbed by her mother's restlessness and her own worries about her father. She hadn't realised he was so ill. She thought about her love for the kind, gentle man she called Dad, and wondered about that other faceless man who was responsible for her existence. Who was he, and what sort of father would he have been? Did he even know she existed? Did he ever think of her? Had he loved and grieved for her mother? And, most of all, would any of her questions ever be answered?

It was mid-afternoon the following day before Jack was out of surgery. Eve had been telephoning at half-hourly intervals since lunchtime and by three-thirty had worked herself into a frenzy of anguish, convinced that they were keeping something from her. In the end it was Carol who made the call and received the message that the operation had been a complete success and her father had regained consciousness. News that she quickly relayed to her mother.

'Oh, thank God! When can we see him?' Eve asked, weak with relief.

'Not till tomorrow evening,' Carol told her. 'They say he'll sleep for hours now and needs all the rest he can get. But we can go tomorrow at the usual visiting time.'

Eve burst into tears. 'Oh, thank God!' she said again, mopping her eyes. 'Thank God it's over.'

Jack looked pale and gaunt when they visited the following evening. Propped against the pillows, his face looked grey, but his eyes were bright and his smile as sunny as ever.

'The doc says I came through it well,' he told them. 'A few weeks and I'll be as good as new.'

Eve fussed over him, tweaking the bed covers, plumping his pillows and rearranging the items on his locker. 'It'll be nice for you to come home to your own bed,' she said. 'Where I can look after you properly.'

Over her head Jack winked at Carol. 'Oh, I don't know, love,' he said. 'The nurses in here aren't doing such a bad job. In fact, between you and me I think they're fighting over which of them takes my temperature next!'

Eve laughed in spite of herself. 'Jack Kenning! Now I know you're getting better,' she said.

The spring term settled in. Kitty got the syllabus through for the gold medal examination and Carol started studying the plays. A letter came from Michael. It was a wonderful letter, full of news and amusing anecdotes, but the last few lines troubled Carol a little.

*I think about you all the time, Carol, especially the last
evening we spent together. I can't wait to see you again.
Please write soon, darling. I love you.
Always yours, Mike*

She liked Michael a lot, of course, but wasn't at all sure
that what she felt for him was love. And she wasn't
completely happy with the notion that he was in love with
her. She confided her doubts to Janet when they met, but
the other girl laughed away her fears.

'Get you!' she said. 'Fellers falling over themselves,
expiring for love of you. And here you are turning them
away. What do you want, little Miss Choosy?'

'It's not that,' Carol protested. 'I just don't want to feel
responsible for making anyone unhappy.'

'Then don't!' Janet said. 'Make hay while the sun
shines, that's my motto. They have some fabulous dos at
Cambridge, so I hear. The May Balls to name but a few!
You wouldn't catch yours truly turning up her nose at the
chance of an invite to one.' She peered at her friend.
'Your trouble, my infant, is that you're still carrying a
torch for that drip Steven Manson.'

'He's *not* a drip!' Too late, Carol realised she'd fallen
into Janet's trap. The other girl laughed triumphantly.

'There! Caught you! Take my advice and let him go,
kid. He's an old man compared to you. Anyway, looks as
if he's well and truly hooked by this Chrissie woman.'

'*Clarissa*,' Carol corrected. 'Why can you never get
anyone's name right?'

Janet shook her head. 'I can't remember people who
aren't important. And neither should you, my child!
Forget Steven and have a good time while you can. After
all, *he* obviously is, isn't he?'

Carol decided to take Janet's advice. She wrote back to
Michael – a chatty letter, telling him the family news and

what was happening to people they both knew. She tried to strike a balance between affection and friendship, and hoped he wouldn't read too much into it.

Just after Jack went into hospital Kitty had friends to stay at Chine Way. Martin and Zelda Waring were old friends from her days with a touring rep company many years ago. To Carol the Warings were enchanting, exotic people and she was fascinated by them.

Neither was young, but both still had the glamour that comes from years of living and breathing theatre. Marty, whose favourite attire was slacks and casual shirts worn with a jaunty cravat, was about fifty. Tall, with thinning brown wavy hair, he had a face that had once been handsome and was now craggily attractive. His bright blue eyes and mobile mouth were etched with laughter lines. Zelda, a little younger, wore her long black hair loosely coiled at the nape of her neck. She had a tall elegant figure and her voice had the kind of honeyed huskiness that Carol envied. They were about to start up a touring company, playing short seasons in small places where live theatre did not normally reach. They had already engaged artists and stage staff and booked a series of dates and they were taking a short respite at Kitty's before beginning rehearsals.

Much to her embarrassment, Carol was introduced to them by Kitty as her 'star student'. Marty took her hand and held it softly to his lips as he looked deep into her eyes.

'Oh, and I can see why, Kitty, my darling,' he said. 'Quite enchanting. If you're looking for a job we still have a vacancy for an ASM, Carol.'

'That's right,' Zelda confirmed. 'How would you fancy touring the outposts of darkest Britain with a group of strolling players?'

Kitty broke in. 'Hands off, both of you. Carol will be

studying hard for her gold medal for the next few months. She's not ready to take a job yet.'

'Nonsense!' Marty said expansively. 'You'd learn far more with our little outfit in a fortnight than you would rehearsing the same old scene for months on end. All the gold medals in the world won't count for anything without practical experience, you know, darling.'

Zelda nodded in agreement. 'It's going to be *enormous* fun too. Let her come, Kitty. Why not? She could stay with us for the summer then come back and take her gold next winter.'

All this time Carol was staring from one to the other with eyes as big as saucers. Kitty caught her expression and laughed.

'We're talking about the poor child as though she's something in a slave market!' she said. 'She probably hates the idea. Anyway, I don't imagine her parents would be very happy about her leaving home at such a tender age.'

Carol found her voice. 'I wish I could come,' she said. 'It sounds lovely. But would I get the chance to play any parts as assistant stage manager?'

'Oh, yes,' Marty assured her. 'You'd have to understudy all the juvenile leads and I'm sure you'd get the odd chance to go on. Then there'd be lots of walk-on parts. You're small enough to play children too, at a pinch. That would save us having to rope in some ghastly local urchin!'

'Stop trying to tempt her,' Kitty demanded. 'She's already entered for the exam and that's that.'

Nevertheless, Carol dreamed wistfully of what it would be like to join the Warings' touring company. 'Fancy being offered a job and not being able to accept,' she told Janet. 'I bet I won't get another chance like that. It's just my luck!'

Jack continued to make good progress. Eve visited him

169

every day, taking him magazines and any delicacies he was allowed to eat. After his stitches were out and he was allowed to get up he began to discuss the future. At first she refused to talk about it, remembering that the consultant had said he was not to be worried. But it soon became clear that not being allowed to talk about it was worrying him far more.

'I've been thinking about what you said about selling up, love,' he said. 'I don't want to – I love that little old shop. I'm proud of what we've done there. Lying here, I've been thinking. Maybe now that I'm going to be fit again we'll do more. Perhaps some day we could buy the house next door if it came on the market and expand again. It means a lot to me. It's hard to explain.' He frowned with the effort of trying to express himself. 'It's a sort of symbol of winning the war for me.' He gave her an embarrassed, half apologetic smile. 'Does that sound barmy?'

Eve swallowed the lump in her throat. 'Of course it doesn't. If you don't want to sell, then we won't,' she told him stoutly. But as she travelled home on the bus she couldn't help thinking of Eddie Wilson and wondering how he would take the news.

After almost two weeks in hospital Jack left for a convalescent home on the Norfolk coast where he was to stay for a week. It was Freda who suggested that Eve should take him to Auntie Kate's boarding house in Hunstanton afterwards.

'Take a couple of weeks off and relax together,' she urged. 'You deserve it after all the worry. And Auntie Kate will love having you. She won't be busy at this time of year.' She offered to come in each day and manage the shop while they were away and it was arranged that Janet should come and stay in the flat with Carol, a treat both girls looked forward to.

It was on the day before Eve was to travel down to

Hunstanton that Eddie called at the shop. As before, he arrived early in the morning while she was busy marking the papers. She didn't notice the car draw up outside and experienced a sharp stab of apprehension when the door bell rang and she looked up to see him standing there.

'Morning, Eve. I was in the vicinity and thought I'd pop in and ask after your hubby,' he said smoothly.

'He's fine, thanks,' she said, going back to her marking. 'He's been at a convalescent home in Heacham, but I'm joining him tomorrow for a couple of weeks in Hunstanton.'

'Winter holidays, eh?' he said. 'Very nice too. All right for some, I must say.'

'Jack's been very poorly. It was major surgery he had,' she said, annoyed at her own defensiveness.

'So I gather. And I wish him well, of course.'

'I'll pass your good wishes on,' she said crisply. 'Now, if you'll excuse me . . .'

'I daresay you know why I'm here,' Eddie said. 'You were going to think over my offer. I've been very patient because of Jack's illness, but I think you must have had time to consider by now.'

'As a matter of fact we have,' Eve said, her heart lurching uncomfortably. Briefly she asked herself resentfully why she should feel so nervous? After all, the shop was theirs to sell or not to sell. What could Eddie really do? Even if he knew anything, he had no proof. She straightened her shoulders and looked him in the eye. 'Jack wants to stay on. He doesn't want to sell.'

His face remained impassive. 'And you?' he asked. 'What about you, Eve?'

Something about the sudden darkening of those pale eyes eroded her confidence. She swallowed. 'I agree with him – of course.'

'I see. And is that your final word?'

'I'm afraid it is.'

'You're not worried by the consequences?'

Eve's heart missed a beat. 'What do you mean? What consequences?'

There was a long pause before he said, 'You're not afraid of your husband overdoing things? After all, he is a sick man.'

'He's better now. Anyway, I shall see that he doesn't do too much. My family are very helpful and supportive.'

He nodded. 'Of course. Your sister Rose and your mother. Yes, you're very lucky there.' He took out his cigarette case and carefully selected a cigarette, lighting it with the flashy lighter Eve had come to know so well. Taking a long pull at the cigarette, he picked a shred of tobacco from his lower lip and inspected it. 'And there's Carol too, isn't there? Lovely little Carol,' he said. 'We mustn't forget her, must we?'

'Carol helps all she can,' Eve said. 'She's a good girl. Always has been, but she's busy with her studies. I wouldn't expect . . .' She stopped, suddenly aware that neither of them was talking about help in the shop any more. She decided on a defiant stance. 'I don't know what you're getting at, but there's nothing you can do to scare me, Eddie,' she told him. 'This shop belongs to Jack and me. We've worked hard to make it what it is. It's our home and our living. All of it will benefit Carol in the end. All I've ever done has been for her.'

He smiled. 'Precisely. You and I – we both know that, don't we? But you haven't always known best, Eve. There have been times when you've let your heart rule your head. This could be one of them.' He shrugged his shoulders. 'Still, it's your decision in the end.' He walked to the door, then paused to look back at her. 'But if things go wrong you'll remember that I did offer, won't you? You'll remember that it was your choice?'

Eve heaved a sigh of relief when he had gone. There was nothing he could do, and she was determined to put Eddie Wilson and his dubious methods out of her mind. Jack should have her undivided attention for the next two weeks. She owed him that much.

Carol and Janet enjoyed sharing the flat on their own. They moved into the bedroom that Eve and Jack shared so that they could lie awake into the small hours, talking and giggling, each of them confiding their dreams for the future. In the evenings they washed each other's hair and tried on each other's clothes. They tried out new make-up and experimented in the kitchen with exotic recipes they found in magazines. Each morning Carol rose at dawn to receive and mark the papers before the boys picked them up. When this task was completed she would go up to the flat to wake Janet with a cup of tea before making breakfast for them both.

It was towards the end of the first week that Eddie Wilson put in an appearance. Carol was surprised when she saw him sauntering into the shop.

'Oh! I don't think we need anything this week, Mr Wilson,' she said. 'Mum and Dad are away and . . .'

'I know that, my duck.' Eddie leaned on the counter and looked at her in a way that made her take an involuntary step backwards. 'I told your mum I'd look in while she was away,' he said. 'Make sure you were all right.'

'Did you? She never said.'

'Oh, yes.' He smiled. 'Your mum and I go back a long, long way, you know. I used to know her when she worked in the canteen at Samson's during the war.'

'Really?'

'Too true. I knew her friend Sally Tyler too.' He looked searchingly at her. 'Ever hear tell of Sally Tyler, did you, Carol?'

Carol felt a sudden prickling down her spine. 'My – my real mother, you mean?'

'Ah.' He nodded. 'I see you do know.' He shook his head. 'Naughty girl, young Sally was.' He leered. 'Nice though. Ooh, yes, a bit *too* nice, as she found out to her cost in the end.'

'I don't think I want to hear . . .'

'Come on now, everyone wants to know about their background,' he said. 'Don't tell me you haven't wondered about your real mum?'

Carol was silent. Of course she had wondered. 'Mum told me about her,' she said.

Eddie laughed. 'Told you what she thought you'd like to hear, I daresay. And who can blame her? Always been very protective, has Eve, I'll give her that. But forewarned is forearmed, that's what I always say.'

'Why are you telling me this?' Carol asked boldly.

'For the same reason your mother should have told you,' he said, his smile vanishing. 'You've got a right to know what's in you. Sally was a bit too fond of a good time. A bit too free with her favours, if you know what I mean, and it got her into trouble in the end. But she didn't deserve to be bullied like Eve bullied her. Couldn't have kids of her own so she made up her mind she was going to have Sally's. Pestered her day and night to give you up, till the poor girl didn't know which way to turn. I bet Eve never told you that on the night Sally was killed she was running away . . .'

'I don't want to hear any more,' Carol said, her face burning with humiliation. 'I didn't ask you to tell me. Anyway, what right do you think you've got to come here and talk to me like this? It's none of your business what my mother did.'

'Ah, but you're wrong there, my duck.' For a long moment his eyes held hers in their colourless mesmeric

174

gaze. 'I think it's high time you knew the truth, Carol,' he said. Leaning closer he said softly, 'A few months ago your mum came to see me. In a right old state she was because of some young feller you'd brought home, remember? You must've wondered why she got so steamed up. And now you're wondering why she came to see me, eh? Well, I'll tell you, shall I? It was because that young feller is *your half-brother*!'

Every vestige of colour left Carol's face. Stunned, she stood staring blankly at him, the implication of what he had just said refusing to sink in.

He raised an eyebrow. 'Get it? I'm your dad, Carol. Your real dad, I mean. How else do you think I know so much about you? You're my only daughter. No, don't look like that. In spite of what your mum was like I was fond of her, and I know she was telling the truth when she told me she was having my baby.'

'No! It's not true. I don't believe you!' Carol shook her head. 'Go away. And – and don't come back. I don't want to see you!'

He held up his hands. 'Okay, okay, you're upset now, but you won't be when you've had time to think about it. You should thank me for being straight with you. It's more than Eve was after all. She should have warned you, Carol. Girls tend to take after their mothers. You're the spitting image of Sal as she was when I knew her, but you don't want to end up like she did, do you?'

Carol put her hands over her ears 'Stop it! I don't want to hear any more. I *won't*!'

'Okay, I'm going.' Eddie shook his head. 'But it makes no difference, love. Nothing can change the fact that you're Sally's girl. One look at you proves that. You're my girl too. And blood will out, as they say. Unless you're very careful.' At the door he stopped. 'Whatever you're feeling now, Carol, however much you're hating me at this moment, I want you to remember that it was me who warned you. And if you ever need anything – if you're ever in any kind of bother – you can come to me. I owe poor Sally that at least.' He held up his hand. ' 'Bye, Carol. Be good.'

When he had gone, she stood for a long moment behind the counter in the shop, unable to move a muscle, almost as though she were paralysed. The impact of what Eddie had told her reverberated through her mind and body like shock waves, shaking her to the core. She had suspected that what Eve had told her about her mother was white-washed, but had never for a moment imagined that the truth would be something like this. Now so much was clear. No wonder Eve had become agitated on the day Carol had brought Paul home. True, she had told her daughter that Sally had been fond of the opposite sex, but Eddie had hinted that she was more than just flighty, promiscuous, even immoral. Eve had admitted that Sally hadn't wanted to part with her baby once she was born. So was it true that Eve had actually bullied her into giving up her child – so much so that she had tried to run away? Carol bit her lip in anguish. Eve must also have known that Eddie Wilson was her true father. It explained her dislike of the man. Everything was clear now. Horribly, hideously clear.

Carol closed her eyes and drew a long shuddering breath. She had always detested Eddie; always made a point of keeping out of the way whenever he was on the premises. Now, the knowledge that he was the closest relative she had – her own father – made her feel physically, wretchedly sick.

The paper boys arrived and collected their bags, but Carol didn't go upstairs. Icy cold, her teeth chattering, she remained where she stood behind the counter, unable to think straight. Her mind was a mad jumble of facts, most of them totally unacceptable, even though she knew instinctively that they must be true. Only one thing was clear: she couldn't stay here. She longed to face Eve with Eddie's accusations, but hadn't the courage to hear her confirm them. She couldn't stay here in this town, this shop, where every day brought the likelihood of running into the hated man who was her father, of seeing the knowing look that would remind her of the loathsome secret they shared.

'Carol? *Carol*, what's the matter? Are you all right?'

She came back to reality with a jolt and focused her eyes on Janet, who was peering at her with concern.

'It's almost seven.' The other girl reached out to touch her hand. 'Carol, you're *freezing*! What is it?'

'I – someone came,' she stammered. 'He said . . .' She swallowed hard. 'I'm all right, Jan. I'm sorry. I forgot your tea.'

'Never mind the *tea*. Tell me what happened. Who came? What did they say – do?'

Carol shook her head. 'It's all right. He's gone now.'

'Who's gone? You're not making any sense.'

'A man. A stranger. He was a bit odd, that's all. I thought he might – might be going to try to rob the shop.'

'Good heavens! We should call the police,' Janet said. 'Haven't you done it?'

'No! It was a mistake. Just me being silly. He was harmless after all. He just scared me, that's all.'

'How awful for you!' Janet came round the counter and took her arm. 'Poor old you. He obviously frightened the life out of you! Look, from tomorrow morning on I'll get up and help you with the papers. Come on upstairs. I'll make you some tea. You're still shaking.'

Carol locked the shop door and allowed Janet to take her upstairs. She felt bad about making up the story of the fictitious man, but she couldn't bring herself to share

Eddie's revelations even with Janet, her best friend. There was no way in the world she would ever acknowledge him as her father.

She made a pretence of eating some breakfast. Janet prepared to leave for school, still concerned at her friend's withdrawn preoccupation.

'Will you be all right? You look very shaky.'

Carol nodded and made herself smile. 'I'll be fine. You go. Gran will be here soon anyway, then I'll be off to Kitty's.'

When Janet had gone she cleared the table and washed up the breakfast dishes. Mentioning Kitty had given her an idea. One that made her heart beat faster as she saw a possible answer to her dilemma.

At Chine Way Zelda and Marty were preparing for their departure the following day. When Carol had taken off her coat in the hall she went upstairs and tapped on their bedroom door.

'Come in!' Zelda was alone, struggling to fasten the largest of their cases, which was to go on in advance. She smiled when she saw Carol. 'Oh, good. You've arrived in the nick of time. You can sit on this case for me. I'm sure we've got twice as much stuff as we came with.'

Carol did as she asked and Zelda snapped the case shut with a sigh of relief. 'Well now,' she said, straightening her back, 'you didn't come up here just to do that. Does Kitty want me?'

'No. It's me actually.' Carol paused. 'You know you asked me if I wanted a job as ASM?' She looked at Zelda apprehensively. 'You weren't joking, were you?'

'Of course not. You're just the kind of girl we'd love to have.' Zelda frowned. 'Why, have you changed your mind?'

'I always wanted to accept,' Carol said. 'It was just that I was studying for my gold and everything. But . . .' She

178

picked at the hem of her skirt. 'Something has happened. I want – *need* – a job. Now.'

Zelda sat down on the edge of the bed beside her. 'You've had a row with your parents. Am I right?'

'No. They're away at the moment.' Carol looked up at her. 'Look, I can't explain, but I really *do* want that job.'

Zelda looked thoughtful for a moment. 'Maybe we'd better see what Kitty says,' she said at last.

'Okay then, but let me talk to her first.'

Downstairs in the kitchen Kitty was preoccupied. She looked up with a smile as Carol came into the room.

'Guess what? I've just had a call from Steven. He's coming home this afternoon on a flying visit. He's off on a tour of Canada with the ballet company and . . .' She trailed off as she noticed Carol's expression. 'Darling, what is it?'

'I've just been upstairs to talk to Zelda. I want to take that job they offered me as ASM.'

Kitty's smile vanished. 'Just like that? Why this sudden decision, Carol?' she asked. 'Do your parents know?'

'No.'

'Then don't you think you should at least phone them and ask what they think?'

'I can't. They'll only talk me out of it and I really want to go.' Carol looked up at her. 'Will you do it for me, Kitty – please? You'll know what to say. How to make it sound good. Tell them it's a marvellous opportunity to gain experience. You know, boost it up.'

'You mean, you're planning to go now? Before they get home?'

'Yes. I have to.' Seeing that Kitty was about to argue with her, she added quickly. 'I'm going anyway, Kitty. If Zelda and Marty won't have me, if you won't help, I'll go out and buy a copy of *The Stage* and apply for the first job I see advertised.'

179

'Now – wait a minute!' Kitty was seriously disturbed by the sudden change in the girl's manner. Clearly something traumatic had happened. 'Carol darling, can't you tell me what all this is about?' she asked. When she received no reply, she took the girl by the shoulders and pressed her into a chair. 'Now – take your time. Just tell me,' she said. 'I can't help you unless you tell me the truth.'

Carol racked her brain for a plausible explanation. 'Mum and Dad have let me study for the stage but I know that they'll never let me go away from home unless I do it this way. Mum always wanted me to be a dancer because she thought I'd make a name for myself locally in amateur shows and stay at home. That's what she's still hoping. That I'll go on for years, passing exams and getting my name in the local paper. You know I want more than that, Kitty. I have to do it like this. To prove to them that I'm serious.'

'Well, I see that, darling. But your gold . . . You've been doing so brilliantly and it's only a few weeks away now. Are you going to pass all that up?'

'Marty says that when it comes to getting a job, exams mean nothing. It's the practical experience that really counts. You know that's true, Kitty, And I can always come back and take my gold another time.'

'Well, that's true enough, I suppose.'

'So will you ring them and say that I've had this wonderful offer? Make sure they know that Zelda and Marty are old friends of yours and that I'll be all right?'

Kitty looked at the two bright spots of colour on the girl's cheeks and the light of something very close to desperation in her eyes. Besides her concern for Carol's state of mind she wasn't at all happy with the responsibility that was being placed on her. 'Look, I can see it means a lot to you, darling, but before I ring your parents, will you talk to Steven first? A few hours' delay can't make much difference, can it?'

For the first time Carol registered the words that Kitty had spoken earlier and realised how wonderful it would be to see him and talk to him again. 'All right then,' she said. 'But I won't let him change my mind.'

'Just the same, I'd be happier if you heard his point of view.' Kitty smiled resignedly. 'Now, you'd better give me the number of this boarding house where your folks are staying.'

Carol's eyes filled with tears and she jumped up and threw her arms around her. 'Oh, thank you, Kitty! Thank you so much. You're the best person in the whole world and I love you.'

Kitty held the girl in her arms, moved by her emotional outburst. There was more to this than met the eye, she told herself. She only hoped she was doing the right thing.

Carol was waiting on the platform at Castle Station when the two-fifteen from London steamed in. She stood by the barrier, watching as the train discharged its passengers and when she spotted Steven swinging down the platform with his familiar rangy walk, an overnight holdall hanging from one hand, her heart missed a beat.

She'd gone home after lunch to change. Suddenly her cherry red winter coat made her feel over conspicuous. She imagined it was the kind of thing Sally Tyler might have worn. Behind the closed door of her bedroom, she hung it at the back of the wardrobe, taking out instead the brown jacket she'd worn last year. She covered her bright hair with a green beret.

Steven didn't see her until he was almost at the barrier, then his face lit up with delighted surprise.

'Carrie! How nice.' He handed in his ticket then turned to her. 'This is a surprise. I wasn't expecting to be met.'

As they walked out on to the forecourt together she said, 'Can we go somewhere and have a talk before we go home, Steven?'

'Fine. How about some tea?' He grinned. 'Shall we go to The Clipper?' He took her hand and began to run. 'Come on, there's a bus waiting.'

It was quiet in the little restaurant. Too late for lunch and too early for the afternoon shoppers' teas, they had the place almost to themselves. Steven looked at her inquiringly when the waitress arrived.

'What's it to be – muffins and strawberry jam?'

She shook her head. 'Just tea, please.'

When the girl had gone he leaned forward to look at her. 'Something's up, isn't it, Carrie?'

She nodded. 'I've decided to take a job I've been offered. The Warnings have been staying with Kitty.'

He grinned. 'Zelda and old Marty! How are they?'

'Fine. They're taking a rep company on tour round the country. Remote places, mostly up north where live theatre doesn't reach. They've offered me ASM.'

'Great! When do you start?'

'Right away. The thing is that Mum and Dad are away on holiday. Kitty's not too happy, but says she'll ring them and persuade them it's okay for me to go.' She looked up at him. 'The things is, she made me promise to talk to you before she'll do it.'

'Talk to *me*!' He pulled a startled face. 'What the hell does she expect me to say to you?'

'I don't know. But I agreed because she made it a condition.'

'Oh, I see. So you're saying you don't need my advice?'

'I'm saying that I'm going anyway, so advice doesn't really come into it.' She bit her lip. 'But I did want to talk to you.'

The waitress brought their tea and Steven poured for

them both. 'I seem to remember that last time I tried to give you the benefit of my vast store of wisdom, I got a flea in my ear.'

'I know. I'm sorry about that.' Carol spooned sugar into her tea and stirred thoughtfully.

'It's okay. I daresay I deserved it, poking my nose in where it wasn't wanted. So – are you still seeing whatsisname, Paul?' To his horror he saw her eyes fill with tears and her mouth crumple. He pulled a clean handkerchief out of his pocket and passed it across the table. 'Is it because of him you want to leave in such a hurry? Poor Carrie. Has he broken your heart? I'll break his smarmy little neck for him if he has.'

'Oh, Steven, if only it were that simple. If only I could tell you,' she whispered. 'It's so much more than that. It's – it's horrible. A nightmare!'

His eyes widened. 'God! What are you saying? Carrie – he hasn't – you're not . . . ?'

'*No!*' Her cheeks flamed as she looked up at him. 'I'm not pregnant if that's what you think! It's worse than that. Much worse.'

He quickly drank the last of his tea and reached across the table to cover her hand with his. 'Look, let's go somewhere quiet then you can tell me. Carrie, look at me.' She looked up and their eyes met. 'You *are* going to tell me, aren't you? All of it, I mean. The truth. Because you have to tell someone what this is all about. I think you know that, don't you?'

She nodded.

'Right.' He put his hand in his pocket and pulled out some coins. 'Just let me pay for the tea and we'll go.'

They set out towards The Meadow, taking the diagonal path across it down to the river by silent mutual agreement. As they walked Steven told her that the tour of Canada was to last twelve months.

'Is Clarissa going with you?' she asked.

'No. She'll stay on at the flat. She has her job.'

Carol glanced at him. 'Will you get married before you go?'

He shook his head. 'We're fine as we are – for now.'

They reached the river bank and found a bench. As they sat down Steven took her hand and pulled her arm through his. 'Okay,' he said. 'Let's have it.'

'I told you Mum and Dad are away. They're taking a holiday after Dad's operation. I've been getting up early and doing the papers each morning.' She paused for breath and Steven nodded encouragement.

'Right. Go on.'

'It was this morning.' She paused again, frowning a little, incredulous that it was only this morning – just a few hours ago – that Eddie had dropped his bombshell.

'Yes? What happened this morning?'

'Eddie Wilson came into the shop.'

'Eddie Wilson? Oh, yes, I remember. He's the oily little wholesaler. Paul's father, yes?'

Carol shuddered. 'Yes. He told me a lot of things about my real mother. I always knew she was promiscuous, Mum told me that. But he made her sound like a . . .' She swallowed, shaking her head, unable to say the word.

Steven slipped an arm round her shoulders and hugged her. 'He sounds like a really nasty type. Was all this because you've been seeing his son? Anyway, how did he know so much about your mother?'

'Because he's – *my father*.' Saying the word still made her shrivel up inside with shame and revulsion. She turned her face up to him, pale and taut with pain. 'He's my real father, Steven. He told me I was the spitting image of my mother and that if I'm not careful I'll be like her in – in other ways too. I've got so much bad in me, Steven,' she said brokenly. 'Bad right through.'

184

'No – no, you're not! Don't ever let me hear you say that again.'

'It's true, though. It must be. How can I not have bad blood with parents like that?'

His hand cradled her head tenderly as she turned her face in to his shoulder. 'Listen, Carrie. Whoever your real parents were, you're still *you*.'

'But I don't *know* who I am any more,' she said, her words muffled against the stuff of his jacket. 'It's like I've been shut up in a box all these years and suddenly the lid's been taken off. I'm afraid to look inside. I'm afraid to look myself in the face.'

'And you think running away is the answer?'

'I'm not running away. I just have to get away from here, where I might meet him – Eddie – round every corner. He's not going to leave me alone now that I know, I can see that. If I go away maybe I can start finding out what kind of person I am. Whether I'm really any good at acting. Who I am and where I'm going.' She looked up at him. 'It's something I've got to do, Steven.'

When he didn't reply she drew her head back to look at him, 'Do you think it's going to be easy? I've never been away from home before. Never stood on my own feet. Do you think I won't miss Mum and Dad, Janet and Kitty and everyone? I've got so much to find out but if I don't make a start now I might never know whether there's any good in me.' She drew a deep shuddering breath. 'Steven, you won't tell anyone what I've told you, will you? I don't want anyone to know. Not even Kitty.'

He shook his head. 'Of course I won't tell anyone if you don't want me to.'

'I haven't even told Janet.' Her eyes widened. 'You won't tell Clarissa, will you?'

'Listen to me, Carrie.' His hands held her shoulders tightly as he looked into her eyes. 'You have absolutely nothing to be ashamed of. I've known you since you were a little girl and I know that you're good, hard-working, sincere and completely – utterly – beautiful.'

For a long moment they looked at each other, then he drew her close and kissed her. Not the chaste, brotherly kiss she was used to but an intense, almost passionate kiss that stopped the breath in her throat and set every fibre of her body singing. When they drew apart he held her very close and she heard her own heartbeat drumming in her ears.

'Whatever happens, never change, Carrie,' he whispered, his lips caressing her ear. 'Promise me you'll stay just exactly as you are, always?'

With his arms around her and her face against the warmth of his shoulder she was sharply aware of the moment; of the sun going down like a ball of fire in the turquoise and gold winter sky, setting the river ablaze with its radiant reflection. She saw too that the gently swaying wands of the willow trees were faintly brushed with gold. It was the first sign of spring, and she felt her heavy heart begin to lift a little.

'I promise I'll always be the same for you, Steven,' she whispered. And in her heart she added: *Because I'll always – always – love you.*

Chapter Six

June 1963

Eve stood at the kitchen window, waiting for the kettle to boil. This was her favourite view. One of the many things that had attracted her to the new house was that the kitchen looked out on to the garden.

Jack had taken to gardening like the proverbial duck to water. He had never had anything more than a tiny patch of grass surrounded by concrete to tend and now attacked his new hobby with all the fervour of the newly converted. During the time that they were waiting to move he had made frequent trips to the library, taking out all the books they had to offer on gardening and studying them for hours. The result was that now, just two years after they had moved into number 8 Sunnyside Crescent, the Kennings' garden was the pride of the neighbourhood.

Eve made the tea and set it to brew while she laid the breakfast table. It was hard to believe that their lives had changed so much in just five years. The turning point seemed to have been Jack's operation. It had been a shock, hearing that Carol had been offered a job and was planning to be gone before their return.

When Kitty Manson had rung them at Auntie Kate's to tell them about it they hadn't felt they could forbid Carol to go, yet neither had been completely happy about it. After all, she'd never been away from home before, and there had been no chance to meet these friends of Mrs Manson's or discuss the job or its prospects. They were hurt that she hadn't felt the need to ask their advice. Eve's mother had been upset too, feeling that she was in some way responsible.

It had been strange, coming home to the empty flat, and getting used to life without their daughter. But no sooner had they begun to settle down again than another bolt had hit them right out of the blue.

The letter had arrived one wet Monday morning. Jack had read it through twice before he passed it over to Eve across the breakfast table. It was neatly typed on the smart headed notepaper of a firm of commercial speculators. It explained that they had received planning permission from the local council to redevelop this part of the town, building a new shopping centre, complete with one of the new supermarkets that were springing up all over the country. Eve stared hard at the figure they were being offered for their shop and buildings. She looked incredulously across the table at Jack.

'How can it be worth so *much*?' she whispered.

'Because without our agreeing they can't go ahead with their plan,' he told her. 'All the properties round here are old like this, and they're mostly rented. That means the rest of the neighbourhood is owned by just one or two people. Obviously they've already agreed to sell. Makes sense after all. They stand to make a packet out of it. We could prove a serious stumbling block if we dug our heels in. Hence their generous offer.'

'I see.' Eve looked again at the figure, shaking her head in disbelief. 'It's more than twice what Eddie Wilson offered us,' she said.

'Exactly!' Jack laughed. 'Now we can see why he was so desperate to buy, can't we? Crafty devil! He must have had wind of this some time ago and seen his way to making some easy cash!' He pointed to the last few lines of the letter. 'And do you see what it says here? We can have first refusal to rent a similar business in the new centre. Can't say fairer than that, can they?'

Jack had written off right away to accept the offer and after that things had moved fast with visits to the firm's solicitor and the drawing up of contracts. There would be no living accommodation with the new shop so one of their priorities was to start looking for a new house.

The moment Eve had seen the newly completed houses in Sunnyside Crescent she had fallen in love with them. They were just three miles out of town. Near enough to have easy access to all the amenities, yet almost in the country. The bright, airy little detached houses on the new estate had all the features she had admired in magazines but would never have dreamed of owning if she'd lived to be a hundred. There was central heating, fired by gas, so no messy fires to light and clean. A wonderful fitted kitchen with lots of cupboards and a shining stainless steel sink. A downstairs cloakroom and large lounge with French windows opening on to the garden. And upstairs, three lovely bedrooms and a pretty pink bathroom complete with a shower. After the agent had shown them round Eve looked at Jack with shining eyes.

'Oh, Jack. Isn't it *beautiful*? If only we could live in one of these.'

He had laughed. 'But we can! And I'll tell you something else, love. We won't need a mortgage either!'

Just before they moved in Jack had bought himself a brand new car to put in the neat integral garage: one of the new Minis that had just come out, compact and racy in pillarbox red. Next to the garden it was his most prized possession and every morning he and Eve travelled in it to the new newsagent's shop they ran in the Clarence Centre. The whole thing was still like a dream come true to Eve.

Since they'd been at Sunnyside Crescent, baby Wendy had occupied her thoughts almost constantly. Until the move the memory of the baby had been so deeply buried that whole weeks could go by without her remembering. But when the Queen gave birth to a new baby prince in 1960 and the newspapers and magazines in the shop were all full of baby pictures, the heart-aching grief for the child she had lost was triggered afresh.

It seemed to Eve then that the bright, modern house was just made for bringing up a child. The little bedroom at the back which caught the early-morning sun and overlooked the garden would have been perfect for the growing Wendy. Time and again she would find herself drawn towards the room, where she would stand at the window, imagining her life as it might have been.

Wendy would have been twelve now. A lovely, companionable age for a daughter. Eve visualised what she would have been like: dark-haired and brown eyed like her; bright and sunny-natured like Jack. Their own child. She would have been such a comfort to them now. She would have made up for everything that had happened in the past – especially now that the much-loved adoptive daughter, in whom she had invested so much more than she could ever tell, had gone.

Carol came home now and again, of course, mainly on flying visits, because even when she was 'resting' as she called it, she insisted that she needed to be close to London where all the auditions seemed to be held. Since she'd left home things between them had become subtly different. She was still a dutiful daughter, remembering birthdays and anniversaries meticulously and phoning home every few weeks, but there was a barrier between them, something Eve could not quite put her finger on. Jack seemed not to notice. He tried to persuade her that Carol was a grown woman now with a life of her own, that it was all in her mind, but Eve knew it wasn't.

Sometimes when she lay awake at night worrying over

it, she was sure that there was more to Carol's sudden departure than the offer of a job. Could something have happened during the time they had been away? Could Eddie Wilson have had anything to do with it? After Carol had gone there had been a sly look about him when he'd asked after her, and once Eve had asked him outright if he had seen and spoken to her while they were away – said anything that might have driven her away from home? He had denied it vehemently.

'Never been near the girl!' He protested indignantly. 'Anyway, why should I be the cause of her leaving home? I mean, it was always on the cards, wasn't it, her taking up the stage? Why blame me for everything?'

But still Eve wasn't convinced that he hadn't had some hand in it. He had been so angry when she'd turned down his offer to buy the shop, and now that it was clear how much money he could have made from the deal she could understand why. It would be just the kind of spiteful, vindictive thing he would do to pay her back.

Often in the small hours of a sleepless night she would agonise over all the mistakes she had made. She saw now that she should have told Carol she was adopted at a much earlier age. Should she also have told her the real reason behind her distress over her friendship with the Wilson boy? She promised herself that one of these days she would talk to her heart to heart; lay her cards on the table and break the news that Eddie Wilson was her father as gently and sensitively as she could. But every time Carol did come home she put it off, reluctant to spoil her brief visit with anything so unpleasant.

Nowadays she saw Eddie only occasionally. The new shop was much smaller and they sold only tobacco and confectionery along with the magazines and papers, so they didn't trade with him any more. But Eve was still only too aware of his menacing presence hovering in the shadowy corners of her mind. She still felt threatened by him, afraid of how much he really knew about Sally – and how much of it he might have hinted at to Carol.

The kitchen door opened and Jack came in, interrupting her reverie.

'Mmm, bacon and eggs,' he said, rubbing his hands. 'Nothing sets a chap up like his bacon and egg breakfast.' He sat down at the table.

Eve smiled. It was what he said every morning and never failed to put things in perspective for her. Last October she'd been terrified when it looked as though the Cuban missile crisis would plunge them all into a nuclear war. Thank God President Kennedy had saved them all from that! Jack's enthusiastic presence at the breakfast table reminded her of how lucky she was to have him still, and how secure they were in their new business and home. She had a lot to be grateful for.

Carol got out of bed and padded to the window to draw the curtains. She had arrived late the previous evening at the house in Hackney that Janet and three other young medics shared. All she had seen last night was the front of a three-storey Victorian terraced house so she was slightly surprised to find that there was a garden at the rear; or at least, if not a garden, a long narrow strip of land, bordered on either side by walls. It consisted mainly of dry, wiry grass, but at the far end stood a gnarled old apple tree and a patch of earth where someone was attempting to grow vegetables.

'Are those peas?' she asked the humped shape in the other bed.

Janet raised her head, her eyes squinting against the sudden flood of bright sunlight. 'What?'

'Peas. There at the end of the garden. It would be lovely to have fresh peas for lunch.'

Janet pulled herself into a sitting position. '*Peas*? Wouldn't know. Some little man from next door has that bit of the garden.' She rubbed her eyes and looked at Carol. 'Honestly, I don't believe you! Here you are, out of a job, and all you can think of is fresh peas!'

Carol laughed and sat down on the end of Janet's bed. 'In our business, being out of work is an occupational hazard. One gets used to it. Anyway, I like the house.'

Janet wrinkled her nose. 'It's okay, I suppose. Better than that poky little room I had at the hospital. Even if my fellow tenants do leave a lot to be desired! At least I can have Geoff here to stay on the rare occasions when he can make it down from Edinburgh.'

'You must miss him?'

'Only like hell!' Janet got out of bed and pulled on her dressing gown. 'Thank God I'm not on duty till this afternoon. Shall we go and make some tea and toast and bring it back up here?' she suggested. 'I don't think I could face the others this morning.'

Janet's house-mates consisted of Harry Billings and Jim Thresher, junior housemen like herself. The fourth tenant was Mary Granger, a medical student in her final year. Where Harry and Jim were boisterous and gregarious even at seven o'clock in the morning, Mary was profoundly serious, her thin bespectacled face forever buried in a medical textbook. The boys, tired of their teasing and boyish jokes falling on deaf ears, had dubbed her 'The Prof'.

The kitchen, when they reached it, was mercifully empty but bore the traces of the previous night's hastily prepared and consumed supper. The elderly gas cooker was liberally splashed with fat and in the sink plates coated with congealed fat and egg yolk jostled for position with a used frying pan and two mugs rimmed with dried-on coffee. Janet took one look and pulled a disgusted face.

'Ugh! It's like living with a bunch of un-house-trained

mongrels,' she said. 'Those two blokes are repulsively undomesticated and Mary is too preoccupied to notice. How I *long* for the day when Geoff and I can have a place of our own.'

'When will that be?' Carol asked, running hot water into the sink and squirting washing up liquid on to the offending mess.

'Not too long with a bit of luck. At the end of this pre-reg year I'm going to do a GP course.'

Carol turned to look at her friend. 'But I thought you wanted to specialise in obstetrics?'

Janet sighed. 'I did, but if Geoff and I want to get married this side of sixty-five, one of us is going to have to earn some proper money.'

'He's definitely going on with cardiology then?'

Geoffrey had been 'student of the year' on taking his finals. He'd managed to get on the firm of a consultant cardiologist in Edinburgh for his pre-reg year and his ambition was to achieve a consultancy by the time he was thirty-five.

'Yes. I know he can do it and if I support him while he studies, we can get married too. He's brilliant,' Janet told Carol with a sigh as she popped the sliced bread under the grill. 'Far more brilliant than I'll ever be, so it makes sense.' She turned to Carol. 'Anyway, that's enough about us. Tell me your news. All I got from you on the phone yesterday was that the theatre in Bradwich had closed and the company is collectively out of work.'

'Well, that's it in a nutshell,' Carol said. 'I'm afraid television has a lot to answer for as far as the provincial theatre is concerned. Kitty always said it would happen. Of course once the novelty has worn off . . .' She shrugged. 'But who knows how long that will take?'

Janet buttered the toast thoughtfully. 'What *about* television? Are there any openings there?'

'I don't know. It's a totally different medium,' Carol said. 'I trained for the stage. It must have been a bit like this for all those actors in silent films when talkies came in.'

Janet nodded sympathetically. 'In a way it's like me going into general practice after a hospital environment. From what I can gather one has to be much more of a psychologist.' She reached into the cupboard for the marmalade and found the jar covered in sticky finger marks. 'Oh, really!' she said, pulling a disgusted face. 'Hand me the cloth, will you?'

'Shouldn't you have an agent?' she asked as she handed the cloth back.

'I suppose I should,' Carol said. 'Maybe I should start looking for one. I'm off to see the Warings this afternoon. They bought a house out at Stanmore and went into semi-retirement a few months ago, but they still have all their old contacts.'

During the year that Carol had been with the Warings they had toured the north of England extensively with a repertory of plays. For the first month she'd been terribly homesick, but Marty and Zelda were kind and sympathetic in their casual, easygoing way. During those early weeks they'd been patient and understanding and a strong, lasting bond had formed between the three of them. She'd gained a lot of valuable experience in the twelve months she'd worked with them in her job as assistant stage manager, even getting the chance to play several good roles. But the tour had eventually come to an end because of dwindling audiences. TV had penetrated even to the remote villages of the far north, and as the winter weather began to bite people were reluctant to leave their firesides when entertainment was so close at hand.

Mary Waring had put Carol in touch with a friend who was producer of a rep in Broadstairs and she had spent a year and a half there, leaving when she was offered a small part in a play that was tipped to come into the West End after touring. Unfortunately the play had failed and the hoped-for London season had never materialised. She had been with the rep in Bradwich ever since. But last week the notice had gone up. The theatre had been running at a loss for three months now and the local council, who owned it, were refusing to put any more money into a failing project.

'We put on *The Corn Is Green* for our last production,' Carol said wistfully as she dried the last of the dishes. 'The irony was that we played to packed houses every single night. And I played a part I've always wanted to play: Bessie Watty, the cockney bad girl. If only people had patronised us more over the past months, perhaps we wouldn't have had to close.'

'Always the way, isn't it?' Janet said, setting the teapot and cups on the tray. 'People don't realise they've got something good until it's taken from them. Well, serves them right if you ask me.' She shot Carol a curious look. 'So – what about this Mr Wonderful I've heard so much about in your letters? You haven't mentioned him at all yet. What's his name – Quinn, isn't it?'

Carol sighed. 'Really, Jan! It was *Finn*, not Quinn. Finn O'Connor. I hope you remember your patients' names better when you're a GP.'

'Okay, so I've got a bad memory for people I've never met. I notice you speak of him in the past tense, so are you and he still on?'

Carol shook her head. 'It was over some weeks ago.'

Janet cocked an inquisitive eyebrow. 'And . . . ?'

'And nothing. It's over. End of story.'

'Okay. Tell me to mind my own business, why don't you?' Janet laughed. Sensing her friend's reluctance to pursue the subject, she picked up the tray and opened the kitchen door. 'Come on, let's scarper upstairs again before that revolting crew gets down here and starts messing the place up again. And be warned, the sight of Harry and Jim first thing in the morning is definitely not for those of a nervous disposition!'

Upstairs in Janet's room, as they sat on the beds eating their breakfast, Janet laughed. 'Hey, you know what this reminds me of?' she said. 'That time when I came and stayed with you when your parents were on holiday. The time when you made your monumental decision to leave home.'

Carol smiled reminiscently. 'It was fun, playing at sharing the flat, wasn't it?'

'It was while it lasted! I was really cut up when you upped and ran off like that, you know,' Janet said, chewing her toast. 'You left me trying to calm your poor gran's ruffled feathers too. I thought you were bloody selfish at the time.'

'I know. You've said so enough times for me to have got the message by now.'

'Well, it's true. It was so unlike you.'

'I suppose it must have seemed like that at the time,' Carol said. 'But when chances come in this business, you have to grab them.'

'Well, it's ancient history now anyway. I daresay all is forgiven and forgotten at home.' Janet poured them both another cup of tea. 'Are you planning to visit your folks while you're between jobs by the way?'

'I don't know. It depends.'

'Do you still write to your cousin Mike?'

'Oh, yes. He keeps me up with all the gossip. He's been up to Bradwich to see me a couple of times. He came up to see me in *The Corn Is Green*.'

'Oh – you don't *say*?' Janet looked intrigued.

'Yes. We went to see it once at the local rep and he said

197

then that he could see me in the part of Bessie, so I invited him up to see if his confidence had been justified.'

'And was it?'

Carol smiled. 'I think I can safely say that he enjoyed his weekend visit.'

Janet's eyebrows rose. 'A whole weekend, eh?'

'No need to look like that. It was strictly separate rooms. I told you about my digs. All brass bedsteads and Victorian framed photographs. Mike stayed at the local pub.'

'Mmm.' Janet looked unconvinced. 'So – what did the fabulous Finn think of you having a boyfriend to visit?'

'I've no idea. I told you, that's history,' Carol said dismissively. She didn't tell Janet that Mike had urged her to let him take her home with him when he went, neither did she mention that she had turned down his proposal of marriage. Instead she said, 'Mike has passed his Law Society part two exam, by the way.'

'Great! Good for him.'

'He's working as a junior solicitor for Webb and Mather in York Road.'

'At *home*, you mean? He's opted to stay in the town where he grew up?' Janet pulled a face. 'You'll be telling me next that he still lives with his folks.'

'He does, actually.'

'My God! How parochial can you get? And the vitriolic Liz?'

'Her too. She teaches juniors at Barry Street Primary.'

'Poor little buggers!' Janet glanced at her. 'And Steven? Still hear from him?'

'We keep in touch,' Carol said lightly. 'He was working on the P&O line for eighteen months. Playing on luxury cruise liners.'

'Nice work if you can get it!' Janet said.

'Now he's freelancing. Film and TV jobs mainly. You

know, background music and that kind of thing. But he's met a talented lyricist and they're working together on some sort of project.'

'And the faithful Clarissa is still in the picture, I take it?'

'Sort of.'

'You surprise me. I think I'd have taken the hint by now, wouldn't you? I mean, from what you say, he's been away more than he's been at home over the past five years and she's still sitting at home with her knitting, waiting for him?'

'Hardly that! She's got a very absorbing job with the film company. From what I gather Steven seems to crash out anywhere he can lay his head these days. Sometimes it's at Clarissa's flat – sometimes with a friend. I think she understands that he needs his freedom.' Carol shrugged. 'I think she probably does too.'

'But she must still be carrying a torch for him, mustn't she? I mean, she doesn't seem to have found anyone else.'

'I've no idea.' Carol buttered her last slice of toast. 'Last autumn she came up to Yorkshire on location with the film company she works with. They were there for six weeks, near Bradwich, and we saw quite a bit of each other. I got to know her better. She's a nice person.'

'Mmm, she'd have to be,' Janet said with a hint of irony.

'She offered to put me up at the flat any time I was in Town.'

'And you turned down Earl's Court in favour of my squalid East End pad?' Janet laughed.

'There's no comparison, Jan. You know I'd rather stay with you. Besides, now that Steven's settled in London again for a while he's probably living at the flat and I wouldn't want to intrude.'

Janet said nothing but Carol's averted eyes when she

spoke of Steven confirmed what she'd guessed – that Carol still cherished her teenage passion for him.

'Right then,' she said piling the breakfast things back on to the tray, 'I'm free till two. Let's get dressed and go "Up West" window shopping. We could go and see what Carnaby Street has to offer. You look so damned glamorous with your new haircut and clothes, you make me feel positively frumpy! You can help me do something about my image.' She looked at her watch. 'If we get a move on we'll have time for lunch too, before I have to get back to the grindstone.'

The Warings' semi-detached villa in Stanmore was easily distinguishable from the other identical ones in the pleasant tree-lined road by its purple front door and bright yellow curtains. It was almost three when Carol arrived there and, getting no answer to her ring at the front doorbell, she walked round to the back to find them sitting in the garden in deckchairs. Marty wore a pair of ancient tennis shorts that reached to just above his bony knees, Zelda a colourful Indian caftan. Between them on a rickety green-painted table stood a bottle of gin, tonic and a thermos of ice. Zelda rose and came towards her with open arms.

'Darling! How lovely to see you.' She kissed Carol on both cheeks. 'You know, it's the oddest thing. Marty and I were only talking about you last night, just before you rang. What a shame, the rep at Bradwich closing like that. Come and sit down, and tell us everything you've been doing. We're always hungry for all the gossip now that we're out of the swim as it were.' She unfolded a third deckchair and nudged her husband. 'Marty, pour Carol a snifter, darling. I'm sure she's gasping for one.'

He did as he was told. 'You're looking ravishing, Carol love,' he said. 'Lost a little weight perhaps but ravishing just the same.'

Zelda laughed her throaty laugh. 'Well, you know what the Duchess of Windsor always says: "You can never be too rich or too thin". Carol's got the thin, now all she needs is the riches!' She leaned forward. 'We've got some news, darling.' She looked across the table at Marty. 'Go on, tell her.'

'Well, it's a bit previous really. Nothing's final yet but . . .' He cleared his throat. ' 'S' matter of fact, we've bought an agency,' he said. 'At the moment it's still going through, but it's all agreed. When we knew it was coming up, Zelda and I thought it would be a good investment. Neither of us wanted to retire from the business completely and we're both choked off with middle-class bloody suburbia. This way we could still stay in touch with all our old chums.'

Carol smiled. 'That's wonderful!'

'It's old Asa Marks's agency,' Zelda said. 'He's been a dear friend of ours for years and of course we're hoping that we'll inherit most of his clientele. But once all the details are sorted out we'd like you on our books too, darling.'

'I'd love that.'

'Meanwhile . . .' Zelda looked at her husband. 'Do we know of any good opportunities?'

He frowned and sucked in his breath. 'Not the best time of year. Summer season already under way. Panto's not yet casting. And you know as well as I do what the state of rep is at the moment. Why don't you leave it with us and go home for a while?' he suggested. 'We had Kitty up for a weekend recently to see a few shows. She was saying she hadn't seen you for ages. Then there's your family, of course. Got to fit them all in sometime, haven't you, darling? This might be as good a time as any, eh? If we hear of anything we'll give Kitty a ring and you can hop on a train post haste.'

It was still early when Carol got off the train at Baker Street. She knew that Janet would be on duty till much later that evening and wondered what to do to while away the time. Impulsively, she went into a phone box and dialled the number of Clarissa's flat.

'Oh, hi, Clarissa. It's Carol. I'm in Town and I thought . . .'

'Wonderful! How long for?'

'Oh, just a few days.'

'And you want to come and stay with me – yes?'

'Oh, no – thanks. I'm staying with my friend Janet. She's a houseman at St Gregory's in Hackney. But I would like to pop over and see you.'

'I should just hope you would! I'd have been very upset if you hadn't. I'd love to see you and hear all your news. Steven's here by the way. I know he'd love to see you too.'

Carol's heart lurched. 'Oh, really?'

Clarissa laughed. 'Yes. He and Freddie are working here at the moment. Steven keeps his piano here as you probably know, so as I'm out a lot of the time, I said they could have the use of the flat.'

'Oh – well, I wouldn't want to interrupt . . .'

'Don't be silly, of course you won't.' Clarissa laughed. 'As far as I can see they're always game for an excuse to stop working! Don't waste any more time talking. Jump on a train right away and I'll have the kettle on waiting. 'Bye!'

Carol replaced the receiver slowly. If she were completely honest she had hoped that Steven would be there. Yet, perversely, now that she knew he would be she would have done anything – made any excuse – not to go. For reasons she preferred not to examine.

There had been one or two tepid affairs during the past five years but none of them had ever really got off the ground until she met Finn O'Connor, the stage manager

202

at Bradwich. Finn was dark and brooding. Very Irish and very demanding. In his uncompromising way he had made it clear from the first that they were destined to fall in love and had swept her completely off her feet. For a while, Carol had thought that the spell under which Steven had held her all these years might at last have been broken. Naively trusting and dazzled by Finn's flamboyant character and romantic eloquence, she had allowed him to become her first lover. Convinced that she was head over heels in love, she had thought herself deliriously happy – until the day that his wife had arrived out of the blue and dealt a heavy blow to her confidence and self-esteem. She had confided all this to Mike during that last week, when he had come up to Bradfield, grateful for his broad shoulder to cry on. But she had been dismayed when he then had asked her to marry him.

Now, standing hesitantly by the telephone kiosk, she was forced to acknowledge that her feeling for Steven was as strong as ever in spite of the emotional upheaval she had gone through. Just knowing that he was within reach, that she would be seeing him in less than half an hour, made her heart quicken as it had all those years ago when they were both growing up.

She bought her ticket and caught the Circle line train to Earls Court, then walked the short distance to Abingdon Court. As she stood waiting for someone to answer her ring at the bell she could hear the piano playing. The sound was so evocative it brought a lump to her throat. For her, the sound of the piano would always bring back memories of the Mansons' house, of Kitty's kindness and all the good times she had had there. But most of all, of Steven.

Clarissa opened the door.

'Come in and take off your coat.' She hugged Carol warmly. 'It's lovely to see you. Tea's all ready. I'm sure you're dying for a cup? London is so dusty in summer, isn't it?'

As she stood there in the narrow hallway, taking off her jacket, the piano stopped, the door of the living room opened – and suddenly Steven was there.

'*Carrie*!' His arms tightly round her, he lifted her off the floor in an enthusiastic hug. 'God! It's so long since we last met, I can't even remember when it was. You look marvellous!' He held her at arms' length to inspect her better. 'You've had your hair cut. It suits you.' He peered at her. 'Wait, though. Does your being here mean you're "resting" again?'

' 'Fraid so.'

'Damn! Never mind. Talent like yours doesn't lie idle for long.'

'I've just been out to Stanmore to see Marty and Zelda,' she told him.

He laughed. 'I guessed as much. I can smell the gin!'

'They're buying an agency.'

'Good for them! Hear that, Rissa?'

'I hear!' she laughed. 'Let the poor girl come in and sit down. She's dying for some tea. You can hear all her news then.'

Carol was briefly introduced to Freddie Manners, a fair-haired, rather stocky young man who was Steven's lyricist friend. When they came into the room he was standing by the piano, packing manuscripts into a briefcase. He shook hands with Carol and declined Clarissa's offer of tea, explaining that he had a pile of work to catch up on at home. When he had gone, Steven laughed.

'Poor Freddie! Trying to juggle his other job with writing lyrics is a constant struggle.'

Clarissa passed Carol a cup of tea. 'You will stay for dinner, won't you? There's plenty for all of us.'

'Well, if you're sure?'

'I am. Now, I'll leave the two of you to catch up while I go and see to it.'

When the door closed behind her, Steven looked at Carol. 'I can't get over how marvellous you look,' he said. 'You know, every time I see you it's like being introduced to a brand new person.'

Carol sipped her tea. 'I'm no different really. It's only because the intervals between our meetings are so long!'

'I know. I only wish it could be different. But with both of us gadding about all over the country . . .' He leaned forward and took her hand. 'Tell me, how have you been, Carrie? Is life being good to you?'

She shrugged. 'Not bad. I could do with that big lucky break.'

He laughed. 'Couldn't we all? I'm planning to stay on in London at the moment, for a while at least. Have you noticed how the old girl's waking up at last after the war? How about the new National Theatre on the South Bank? It's actually opening at last. I'm sure that must excite you, especially with Sir Laurence directing? Everything is changing, Carrie. Don't you feel it? There's kind of buzz in the air. And there are all sorts of innovations in the world of music, especially musical theatre. No more lightweight fairytale stuff, it's all new punchy themes like *West Side Story*. It's the beginning of a vibrant new era and I want to be part of it.'

'You forget I've been vegetating in the sticks!' she laughed. "Up North" one tends to become insular. I'm a bit out of touch as far as the latest trends are concerned.'

'But you must have heard of the new group from Liverpool, the Beatles?' he said. 'They write all their own stuff. Really different and refreshing. There are other exciting groups coming up too, like the Rolling Stones. Then there's the satire on TV. It's like a breath of fresh air blowing away all the dusty old cobwebs! Things are beginning to take off in a big way.'

'Well, of course, I've heard of things like that,' she said, catching some of his enthusiasm. 'I haven't exactly been buried alive up in Bradwich! There are some new playwrights who are doing different things too, like Harold Pinter and John Osborne. Unfortunately their plays aren't going to help save provincial rep! Live theatre is dying, Steven – in the provinces anyway.'

'It'll come back, Carrie,' he said encouragingly. 'Given time.' He smiled. 'I can see you're definitely not behind when it comes to fashion trends anyway.' He looked appreciatively at the slim, pale pink cotton shift dress she wore and the smooth, shining hair, cut in a bouncy tulip shape that enhanced her delicate bone structure. She was slimmer than the last time he had seen her. She seemed taller, too, but he thought that was probably due to the way she carried herself. The expressive, violet-blue eyes hadn't changed at all, though. There was still a heart-stopping hint of vulnerability in their dreamy depths. He reached for her other hand and squeezed them both. 'Is your heart still in one piece, Carrie?' he asked. 'Has anyone swept you off your feet yet?'

She shrugged. 'There was one near miss,' she said lightly. 'He turned out to be suffering from amnesia.'

'Really?' He looked at her inquiringly.

'Yes. The convenient kind. He'd forgotten he already had a wife.'

'Oh!' He nodded. 'Poor Carrie.'

'Not a bit. Actresses need experience. All grist to the mill as they say.'

'Ah.' Her glibness didn't fool him. 'He hurt you badly?'

'No.' She waved a dismissive hand. 'Tell me about you. Are you and Clarissa . . . ?'

'Did she tell you that Freddie and I are trying to write a

206

musical?' he interrupted. 'We've got high hopes of it, but we're not kidding ourselves we'll be an overnight success. Neither of us is giving up the day job as they say. I've got a good agent who gets me all the freelance work I can handle, and Freddie is still working in his father's firm of accountants. As his elder brother is his boss, he's allowed to work in his own time as long as he gets it all done.' He pulled a face. 'Poor Freddie. Can you imagine a creative bloke like him slaving away with boring figures? He had a good musical training but his father insisted on his joining the family firm. Still, he knows he can come up here to the flat whenever he wants to get away and try out a new idea on the piano.'

Carol smiled. 'She's very good to you both, isn't she?'

'Rissa? An absolute gem. Cooking us meals when we forget to eat. Encouraging us. Cheering us up when we get depressed. I don't know what we'd do without her.' He looked at her. 'Kitty came up to Town a few weeks ago. She stayed with the Warings but we did manage to spend some time together. She tells me she hasn't seen you for ages. Don't you get home much?'

'It's a long way down from Bradwich. You know how much time we get off. Sundays and that's about it.'

'Between jobs though?'

'Oh, yes. Between jobs. The odd week out. Flying visits. Now and then.'

'So – are you going home this time?'

She shrugged. 'I might.'

'You're not still upset about that little creep Wilson, are you?'

'That *little creep, Wilson*, as you call him, happens to be my father,' she said bitterly. 'There's no getting away from the fact. I try not to think about him. He's one of the reasons I don't go home.'

'So you've never spoken to your folks about what

happened?' When she shook her head, he said, 'Carrie, have you ever considered the possibility that he could have been lying?'

'Why should he lie about a thing like that?'

'I don't know. Spite – sheer bloody-mindedness – who knows how a mind like his works? If I were you I'd forget all about it. You've never known any other father but Jack Kenning. Why not just leave it at that?'

Carol shook her head impatiently. 'You *know* why, Steven.'

'You're not still worrying about the heredity thing?' He shook his head. 'Look, Carrie, from what Kitty tells me my own father was no great shakes; a wastrel and a womaniser and God only knows what else. But I haven't allowed it to give me a bunch of hang-ups and mess up my life, have I?'

'You had a marvellous mother who was around long enough to bring you up. I'm sure you take after her, not him.'

'But you might easily . . .'

'Please, Steven.' She shook her head at him impatiently. 'Let's talk about something else.' She gave him an ironic little smile. 'Sorry. This is one dragon not even you will ever be able to kill.'

Clarissa joined them then, announcing that the meal was ready. They ate companionably together, catching up on each other's news and chatting light-heatedly until, at ten o'clock, Carol decided it was time to go.

'You're not going all the way back to Hackney on your own!' Steven said. 'I'll drive you.' He grinned. 'Didn't know I had a car, did you? She's a bit of an old tank but she gets me from A to B. Come on, get your coat.'

Carol gave Clarissa a hug and as she did so the other girl said quietly, 'Can you meet me for a coffee tomorrow morning?'

Carol was about to make an excuse when she looked into Clarissa's eyes and saw that there was an urgency behind her request. 'All right, where? And what time?'

'There's a little coffee bar in Argyle Street, almost next door to the Palladium. It's called The Crocodile. See you there at eleven. Okay?'

'Okay.'

Steven appeared in the doorway. 'Your carriage awaits, madam.' He dangled the car keys. 'Come on, she's parked in the underground car park. We'll take the lift down.' He dropped a kiss on Clarissa's head. 'See you tomorrow sometime, Rissa. Thanks for dinner. 'Night.'

Steven's car was a ten-year-old Austin A40, but it seemed serviceable enough. As they negotiated the London streets Carol glanced at him speculatively. His remark to Clarissa hadn't escaped her. 'You don't live at the flat any more then?'

Without taking his eyes from the road, he shook his head. 'No. When I came back to Town to stay, I found myself a place of my own. It's a bedsit but I'm only there to sleep so it doesn't matter. I can come and go as I please.' He shot her a quick look. 'I reckoned Rissa deserved to have the place to herself occasionally. She puts up with Freddie and me enough as it is. I do stay on occasionally,' he added. 'If we've worked on till late or I've had a few drinks.'

When they reached the house in Hackney he pulled into the kerb and switched off the engine. Carol looked at him.

'Coming in for a coffee?'

He shook his head. 'Better not. It's late and your friend . . .'

'She's on duty. Will be until late.' She laughed. 'Anyway, it's Liberty Hall here. No one seems to give a damn who comes and goes. I know Janet would want me to invite you in.'

He smiled. 'Another time, eh?' Reaching out an arm he encircled her shoulders. 'It's been wonderful seeing you, Carrie. You won't leave it so long again, will you?'

Her heart sinking, she shook her head. She was so disappointed. As he wasn't in a hurry to get back she had visualised sitting with him in Janet's room, talking for hours over coffee, recapturing the companionable closeness they had once had – perhaps something more that she wouldn't even let herself think about.

'I'll be in touch,' she said. 'Are there any messages if I go home?' 'Just give everyone my best,' he said. 'And a big hug for Kitty of course.'

'Right. Well – better go in, I suppose.' She reached for the door handle, but his arm tightened round her shoulders.

'Hey, hold on! Was it something I said?'

'Sorry?'

He smiled. 'Don't I get a kiss?'

She laughed shakily. 'Of course.' She held up her face, closing her eyes as their lips met, trying hard not to let him feel the tremor that went through her or sense the heart-wrenching need that threatened to tear her in two. His mouth on hers felt as familiar and sweet as it was in dreams. And just as distant and unattainable. She drew away and touched his cheek briefly.

'Goodnight, Steven. It's been lovely, seeing you. Thanks for bringing me home.'

'Goodnight. And don't forget to keep in touch, will you? I do miss you, you know.'

She swallowed hard. 'Me too.' For a moment their eyes held. She was first to break the contact, turning to open the door. 'I'll write,' she called. Already she was running up the steps. At the top she stood in the shadows and watched as he drove away, holding on to the sight of the car's red tail lights until they merged into the traffic and were finally swallowed up. She was always saying goodbye to him, she reflected wistfully. Maybe she always would be.

The Crocodile was crowded when she got there at five to eleven the following morning. It seemed to be a popular coffee bar, much like all the others springing up all over London. The decor was black and white with lots of gleaming chrome, and the furnishings were brashly geometric in design. Behind the bar loud speakers were blaring out Acker Bilk's hit, *Stranger on the Shore*. Carol spotted two people leaving their stools at the far end of the long bar where the espresso machine hissed and spluttered. She quickly grabbed them, climbing on to one and reserving the other with her handbag. Catching the eye of the girl behind the bar, she ordered two cappuccinos and settled down to wait. Looking around her she couldn't help nostalgically comparing the atmosphere here with the cosy charm of The Clipper. Steven had been right. Things were changing.

Clarissa didn't see her at first, almost hidden behind the coffee machine. Carol waved frantically.

'Clarissa! Over here!'

As the other girl hoisted herself on to the bar stool next to her, Carol thought she looked tired and a little drawn.

'Good of you to meet me like this, Carol,' she said. 'We're terribly busy at work. I just slipped out in my coffee break to do some shopping. Promised I wouldn't be any more than half an hour.'

'There was no need to rush. I could have come round to the flat after work.'

Clarissa spooned at the froth on her coffee, then made a face and pushed the cup away. 'There's always someone there nowadays,' she said. 'Not that it's any

211

more private in here. Or quieter,' she added, wincing as the coffee machine at her elbow let out a sudden angry hiss. 'It's just that it's close to the office and handy. I wanted to tell you something – ask your advice really. You've known Steven so long. You probably know him better than anyone.'

Carol smiled. 'I doubt that. There have been some very long gaps in our acquaintance.'

'Nevertheless, you've known him since childhood. He always says you're like family.'

'Does he?' Carol looked at her. Something was obviously bothering her. 'What's wrong, Clarissa? If there's anything I can do . . .'

'There isn't. Not about – unless . . .' She glanced at her watch. 'Oh, God, look at the time. I'll have to go in a minute. I must get to the point.' She looked at Carol. 'I take it Steven has told you about Freddie – the set up?'

'That they're writing a musical – using your flat? Yes.'

'And that he, Steven, moved out a while ago?'

'Yes.'

'There was a time when I thought we might get married, but that passed. We haven't been what you'd call serious for some time. But he's still special to me.'

'I sort of gathered that.'

'Well, there's a complication now.' Clarissa took a deep breath. 'You see, the thing is, Carol – I'm pregnant.'

The word hung in the air between them. Carol felt as though someone had delivered a hefty kick to her stomach, knocking all the breath from her body. For a moment she was speechless. 'You're – you're sure?' she asked lamely.

'Positive. Look, Carol, you know Steven. How do you think he'll take it?'

'Well . . .' Carol swallowed. Her mouth was dry and her tongue felt too big for her mouth. 'I've no idea.' She looked at the other girl. 'Are you planning to go ahead with it? Or . . .'

'Have an abortion?' Clarissa shook her head. 'Good God, no! I couldn't do that.'

'Then you'll just have to – tell him,' Carol said, nonplussed. 'After all he must have known it was a possibility?'

'Well – yes.'

'He'll be pleased. Of course.'

'But I'm so afraid it'll mess everything up.'

'Surely not?' Carol had no idea what Clarissa wanted her to say. She felt totally inadequate. But Clarissa hardly seemed to be listening anyway.

'I want the baby so much, Carol,' she was saying. 'I'm thirty-one and I've always wanted a family. Time's ticking away for me. But I don't want Steven to be upset. It could be disastrous.'

'I don't see why. It won't be, I'm sure.'

'Are you? Are you *really*?' Clarissa turned to look at her. 'I've been so worried about it, but when you were at the flat last night I suddenly saw how close you two were and I knew I could ask you to – ask you . . .' She shook her head. 'No, it's my problem. I have no right . . .'

Carol was shocked. Clarissa *surely* hadn't expected her to speak to Steven on her behalf? The very idea was anathema – unthinkable, like rubbing salt into an open wound. Unable to meet the other girl's eyes she said quietly, 'I think you should tell him, Clarissa. As soon as possible.'

'Yes. Yes, of course. You're right. I'm being cowardly.' Clarissa looked again at her watch. 'Oh, *no*! It's twenty to twelve. I'm sorry, love, I'll have to run now. It was so good of you to come. It's helped a lot to talk even if . . . Well, you know.' She slipped down from the stool and gathered up her bag. 'Goodbye. I'll write and let you know what happens. Keep your fingers crossed for us. See you again soon, I hope.'

Eve was at the shop when she got the call. It had been a busy year. Ever since March, when the Profumo affair broke, the sales of newspapers had rocketed. It never failed to disturb Eve that people were so thrilled and titillated by scandal and the downfall of others. She was making their afternoon cup of tea in the little office at the rear of the shop when the telephone rang. She lifted the receiver.

'Kenning's newsagent's?'

'Mum? It's me – Carol. I wondered if it would be all right if I came home?'

'Carol, love! Of course it is. You know you don't have to ask.'

'Right. I'd like to come this afternoon if it's okay?'

'Of course. I'll go home right away and get your room ready.'

'No, don't go to any trouble. I'll do it when I get there. I'm at Euston now.'

'All right. How long will you be staying, love?'

'I don't know. A week or so. Maybe more.'

'That's lovely! Your dad will be thrilled.' Eve frowned. The girl sounded strained. 'Carol – there's nothing wrong, is there?'

'No. Oh, only that the company in Bradwich has disbanded and I'm looking for a job. But I wanted to see you too,' she added quickly.

'And we want to see you. It's been so long and . . .' Eve was interrupted by the beeping sound.

'Oh, there are the pips, Mum. I've no more change. See you later.'

'Do you want your dad to meet . . .' Eve was left with the buzzing receiver in her hand. She replaced it and went through to the shop.

'That was Carol on the phone,' she told Jack. 'And guess what – she's coming home.'

Jack's eyes lit up. 'Oh, that's great! When?'

'This afternoon. She was ringing from the station.'

'Does she want me to meet the train?'

'I asked her but the money had run out.'

Jack was already pulling out the railway timetable he kept under the counter, his face pink with excitement. 'If she was already at the station there must be a train due. I can easily work it out. Won't matter if I have to wait a while. You can hold the fort here, eh?'

She saw him waiting as soon as she got off the train and was taken aback to see how much he had aged since her last visit. He seemed shorter somehow and the broad shoulders he had carried her on as a little girl were now slightly stooped – almost frail looking. With a small shock she realised for the first time that he was getting older. But when he caught sight of her and waved she was relieved to see that the light in his eyes was a bright as ever.

'Carol, love! Oh, it *is* good to see you.' He hugged her warmly. 'Your mum was thrilled to bits when you rang.' He took the case from her hand. 'Here, let me have that. The car's waiting. Mum says I'm to take you straight home then go back to the shop for her at closing time.'

The house was as bright as a new pin, the garden ablaze with Jack's beloved roses and every kind of colourful bedding plant imaginable. When they had drunk a cup of tea together in the kitchen and Jack had set off into town again to fetch Eve, Carol made up the bed in the spare room and unpacked her things. It was a lovely house, but somehow for Carol it had never really felt like coming home since the family had moved away from Clarence Street.

Standing at the open window of the silent house, she let her mind dwell on the events of the past two days. Clarissa's news had shocked her deeply. All she could think about was getting as far away as she could, as soon as possible. Janet had been disappointed and slightly put out when Carol had announced that she was leaving so soon.

'What's the matter with you?' she'd asked bluntly. 'There was a time when we told each other everything, but these days you're so close. You bottle things up.'

'I don't!'

'Yes, you do. And it can't be good for you. I've known there was something wrong ever since you arrived. You and I used to be such close friends. What's wrong, don't you trust me any more?'

Carol, already close to tears, felt the lump in her throat almost choking her as she sank down on the edge of the bed. 'Oh, Jan, I'm sorry,' she said. 'I don't mean to be a bore. It's just that nothing ever seems to go right for me.'

Relenting, Janet sat down on the bed beside her and laid a hand gently on her arm. 'What is it, love? Come on, you've got to tell someone.'

Carol glanced sideways at her friend. 'First there was Finn. What I didn't tell you was that he turned out to be married.'

'Swine!' Janet said dispassionately. 'I thought it might be something like that. But you're better off without a creep like that. And you're over it now, aren't you?'

Carol nodded. 'It wasn't easy, working with him afterwards. Then the notice went up and I found myself out of work again.' She sighed. 'Then, this morning, I met Clarissa for coffee.'

'Yes?' Janet prompted.

'And she told me – told me that she's pregnant.' Carol bit her lip hard to stop it from trembling. 'She actually wanted *me* to tell Steven for her, because she's afraid he'll be upset.'

216

'Oh, *no*!' Janet slipped an arm round her shoulders. 'Oh, poor Carol. You still love him, don't you? I've always known how you felt. It was more than just a schoolgirl crush, wasn't it?'

'Was it really that obvious?' she asked miserably.

'Only to me. Because I know you so well.'

'Well, anyway, I couldn't do it. I told her she should tell him herself.'

'So I should damned well think!'

'I've had enough, Jan. This was about the last straw, so I thought I'd go home for a while and try to recharge my batteries. If that's possible.'

'Of course. A break is just what you need. And you know you're always welcome to stay here if you need to come up for auditions or anything.'

'Thanks, Jan.' Carol looked gratefully at her friend. 'I haven't meant to be cold and unconfiding. I can't afford to lose a friend like you. It's just that I hate moaners and I wouldn't want you thinking of me as one.' She smiled a little shamefacedly. 'Besides, your life always seems to be so well ordered compared to mine.'

'Well ordered? You're joking!' Janet pulled a face. 'That'll be the day! Come on, I'll help you pack, then we'll ask Harry and Jim to take us out for a drink. They'll jump at the chance of being seen with my glamorous actress friend and they'll be sure to cheer you up.' She laughed. 'I have to admit they do have their uses, even if they are a pair of slobs!'

And now here she was.

'I'm back to square one,' Carol told her reflection in the dressing-table mirror.

When Eve and Jack arrived home, Eve ran into the house ahead of her husband and met Carol in the hall.

'Carol love! Oh, it's so good to see you. I can't tell you

how much we've hoped you'd come home.' She threw her arms wide and Carol stepped obligingly into them. 'Not that we wanted you to be out of work of course,' Eve added. 'Now – is your room all right?'

'Yes, Mum. I've made up the bed. There's nothing more to do.'

'Well, better slip a hot bottle in to air it,' she fussed. 'I know it's summer but it hasn't been slept in since last time you were home. Don't want you catching a cold, do we?' She bustled into the kitchen and filled the kettle at the sink. Carol laughed.

'Mum! I think it'll wait till you've taken your coat off!'

'What? Oh, yes.' Eve laughed and slipped off her outdoor things, hanging them in the hall cupboard. 'Now – you must be starving,' she said, returning to the kitchen. 'I made a casserole last night. It's in the fridge. There's plenty for all of us.'

'Shall I get it out?'

'If you wouldn't mind, dear.' Eve bent to turn on the oven, then took a basket of potatoes out of the pantry. As she tipped them into the sink she eyed her daughter anxiously.

'You are all right, aren't you, love? You're looking a bit peaky.'

Carol took a vegetable knife from the drawer and began to peel the potatoes. 'I'm fine, thanks.'

'It is *just* that you're out of work that you've come home, isn't it, dear?'

Carol shot her a warning look. 'Mum – don't start.'

'No. I'm not. It's just that . . .'

'I'm *fine*. I've come home because I wanted to see you and Dad. If you're going to start cross-questioning me the minute I walk in the door . . .'

'No, It's only – I was just . . .' Eve turned away and dried her hands. 'You look so tired, Carol, and you've lost weight since you were last home. I am your mother, you know. I'm entitled to be concerned about you.'

Carol sighed. 'I know, Mum. I know,' she said wearily. 'Look, as you say, I'm tired. I stayed with Janet in London for a couple of days. Last night we went out – had a late night. Okay?'

'If you say so,' Eve said unhappily. 'But if anything were wrong, you would tell me, wouldn't you?'

Behind her mother's back Carol raised her eyes ceilingwards. 'Yes, Mum. I'd tell you,' she said between clenched teeth.

'Good.' Eve began to lay the table. 'All right if we eat in here, love?'

'Of course.' Carol looked at her mother. 'Mum, while we're on the subject of health, is Dad all right?'

'Of course. Why?'

'Oh, nothing, I just thought he looked – I don't know. Older, I suppose.'

'We're all getting older,' Eve said. 'Sometimes his old problem bothers him a bit, but he has some tablets from the doctor and they soon clear it up. There's no need to worry, he's fine.' She smiled wryly at Carol. 'Now who's *starting* as you call it?'

'Sorry.'

They worked in silence for a moment or two then Eve cleared her throat. 'After you'd called I rang your Auntie Rose,' she said with a tentative glance at Carol's back. 'She's asked us all round for tea on Sunday. Grandad and both Grans too. It'll be like a family reunion.'

'Oh?' Carol's heart sank. 'I was hoping for a few days' peace and quiet.'

'Well, you hardly ever come home, love,' Eve said pointedly. 'So it's a bit of an occasion. And you surely can't complain if your relations want to see you.' She

219

smiled. 'Did I tell you how miffed our Rose was when your dad and I sold the shop and moved here?'

Carol had heard it all before but feigned ignorance.

'She got Ted to buy a whole new set of furniture for the lounge *and* the dining room,' Eve told her. 'And you should have seen her face the first time she saw this house!'

Later, upstairs in her room after pleading that she needed an early night, Carol lay on the bed and wondered how she was to survive the so-called family reunion. *If I needed reminding why I don't come home more often, that should do it,* she told herself wryly.

They were all there, assembled in Rose's front room, dressed in their Sunday best and perched stiffly on the edges of her new beige Dralon three-piece suite. Each of them greeted Carol and asked polite questions about her health, all of them carefully avoiding inquiring about her work which they didn't understand. Only Elizabeth brashly drew attention to the fact that Carol was out of a job.

'As a matter of interest, I suppose actresses *can* draw the dole the same as anyone else?' she asked.

Carol looked at her coldly. 'It's necessary to sign on if one wants the National Insurance stamps paid up,' she said coolly. 'That's the law.'

'Oh, well, it's a good thing you've got your parents to fall back on,' her cousin said with a smirk. 'At least you won't starve.' She stared challengingly at Carol, one heavy black eyebrow raised. 'Isn't that what you arty types are supposed to do – starve in a garret for the sake of your art?'

'I haven't come home to sponge on my family, if that's what you mean,' Carol said, flushing hotly.

'Really? You don't come home when you're working, I notice!'

'That's because we only get Sundays off!'

Seeing Carol's heightened colour, Mike stood up and held out his hand to her. 'Come and see the rockery and pond Dad and I have built,' he invited. 'You haven't been home since we made it.' He took her hand and drew her firmly out of the room. Once outside in the garden he smiled calmly at her pink cheeks and blazing blue eyes. 'You shouldn't let Liz get to you like that,' he said. 'You know she's always liked nothing better than having a go at you.'

'You can say that again!' Carol said grimly. 'Honestly, Mike, your *sister*!'

He grinned. 'In a way it's comforting to know that nothing changes.'

She smiled in spite of herself. 'You're right, I rise to it every time, don't I?'

'It's not as if you don't know the reason. She's green with envy. I mean, it's obvious, isn't it? Liz gets plainer and you get prettier with every year that passes. She's got a boring, mundane job whilst you . . .'

'Are on the dole,' Carol finished for him. 'And she's going to make sure I get my nose well and truly rubbed in it.'

'I was about to say that your job is exciting and glamorous,' he said, squeezing her hand.

'Liz chose teaching. It's fascinating and rewarding, I daresay. And to give her her due, she worked hard for it. My job is sheer hard graft for very little reward and few prospects,' Carol told him bitterly. 'That's when I can get any work at all.'

'Ah, but one of these days you're going to be a big star,' he said. 'While Liz will never be anything more than a teacher, so you can afford to put up with her sniping, eh?'

'Your faith is touching.' Carol said dryly. 'But I don't see why I should let her get away with it.'

Mike shook his head. 'A confident smile would be more effective than a defensive remark,' he said wisely. 'Let her know that you can rise above her bitchiness.' He tucked her hand through his arm. 'Now come and look at our handiwork.'

Rose had put on an impressive spread. Just the kind of family high tea that Carol remembered from her childhood. There was tinned salmon, and boiled ham and salad with home-made chutney and pickles. Tinned fruit and cream, and, to finish up, chocolate biscuits, jam sponge and fruit cake. The family did justice to it all, clearing the plates like locusts, especially Elizabeth who, Carol couldn't help noticing, had put on at least a stone since last she'd seen her; most of it on her already ample hips.

After tea Carol and Mike volunteered to wash up and the older family members decided to play Newmarket. Liz disappeared upstairs, reappearing a little later having changed into a different dress and wearing a lot of lipstick in an unbecoming shade of bright orange.

'Her boyfriend is calling for her,' Mike explained to Carol in a whisper. And, sure enough, a few minutes later a ring at the front door bell heralded a gangling young man with horn-rimmed spectacles and a nervously bobbing Adam's apple. Elizabeth led him into the kitchen like a lamb to the slaughter.

'This is Harold Roper,' she said, looking at Carol defiantly. 'My cousin, Carol Kenning.'

Harold blushed and held out a large perspiring hand, muttering a muffled greeting.

'We're going to the tennis club social evening,' Elizabeth said. Grabbing Harold's arm, she yanked him towards the front door. 'See you later. Goodbye, Carol.'

'Goodbye. Have a nice evening.' Carol and Mike exchanged amused glances.

'How did she meet him?' Carol asked.

'Old Harold? At work. He teaches at the same school. I'm afraid the poor blighter's had it. If Liz decides he's the one she wants to marry, his goose will be cooked. There'll be no escape.'

They laughed, then, suddenly serious, Mike looked at her. 'I suppose you haven't had any more thoughts about marrying me?'

Carol sighed. 'Oh, Mike. You know how fond of you I am.'

He winced. '*Ouch!* Don't go on. Forget I asked.'

'I certainly won't do that,' she said, putting away the last of the clean dishes. 'I'm deeply flattered that you asked me, Mike. But with your work and mine, I'm afraid it would never be on.'

'So – are you saying that's the only reason?'

Carol shrugged. 'Well, it's an important consideration, isn't it?'

'Love is another,' he reminded her. 'But you're too nice to mention that that isn't on the cards.' He smiled at her ruefully. 'Still, you never know,' he said. 'I shan't give up hope till you actually tell me to go and take a running jump at myself.'

She laughed. 'As if I would!'

Putting his arms around her waist, he drew her close and kissed her gently. 'Bless you for that,' he said against her hair. 'Shall I tell you something? You're like a bright jewel shining in the dark for me. And just as long as I can see you twinkling away somewhere, I'll be content.' He smiled down at her and kissed the tip of her nose. 'At least, I think I will,' he added wistfully. 'For now.'

It was the following Saturday morning before Carol got around to visiting Kitty. The house in Chine Way looked just the same as she stood in the porch waiting for someone to answer her ring at the bell. From above she could hear the familiar tapping of two dozen feet and the ring of Kitty's voice as she called out above the music. The teenage girl who opened the door to her was different, though. Small and bright-looking with a mop of ginger hair and freckles, she was a definite improvement on the dour and taciturn Mrs Gammon who used to be Kitty's 'daily'. She looked Carol up and down with undisguised interest.

' 'Morning. Can I help you?'

'Oh, hello.' Carol smiled at the girl. 'I'm an old pupil of Mrs Manson's,' she said. 'I've just popped in to see her, but don't disturb her. I'll wait till the class is over.'

'It's all right, miss. They've about finished,' the girl said.

Even as she spoke the music stopped and the clatter of tap shoes on the uncarpeted stairs heralded a stream of little girls in practice tunics swarming down to the ground-floor changing room. Their chatter filled the house with a life and vitality that Carol found painfully nostalgic. Kitty leaned over the banisters.

'Gloria! Did I hear the door bell . . . Oh! *Carol!*' She ran lightly down the stairs, her loose practice dress floating about her and her hair, redder than ever, bouncing. She embraced Carol, kissing her soundly on both cheeks. '*Darling*! How lovely to see you. Steven told me you'd been to see him when he rang me the other evening. He said you were going to try to get home for a few days and I've been hoping you'd find time to look me up.'

Holding fast to Carol's hand, she pulled her into the office. 'Come and tell me all your news, darling. Gloria, be an angel and make us some coffee, will you?'

Over the coffee Carol told Kitty about the rep in Bradwich and its failure. 'I went to see Zelda and Marty

224

while I was in Town,' she said. 'Did you know they've bought an agency?'

Kitty laughed. 'Yes. I knew suburban retirement was going to pall before long. When I went up to spend a weekend with them recently Marty told me they'd been asked to join the local Darby and Joan Club,' She chuckled huskily, spluttering into her coffee cup. 'Darling, can you *imagine* it? But that's not the best bit. Apparently the chairman thought they'd come in handy for organising concert parties! I wish you could have seen the expression on Marty's face. It was an absolute *study*!' She reached across to pat Carol's hand. 'I'm sure they'll help you all they can darling. You're a great favourite of theirs, you know.'

'I hope so,' Carol said with a sigh. 'I don't know how long I can stand it here at home.'

Kitty frowned. 'Why?'

Carol shrugged, slightly ashamed of her disloyalty. 'I don't know. It's me, I suppose. After being away, it all feels slightly claustrophobic.'

Kitty patted her hand. 'Well, I'll keep my fingers crossed for you. And in the meantime, I can always use some help with classes here if you want to keep your hand in.'

'Thanks, Kitty. I might just take you up on that.' Carol paused, wondering if Kitty knew about Clarissa's pregnancy. Surely they would tell her soon? After all, they were about to make her a grandmother. She'd said that Steven had rung her recently. Hadn't he mentioned it? But she couldn't bring herself to talk about him or to broach the subject of Clarissa's baby. It was all too painful still and she was afraid that Kitty with her needle-sharp perception would pick up on her unhappiness. It wasn't her secret to tell, Carol told herself firmly. For all she knew Steven was still unaware of it himself.

225

She was on the way home, walking to the town centre to catch the bus from All Saints, when a long, low car purred to a stop beside her.

'Hel-*lo*! Well, I'm blowed! If it isn't Carol.'

Her blood froze as she recognised the man at the wheel. It was Eddie Wilson.

'I can't stop,' she said. 'I have a bus to catch.'

'No problem. Hop in and I'll take you wherever you're going.'

'It's all right, really. I'm – I'm meeting someone.'

He smiled disbelievingly. 'It's all right. I won't eat you, Carol.'

'I've got to go!' Her heart was beating fast as she quickened her pace. But he drove slowly along beside her, still smiling up at her through the car window. 'It's coming to something when you haven't got time for your poor old dad, isn't it, Carol?' he taunted. 'Come on, relax. I want to hear all about this stage career of yours. When are we going to see you on the pictures then, eh?'

She stopped walking and turned to face him. 'Does your wife know about me?' she challenged. 'And your sons – do they know what kind of father you are?'

Eddie's smile didn't flicker, but the pale eyes became opaque. 'My wife left me last year,' he told her. 'After all these years. Talk about gratitude! Everything of the best that woman had from me. And the boys have left home and gone their own ways. All except Paul. Remember Paul?' He cocked a cynical eyebrow at her. 'But he works for me now and he's got the sense to know which side his bread is buttered, so you needn't get any ideas about him.' He winked at her. 'Now – want that lift, do you?'

'No!' she said, walking on.

'Okay, I can wait.' His voice hardened as he revved the engine noisily. 'You're my daughter, Carol. That means a lot to me now I'm all alone. We could be close, you and me. I could do a lot for you.'

'I don't think so.'

'Don't think so, eh? You want to count yourself lucky. I could make things unpleasant for you and your folks if I was the vindictive sort. Good thing I'm not, eh?' He leaned his head out of the window to look at her. 'One of these days you'll come to me on bended knees, Carol. You mark my words if you don't.' He withdrew into the car and began to wind up the window. 'Be seeing you, sweetheart.'

He drove on, leaving her trembling. The encounter had shaken her. Eddie's veiled threats might leave her with feelings of revulsion but they were empty and stupid, she told herself. There wasn't a thing he could do – not a single claim he could make on her. All the same, he gave her the creeps and she knew for certain that she couldn't stay here now. She loathed the thought that Eddie Wilson was her father, that she was his flesh and blood. But while she remained here at home she would be reminded of the fact constantly.

Chapter Seven

'I've suggested a June wedding,' Rose announced. 'At St
Matthew's. And a sit down meal afterwards. They say the
Co-op is very good, but I shall have to get some estimates,
of course.'

Still breathless from the effort of pedalling her bike two
miles at top speed, she deposited her bulk on a chair at
Eve's kitchen table. Her face was flushed and her eyes
gleamed with relish as she imparted her news. 'If they agree
on June that'll give me a good eight months to organise
everything. Oh, she's going to make such a *handsome* bride.'

'Yes, well, very nice,' Eve said coolly. 'You'll have a
cup of tea, won't you, Rose?' She turned to put the kettle
on. 'You look as if you could do with one.'

'Oh, I could! Oh, dear, I'm all of a doo-dah,' Rose said,
blowing out her crimson cheeks. 'Never slept a wink last
night. I mean, it came as such a *shock*. They went off out
last night as if nothing was any different. Then Elizabeth
suddenly announced at breakfast this morning that
Harold had popped the question! Exciting, isn't it, the
wedding of our only daughter? It'll be a big do all right.
Well, it's the least we can do, isn't it? She's always been
such a good girl, our Elizabeth. Deserves a good send off.'
She smiled proudly. 'Harold's coming round tonight to
see Ted,' she added. 'You know – to ask for her hand, as
they say. Oh, he knows how to do things properly, does
Harold.' She looked at Carol who was still washing up the
breakfast things. 'I bet you never thought she'd beat you
to it, did you, Carol?'

228

'Beat me to what?'

'Getting engaged, of course.'

'I can't say I've really thought about it,' Carol said truthfully.

'Not *thought* about it?' Rose laughed disbelievingly. 'Pull the other one, dear! It's all girls of your age ever talk about, getting married. Eh, Eve?' She cocked her head at her sister. 'Remember what we were like at that age? And I beat you to it, didn't I?' She laughed. 'You should have seen her face, Carol, the day I came home with a ring on my finger.'

Eve's cheeks flushed slightly as she poured boiling water into the teapot. 'As I remember it, you didn't *have* an engagement ring.'

It was Rose's turn to colour. 'Well, you know what I mean. Anyway neither did you – even after five years!'

'No. We thought that saving the money to buy our own home was more important,' Eve said. 'And it paid off in the end, didn't it? Helped us up in the world.' This was a direct hit at Rose who still lived in the rented house she and Ted had moved into when Michael was born. The barb found its target. Rose turned a dull red and, for the first time since she'd breezed into the house that morning, fell silent.

'What's Elizabeth's ring like?' Carol asked in an attempt to avert the usual squabble. 'I can't wait to see it.'

Rose's enthusiasm returned with a rush. 'It's gorgeous. Cost a *fortune*. Well, Harold's in line for the job of deputy headmaster at Barry Street Primary, you know. And he comes from a very nice family. His father's a master plumber.'

'So what's it like – the ring?' Out of the corner of her eye Carol was watching her mother's tight-lipped expression as she poured the tea.

Rose held out a plump left hand so as to demonstrate.

'A big ruby in the centre, surrounded by diamonds. And the stones are set in platinum. That's much stronger than gold, you know.'

'It sounds beautiful,' Carol said. 'I expect she'll be over to show it to us this afternoon.'

Rose frowned. 'Oh, she hasn't actually got it yet. I think they're getting it next weekend.'

Eve passed her sister a cup of tea and the biscuit tin. 'So how do you know what it's like?' she asked.

'She showed it to me in the window of Granville's when we went down town shopping together last week.'

'So she already *knew* she was getting engaged then?' Eve said, picking up quickly on her sister's slip. 'It couldn't have been that much of a shock to you then, could it?' She smiled grimly. 'Perhaps it was just Harold who didn't know?'

Rose bridled. 'What I mean is that she showed me the ring she'd choose if ever he *did* ask her, that's all.' She smiled at Carol. 'I daresay she'll be asking you to be bridesmaid,' she said archly.

'I wouldn't rely on it if I were you,' Eve cut in. 'Carol's very much in demand, you know. I daresay she'll be snapped up for some important part long before next June.'

Rose sniffed. 'The length of time these stage jobs seem to last she'll be gone and back again.' She looked at Carol. 'So, what do you say?'

'I'd love to. If she asks me and if I'm not too far away.'

Eve lifted the teapot and refilled their cups. 'Let's wait and see what happens, shall we?' she said. 'June is a long way off yet, isn't it? "Many a slip twixt cup and lip", as they say. Let's wait till Elizabeth has actually got that ring on her finger and the announcement is in the paper before we start cutting the sandwiches.'

Carol had been home just over three months, but it felt more like three years. She had been helping Eve and Jack at the shop in the daytime and taking evening classes for Kitty at Chine Way. She enjoyed keeping busy and, as Kitty and Jack each paid her a small wage, it meant that she could sign off the unemployed register. It also helped to take her mind off Steven and Clarissa, not to mention the total silence on the work front.

Each week she combed the pages of *The Stage* for suitable jobs, but there seemed to be nothing apart from the usual advertisements for chorus and showgirls wanted for dubious-sounding dates in the Far East and on the Continent. She'd even gone cap-in-hand to the local rep, asking if they had any vacancies. There was nothing, the producer told her regretfully. Either now or in the foreseeable future.

She telephoned the Warings who, Kitty told her, had now officially taken over the Marks agency which was open for business again. Zelda answered the phone.

'Carol love! How nice to hear from you.'

'Hello, Zelda. I heard that you and Marty were up and running and just wondered if there was anything going in my line?' she asked tentatively.

'Sorry no. I keep asking and looking out with you in mind, darling,' Zelda said. 'It's just that jobs in rep are so few and far between these days. But the very *second* anything promising comes up, I'll ring you at once.' She paused. 'There might be some work in telly commercials. Would you be willing to take something like that?'

'Well, I don't know . . .'

'Never know who you might meet,' Zelda said encouragingly. 'Contacts and all that. Better than nothing love.'

'Okay then. If something comes up, I'll give it a go.'

'Fabulous! I'll make a note.'

They exchanged pleasantries and Carol hung up, feeling dispirited. Sometimes she wondered if she would ever get another job. Perhaps she'd still be here in ten years' time when her parents retired, taking over the shop from them. She pictured herself, a little grey-haired lady with spectacles perched on her nose, serving sweeties to the school-children and relating endless boring anecdotes of her life as an actress while they sniggered behind her back.

Mike was a tower of strength to her during this time, laughing her out of her depression and organising little treats to cheer her up. His sister's wedding was the chief topic of conversation at home. Mike thought it all a great joke.

'What did I tell you?' he laughed. 'She'd got it all cut and dried. I bet poor old Harold didn't know what had hit him! He walked smack into it like the mutt he is. Poor devil! She'll make mincemeat of him.'

But Rose's feigned shock at the news of the engagement became reality two weeks later when Elizabeth suddenly announced defiantly that there would be no June wedding because she was pregnant and intended to marry Harold in a quiet register office ceremony at half term. Rose's plans for an opulent white wedding with all the trimmings went right out of the window, leaving her shamed and devastated.

Although Eve was outwardly sympathetic she couldn't help feeling the tiniest bit triumphant. 'I know I'm awful, but I can't help feeling it serves her right,' she told Jack in the privacy of their bedroom. 'She's had enough to say about others it's happened to, calling them sluts and tarts. Now she knows what it feels like when the boot is on the other foot!'

Mike, who wisely kept his opinions very much to himself at home, confided to Carol one evening on the way back from the cinema that, in his opinion, Elizabeth's pregnancy was in fact planned.

'I mean, let's face it, getting pregnant was the only way

Liz was ever going to get anyone to marry her,' he said unkindly. 'The biggest mystery to me is how she persuaded him to *get* her pregnant in the first place. You have to hand it to her for that!' He shook his head. 'Poor old Harold . . . what a price to pay for a moment's idiocy!'

'Mike! I think you're being a bit hard on them both,' Carol said, trying hard not to laugh at his irreverent remarks. 'I daresay they're very well suited. They'll probably be extremely happy.'

He looked at her, suddenly serious. 'Carol, I've been thinking. Once Liz is married I'm planning on getting a flat of my own. I've joked about it but this business has hit Mum really hard. You know how her generation feels about things like this. To her it's a deep disgrace and she's taken what she sees as the shame of it on herself. She's been on at Dad to buy a nice little modern bungalow further out of town so that they can move right away from all the neighbours. If they do move, I think they deserve to have their home to themselves.'

'That's a good idea.' Carol pretended not to know what was coming, but she'd already guessed that another proposal was on its way.

'You and I would be able to spend more time together too,' he said, slipping an arm round her shoulders. 'I'd like that. The thing is, would you?' Before she had time to reply he went on, 'I know you find it a bit claustrophobic, being in your parents' pockets all the time. If I had a place of my own you could have your own key – go there whenever you felt the need for a bit of space.' He gave her his gentle, lop-sided smile. 'Or be with me, of course.'

Carol laid her head on his shoulder. 'Oh, Mike. You are sweet.'

'*Sweet*?' He bent forward to look at her inquiringly. 'How do I interpret that?'

'You're my very best friend,' she told him.

233

'It gets worse! Anyway, the offer's there if you want it. No strings attached. Okay?'

She kissed him. 'Bless you, Mike. What would I do without you?'

'You'd find some other adoring admirer,' he said ruefully. 'You'll never be short of those, Carol, believe me. Whether you want them or not.' He switched on the ignition and began to drive her home. Sitting beside him in the passenger seat she wondered wistfully why the 'adoring admirers' Mike spoke of were never the one man she really wanted.

It was two days later that the telephone rang one morning just as Carol and her parents were leaving for the shop.

'Drat the thing. Let it ring,' Jack said, his hand on the door handle.

'Yes. If it's anything important they'll ring back,' Eve said. 'Or catch us at the shop.'

But Carol was already retracing her steps and lifting the receiver.

'Hello?'

It was Zelda's husky voice at the other end. 'Darling, thank goodness I've caught you. I'm ringing from home because I don't know the number of your parents' shop and I was afraid you might have left. Look – can you come up to Town?'

'When?'

'Today, of course!'

Carol felt her heart jump violently. '*Today*! Well, I suppose so. What's it for?'

'There are auditions for a new play by Carl Gibson. It's going out on tour and then opening in London next spring. They've already got the backing *and* a theatre. The Adelphi. I only heard about it on the grapevine last night, which is why I couldn't let you know before. I'd like to

234

have sent you a script to read, but that can't be helped. If you're interested I'll ring the producer right away. He's someone I know from yonks ago. What do you think?'

A new play by Carl Gibson! What did she *think*? Carol's heart was beating so fast she could scarcely breathe. 'Oh, Zelda! What time are the auditions? And where? I'll have to look up the trains and everything. Oh, I wish I'd had time to get my hair done!'

'Never mind all that! Just get your delightful self there on time. Two-thirty, 84 Martha Street, just off St Martin's Lane. It used to be a warehouse but now it's used as a rehearsal room. Okay?'

'I'll be there. And thanks, Zelda.'

'Not a bit. It's what we're here for. Pop in and see us afterwards if you have time. Let us know how it goes, eh?'

'Of course I will.'

'Fine then, I'll ring them as soon as I get to the office and tell them to expect you. Good luck, darling. I'll keep my fingers crossed for you.'

Jack was as excited as she was. 'What a marvellous chance!' he said. 'Drive into town with us and I'll look up the trains for you. Then you can take the car and drive yourself to the station. If you leave it in the car park I'll walk down and pick it up later.'

Eve was silent as she sat in the back on the way into town and Carol sensed her disapproval. Although she boasted to Rose about her daughter's success, underneath it all she secretly wished that Carol would stay at home and do an ordinary job like Elizabeth. These past weeks they had almost grown back into the family they used to be and Eve hated the thought that it was all about to end.

'I just hope you know what you're doing,' she said as they waited for Jack to unlock the shop. 'Forever dashing off like this at a moment's notice. Getting yourself into Lord knows what!'

'It's a West End play, Mum,' Carol said exasperatedly. 'By Carl Gibson. He's just about the most successful playwright there is! Chances like this don't grow on trees.'

'Well, just you make sure they're going to make it worth your while,' her mother said dourly. 'And don't forget that you can always come home if you don't like it.'

Carol hugged her. 'I know, Mum. But I'll be home again tonight anyway. I'm only auditioning. I might not even get the part.'

She reached Euston with time for a quick lunch for which she had no appetite. Finding a coffee bar, she bought a bun and a cup of coffee which she was too nervous to swallow. She arrived early at the rehearsal room and went inside, giving her name to the young man in charge who handed her a script.

'Your agent did tell you that we're auditioning today for supporting roles?' he inquired.

She nodded. 'Yes. I've come at short notice so I haven't had time to read the play, I'm afraid.'

He grinned. 'Never mind. I expect you'll be up for the part of Daisy.' He pointed to his schedule. 'The scene they'll want you to read is on page twenty. Act Two. And I take it there's something of your own you can do?'

'Yes, of course.' Her mind was working quickly. Already she'd decided to give them one of Bessie's scenes from *The Corn is Green*.

She took a seat on the row of chairs the young man pointed out to her, already half occupied with other hopefuls, all eyeing each other speculatively. Carol's heart was beating fast as she quickly read through the scene she would be required to read. It was a small part but it looked extremely good.

She guessed that the sudden movement at the back of the hall heralded the arrival of the producer and director, but didn't dare turn to look. The little group, producer, director and casting director, walked down to the front and took their seats at the table set up for them.

Carol sat through the auditioning of other minor parts, both male and female. The standard was good. She guessed that most of them were far more experienced than she was and her hopes began to fade. From what she had managed to read it looked like an outstandingly good play and, being by Carl Gibson, it was obviously destined for success. Playing a part in it – even a small one – would really set her up; give her the chance to be seen by London audiences as well as more important producers. She hardly dared to hope she might stand a chance of getting it.

The time arrived to audition for the part of Daisy. The director stood up to describe the character for them.

'She seems on the face of it like the average dumb blonde,' he said. 'But there is a depth to her character which needs to be put across to the audience. It's a small part but pivotal to the plot and quite showy.' He smiled. 'A chance to show off your acting ability. So – can we have the first, please?' He looked at his list. 'Miss Frazer, I think.'

The girl sitting in front of Carol stood up and went forward. But Carol was too preoccupied to notice her. It was the director who was taking all her attention. She had met him before: it was Gareth Dean, who had been the adjudicator when she took her silver medal examination. Would he remember her? she wondered. Then cast the notion aside. Of course he wouldn't. It was years ago. Why should he?

Suddenly she came to with a shock as she realised that the girl had finished and her own name was being called. She stood up on trembling legs and walked forward. Opening the script, she read the scene, putting as much into it as she could. When she had finished there was silence. The director cleared his throat.

'Thank you. Would you like to continue with your own choice, Miss Kenning?'

Carol put down her script and launched into Bessie's scene, the one where she returns to Wales from London in all her finery. It ended and she paused, then walked back to her seat, wishing she could go back and do it all again. In her head she was already criticising her performance, wondering why she had read a certain line this way, moved so – wishing she could do it all again. She sat down and closed her eyes, taking several deep breaths. When she opened them Gareth Dean was handing a slip of paper to the young man in charge. He looked at it and read out the names of those who were to remain behind. Carol's was the last on the list.

She waited patiently to be interviewed. When it was her turn Gareth Dean looked up from the table where he was busy scribbling notes and smiled at her.

'Miss Kenning. I think we've met before?'

'That's right.' She smiled. 'When I took my silver medal. You were adjudicating.'

'I remember.' He nodded. 'Your agent has told me what you've done over the past few years, so I already know your experience. As you must have guessed, the choice is between you and one other girl: Melissa Frazer. She has already had experience of the West End stage and is the obvious choice. However, I was impressed by your audition.' He grinned. 'And I liked your spirited interpretation of Bessie.' He looked down at his notes. 'Over the next two days we'll be conferring. We want to have the play fully cast by the end of next week so we'll be in touch quite soon.' He held out his hand. 'Thank you for coming, Miss Kenning. Good afternoon.'

Carol called in to see the Warings. They were very busy but showed her round the offices, gave her tea and made encouraging noises when she expressed doubt that she would get the part for which she'd auditioned. With an hour to spare before her train, she rang Janet to tell her too about the audition. Her friend was impressed and excited.

'Carl Gibson eh? Fantastic! Geoff and I went to see *Tell Me A Secret* last time he came up to Town. It was fab. What's this one called?'

'*Dance With Angels*,' Carol told her. 'But don't get excited. I've already been told that another girl is the obvious choice so it doesn't look very promising.'

'I bet you anything you'll get it,' Janet said optimistically. 'And if you do, you can come and stay here while you're rehearsing. Save money on digs.'

Carol laughed. 'Thanks, Jan. You're on.'

As she replaced the receiver she looked at her watch. Should she ring Clarissa's flat? Was there a chance she might get to speak to Steven? For a moment she stood staring at the receiver, then quickly lifted it, inserted her coins and dialled the number. A man's voice answered. It wasn't Steven's.

'Oh. Hello,' she said hesitantly. 'Is Clarissa there? Or Steven?'

'Sorry, neither. It's Freddie Manners speaking. Can I help?'

'Well – no, not really. This is Carol Kenning. I'm up in Town for the day. An audition. I'm catching the six-thirty train home but I thought I'd just say hello.'

'What a pity. They'll both be sorry they missed you. I'll pass the message on, though.'

'Thanks. Goodbye.' Carol felt bitterly disappointed. Steven hadn't been home to stay with his mother in the three months she had been at home, and she couldn't bring herself to ask Kitty if there was any news of a coming wedding. She was hungry now and bought herself

239

a sandwich and a cup of coffee in the buffet at the station. Then she walked across the concourse to her platform to wait for her train to come in.

She was just about to climb aboard when she heard a voice calling her name and turned to see a tall figure tearing down the platform.

'Carrie! Hi, *Carrie*!'

Her heart somersaulted as she watched him zig-zagging in and out of the startled passengers in his hurry to get to her. Finally he stood in front of her, breathless and dishevelled.

'*Carrie*!' He enveloped her in a bearlike hug, kissing her soundly. 'God, I've never moved so fast in my life. I was so afraid I'd miss you!' He laughed and raked his fingers through his hair. 'I arrived just after you rang. Freddie said you were up for an audition.'

'That's right. It's a new Carl Gibson play. But I don't think I stand an earthly of getting it.'

'Think positively. You never know,' he said. 'I'll keep my fingers crossed for you. Listen, Carrie, I've got some wonderful news! I'm so glad to be able to tell you like this. It's never the same second-hand or in letters.'

Her heart missed a beat. She knew what was coming, but wouldn't steal his thunder – wouldn't tell him she already knew about the baby.

'Good news? Super! Just what I could do with,' she said with forced gaiety. She glanced around at the empty platform. Everyone was aboard the train now. 'You'd better tell me quick. I think the train's about to leave.'

'Right. I'll be brief. Freddie and I sent an outline of our show, along with some of the numbers, to Graham Lang.' He grinned. 'We thought we might as well start at the top.'

'Graham Lang?' Carol's eyebrows rose. 'The impresario, you mean? The one who stages all the big Broadway and West End musicals?'

'The very same. Anyway, guess what? He likes it. He actually bloody well *likes* it! Can you believe it, Carrie?'

She laughed. 'Of course I can. Congratulations!'

'He'll need a lot of alterations – probably want to revamp the whole thing. But he likes the music and lyrics and says he definitely thinks Fred and I have something.' He paused for breath. '*And* – this is the best bit, Carrie – he wants us to go over to New York and see some of his productions. Talk to people from his company – have some script conferences.'

'That's fantastic!' She saw that the guard was about to flag the train out. 'This is it, Steven. I think we're off.'

'Okay, love.' He pulled her to him, hugging her close. 'Better get in now.'

She climbed hurriedly in and he took her hand as she leaned out of the window. 'When are you going, Steven – to New York?'

'Next week!' he said. 'That's why it's so good to see you. You'll tell Kitty that you've seen me, won't you?' He kissed her hand and let it drop.

'Of course I will.' The train began to move and he walked along with it. Suddenly Carol realised that he hadn't mentioned Clarissa. She had to ask – had to know. 'Steven . . .' She leaned out of the window as the train began to gather speed. 'What about Clarissa?'

For a moment he looked puzzled. 'Rissa? Oh, we'll be back in plenty of time for the wedding!' She only just caught his next words as they neared the platform's end. 'It's fixed for November the fifteenth. Hope you'll be coming!'

The distance between them had widened too much for her to reply, but she could still see him standing at the end of the platform, his arm raised, the smile still on his face. She waved back. So it was true then? It was really going to happen? When she could no longer see him she sat down in her seat, staring unseeingly out at the urban sprawl as it sped past. Her eyes still held that image of Steven's face, alight with excitement and expectation. It's over, she told herself bleakly. I've lost him. This time we've said goodbye for the last time.

Carol felt drained and dispirited when she reached Castle Station. She caught the bus up to the town centre, then queued at All Saints for the bus out to Sunnyside Crescent. When she got home Eve and Jack were all agog to hear about her day, but she felt disinclined to talk about it.

'They were all much more experienced than me,' she said dismissively. 'I don't stand a chance of getting the part. The director more or less told me so. I can't think why Zelda thought I should try for it.'

She felt slightly ashamed of the curt manner with which she pushed aside their inquiries, but she felt too exhausted to put on a show of enthusiasm. She picked at the supper Eve had prepared for her and went early to bed, pleading a headache.

In their own bedroom, Eve and Jack were bewildered.

'I can't understand it. She went off so excited this morning,' he said. 'And it's not as if they've turned her down. You'd think she'd be more hopeful.'

Eve shook her head. 'Sometimes I wish I'd never encouraged her to go in for this stage lark,' she said. 'If you ask me, it's all up in the clouds or down in the dumps. It'd be nice to see her settled down to a good steady job. Or married,' she added wistfully. It was something she'd secretly wished for for some time now. And if Carol got fed up with looking for fame and fortune on the stage maybe Eve might actually get her wish. Carol and Michael had always got along well together, and they made a lovely couple, Carol so fair and petite and Michael so tall and dark. Eve climbed into bed and pulled the eiderdown round her.

'Oh, I don't know about marriage,' Jack said doubtfully as he carefully folded his trousers and hung them on their hanger. 'Plenty of time for that. The girl's hardly more than a kiddie yet.'

But Eve was thinking ahead – visualising the wonderful wedding they would have. Carol would look a perfect picture in white lace, and orange blossom. A full-length veil, she'd have, and a train. Eve could just see her floating down the aisle, ethereal and dainty as thistle-down. And Michael would make the perfect foil. He was such a handsome lad. Top hats and morning dress the men would wear, she decided. Like the posh society weddings in the magazines. You could hire them all from Moss Bros. That'd show Rose! Their Elizabeth would never have suited white anyway. Really sallow, she'd have looked, not to mention lumpy, expecting or not! That girl hadn't an ounce of grace in her. Just as well she was marrying in a two-piece and hat if they asked Eve. She pulled the pillow around her shoulders and sighed, indulging in her favourite fantasy. Oh, if only it could all happen. She couldn't wait to see the look on Rose's face then!

As Carol lifted the receiver her heart was already sinking. She couldn't help feeling that the result of her call wouldn't be good news. It was two weeks since her audition, since when she'd heard nothing. This morning unable to bear the uncertainty any longer, she'd decided to ring Zelda as soon as she and her parents arrived at the shop.

'Carol! Funny you should ring now, darling,' Zelda said. 'I've just opened my post and it's here. *Dancing with*

243

Angels has been fully cast.' She paused and Carol's heart sank. 'I'm sorry, darling, but the part of Daisy has gone to Melissa Frazer.'

'I see. Well, I guessed she'd get it,' Carol said. 'Thanks for putting me in for it anyway, Zelda. There's nothing else, I suppose?'

'Not at the moment, love. I'm sorry. And of course it goes without saying that the minute there is, I'll ring you.'

'Of course. 'Bye then. Love to Marty.'

Jack looked up as his daughter walked back into the shop. He saw immediately from her expression that she hadn't got the part. As she walked round the counter and began to unpack a box of chocolate bars, he laid a hand on her arm.

'No luck, duckie?' he asked, his eyes gentle with sympathy.

She bit back the tears. 'No, Dad. No luck. I told you the other girl would get it.'

He squeezed her arm comfortingly. 'They're barmy to let you go, if you ask me. Never mind, sweetheart. You'll get that big break soon, you see if you don't.'

She smiled. 'I wish everyone had as much faith in me as you, Dad.'

From the other side of the shop Eve watched them. It was clear that Carol hadn't got that part she was after. Of course she felt for the girl. Anyone could see she was disappointed. But all the same, Eve couldn't help feeling that this was one step closer to what Carol really needed: a nice husband like Michael, a cosy home and a couple of dear little children. She smiled at the delightful prospect of holding her grand-children in her arms. If Carol had a baby girl perhaps they'd call her Wendy . . .

The Saturday of Elizabeth's wedding dawned grey and drizzly. Jack drove Eve over to Rose's after breakfast so that she could help prepare the food. It was to be a small reception, just relations and a few of the couple's friends round at the house after the register office ceremony. Rose felt no enthusiasm for the occasion. She still hadn't forgiven her only daughter for disgracing the family, not to mention doing her out of the white wedding she had so looked forward to. In fact she'd been on the telephone to Eve in tears so many times during the past weeks that Jack had resorted to taking the phone off the hook when he came downstairs this morning, afraid none of them would ever be allowed to have any breakfast.

As Carol was getting ready in her room she heard her father give a muffled cry from the bathroom. Stepping out on to the landing, she called out, 'Dad – are you all right?'

There was a short pause before he said, 'I'm fine, love. Just a twinge of indigestion, that's all.' He opened the door and smiled reassuringly at her. 'Fine one, aren't I, getting indigestion just before a wedding?' He tapped at his chest with his fist. 'Reckon it must have been those sausages your mum cooked for breakfast. Keep giving me right old gyp.'

'I'll get you some Rennies,' Carol said, slipping down to the kitchen. 'They'll soon do the trick.'

Back in her room, she put the finishing touches to her appearance. She had bought a new outfit for the wedding, a bouclé suit in a pretty shade of rose pink with a little matching pillbox hat. When she came downstairs her father was waiting for her at the bottom. He smiled and held out his hand.

'You look a picture, love,' he said, taking her hand. 'You know, your mum and I are very proud of our beautiful daughter.'

Carol looked into his gentle brown eyes and felt a warm rush of love for the man she had always called Dad. She put her arms around him and hugged him close.

'I'm proud of you too, Dad,' she said huskily. 'And I love you both very much, even if I don't always show it.'

'Good heavens!' Jack cleared his throat loudly. 'Listen to the pair of us, getting all soppy. We'd better get going before that cousin of yours gets herself wed without us!'

The little group was waiting in the dimly lit hallway of the register office. Elizabeth wore a brown tweed suit and velvet hat and carried her posy of rosebuds and carnations awkwardly, dangling it from one hand. She also wore a defiant expression, born of the long, reproachful conversations she had had with her mother over the past weeks. Her bridegroom was in a new grey pinstripe suit with a white carnation button-hole. Rose had decided that her 'best blue' would do for the wedding, having flatly refused to waste money on a new outfit. Her only concession to the occasion was a large spray of freesias which hung dejectedly upside-down on her bosom. Ted wore his dark blue 'weddings and funerals' suit and a deeply anxious expression, whilst the grandparents stood in the corner, looking subdued.

Jack dropped Carol off and went to park the car. She found her mother waiting for her just inside the door.

'Mum. Everything all right?' she whispered.

Eve shook her head and drew her to one side. 'No, it isn't! I really don't know what's got into our Rose,' she said. 'I understand she hasn't had the heart for this wedding, but she could have made a bit more of an effort. When I went to the cupboard there wasn't a doily in the place!'

Carol tried not to laugh at the scandalised expression on her mother's face. 'No doilies, eh?'

Eve frowned. 'I mean, what will folks think? No need to go putting a poor show on, is there? Does she want people to go away thinking she knows no better? I don't

246

know what our Rose is thinking of.' She looked at Carol. 'Will you take the car and slip home again, love? You'll find a new packet of assorted sized ones in the sideboard cupboard. You can bring them back here with you and we'll slip them on to the plates when we get round to Rose's.'

'Now?' Carol looked doubtful. 'Have I got time?'

'Yes. The couple before Elizabeth and Harold were late. They've only just gone in. I'd ask your dad but you know what men are. He'd never find them. Probably come back here with a stack of tea towels or something. You'll just make it if you take the car and go now.' She demanded the car keys from a bewildered Jack as he walked up the steps.

'There. Off you go, love,' she said, pushing them into Carol's hand. 'See you later.'

Carol drove home as fast as she could, taking the quieter roads to avoid the busy Saturday morning traffic. At home she unlocked the front door and ran in. She located the required packet of doilies quickly and retraced her steps. It was only then that she noticed the yellow envelope of the telegram lying on the mat. It hadn't been there when they left. Stooping, she picked it up and saw that it was addressed to her. Tearing it open, she read the printed words with mounting excitement.

Telephone not answering. Urgent you ring me earliest – Z.

Picking up the receiver from where Jack had laid it beside the telephone, Carol dialled her agent's home number with trembling fingers. Zelda picked it up almost at once.

'Carol! Thank God you've rung. Listen, Gareth Dean has been on to me to see if you're still available. The Frazer girl has had a better offer and turned the part down. It's yours if you still want it. But he must know right away. Today.' There was a pause as Carol tried to

247

take in what she had just heard. '*Carol!*' Zelda's voice rang out at the other end of the line. 'Are you still there?'

'Yes, I'm still here.' She laughed shakily. 'And of course I want the part. What did you think?'

'I knew you would, but I couldn't say yes without asking you. Right, I'll ring him right away. Rehearsals start next Wednesday at the same place you took the audition. I'll put the contract and details in the post. Congratulations darling. Be in touch. 'Bye!'

' 'Bye, Zelda. And thanks, thanks so *much*!' Carol put the receiver down and stood for a moment, pinching herself to see if she was dreaming. If it hadn't been for Mum and her insistence on doilies she might not have known about the part until it was too late! There must be something in the belief that fate shaped one's life. Suddenly she remembered that time was ticking away and snatched up the packet of doilies. There was a wedding to get through before she could tell anyone. Her big news would have to wait until afterwards. Aunt Rose would never forgive her for stealing the scene on Elizabeth's wedding day, even if it wasn't what she had planned.

She arrived back at the register office just as the party was making its way into the room where the ceremony was to take place. Tacking on to the tail end of the procession, she edged into the end of the row of chairs and took her place next to Michael. He turned to look at her.

'Hi, gorgeous! You look all sparkly. What's up?'

'Just went home for something Mum wanted,' she whispered. 'There was wire – a message to ring my agent.'

'Yes. And . . . ?' He looked at her expectantly.

The registrar was staring at them. Running late and having completed the preliminaries, he was obviously impatient to begin.

'I call upon these persons here present . . .'
Carol shook her head. 'Tell you later,' she whispered.

Back at Rose and Ted's the atmosphere felt noticeably lighter. Now that the knot was tied everyone felt they could relax. Ted poured sherry for all the guests and they drank the health of bride and groom. Eve had hurried to the kitchen to carry out her damage limitation exercise and the buffet duly appeared decently arranged on doilies and garnished with parsley from the back garden.

A full plate in one hand, glass in the other, Michael made his way over to Carol. 'Well, I have to say that I've never seen Liz looking happier,' he said. 'Not that I can say the same for poor old Harold. He has the resigned look of a man about to board a tumbril on his way to the guillotine.'

Carol nudged him. 'Mike! You mustn't say such things. I think he's just shy and nervous. All this is probably an ordeal for him. He'll be fine once they get away, just the two of them.' She took a sip of her sherry, looking at him over the glass's rim. 'Where are they going for their honeymoon?'

'Haven't you guessed?' Mike grinned. 'Auntie Kate's at Hunstanton. They would have gone to Paris but Liz only has to look at a puddle to get seasick. Something to do with her *interesting condition*, so I'm told'. He looked at her. 'So – what's this news of yours then?'

Carol shook her head. 'I promised myself I wouldn't say anything until the wedding was over.'

'You can tell me, though. Come on, you can see I'm dying of curiosity.'

'Well, you know I told you I had to ring my agent?'

'Yes?'

'Well, apparently the . . .' Her next words were drowned by a shrill cry of panic from the other side of

249

the room. Eve was shouting, 'Jack! *Jack!* Oh, my God – what's wrong?'

Carol pushed her way through the crowding guests to where her mother knelt on the floor beside the prone figure of Jack, who had collapsed, grey-faced, on the floor.

'Stand back, everyone. Let him get some air!' Mike took charge, bending to loosen Jack's collar and turn him on his side. 'Open a window, someone.' He looked up at Carol. 'Better ring for an ambulance. I'm afraid it looks like a heart attack.'

Carol went to the hospital with her parents in the ambulance. The moment they arrived Jack, who remained unconscious, was wheeled hurriedly away to the intensive care unit.

They sat in the waiting room for what felt like hours, hoping for someone to come and tell him how he was. Eve, her face drained of colour, shoulders slumped and hands clasped together in her lap, looked suddenly ten years older and Carol felt at a loss to know what to do or say to comfort her. She remembered Jack's 'indigestion' attack that morning and wondered if she should have mentioned it to her mother. Maybe if Eve hadn't fussed over those wretched doilies she would have. Could something have been done to prevent this? Was she to blame?

At eleven o'clock Rose walked down the corridor and joined them. She looked pale and exhausted.

'I've packed Elizabeth and Harold off to Hunstanton,' she told Carol. 'They didn't want to go but I made them. There's nothing they could have done here anyway.' Without another word she took Eve in her arms and held her close, weeping with her. The sisters for all their squabbling rivalry, were united by shared fear and anxiety.

Carol slipped out into the corridor to get tea for them

250

all. As she came back she saw through the glass panel of the waiting-room door that a doctor was with them. As she pushed the door open she heard the last few vital words he spoke.

'. . . a massive coronary, I'm afraid. We tried to resuscitate him, Mrs Kenning. Everything possible was done. But I'm afraid it was no use.'

For a moment Eve stared up at him, her eyes wide with disbelief. Then her hand flew to her mouth and she cried out, '*No*! Oh my God, no! He can't be. *He can't be!*'

In that instant Carol knew that Jack, the sweet man she had always known as her father and loved so much, had gone from them forever. Blinded by tears, she put down the tray and went to Eve, gathering her close.

'Carol – oh, Carol, what shall I do without him?' her mother sobbed. 'Oh, I'm so grateful you're here, love. I'm so glad you're not going away. Thank God I've got you, I couldn't face this on my own.'

Carol looked up at Rose who stood beside her mother, one hand resting on her shoulder. Her aunt nodded.

'She's going to need you now, Carol,' she said. 'You're all she's got.'

It was early next morning before Carol found the opportunity to ring Zelda. Their GP had given Eve a sleeping tablet late the previous night and at eight a.m. she was still sound asleep. Carol hadn't slept at all.

Downstairs in the hall she lifted the receiver quietly and dialled the Warings' number. As she waited for one of them to pick up the phone the tears streamed down her cheeks. Grief for her father was mingled with self-pity. And because of that there was guilt too – in abundance. She despised herself. Why couldn't she forget her own needs? A good daughter would put her mother before everything else.

But she had waited so long – wanted that part so badly. She knew that if she were to tell Eve about the offer she would urge her to go. She would say that Jack would not have wanted her to miss the chance. She also knew that if she allowed herself to be persuaded she would never be able to live with herself. Thank God she hadn't had time to tell anyone about it. At least she would be spared that much.

Standing there in the hall, shivering in the November morning chill, she longed with all her heart for Steven. Never had she needed him as she did now. He would have known what to do, or at least how to offer support and make her feel better. It was dragon-killing time again. But this was the worst dragon she had ever faced. Worse even than finding out that Eddie Wilson was her father.

But Steven couldn't help her this time. He was thousands of miles away, in New York, busy making his own dream come true. And anyway, he belonged to someone else. This time she was on her own with her dilemma.

Gareth Dean's offer was the kind of opportunity that came only once in a lifetime. There would never be another chance like this. Turning it down was the hardest thing Carol had ever done. The thought of it was like an ache deep inside her.

She heard the click of the receiver being lifted at the other end and Zelda's sleepy voice saying, 'Hello? Zelda Waring here.'

Carol took a deep breath, her heart as heavy as lead, knowing that she was about to put an end to a dream and wake up to cold reality.

Chapter Eight

The funeral was a dismal affair. It was a bitterly cold day. A chill mist hung over the churchyard and to Carol the whole thing seemed somehow unreal. Later all she remembered was a blur of mist and dripping trees and the sound of the vicar's voice droning while her feet grew numb from the wet grass soaking through her shoes. Eve, weak with grief, leaned on her arm throughout the service, a handkerchief pressed to her trembling mouth as she suppressed the sobs.

After the interment the family and a few friends went back to Sunnyside Crescent where Rose and Freda had laid on tea to warm everyone up. As Carol helped carry plates of sandwiches through to the dining room she noticed with irony that the doilies on the plates were from the same packet she had been sent to fetch on the day of Elizabeth's wedding less than a week ago. It was hard to believe that only a few days had passed since then. To her it felt like an eternity.

The following day she accompanied her mother to the solicitor's office where Jack's will was held. Predictably, everything was left to Eve and his affairs seemed to be in order. They returned home to tackle the desk in the dining room where he kept all the family and business paperwork. That was when they received the first shock.

Eve had been happily confident about their financial situation; sure that they were completely solvent and secure. But a quick examination of the books and bank statements showed that there was an alarmingly small amount of money in credit at the bank. Most of their investments seemed to have been cashed in too. When Carol checked the balance against outstanding bills she discovered with dismay that, once paid, they would be down to almost nothing. She broke the news to Eve and the two of them looked at one other across the paper-strewn dining table.

'But what are we going to do?' Eve's eyes were wide with panic and disbelief. 'I always left the money and business side of things to your dad. I'd no idea we were almost down to our last penny. He never said a word to me. How could he have let things slide like this?'

Carol tried to stay calm for her mother's sake. 'He wasn't expecting to die so suddenly, Mum,' she said. 'He paid cash for the house and car. Then there was the franchise for the newsagent's business. Most of these bills are quarterly ones, so I daresay it looks worse than it is. Once they're paid . . .'

'Once they're paid we'll have nothing! I can't understand it.' Eve got up and walked across to the window, her arms clasped protectively around herself. 'We'll have to sell the house, Carol.'

'No, Mum. There's no need to overreact like that.' She got up and went to her mother. 'Business is like this, I daresay. Up and down. Why don't you make an appointment to see the bank manager? He'll advise you. Christmas is coming, that'll boost business, and once you're in credit again . . .'

'No, I mean it.' Eve half-turned, holding up her hand. 'It's not just the money. Look out there.' She pointed. 'That garden was his pride and joy. I can't keep that up and run the business as well. Not the way he'd have wanted it kept. I'd never have the time, let alone the know-how. I won't need a place this size either – or a car, when I can't even drive.' Her eyes filled with tears. 'It can all go. *All* of it. The business as well. I don't want it any more. Without your dad, it's nothing to me.' She fumbled for her handkerchief. 'I wish I could have gone too, Carol,' she said brokenly. 'I don't want to go on without him. My life is over anyway now.'

'Now, now.' Carol put an arm round her shoulders, her throat tight with compassion. 'Mum, come and sit down. Things look black, but Dad wouldn't want you to give up like this. You're not old and you love the shop. Look how you managed in the war when he was away. You can do it. I'll be here to help.' She bent to look into Eve's brimming eyes. 'I need you too, remember, Mum?'

Eve dabbed at her tearstained face and made an effort to pull herself together. 'I know, love. And I know you'll help. You already have – so much. You're such a good girl, Carol. Thank heaven you were at home with us when it happened.'

After Carol had packed Eve off to bed that night she went back to Jack's desk and got out the folder of bank statements again. Earlier she had seen something that puzzled her. Regular monthly payments had been paid as a standing order into an account in another bank. They were the only entries she didn't understand. The overhead bills – gas and electricity – supplies and stock for the shop, were all clear, with corresponding invoices and receipts. Jack was very methodical. Only these substantial monthly payments puzzled her. The regular amounts were paid to a firm called Trident. A name unfamiliar to her. Searching back, she found that the order had begun four years before. Jack had been paying this money out since soon after they moved from Clarence Street. She decided to pay a visit to the bank the following morning and find out who or what Trident was and what Jack had been receiving for the money paid to them.

'I'm sorry, Miss Kenning. All I can tell you is that Trident is a wholesale firm. I believe they deal in grocery. Dry goods.' Mr Masters, the bank manager, looked apologetically at Carol across his desk.

'But Kenning's is a newsagent's,' she pointed out. 'My father stopped dealing in groceries over five years ago. It must be a mistake. Is it possible to find out the name of the person who owns the firm?' she asked. Mr Masters pursed his lips doubtfully and Carol felt a stab of impatience. 'I need to know what this money was paid out for, Mr Masters.'

The manager frowned. 'Isn't there anything among your father's effects to tell you?'

'Nothing at all. There are no receipts, no invoices. Nothing with a signature on. I've looked thoroughly.'

'Well, I do see your dilemma, of course.' He hesitated. 'But I'm sure you understand that all arrangements undertaken by the bank are highly confidential?'

'We are talking about my late father's estate, Mr Masters,' Carol reminded him. 'I'm trying to get things cleared up for my mother. If there are any debts that are still outstanding, or any money owing to Kenning's, it must be paid. I'm sure that if you were to ring the manager at Barfield's and ask . . .'

'Yes, yes, I see of course.' Mr Masters frowned. 'Perhaps in this case . . .' He rose from the desk, and opened the door. 'If you wouldn't mind waiting outside for a moment?'

Carol left the office reluctantly. Why were they so cagey about something she felt she had every right to know? After all, how could she sort out her father's financial difficulties blindfold and with one hand tied behind her back? She paced the corridor restlessly until the manager opened the door and invited her inside again. He smiled apologetically, indicating a chair.

'Do sit down. I'm sorry about that, Miss Kenning, but I'm sure you understand the difficulty?'

She wanted to say no, she didn't. Instead she nodded. 'Did you get the name of the person behind this Trident firm?'

'I did. And I'm sure there's no mystery about the payments. The monthly standing order in question was for wholesale supplies, as I thought. The payments must have been some sort of mutual business arrangement.'

'And the name of the proprietor?'

Mr Masters glanced at the note he had made on his pad. 'A Mr Edward Wilson. He has been a wholesaler in the town for many years. I daresay you've heard of him through your parents. What I would advise is that you get in touch with him direct. I'm sure you can sort out things between you.'

Carol's blood froze. Why had Jack been paying out money to Eddie Wilson? They didn't even trade with him any more. Yet now it seemed that Eddie had been draining her parents dry for years. He was the reason Eve was now so short of money she might have to sell the home she loved so much. He could even have been indirectly responsible for Jack's heart attack! Anger burned in Carol, making her cheeks flame. She stood up.

'I see. Thank you for your help, Mr Masters.'

'Not at all. If I can be of any further service, you only have to ask.'

She left the bank on trembling legs. Standing outside in the street, grateful for the cool air on her burning face, she took several deep breaths to steady her pounding heart. Then she made up her mind. Although she shrank from the idea, she would have to do as Mr Masters said – go and see Eddie herself; find out how and why he had been able to extract money from Jack.

'Carol! Well, what a surprise.' Eddie looked up as the typist from the outer office showed her in. 'Come in and sit yourself down. I was sorry to hear of poor Jack's passing.' He looked perfectly relaxed, sitting there in his swivel chair on the other side of his desk.

'I daresay you were.' Carol ignored his invitation. The sight of his smug smile sent a rush of adrenalin coursing through her veins, giving her the courage she needed. Her blue eyes blazed at him. 'Especially as it means you won't be getting any more monthly payments!' She rested her hands on the desk and stared into his face. 'What was the money for? Why was he paying you?'

Eddie affected an expression of pained surprise. 'Payments? The only money Jack Kenning ever paid me was for goods supplied. What else would he pay me for?'

'You tell me,' Carol challenged. Opening her bag, she held up the folder containing Jack's bank statements. 'Every month for the past four years he has been paying you a regular sum of money. A substantial one. You know as well as I do that you stopped supplying my parents when they moved from the Clarence Street shop. So what were these payments for?'

Eddie picked up a pencil and rolled it between his fingers. 'That's confidential. Between me and Jack. If he'd wanted you to know, he'd have told you.'

Carol was seething now. 'You were blackmailing him, weren't you? You told him what you told me, about our blood relationship.' Her voice was little more than a whisper. 'You threatened to tell me and he was paying you not to. And all the time – *all the time I already knew*!'

'That's pure fantasy.' Eddie shrugged his shoulders. 'You're just guessing.'

'And guessing right, I'd bet my life on it. You're a despicable little rat! You've been bleeding my father dry all this time. Don't you think it's bad enough for my mother, losing him, without finding out she's going to be short of money too?'

258

'Despicable little rat, am I?' Eddie was on his feet now, bristling with anger, his colourless eyes as cold and sharp as chips of ice. 'I'd like to remind you that Jack Kenning was *not* your father. *I* am.'

'No!' Carol shouted. She was trembling. 'You're no father of mine.'

Eddie shook his head. 'Ah, but I am, Carol. Ours is a tie that's impossible to break. There's no getting away from it. But if you really want me to keep out of your life, you'll keep your mouth shut about the money Jack paid me. If anyone's to blame it's Eve – keeping everything so secret all these years. If she'd come out into the open with it years ago there'd have been no mystery. As it is, I take it you wouldn't want her to know about this?' Carol's silence confirmed it. 'Right. Supplies are what he paid me for. All legitimate and above board.'

'So how do I explain the lack of invoices?'

Again he shrugged. 'How should I know? If Jack mislaid them that was his fault.'

'If I were to go to the police . . .'

His eyes narrowed dangerously. '*Go* to them if you think it'll get you anywhere!' he hissed. 'If you've got a nasty suspicious mind that's your problem. But you'd need to have concrete proof before you could get them to listen to you.' He leaned across the desk, his eyes glinting with pure malevolence. 'I'm warning you, Carol, don't get on the wrong side of me. You'll be sorry if you do. I've given you the chance to be a daughter to me and you've turned it down – don't want anything to do with me. Well, that's your choice. It won't be offered again.' His eyes bored into hers. 'There's a lot more you don't know. A lot you wouldn't *want* to know, believe me. So unless you want to open a can of worms – if you've got the sense to know what's good for you and Eve. Oh, yes, *especially* Eve – you'll leave well alone and keep your trap shut.'

The air almost crackled with tension as they stared at each other. Then Eddie walked to the door and opened it. 'Good morning, Carol. It was nice seeing you,' he said, loud enough for his typist to hear. As she passed through the door, he added, 'Oh, and please give my condolences to your poor mum, won't you?'

Sitting in the bus on her way home Carol's mind teemed with anger at Eddie's arrogance. She was sure she was right. He had been blackmailing Jack. And all for nothing. If only Jack had spoken to her. If only there was some way she could prove what Eddie had done. But she knew there wasn't. Besides, she couldn't upset Eve by bringing it all out into the open. Not yet anyway. After losing Jack it would be too traumatic for her and Eddie knew it. His later remarks troubled her though. It was his nature to be devious, to talk in riddles, but what had he meant when he'd said there was a lot more she didn't know – wouldn't *want* to know? It seemed it was all tied up with her mother somehow. Had Eve told her the whole truth about her birth? How many more secrets were there lurking in the past? Of one thing she was sure. There must be no more between Eve and herself. Telling her how Eddie had blackmailed Jack would be too painful, so close to Jack's death, but if they were to safeguard their future, mutual trust and honesty from now on were essential.

That evening she told Eve about Eddie's visit to the shop in Clarence Street and his revelation that he was her true father.

'He'd have done it out of spite and vindictiveness because we wouldn't sell the shop to him,' Eve said. 'He was hoping to make a lot of money, you see. He knew about the new development before anyone else. Probably got wind of it through someone in the know. We nearly let him swindle us. When he didn't get his way, he must have made up his mind to get even through you.'

Carol's mind was working fast. Eddie's greed had been satisfied after all. When his devious business methods failed, he got what he wanted through blackmail. Obviously he didn't care how low he stooped to get his way.

The implications of what Carol had just told her began to sink in for Eve. Now so many things were becoming clear. 'So – was that why you left home so suddenly?' she asked.

Carol nodded. 'In a way. I probably wouldn't have accepted Marty and Zelda's offer if it hadn't been for that. At the time I just wanted to get away. It was an awful shock, Mum. I suppose I blamed you a bit too, for not preparing me. I thought hearing that I was adopted was bad enough, but finding out I was Eddie Wilson's daughter was . . .' She broke off, shuddering. 'It devastated me. You know how much I've always hated him. I can't begin to tell you how it made me feel. It still does.'

'I'm sorry.' Eve sighed. 'I should have told you, love. But yours wasn't a straightforward adoption. Normally the child doesn't get to know who her real parents are. The natural parents never know where the child has been placed either. You can see the sense of it, can't you?' She sighed. 'I never told Jack Eddie was your real father. Maybe I should have, but something always held me back. You see, I wanted him to feel you were truly his. And I know he always did. He couldn't have loved you any more if you had been.'

'I doubt whether it would have made any difference between Dad and me,' Carol said ironically. 'But I do understand why you kept it from him. But, Mum . . .' She looked hard at her mother. 'If there's anything else I should know, perhaps this would be a good time to tell me about it now?'

'Anything else?' Eve felt her heart begin to race. 'What did Eddie tell you?' she asked fearfully. 'Apart from the fact that he was your natural father?'

'He said that you bullied Sally into giving me up,' Carol said. 'That you made her life a misery.'

Eve bit her lip. Was that really what Sally had told him, or had he been lying about that too? Who could tell with Eddie? 'If she felt like that then I'm sorry,' she said uneasily. 'She was all for letting me adopt you at first. It was a big relief – an easy way out for her – especially when she heard that her husband was lost at sea and she was about to become an unmarried mother. After you were born she began to feel differently, and then, when she heard her Dave was safe, she made up her mind. Decided to keep you, convinced that her husband would forgive her and accept you.' She frowned. 'At least, that's what she told me.'

'You didn't believe her?'

Eve shook her head. 'Then, I did. It scared me because I was losing you. That's when I tried to persuade her. If she saw it as bullying and it made her miserable, I'm sorry. But I wanted to keep you so badly, love. You meant everything to me. I'd done everything for you since birth and by then you were like my own child. But . . .' She broke off, biting her lip.

'Yes?' Carol leaned forward. 'There was something else?'

'Just that Eddie told me a long time after that that Sally'd had no intention of going back to her husband at all. He said she'd arranged to run away with him – and take you with her.'

'On the night she was killed?'

'Yes.'

'But she left me with you that night.'

'Yes, but not – not willingly. I – I made her. But even

then I didn't know she meant to go away for keeps. Because of the raid and because you had a cold, I – I persuaded her to leave you behind.' Her eyes met Carol's appealingly. 'And, Carol love – if I hadn't taken you from her . . .' Her hand went to her mouth, stifling the sob that stopped her from continuing. 'Oh my God . . .'

'I'd have been killed too.' Carol put her arms round Eve. 'It doesn't bear thinking about. Oh, Mum, don't get upset. Don't feel guilty. If you hadn't done what you did, I wouldn't be here now. I owe my whole life to you, I'll never forget that.'

Eve held her daughter close and shut her eyes tight, saying a silent prayer to herself. She couldn't tell her the whole truth and prayed to God Carol need never find out. If ever she did, it would not be of Eve's doing.

Jack had been dead only a month when Eddie rang one morning, asking Eve to visit him at his office. She wanted to refuse to go but he sounded so threatening she didn't dare defy him.

In his stuffy little office, seated opposite him, she learned with revulsion the reason why Jack had left her so badly off. Eddie explained it all so calmly and dispassionately he might have been reading from a stock sheet.

He had been to see Jack without Eve's knowledge and told him everything: that he was Carol's natural father and, worse, what he had witnessed that night on the old railway bridge when Sally had been killed. *Jack knew her terrible secret and had kept it to himself all this time*. Never said a word. Not only that, he had paid Eddie to keep quiet about it to Carol. It had cut Eve to the heart to know what he had done for them. She had been determined to keep it from him all these years, afraid that if he'd known Eddie was Carol's father the relationship that meant so much to him might have been soured.

Now she knew how much she had underestimated Jack, and how wrong she had been not to be open with him from the first.

Shocked and deeply wounded by Eddie's calm revelation, she railed at him. With tears pouring down her cheeks, she called him every name she could lay her tongue to. But she might as well have saved her breath. It was like so much water off a duck's back. He simply sat there, smiling at her. Eventually she discovered he had not invited her there simply to shock her with a summary of past events. Jack might be dead but Eddie had not done with the Kennings yet. His reason for asking her to visit him had been to demand yet more money. The monthly payments would be less of course, because even Eddie knew you couldn't get blood out of a stone, but nevertheless he insisted they be paid regularly if she wanted to keep the truth from Carol. Her poor devoted Jack had paid dearly – probably with his very life to save them from anguish – and she couldn't let his sacrifice count for nothing now. She hated herself for giving in to Eddie, but what choice did she have? He reminded her that even after all these years she could probably still go to prison for manslaughter at least. She shuddered, chilled to the marrow by the thought.

Now, holding Carol close, she prayed that God would forgive her. She *couldn't* tell it to her the way it really was. And the girl was right about one thing. She certainly wouldn't be here now if it hadn't been for that last desperate struggle on the bridge that terrible night. Surely that at least was in Eve's favour?

In the weeks that followed Carol worked hard alongside her mother at the shop. They sold the car and used the money to buy in extra stock and fancy goods for Christmas to attract the customers. The outstanding bills were paid off too and it began to look as if they would manage to keep afloat in spite of their insolvency. Eve even insisted on taking over the shop's books, pointing out that when Carol went away again she would have to do them. Then, on 22 November, came the shocking news of President Jack Kennedy's tragic assassination.

On the evening the news broke Carol and her mother were watching TV together, supper trays on their laps in front of the fire after a long day at the shop. The news seemed to floor Eve. Although it was happening to people outside her sphere and thousands of miles away she identified strongly with the suddenness and horror of the tragedy. It seemed to bring back all the trauma of Jack's death once again. The two men even had the same name and every time it was mentioned on TV or radio she would burst into inconsolable tears. Carol found it hard to cope with, coming on top of all her other recent traumas.

She found comfort in regular visits to Chine Way, relaxing in Kitty's warm, undemanding companionship. It was Christmas Concert time again and Carol jumped eagerly at the chance to occupy herself in helping with the preparations. Sitting in the basement kitchen, she and Kitty planned the programme together. But Kitty sensed a marked change in Carol since the happy days when she had been a favourite pupil. Stress and fatigue showed in the dark rings under her eyes, and where she had once been open and confiding she now kept her problems firmly to herself, hiding her sorrow under a new false brightness that seemed to put her frustratingly out of reach.

Kitty had heard through Zelda and Marty about Gareth Dean's offer and how Carol had been obliged to turn it down when her father died. She of all people knew that chances like that were few and far between. Being forced to turn it down must have meant so much to the girl. But Carol had never mentioned it to her so she had remained tactfully silent on the matter.

In the same week as Jack Kenning's death Kitty had been up to London to attend the wedding, but had kept quiet about this too. It had seemed inappropriate to speak of celebrations when Carol was recovering from a bereavement. Instead they worked hard together, planning the concert, making costumes and rehearsing, keeping their conversation safely unemotional.

It was three weeks before the concert when Kitty's electrician suddenly let her down. He had decided to move south with his family so as to be closer to his youngest daughter who had recently married. For Kitty it was a crisis. Good lighting was essential to the show and she didn't know where to look for another suitable electrician at such short notice.

When Mike heard about it through Carol, he volunteered to fill the gap.

'I'm only an amateur, of course,' he said modestly. 'But I'm pretty good with the old sparks if I do say so myself.'

During these traumatic weeks he had done his best to support Carol and she was grateful for it. She had had a dozen or more picture postcards from Steven while he was in New York; views of Times Square, Central Park, Broadway. They all had short, excited messages scribbled on the back, about visits to famous places, shows they had seen and people he and Freddie had met. There had been a short note of condolence after Jack's death, but since then nothing. Kitty had mentioned in passing that he and Freddie were working hard on the revisions to the show now that they were home again. The talk was all of financial backing and the choosing of a catchy new title, but Carol hadn't the heart to listen very attentively. She was well aware that the date for the wedding had come

266

and gone. Although she had not received an invitation she had sent a telegram on the day, addressed to the Bride and Groom. She knew that Kitty had attended, though she hadn't mentioned it once. Carol felt hurt, left out and slighted. So when Mike had asked her to help him move into his new flat, she had agreed willingly.

The flat consisted of two rooms, a bathroom and a tiny kitchen. It was all on one floor above a wine shop in Marefair and as it was unfurnished there were plenty of things to buy. Carol accompanied Mike to salerooms and furniture shops and found it enjoyable, helping him choose. He had little idea about colour schemes or soft furnishings and she found herself advising him on the purchase of fabrics and running up curtains for him on Eve's sewing machine.

Rose was busy with her own house move. Elizabeth and Harold had moved in temporarily with Harold's parents, and Rose and Ted had bought a bungalow on a newly built estate at Spinney Hill. Rose's entire topic of conversation was oil versus gas heating, stainless steel sinks as opposed to enamel, and the beautiful picture windows in the new lounge that were going to take simply *acres* of material to curtain.

Eve, on the other hand, was keeping quiet about her own plans to move from the house in Sunnyside Crescent into something smaller. Feeling unequal to facing the triumph in her sister's eyes when she heard that the modest affluence the Kennings had been so proud of was now over, she had shelved breaking the news until the new year. The bank manager had advised her to delay putting the house on the market till spring and for the moment Eve was content to go along with that.

In return for Carol's help with the flat, Mike gave over all his spare time to helping Kitty and her prepare for the concert. He proved to be talented and innovative when it came to stage lighting and Kitty was delighted with his work. The day of the concert arrived with all its attendant panic and nerves in the hours before curtain-up. It proved to be its usual success and when the big night was over and the weeks of frantic activity gave way to comparative leisure once more, Mike insisted on taking Carol out to dinner.

Although they had seen a lot of each other and worked together on the concert, they hadn't really talked since Jack's death. Knowing her as he did, Mike could see Carol's unhappiness in the shadows under her eyes and the sadness half hidden in her smile. He decided to try to get her to open up over the meal, feeling it was time she let her own grief out.

'It can't have been easy for you these past few weeks,' he said tentatively as he sensed her beginning to relax.

She gave him a wan smile. 'Poor Mum. It hit her very hard.'

'And you?' He reached across the table till his fingertips touched hers. 'What about you, Carol?'

She looked up at him in surprise. 'Me? I'm fine.'

'Forgive me, but you're very far from fine,' he contradicted. He paused before he went on, 'Carol – remember on Liz's wedding day, you started to tell me something about your agent calling you? Was it an offer?'

She shook her head, avoiding his eyes. 'Better not talk about it.'

'I don't agree. You've never told anyone, have you?'

She shrugged. 'What was the point? I couldn't take it anyway.'

'Was it important?' He pressed her fingers. 'Carol – tell me. You know you can trust me not to blab.'

She laid down her knife and fork and looked at him. 'Remember that audition I went to? A new play by Carl Gibson – another girl got the part?'

'I remember.'

'Well, the other girl backed out. Had a better offer. They came back to me. On the day Liz got married. The day that Dad . . .'

His fingers curled round hers and held them. 'Oh, Carol. I'm so sorry, darling. That must have been such a terrible sacrifice for you to make.'

She shook her head. 'There was no question of sacrifice. I had no choice. They needed me immediately, you see. I was just glad I hadn't told anyone about it.'

'Your father would have wanted you to take it. He'd have been so proud.'

'I know. But you saw how Mum was. How could I have left her in that state? He wouldn't have wanted that, would he?'

'The rest of the family would have rallied round. I know my mum and yours are always arguing, but when the chips are down there's no one closer.'

'All the same . . .' Carol broke off with a small impatient gesture, unwilling to continue the conversation.

'There'll be other chances,' he said. 'Talent like yours won't go to waste.'

She looked up at him, her eyes bleak. 'Mike, there are dozens of talented young actresses out there. Far more than there are jobs. And any one of them is as good if not better than me. I'll never get another chance like that.'

'You *will*, though. Just you wait and see.'

She smiled ruefully. 'As to that, I haven't much choice, have I?'

As they left the restaurant it was beginning to snow. He slipped an arm around her shoulders. 'Come back to the flat for a nightcap before I run you home. You haven't seen it since I moved in last week, have you?'

'No.' She smiled up at him. 'Okay, why not?'

The flat was reached by a side door to which Mike had

a key. They climbed the dark, uncarpeted staircase and he unlocked the door at the top and switched on the light to reveal a narrow hallway. The gold-coloured carpet Carol had helped him choose made it look warm and welcoming. Mike helped her off with her coat, flicking flakes of snow from her hair. 'You look like the snow princess,' he said.

'The flat's lovely,' she said, glancing round. 'The wallpaper goes even better with the carpet than I thought.'

'Wait till you see the living room.' He pushed open the door with a flourish. 'There – ta-raah!'

The brown leather Chesterfield and wing chairs they had bought at an auction were set off by a carpet in russet reds and yellows. The deep bay window that looked out on to the street below was curtained in copper-coloured velvet while the walls were painted a soft beige and adorned with some hunting prints Mike had found in a little art shop near the station. As he bent to switch on the electric fire, Carol exclaimed with delight.

'Wow! It looks great, Mike. A real bachelor pad. Very masculine.'

'Glad you like it.' He grinned. 'I must say, I'm enjoying my first taste of real freedom and independence. Should have broken away years ago, I suppose. If Mum had her way I'd be married by now with half a dozen kiddie-winks.'

'I don't know why you're not, Mike,' Carol said softly. 'Some girl's going to get a real prize.'

He took a step towards her, his eyes dark with yearning. 'Don't you really know why, Carol? I'll tell you, shall I?' He laid his hands lightly on her shoulders. 'It's because the only girl I've ever wanted isn't really interested.'

She looked into his eyes and suddenly realised how very

270

dear he was to her. If Mike married, something vital would go out of her life. Could she be in love with him? After all these years it was hard to tell where affection stopped and love took over. 'What makes you think she isn't interested, Mike?' she asked him softly.

'Carol?' His eyes widened in wonder as he drew her towards him. 'Oh, God, Carol. If I thought for even one moment that you . . .' Unable to resist the look in her eyes and her closeness any longer, he kissed her, gently at first and then more deeply, his arms closing round her, pressing her body close to his while his mouth hungrily devoured hers. She gave herself up to his kisses, winding her arms around his neck as their bodies pressed closer, cradling his head in both her hands, lacing her fingers into the thick hair at the base of his neck.

'There have been other girls,' he whispered against the corner of her mouth. 'I've tried to fall in love with someone else, but no one has ever made me feel as you do, Carol.' He looked down at her. 'There must have been others for you too – while you were away?'

'Yes,' she told him. 'There was someone – once.'

'You loved him?' His eyes searched hers. 'What happened?'

'He was – he married someone else.'

'So we're not talking about Kitty's son – Steven?'

Her heart gave a painful lurch at the mention of his name. 'It isn't important,' she whispered. 'It's over now, Mike, all of it. It doesn't matter any more. Not now.' She reached up and pulled his head down to hers again. The look of uncertainty and apprehension in his eyes hurt her. She didn't want to answer any more questions, to examine her own feelings too closely at that moment. She wanted to feel his mouth on hers again and his arms, strong and safe, around her. She needed to feel warm and wanted and loved.

When he began to unfasten the buttons of her dress she made no move to stop him. And when he lifted her in his arms and carried her across the hall she did not protest. In the bedroom she kicked off her shoes and stepped out of her dress. Their arms closed around each other and together they sank on to the bed.

He made love to her with infinite tenderness, bringing her to an unexpected climax that brought tears to her eyes. Together they lay in each other's arms, resting as their breathing slowed and their heartbeat settled. Mike raised his head to look at her.

'I'd given up hope of ever being here with you, like this,' he said. 'I want to stay here with you in my arms for ever. I never want to let you go.'

She smiled and kissed him. 'I'm sorry but I'll have to go, Mike. It's getting late.'

'Do you really have to? Can't you at least stay the night?'

'I can't. Since Dad died, Mum frets so if I'm late home.'

'Of course.' He sat up and raked a hand through his hair. 'I'm being selfish. I'll get dressed and take you.' He began to get up, then looked at her. 'Oh lord! I've just remembered. I promised you coffee.'

'Coffee?' She laughed. 'Next time, eh?'

'There'll be a next time?'

Kneeling up on the bed, she put her arms around him. 'Lots of next times, I hope, Mike.'

He kissed her. 'Oh, Carol. I'm so happy. I love you so much, darling.'

Outside the snow had settled and the world was white and sparkling as they drove the four miles out of town. The sky was clear and sprinkled with bright, frosty stars and the full moon made everything look crisp and pure and new. It was like an omen, Carol thought; a sign that from now on her life would change – for the better. She glanced at Mike and, sensing her eyes on him, he turned and smiled.

'Happy?'

She tucked her hand through his arm and snuggled against his shoulder. 'Very happy.'

As he stopped the car outside the house he turned to her again. 'I won't come in,' he said. 'It's late. Aunt Eve has probably gone to bed. Say hello to her for me, will you?'

'I will.' She began to get out of the car but he reached out a hand to stop her.

'Carol.'

'Yes, Mike?'

'Look, maybe this isn't the ideal time or place, but I can't go home – can't leave you without . . .'

'Without what?'

'Carol – will you marry me?'

The breath stopped in her throat and for a long moment she looked at him. 'Oh, Mike, I don't know what to say.' She reached out to touch his cheek. 'You're not just asking because of what happened tonight, are you? Because . . .'

He grasped the hand that touched his face and pressed his lips into the palm. 'You can't think that, surely? I've wanted to ask you for almost as long as I can remember. I've fantasised about the way it would be.' He smiled ruefully. 'And it was never like this: huddled in the car on a cold winter's night. But your answer is the only important part.' He looked into her eyes. 'If you want time to think about it, it's okay. I've know I've rushed you.'

She shook her head. 'No, Mike. I don't need time. I'll marry you, if you're really sure it's me you want?'

'*Sure?*' He pulled her close. 'There's nothing in the world I'm surer of. I've always loved you, Carol. I always

273

will.' He kissed her and held her close, his breath warm against her cheek. 'When shall we tell them?' he asked, his eyes gleaming with excitement.

She laughed a little unsteadily. 'Whenever you like. Christmas?'

'That's ten days away! I can't wait that long. Tell you what, we'll go and buy a ring tomorrow, then we'll get them all together and make our announcement. How's that?'

'Okay, fine, if you like.'

Eve was still up when Carol let herself into the house. She was dozing in front of the fire and looked up with a start when her daughter walked into the room.

'Hello, love.' She blinked. 'What time is it?'

'It's after one. I'm sorry I'm so late, Mum. I've been with Mike.'

Eve smiled. 'I know. I wasn't worried. I never do when you're with him. I know he'll take care of you.'

Making a sudden decision, Carol sat down opposite her mother. 'Mum – I've got something to tell you,' she said. 'It's supposed to be a secret until tomorrow, but you have a right to be the first to know. Mike has asked me to marry him. And I've said yes.'

Eve's eyes lit up with delight. '*Oh!* Oh, Carol, I'm so happy for you both,' she said. 'It's what I've always wanted – prayed for even.' She got up and put her arms round Carol. 'I know he'll make you happy. Your dad would have been so pleased. You'll make such a lovely couple.' Her eyes clouded for a moment. 'We always planned to give you a wedding to remember, but now that money is so tight . . .'

'Oh, Mum.' Carol stood up and hugged her mother tightly. 'You're not to worry about that. I don't want a big wedding and I'm sure Mike doesn't either. A simple register office ceremony will be fine.'

'Like your cousin had?' Eve looked aghast. 'Never! No daughter of mine is going to get wed in that hole and corner fashion. We don't want folks saying I didn't give my only girl a good send off, do we?'

Carol laughed at her mother's scandalised expression. 'All right, Mum. But there's plenty of time to think of all that. Let's sleep on it now, shall we?'

But Carol hardly slept at all that night. She told herself she was too excited to sleep. She was going to marry Mike. It meant saying goodbye to her dreams of success on the stage and settling down in a nice little home. She tried to assimilate this. There would be no more dashed hopes and shattered expectations. No sudden telephone calls, auditions and anxious, tremulous days of waiting. No opening night nerves. No applause. No soaring highs or plunging lows, From now on life would be safe and secure, serene and contented. A tiny traitorous voice whispered the word: *Dull?* But she thrust it angrily aside. Mike was a darling. He'd always been one of her dearest friends, hadn't he? Falling in love with him had been a natural progression. She enjoyed his kisses and the sweet sensual excitement of being held close in his arms and caressed. They had made love and she knew for certain that they could make each other happy. It was all going to be wonderful – *wonderful*.

But when the first pale rays of dawn lightened the sky and she fell into a restless sleep, the face of the shadowy figure who haunted her dream was not Mike's.

'Are you really sure that's the one you like?' Mike and Carol stood together outside the jeweller's shop in Bridge Street, studying the trays of rings in the window.

'I'm sure. I've always loved emeralds.'

He squeezed her hand. 'Right, let's go in and try it on then, shall we?'

275

Mike had been busy all morning making telephone calls. He'd invited his parents and grandparents, Eve, Elizabeth and Harold to dine with them and had booked a table at a restaurant for eight o'clock that evening, warning them to be prepared for a surprise. Carol had sworn her mother to secrecy, warning her to look suitably astonished when they made their announcement.

Inside the shop Carol took off her glove and tried on the square-cut emerald ring. It was a perfect fit. Mike smiled at her.

'You're sure you like it? Really sure?'

She nodded. 'It's beautiful.'

'Right.'

The ring paid for and nestling in its tiny box in Mike's pocket, they left the shop. 'I want to put it on for you this evening,' he said. 'At least that can be as I've always imagined, with all the family looking on.'

Carol wasn't so sure. It would be a bit of an ordeal but she was prepared to put up with it for Mike's sake.

The table was in a quiet, secluded corner of the restaurant as Mike had requested. They had arrived at the coffee stage when he stood up and cleared his throat.

'I just want to say how nice it is, being together, all of us like this,' he began. 'And if you've been wondering why I invited you all at such short notice, it's because I have something very important to tell you.' He smiled down at Carol seated next to him. 'It's probably no secret to any of you that Carol has always been special to me. Well, last night I asked her to marry me, and I'm delighted to tell you that she has accepted. We're engaged!'

The faces round the table wore a variety of expressions. Eve could not conceal her pleasure and her brother-in-law Ted shared her delight, as did Freda and Albert. Elizabeth, already heavy in the fifth month of her pregnancy and suffering agonies of indigestion, turned pink, eyes glittering with envy as they flickered over Carol's slender figure in her new green velvet dress. Rose, however, made no secret of her misgivings.

'Well, I just hope you know what you're taking on, Michael,' she said grimly.

An embarrassed Ted nudged her sharply in the ribs. '*Rose!*'

She glared at him. 'Never mind *Rose*. I'm his mum and I have to say what I think. What are you going to do with a wife who's always off somewhere acting on the stage?' she demanded. 'Acting love scenes and kissing any Tom, Dick or Harry? Taking her clothes off, likely as not, and flaunting herself!'

Michael frowned at her. 'Don't spoil it, Mother,' he warned. 'Things like that are our affair. It's for Carol and me to decide, not you.'

Rose bridled. 'That's as maybe, but I'm your mother, remember,' she said. 'It's me you'll come running to when it all goes wrong. Me who'll have the sleepless nights worrying about you.'

'Nothing's *going* to go wrong,' Eve said, her face white with anger. 'Michael and Carol are both sensible adults, and if I know my Carol she'll be giving up her acting now she's marrying Michael. They know what they're doing. And I for one think they'll make a lovely couple.' She rose to her feet and picked up her glass of wine. 'Here's to you both.' She raised her glass. 'A long and happy marriage, and God bless you.'

'Hear, hear!' Ted echoed, joining her. 'To Michael and Carol!'

The grandparents and Harold joined in. Then Elizabeth grudgingly hauled herself to her feet; lastly Rose, muttering under her breath.

It was hardly the celebration Mike had planned, but, determined not to be done out of his moment of glory, he pulled the jeweller's box from his pocket and opened it, taking out the ring. He slipped it on to Carol's finger. Kissing her cheek, he whispered in her ear, 'Now you're really mine.'

Eve took hold of Carol's hand to look at the ring. 'Oh, it's beautiful, love,' she said. Rose glanced at it and muttered something under her breath about wasting money, but Elizabeth took a long critical look and raised one eyebrow.

'Aren't emeralds supposed to bring bad luck?' she asked.

When Mike took Carol and Eve home, Eve asked him in for a last cup of coffee. Once indoors, though, she announced that she was off to bed.

'It's been a long day for me. I'm sure you young people will have a lot to discuss,' she said tactfully. 'So I'll leave you to it.'

Carol made coffee and they sat by the fire to drink it. 'You mustn't take any notice of Mum,' Mike said. 'Her heart's in the right place really. It's just that blunt manner of hers.' He looked at her. 'I don't really expect you to give up your career. You know that, don't you?'

Carol put down her cup. 'It seems to have given me up anyway,' she said wistfully.

'Shall we set a date for the wedding?' he asked. 'It can't be soon enough for me. And we've already got the flat and everything, haven't we? We can live there until we find the kind of house we want.'

Carol caught her breath. It was all she could do not to beg him to slow down. She felt as though she were being carried along on a flood tide.

'Let's talk about it tomorrow,' she said. 'Or maybe leave it till after Christmas. There's so much to think about at the moment.' She glanced at him. 'I haven't told you, Mike, but Dad left us a bit short of money.' She bit her lip. She was going to have to tell him about Eddie and the fact that he was her natural father at some stage, but didn't feel she could face it yet. 'It means that Mum will have to sell this house and move into something more economical. If I know her, she'll worry about giving me a nice wedding. Maybe we should wait until she's on her feet again?'

Mike looked appalled. 'But all that is so unimportant,' he said. 'I don't want a big wedding and I don't want to wait, Carol. I want you to be all mine as soon as possible.'

She kissed him. 'I know, but it isn't for long. It will mean such a lot to Mum, me being her only daughter, and with losing Dad and everything . . .' She smiled at him. 'The summer maybe?'

He looked dismayed. '*Summer?* That's ages! I was thinking more of January. February at the latest.'

She laughed. 'Mike! No one gets married that quickly. Even a simple wedding needs planning.'

He sighed and pulled her close. 'I suppose you're right. Thank God we've got the flat. At least we can be alone there whenever we want.'

Carol woke on Sunday morning to the sound of voices downstairs in the kitchen. One belonged to her mother, the other to Aunt Rose. It was with a feeling of foreboding that she slipped into her dressing gown and went to the top of the stairs to listen. The kitchen door was open and Rose's voice carried clearly up the stairs.

'Why didn't you tell Ted and me that Jack had left you poorly off?' she was saying. 'You know we would have helped all we could. Now – we've talked it all out and Ted agrees with me that it's the least we can do . . .'

'I've told you, *no!*' Eve's voice was shrill. 'If I can't pay for my own daughter's wedding it's a poor look out. They'll just have to wait a bit longer, that's all.'

'But why make them wait?' Rose insisted. 'I've been thinking about it and if you ask me, the sooner your Carol gets wed, the sooner she'll settle down and give up all these stage-struck ideas of hers. A home and babies are what she needs.'

'Well, y-es.'

Carol could hear her mother's resolve weakening.

Rose went on, 'It's all in the family, after all. We were done out of a proper wedding for our Elizabeth, so we're happy to spend the money on Michael's wedding instead. I can't see there's any problem. What is there to object to?'

Carol crept back to bed and pulled the covers over her head. She hadn't thought it necessary to ask Mike not to mention their financial crisis to his mother. He must have gone straight round and told her about it. Now that Aunt Rose could see a way to score over her sister she seemed to have forgotten all her objections to the marriage. The repercussions were starting already.

The Christmas concert had marked the end of the drama school term and Carol hadn't seen Kitty since. While she was Christmas shopping she had accidentally stumbled on the perfect gift for her: a little porcelain figure of a ballerina. It was already packed in its box and wrapped in Christmassy paper and the following Thursday, which was half-day closing at the shop, she decided to pay a visit to Chine Way. There was so much she had to tell Kitty. She badly needed someone impartial at whose feet she could lay her mounting apprehension about the future.

The snow had begun to thaw now, making the streets slushy and wet. But as she stood on the doorstep, waiting to be admitted, Carol looked out across the still, white expanse of The Meadow, sweeping away to where the leafless willows fringed the river. The snaking ribbon of water was a dull pewter colour, sluggish and bleak on this

280

grey winter afternoon. Carol stamped her numbed feet impatiently on the step. 'I hate this time of year,' she muttered to herself.

She was still looking out over the snow-clad meadow when the door was opened behind her. Expecting to see the freckled face of Gloria looking out at her, she turned.

'Hello, Glor . . .' The words froze on her lips and her heart turned a somersault as she found herself looking into Steven's smiling eyes. He laughed at the shocked expression on her face.

'Hi, Carrie! You look as though you've just seen a ghost! Come in out of the cold.' He reached out and took her arm, pulling her over the threshold. 'What a nice surprise,' he said as he closed the door. 'Kitty didn't mention you were coming?'

'No. I popped round on the off chance.' She held out the parcel she was carrying. 'I've brought her Christmas present.'

'And where's mine then?' Steven laughed at her crestfallen expression. 'Come on, Carrie – *joke*!'

She laughed obligingly.

'Look, Kitty's not here at the moment, but she'll be back soon. She's gone to the hairdresser's. But you'll come and have some tea while we wait for her – yes?'

'Well, I . . .'

He frowned. 'What up, Carrie? You're looking at me as though I'm some kind of dangerous animal escaped from the zoo.'

'Of course I'm not. I just didn't expect to see you, that's all.'

'Is it that much of a shock?' He grasped her arm and drew her towards the basement stairs. 'Come on, it's bloody freezing up here.'

The basement kitchen looked as cosy and untidy as ever. Kitty had decorated it with holly and paper chains and there was a Christmas tree standing in the corner near the back window, festooned with tinsel and sparkling with coloured lights. Carol smiled.

'It looks nice and Chrismassy.'

Steven nodded. 'Kitty's annual attack of tinselitis,' he said. 'Started when I was two and I'm afraid it looks as if it's incurable.' He took her coat. 'When Christmas comes around I'm sure she still sees me as twelve years old. I'm always expecting her to produce electric trains and football boots!'

Carol was looking round. 'Where's Clarissa?' she asked. 'Is she at the hairdresser's too?'

He frowned. 'Rissa? She's not here. Why do you ask?'

'Because, well, I thought . . .'

'Rissa is with Freddie. In London. They moved into a new flat last month. This will be the last Christmas they'll spend on their own, so they're making the most of it.'

'Clarissa and . . .' She was shaking her head. 'And *Freddie*?'

'Of course. You knew they were married?'

Carol swallowed hard and sat down suddenly. 'No.'

He looked puzzled. 'But you knew she was having a baby? She said she told you.'

'She *did*. She didn't say it was Freddie's, though.'

'So whose did you . . . ?' His face cleared and he struck his forehead with his palm. 'Oh, God! You thought that she and I . . . ?'

'Of *course* I did!' Carol's face was red with anger. 'She was your girlfriend, for God's sake, Steven! What was I supposed to think? She told me when we met that morning in the coffee bar that she was pregnant. She asked me how I thought *you* would take it? She even wanted me to break it to you! She said she was afraid it would disrupt your career just when things were going well. She never said *anything* about Freddie.'

282

'Oh, Carrie! Rissa and I hadn't been close, not in that way, for ages. She must have thought you knew.'

'How could I know when you didn't tell me? You've never told me anything about your life. I've never been that important to you,' she said bitterly.

'But you *have!*' He took her hands and pulled her to her feet. 'Of course you're important to me, Carrie.'

'You could have fooled me!'

'Surely it went without saying? With Rissa and Freddie it was a case of love at first sight. They fell for one another the moment they met,' he explained. 'And I was happy for them. As I told you, whatever Rissa and I had was over long before. I introduced her to Fred and the three of us became good mates. But when things got serious, Rissa was afraid that getting married to Fred and plunging him into parenthood might mess up our working relationship.'

'I see.' Carol was going over that conversation in the coffee bar in her mind. Clarissa had been harassed and in a tearing hurry that morning. It was easy now to see how the misunderstanding had arisen. Especially when Clarissa was under the impression that Steven had put Carol in the picture. Because of this her anger with him increased. 'And has it?' she asked him. 'Ruined your working relationship, I mean?'

'Heavens, no! Fred's keener than ever to make a success of things now that he's about to become a father!' He laughed. 'Look, let me make you some tea, then I'll tell you all our news. The play's finished. It's been a long hard grind, but Graham Lang has okayed the revisions at long last and we'll be ready to start casting early in the new year. We're hoping to go into rehearsal by March at the latest.'

Busying himself with the tea things he went on extolling Freddie's brilliance as a lyricist, explaining the changes they had made to the storyline, saying how much Clarissa had helped and supported them. But Carol scarcely heard. While he talked her mind was travelling back over the recent months; recalling the shocks and the anguish she had suffered, to all of which Steven seemed blissfully oblivious. Suddenly, unable to contain her impatience any longer, she said, 'I suppose you wouldn't like to hear *my* news?'

He stopped in mid-sentence, turning to look at her. 'Carrie! Of course I want to hear your news, darling.' He left the tea things and crossed the room to her. 'I'm sorry. I've been rattling on about myself. It's just that it's all so exciting. It's about all I can think of at the moment.'

'That much is obvious,' she said dryly.

'I'm a self-centred swine, aren't I?' He took both her hands. 'I haven't even said how sorry I was to hear about your father,' he said. 'I know how close you were. And to happen on your cousin's wedding day. It must have been awful for all of you?'

She nodded. 'It was devastating. But there were other shocks in store for us. Dad left hardly anything in the bank. Died owing money, in fact. It's been a struggle to pay off the debts, but we've just about done it now. We've sold the car and Mum has decided to sell the house in the new year.'

Steven looked stunned. 'That's terrible. I thought after the new shopping centre was built, your parents were secure?'

'They were, until Eddie Wilson got to Dad. I found out he'd been blackmailing him. Told Dad he was my real father and threatened to tell me.'

Steven frowned. 'But you *knew*!'

'Dad didn't know that, though. I was away from home at the time and I'd never mentioned Eddie's little heart-to-heart to either of them. You were the only person I told. Eddie took a gamble on that. And it paid off.'

'But blackmail is a criminal offence. You should go to the police!'

She shook her head. 'Then it would all come out. It would be in the papers and everyone would know he was my father.'

'So you're going to let him get away with it?'

'I've no choice, Steven. I haven't even told Mum. She'd be so hurt for Dad. And she'd blame herself for not telling him in the first place. She'd be angry too. So angry she'd probably insist on going to the police.'

He was shaking his head. 'My God! Poor Carrie, I had no idea.'

'Of course you hadn't. Why should you?' She found it impossible to keep the bitterness from her voice. 'There's something else too. On the day Dad died I'd been offered the part I auditioned for in Carl Gibson's play.'

'You turned it down?'

'What else could I do?' She sighed. 'Just lately everything in my life seems to have been beyond my control.'

'Oh, Carrie! Here, let me give you a hug.' He put his arms round her. 'What are you going to do? Look, why don't you come back to London with me after Christmas? I know a few people with serious clout now. I'm sure we could get your career off the ground again. There might even be something for you in our show.'

'If I ever get another job, I want it to be by my own efforts.' She stiffened, pushing him away impatiently. 'Anyway, everything's changed now, Steven. I'm not free any more. I have to stay here and help Mum see things through. There's something else too.' She turned away from him. 'I haven't told you all of it. I . . .' But before she could say any more the sound of high heels could be heard clattering down the basement stairs.

The next moment Kitty's voice called: 'I'm home, Stevie! Get that kettle on. I'm freezing!'

The kitchen door flew open and she stood there, bedecked with parcels and flamboyant in a fuchsia pink coat. Her cheeks were rosy and her hair aflame with newly applied colour.

'*Carol*! How lovely to see you, darling!' She dumped her parcels on the table and turned to Steven. 'Make me some tea, love. I'm gasping. I've bought chocolate eclairs, your favourites.' She turned to Carol. 'You are staying, aren't you?'

'I'd better not. I just called in to bring your present,' she said. 'I've been chatting with Steven and hadn't realised how fast the time had gone.' She made a show of looking at her watch. 'Heavens! I'd better be off.' She kissed Kitty and began to pull on her coat. 'I've put your present under the tree. I hope you like it.'

Kitty was rummaging among her many parcels. 'Hang on a minute. Yours is here. You'd better take it with you.' She held up a small square package. 'Here you are. Happy Christmas, darling.'

Steven hurriedly poured the already boiling water into the teapot. 'There you are. Tea's brewed,' he told his mother. 'I'll just run Carol home. Shan't be long.'

Outside it was getting dark as he led her round to the side of the house and opened the passenger door of his car. She saw that he'd exchanged the tatty old Austin for a smart new Vauxhall Cresta. When they were seated he turned to her.

'Look, why don't we go somewhere and finish our talk. The Clipper?'

She shook her head. 'There's nothing much left to say, Steven,' she said.

'You said there was something else. You were about to tell me when Kitty arrived.'

'It was just that – I'm engaged.'

He stared at her, eyes wide with shock. '*Engaged?* What – to be married, you mean?'

'Yes.'

'Anyone I know?'

'Michael Robson.'

'Your cousin?'

'Yes – except that he isn't.'

Steven was shaking his head. 'Look, I don't get this. You're marrying Michael Robson? You're chucking your career down the drain and settling here to be a small-town solicitor's wife?'

'That's slightly insulting, Steven.'

'I don't give a damn what it is! You're making a terrible mistake, Carrie. You can't go through with it.'

'I can. And I will!' She held her left hand under his nose. 'You haven't even noticed that I'm wearing his ring, have you? That's how observant you are, how much you care. All you can think about is your play, your London friends and your own success. Well, I have to think of *my* life and *my* future too.' She turned her head away to look out of the window.

'You're making a mistake, I tell you. You did it on the rebound, didn't you?'

'*Rebound?*' Her eyes blazed up at him. 'Thinking *you* were marrying someone else, you mean? Don't flatter yourself, Steven. I don't care what you do or whom you marry. You have no place in my life any more!' She made to get out of the car but he grasped her arm and held it firmly.

For a long moment he stared at her, his fingers still tightly gripping her arm. 'I meant on the rebound from having to turn down the play actually,' he said quietly.

'*Oh!*' She felt her cheeks colour and tugged at the arm he held. 'Steven – let go of my arm, will you? You're hurting.'

'Sorry.' He loosened his grip on her arm, patting it awkwardly.

'Look, there's no need for you to run me home. I can get the bus,' she said, controlling her voice with difficulty. 'Go back and have your tea now, Steven. Have a nice Christmas and – and I wish you every success with the play. You know that. We've said what we had to say. Too much probably. Now we'd better try and forget it.'

'Forget it! You drop a bombshell like that in my lap and then calmly tell me to forget it? I'm not letting you go like this!' Without another word he turned the ignition key and began to nose the car out through the gates. 'We need to talk,' he said grimly, his eyes on the road.

'No, we *don't*.' She looked at him. 'Look, Steven – your life and mine have always been poles apart. We've had different upbringings – different ideas about – about relationships and so on. Mine are probably more conventional than yours. And when it comes to values . . .' She shrugged helplessly. 'We don't even speak the same language. Nothing has changed. It never will.'

He gave an explosive little snort. 'You're talking in riddles.' He glanced at her. 'You really mean to marry him then?'

'Yes. Of course.'

'But why?'

'Why do you think?'

'You're in love with him?'

'Would I even dream of marrying him if I wasn't?'

'And the theatre – your career?'

She smiled ruefully. 'Maybe I've never had quite the same outlook on that as you have, Steven,' she told him. 'It was something I wanted very badly once. Part of me still does. But to me, people, family, have to come first. That's just the way I am.' She blushed and bit her lip, aware of how sanctimonious and self-righteous she must sound.

He didn't reply and the rest of the drive was made in silence. A silence heavy with their unspoken thoughts. When he pulled up in Sunnyside Crescent he turned to her and in the dusky light she saw with surprise that his eyes were ablaze with anger.

'As long as you're hell-bent on going ahead with this – this self-destruction thing, Carrie, you might as well hear what I think.'

'No.' She reached for the door handle. 'I don't think I want . . .'

'Well, that's too bad because you're bloody well going to!' Reaching across, he grabbed her hand and held it. 'It's time to grow up, Carrie,' he said, his face close to hers. 'Time to face what and who you are. You should have done it a long time ago.'

Her heart began to beat faster. 'What are you *saying*?'

'You blamed your mother for not telling you you were adopted sooner, but you're equally guilty. You blamed the Wilson man for shaming you with the fact that he is your true father, then you tried to bury your head in the sand in the hope that the truth would go away.' He took her shoulders and forced her round to face him. 'Can't you see that much of this is your fault, Carrie? If you'd stayed on and told your parents about Eddie's visit, the three of you could have decided what to do about it. You'd have been in a stronger position. Then the wretched man would have been powerless to hurt you or your family.'

She shook her head, tears stinging her eyes. 'You're saying it's *my* fault that Eddie blackmailed Dad? How can you be so cruel? I seem to remember you telling me to forget Eddie!'

'Only because you obviously weren't going to accept the truth. I'm saying this because I care about you, Carrie. I care about the mess you're making of things. I want you to throw off these self-imposed shackles you're making for yourself and grow into a whole person.'

'I don't have to listen to any more of this.'

But he held her fast, his fingers bruising her shoulders even through her thick coat. 'Can't you see, Carrie? Your whole life has been a series of half-truths. A lot of it isn't your fault, but some of it is. Now you've arrived at a watershed. It's time to look life in the face and come to terms with it before you run into another disaster. Okay, so you're Eddie Wilson's daughter. So *what*? What matters is that you're *you* – Carol Kenning. You're whatever you want. Whatever you decide to be. What do a few genes matter?'

As she looked at him his face was a blur. Tears blinding her, she lashed out at him, 'I can't *believe* how arrogant you are, Steven. You're trying to tell me to kill dragons again. Well, it's just not that simple any more.' She shook her head at him. 'You really don't have a clue about me, how I feel or what I want. How can you know what I've been through? Telling me I'm probably responsible for what's happened isn't helping one bit! So why don't you go back to your friends and your marvellous new, successful life and just forget me? Why should you give a damn what kind of a mess I make of my life?'

He stared down at her. The anger suddenly dissolved from his eyes and in the growing darkness they were almost luminous. 'Oh, Carrie, do you really need to ask me that?'

She pushed his hands away. 'You think you can say what you like – *hurt* all you like and then pretend it's all for my own good – that you care about me. Well, you can't!' She fumbled with the car door. 'Goodbye, Steven.'

'Goodbye sounds very final,' he said. 'I hope we'll still see each other from time to time?'

She hesitated, suddenly afraid. 'Who knows?'

Suddenly he reached out and pulled her to him roughly. His mouth on hers took her breath away and sent her senses reeling. She closed her eyes, sure that even through her thick winter coat he must be able to feel her heart pounding. 'Oh, Carrie, you know I don't want to hurt you,' he whispered against her hair. His lips lingered tenderly on hers and his cheek was warm and slightly rough. The scent of his skin and the stuff he used on his hair was so nostalgically familiar that it made her heart ache painfully. Feeling her throat tighten, she pulled away from him.

'I – I'd better go now.'

He looked down at her, his eyes dark with something she couldn't interpret. 'Carrie, you're really going to marry him? You know what you're doing? You're sure it's what you want?'

'I've never been surer of anything.'

Gently he released her. 'Nothing more to be said then, is there? Goodbye. Take care of yourself. Be happy, Carrie.'

For a long moment his eyes held hers, then she got out of the car and hurried along the pavement, resisting the powerful urge to look back until she reached the gate. When she turned he was still sitting there, watching her through the windscreen. As she looked he half raised his hand. She did not return his wave but turned away and ran up the path, brushing away the tears that streamed down her cheeks with her gloved hand.

His last words, *Nothing more to be said*, taunted her. If he had only said the one thing she longed to hear she would have given up everything for him. Regardless of whom she hurt or let down she would have gone with him – anywhere in the world; done anything he asked, no matter how unreasonable or impossible.

So, she told herself firmly, it was just as well he hadn't said he loved her, wasn't it?

291

Chapter Nine

The wedding date was set for 14 May. Mainly because Elizabeth's baby was due at the beginning of April and Rose had decided that Elizabeth was to be Carol's matron of honour.

Christmas had been a melancholy affair. Carol had been deeply disturbed by Steven's outburst. Lying in the dark night after night she went over and over their conversation in her mind. What hurt most was that deep inside she recognised the truth in what he had said. She had done wrong by not facing up to Eddie's revelation; by not sharing it with her parents. Lingering at the back of her mind was the terrible guilt that it was her fault that Jack had suffered the unnecessary torment of blackmail at Eddie's hands; that it could have brought about the heart attack that killed him. She longed to do something about it, but revenge seemed a very negative option. Nothing would bring Jack back to them, just as nothing would return the money he had needlessly parted with to save her from pain.

Carol and Eve had spent Christmas at Freda's with the rest of the family. But although Eve tried hard to put a brave face on things, she was missing Jack badly and close to tears for much of the time as she remembered past holidays they had shared. Elizabeth, who had just received the news that she was expecting twins, heaved her enormous bulk resentfully from room to room, clutching her back and complaining vociferously. In spite of Michael's good-humoured presence, Carol was glad when it was over and they had returned to their normal routine.

But the moment they embarked upon 1964 Rose began her campaign, organising the coming wedding with the determined single-mindedness of a general planning a military offensive. First it was the venue for the reception. She could not make up her mind between hiring the church hall and engaging a caterer, or handing everything over to a hotel or restaurant. Eve's suggestion that they might do the catering between them was pushed brusquely aside and when Carol tried to intervene she was told to: 'Leave everything to me. All you have to do is pick out what you're going to wear, dear. And don't forget that Uncle Ted and I are paying for everything.'

Carol didn't know whether this was meant as a warning not to spend too much or *carte blanche*. But she soon discovered that in spite of what she said, Rose expected to have the last say even in this. She arbitrarily rejected the smooth ivory brocade sheath that Carol favoured, dismissing it as 'too plain'. Her own choice was a ballerina-length confection with a beaded bodice, puffed sleeves and a skirt made up of layers of spangled tulle, which she purchased before anyone could argue with her over it.

Predictably, it triggered the inevitable row between Eve and her sister, which had been simmering like a volcano for weeks.

'You told her to choose the dress she liked,' Eve protested. 'A girl as slim and dainty as Carol can carry off something plain and elegant. She doesn't need all those flounces. That thing looks more like a tea cosy than a dress! And as for the head-dress . . .' Eve picked up the heavy wreath of silk roses chosen by her sister. 'She's not tall enough for a thing like this. She's going to look like a *mushroom* in it!' she said. 'Why can't you let her have that charming little lily-of-the-valley circlet she likes?'

The next upset was over who should give Carol away. When Eve expressed the wish to do this herself, Rose was appalled.

'Oh, *no*! It wouldn't look right at all, a woman taking the bride down the aisle,' she said. 'Ted is the obvious person for that.'

Eve's mouth tightened. 'Am I to have no part at all in my own daughter's wedding?' she demanded.

'It's our son's wedding too, remember,' Rose reminded her. 'And we *are* standing the cost of it after all.'

'That was your suggestion,' Eve said stiffly. 'It was never what I wanted. And if you ask me, I don't think Carol and Michael want all this fuss either.'

Rose bristled. Drawing herself up to her full height, which was two inches taller than Eve, she glowered down at her sister. 'Well, pardon *me*, I'm sure!' she said. 'I was under the impression everyone was happy with the arrangement. Are you telling me that you'd have let your girl get married in a register office if Jack had been alive?'

'If she really hadn't wanted a church wedding, yes,' Eve told her. 'Anyway, I'm surprised you're so against register offices. You didn't seem to mind your Elizabeth getting wed in one.'

This was a sore point and Rose coloured angrily. 'If Jack hadn't squandered all your money, you could have afforded to give the girl a proper send off yourself,' she said spitefully.

Eve's colour drained and she stood staring at Rose, hands clenched into fists at her sides. 'My Jack never *squandered* anything in his life,' she said, white with fury. 'It wasn't his fault he lost our money. I don't know how you can say such a hurtful thing to me. It'll be a long time before I forget that remark, Rose.'

Her sister, knowing she had overstepped the mark, was immediately defensive. 'Oh, come *on*, there's no need to be like that. You know what I mean.'

'Oh, yes. I know what you mean all right!' Eve was pulling on her coat. 'Just you get on with whatever you want to do,' she said. 'But don't expect any cooperation from me. I shall ask Carol who she wants to give her away. I hope you'll at least give her the chance to choose *that*. She's had no say in anything else, poor girl.' And with that parting shot she strode out of Rose's house and slammed the front door.

At the beginning of February Carol escaped gratefully to spend a day in London with Janet who had been on duty in Casualty all over the Christmas break. She was off for a much-deserved winter sports holiday in Switzerland with Geoffrey and rang to ask Carol to go up for the day and help her choose some skiing gear and holiday clothes.

They met at Oxford Circus Underground station and hugged each other warmly.

'Great to see you!' Janet enthused. 'Coffee first. I want to hear all your news – everything! You could have knocked me down with the proverbial feather when I heard you and Mike were getting hitched!'

They sat in a corner of Dickens and Jones's coffee shop and Janet described the horrors of spending the holiday in Casualty at St Gregory's.

'Everything from street brawls to some silly woman who scalded herself with fat from the turkey! Still, over now. Three whole weeks off to look forward to,' she said, stretching her arms above her head. 'Just Geoff and me and the mountains. *Bliss*! I can't wait!' She peered at Carol. 'Okay, it's your turn. I've seen the ring, now I want to hear all, including the spicy bits. You say that Mike has his own flat, so I take it you and he have been sampling the joys of sex?'

Carol laughed. 'Do ask, won't you? Be my guest!'

Janet leaned forward, unrepentant. 'Well, what's wrong with it anyway? This is the sixties. It's as well to find out if you're compatible in every sense. I take it you are?'

Carol shrugged noncommittally. 'I suspect it's like a lot of other things – takes time to become skilful.'

'Oh, Gawd!' Janet pulled a face. 'You make it sound like shorthand typing or something! I know he's not your first lover, and from what I gather Quinn must have taught you the basics at least.'

'His name was *Finn*, not Quinn! Everything between Mike and me is fine, thanks,' Carol said. 'Sex included.'

Janet pulled a face. 'Come on, this is *me*, Carol. Your oldest friend. The one you used to confide in. Remember?'

'There's nothing to confide, Jan. We've been to bed together, yes. And everything is fine.'

'Okay, okay.' Janet selected a biscuit and bit into it, eyeing her friend thoughtfully. 'So – what about Steven Manson? Where does he fit into the picture these days?'

'What picture?' Carol felt her colour rise in spite of herself. 'It has nothing to do with him.'

'I see. Do I take it he's married to that Melissa person now then?'

'*Clarissa!*' Carol corrected, smiling in spite of herself. 'You do it on purpose, don't you? You know damned well what her name is!'

Janet's face crinkled into an impish grin. 'Well, at least it brought a smile to your face, didn't it? Are they though – married, I mean?'

'As a matter of fact, Clarissa has married Steven's partner and they're expecting a baby very soon.'

'Wow!' Janet's eyes opened wide. 'How did he take that?'

'Apparently he's delighted.'

'And does he know – about you and Mike, I mean?'

'Of course.'

'And was he as delighted about that?'

'I haven't a clue.' Carol sighed. 'Look, Jan, can we talk about something else? I'm sick and tired of wedding talk. My Aunt Rose has hijacked the whole affair. She's even picked out the dress for me. It's covered in frills and sparkly bits and I look as though I've fallen off a Christmas tree in it. She and Mum have got to the spitting stage, and to be honest I'll be glad when it's all over.'

To her relief, Janet dropped the subject and the atmosphere lightened. They enjoyed the rest of their day, shopping, giggling and reminiscing as though they were schoolgirls again. Janet needed her passport renewing and while she was busy with that Carol slipped in to say hello to Marty and Zelda, arranging to meet Janet for tea at a coffee bar in Charing Cross Road.

Climbing the three flights of steep, dusty stairs that led to the small suite of offices her agents occupied she felt a wave of regret and nostalgia for all the hope and excitement she was leaving behind. Both the Warings were in good form and delighted to see her.

'I can't believe you're ditching your career for this Michael person,' Zelda told her. 'You are sure you're not jumping into marriage too quickly, aren't you, darling? I mean – a *solicitor*!' She wrinkled her nose. 'Have you really got enough in common? Things have been looking up a bit lately. I know I could get you plenty of telly commercial work. Might not be exactly what you want, but it does get you seen, you know. It would get you back in circulation again.'

Marty laid a hand on his wife's arm. 'Zelda, the girl's head over heels in love. Can't you remember what it's like? Maybe after a few months,' he said with an indulgent smile. 'After the honeymoon. At the moment the only production she can think about is her wedding.' He patted Carol's arm benignly. 'Aren't I right, sweetie?'

Carol gave him a wan smile. 'It's certainly true that there's a lot to think about, Marty. But Mike has never said he wants me to give up acting. I'll let you know when I'm ready to think about a job again.'

'I saw Gareth Dean at the opening night of *Dance With Angels* down in Brighton,' Zelda went on, giving her husband a scathing look. 'He asked about you. He was genuinely sorry you had to turn down the Carl Gibson play, you know. The opening was a big success, by the way, and it's had super notices since.' She rummaged in the drawer of her desk. 'I've got a copy of *The Stage* here. You can read all about it on your way home. It comes into the West End next month.'

Carol took the paper from her with a sharp pang of regret. She was beginning to wish she hadn't come. 'It really hurt to have to give it up,' she said. 'But it couldn't be helped. Mum needed me.'

Janet went to Euston with Carol when it was time for her train. As they stood on the platform together she said suddenly, 'Hey, listen, take care of yourself. And don't let your aunt walk all over you. And Carol . . .'

'Yes?' She looked into her friend's eyes and saw that they held a look of genuine concern. 'Don't take this the wrong way, love, but are you really sure Mike's the right one for you?'

Just for a moment Carol almost gave in to the urge to break down and tell Janet about her row with Steven and the agony of doubt it had triggered. She took a deep breath and stopped herself. Telling someone else of her misgivings, voicing her thoughts, would force her to listen to them herself and she was keeping her mind firmly shut against that possibility.

'Mike is wonderful,' she said truthfully. 'Any girl would be lucky to get him. He makes me laugh and he's kind and strong. I'm sure he'll make me happy.'

'Yes, but do you *love* him?' Janet was looking closely at her. 'And will you be able to make *him* happy? Because unless you love him, you won't. And that wouldn't be fair to either of you.' She grinned and hugged Carol. 'Hey – listen to me? Never thought you'd catch me giving advice like some whiskery old agony aunt, did you? Tell me to shut up if you like. It's just that I want you to be as happy as I am with Geoff. You see, when it's right there can be no doubt, and frankly – well, you just haven't got that *glow*.'

The guard began slamming doors and Carol climbed quickly on to the train. 'Have a lovely holiday, Jan,' she said. 'It's been super seeing you. Love to Geoff.' She reached out to grasp Janet's hand. 'Bless you for being worried about me. But there's no need – really.' The guard blew his whistle and the train began to move. 'I'm happy,' she called from the window. 'Just tired of all the fuss, that's all. See you at the wedding!'

Janet stood on the platform, watching as the train gathered speed, carrying her friend away, a frown creasing her brow. '*Will* you, Carol?' she asked silently. 'I wonder.'

As the train pulled out of the station Carol pulled the folded copy of *The Stage* from her bag and turned to the review page. Zelda had been right. *Dance With Angels* had received glowing notices. In one, attention was drawn to 'promising young newcomer Phillida Jackson, whose spirited portrayal of the gamine Daisy was a delight. I predict that we shall be seeing much more of this talented young actress'.

Carol folded the paper and stuffed it back into her bag.

Would she have drawn rave notices if she had played the part? she wondered. Would *Dance With Angels* have been the big break she'd been looking for? Would it have set her on the road to a successful career – fame, maybe? Well, now she would never know. Inside her heart felt like lead, the grinding disappointment of the chance she had lost almost a physical pain.

As she stared out of the train window Carol's mind turned to Janet's remarks about her future marriage to Mike. In her mind he and Steven always stood side by side, making it impossible not to compare them. They could hardly have been more dissimilar. She pictured Mike, broad-shouldered and well-built, always immaculately turned out in his white shirts and dark business suits, his hair neatly groomed. Then Steven, tall and rangy in his jeans, casual sweaters and leather jackets. She visualised the expressive 'musician's' hands with their strong palms and long sensitive fingers, and that floppy hair, permanently in need of cutting. But the differences between them amounted to more than just appearance. Mike's mind was clear and logical, a single-track 'legal' mind that neatly compartmentalised life, seeing it in terms of black and white, whereas Steven had the eclectic mind of an artist. Original, imaginative and creative. Some people would call him thoughtless, even selfish, obsessional about his art. But she knew there was more to him than that. He was intrinsically kind and caring. She remembered how, as a teenager, he had steered her tenderly through a difficult phase of her childhood; helped her see a point of view other than her own; comforted and encouraged her. Steven had always been there; almost as much a part of her life as her parents.

Leaning back in her seat, her eyes closed, she had a sudden tantalising vision of that quick smile of his; the way it lifted the corners of his long, mobile mouth and lit up his eyes. How it brought into play the dimple in his left cheek and exposed the tooth that was slightly out of line. The memory pierced her heart like an arrow, and her view of the rushing landscape suddenly swam and danced, blurred by tears.

Mike was waiting to meet her at the station. Even before the train stopped she saw him, standing on the platform eagerly scanning the faces of the passengers for the first glimpse of her. As she stepped down he was waiting, his eyes shining a welcome.

'I've got a meal ready for you at the flat,' he told her, pulling her arm through his. 'You must be cold. Come on. Soon be there.'

The flat was only a short walk from the station and they were there in minutes. Mike had the fire alight and a casserole warming in the oven. When they had eaten he led her to the settee and knelt to slip her shoes off, rubbing her chilled feet. Then he took her in his arms and kissed her.

'I've missed you,' he said.

Carol laughed. 'I've only been gone for the day.'

'I didn't mean that.' He settled himself comfortably beside her and put his arm around her, pulling her close with a sigh. 'We never seem to get any time to ourselves lately. I wish Mum would stop making all this fuss about the wedding. What I'd really like would be for the two of us to slip off somewhere and get married on the quiet.'

'It would be nice to have it all behind us.'

He looked at her, taking her words as encouragement. 'It's not impossible, you know. We could do it. I could get a special licence and we could be out of it all before you could say confetti!'

'We couldn't do that, Mike!'

'Why not? I'm serious. Just think, a week from now we

301

could be an old married couple. Mr and Mrs Robson. What do you think?'

Carol shifted uneasily. At least with another three months between now and the wedding she didn't have to worry about its rapid approach.

'You couldn't do it to your mother, Mike,' she said. 'She's enjoying herself – looking forward to it so much.'

He pulled a wry face. 'If she is, she's the only one. Ask your mother's opinion on that! Besides, I wouldn't mind betting that once Liz's little monsters arrive, the wedding will take second place in her thoughts. She'd probably even thank us.'

Carol was still trying to think of another reason not to elope when he cupped her face in both hands and kissed her hungrily. 'Oh, Carol, *Carol*! You don't know how far off May seems to me. I want us to be together *now*!' He looked at her. 'I shan't believe you're really mine till I've got that marriage certificate in my hand.' He looked at her, eyes burning with desire. 'Stay here with me tonight? Ring your mother and say you won't be home.'

'Mike, I can't.'

'Can't?' His eyes were clouded as they searched hers. 'Or don't want to? You've been – I don't know, a bit distant lately. You're not regretting anything, are you?'

'Of course not,' she said without conviction. She knew he was right. And she knew that her unsettled feelings dated back to her meeting with Steven just before Christmas. But she wouldn't let it spoil things for her, she told herself fiercely. She *did* love Mike. Everything would come right. It *had* to. The heaviness that was weighing her down was due to the fuss over the wedding and the constant squabbling between Aunt Rose and her mother. Mike was right, escaping to a runaway marriage would be the obvious answer. Surely once they were married everything would be all right? And yet . . .

'You don't sound very sure.' He was looking at her anxiously and she felt a sudden rush of affection and remorse.

'Oh, *Mike*!' She put her arms around his neck and drew down his head to hers. 'I'm sorry if I've seemed vague and offhand. What with the dress and the reception, Mum and Aunt Rose rowing, working hard at the shop and everything else . . .'

'I know, darling. You're tired and harassed. All brides go through it, I'm told. I shouldn't have said anything. It's just that I have to know that you're really, truly sure about me?'

Carol hid her face against his neck, afraid of what he might see in her eyes. Afraid that her own doubt would show on her face. It was something she was going to have to resolve by herself. She was so lucky to have someone like Mike in love with her. She would *make* it work.

'I'll stay,' she told him decisively.

'You *will*?'

'Yes. I really want to, Mike, honestly. It's just . . . I'll ring Mum now.'

'What will you say?' His eyes were shining with happiness.

'I'll tell her the truth. After all, we are engaged. What does it matter?'

'Will she mind?'

Carol shook her head. 'Most couples sleep together before the wedding day, if they're honest. I prefer to be truthful than lie about it.' She looked at him. 'And speaking of truth, Mike, there's something I have to talk to you about before we get married. This might be a good time.'

She explained to Eve almost brusquely on the telephone the reason why she wouldn't be home that night.

'You're saying that you're staying with Mike? At the

flat? For the *night*?' Her mother's voice at the other end of the line sounded shocked and worried.

'Yes, Mum. There's no need to sound so upset. We'll be married soon anyway.'

'I know, but all the same . . . Listen – Carol, you do know what you're doing? I mean, I don't want you to . . .'

'Get pregnant?'

'*Carol*!'

'Well, it's what you're really saying, isn't it? There's no need to worry, Mum. Mike will take care of it. Goodnight. I'll see you at the shop in the morning.' She rang off before Eve could say anything else.

She let him undress her, trembling slightly as he reverently kissed every inch of her. She held him close as they made love, giving herself up to the sensual pleasure, trying not to think of anything beyond the reassurance her response would give him. Afterwards as they lay in each other's arms, she tried to take pleasure from his happiness, wishing with all her heart that she could share it, filled with guilt that her own satisfaction was based on sensuality alone.

Mike kissed her. 'I love you,' he whispered against the corner of her mouth. 'I just can't get over the fact that we're going to be married. I'm so afraid I'll wake up and find it's all a dream. I suppose that's partly why I want to whisk you off as soon as possible. I love you so much, Carol.'

She knew he was waiting for her response and paused a fraction too long. 'I love you too,' she murmured. 'Mike.' She turned her head on the pillow. 'Listen, there's something you don't know about me . . .'

He looked at her, eyes dark with the joy of possession. 'I know everything I'll ever want to know about you.'

'But there's something I have to tell you,' she said. 'Please listen, Mike. I *need* to tell you.'

'Heavens! You sound so solemn.' He smiled. 'Let me

304

guess? You robbed a bank when you were in London today and the police are surrounding the building even as we speak!'

'Please, Mike. It's serious. You know, of course, that Mum adopted me? That my real mother was a girl who was billeted on her during the war?'

'Yes, I know all that.'

'Well – it was only a few years ago that I found out who my real father was.'

He raised his head to look at her. 'And?'

'It was a man called Eddie Wilson. He's a grocery wholesaler. Mum and Dad used to deal with him when they had the other shop.'

'So?'

'He's not a very nice person, Mike. Not the kind of father anyone would be proud of. He's shady and underhand, probably sails pretty close to the wind when it comes to business.'

'But he was only your biological father, wasn't he? I mean, he had nothing to do with your upbringing.'

'That's true. But all through my life he's been there, a shadow in the background. I'd always disliked him intensely, so you can guess what a blow it was to find out he was my father.'

'I see.'

'There are complications too. Mum never told Dad that Eddie was my father because she thought it might upset him and cause problems. Eddie tried to buy the Clarence Street shop and when they wouldn't sell it, he cornered me in the shop one day when Mum and Dad were away and told me he was my father. He did it to spite them. I went away without telling them about it.'

'I don't blame you,' Mike said. 'Why let him think he'd scored?'

'But I should have! After Dad died I found out that he

305

knew all along, and had been paying Eddie to stop him from telling me.'

Mike sat up. 'God! You mean the little creep had been blackmailing him? So that's why your mother is so strapped for cash?'

'Yes.'

'But that's a criminal offence! A serious one. You should go to the police at once.'

'I can't. Mum doesn't know about it. I couldn't expose her to all the publicity. There's nothing more Eddie can do to hurt us now, thank goodness. There are no more secrets he can tell, so with luck he'll leave us alone from now on. I just wanted you to know about it, in case – well, in case it made any difference.'

He drew her close. 'As if it could! Nothing could ever change the way I feel about you, Carol. I'll make up to you for all you've been through, I promise.'

When Carol arrived at the shop the following morning Eve was quiet. She obviously disapproved of Carol's staying overnight with Mike, but was determined not to be the first to mention it. Halfway through the morning, unable to bear the long silences any longer, Carol said, 'Mum, what's wrong?'

Eve sniffed. 'I'd have thought *that* was obvious.'

'You're upset because I spent the night at Mike's flat? I'm sorry, but in a few months from now we'll be married so what difference does it make?'

'In my day it made a lot of difference. We waited till we'd got that marriage certificate,' Eve said. 'There's many a slip, you know. Besides, what do you think Rose would say?'

Carol laughed. 'Aunt Rose? Mum, Mike is almost twenty-six! He's a professional man with a life and a home of his own. It's really none of her business.'

'Huh!' Eve's eyebrows rose sceptically. 'Try telling *her* that!' She touched Carol's shoulder. 'You know how pleased I am that you and Michael are getting married. It's been a secret dream of mine for years. He's a lovely man and I'm very fond of him. But I worry that if you're too free with your – your affections now, his opinion of you will lessen.'

'He'll stop respecting me, you mean?'

'Well – yes.'

Carol hid a smile. 'Oh, Mum, all that is a bit Victorian, isn't it? It's the sort of stuff they used to put in magazine agony columns to deter young girls from risking pregnancy. There are other ways nowadays. Besides, I think Mike and I know each other far too well for that.'

Eve sighed. 'You young people nowadays, you think you know it all. But human nature doesn't alter, I don't care what anyone says. Well, I've said what I think. It's up to you. But remember what I said about your Aunt Rose,' she warned. 'She's bad enough now. Don't want to give her anything else to start going on about, do we?'

It was time for Carol's lunch break when Eve suddenly remembered something. Opening her handbag, she took out an envelope. 'I almost forgot,' she said. 'This came for you yesterday after you'd left for London. I thought it might be important so I brought it with me.'

Carol didn't recognise the handwriting, but the envelope bore a London postmark. She tore it open and glanced quickly at the signature. To her surprise she saw that it was from Clarissa.

My dear Carol

Steven doesn't know I'm writing this but I felt I must drop you a line because he has told me about your meeting at Christmas and the misapprehension you were under about us. He's very upset about it and I know that if it weren't for that stubborn pride of his he would be writing to you himself. I realise that I am largely to blame for the misunderstanding between you. Looking back, it was entirely understandable and I hope you can forgive me for not making things clearer.

I'm was so sorry to hear about your father, Carol. It must have been a terrible blow for you. Sorry too about the job you had to turn down. It must have been a great sacrifice.

I hope you didn't mind our not inviting you to the wedding? It was a very quiet affair, with only a couple of witnesses, but it would be lovely if you could come up and spend a couple of days with us. I'd love you to see the new flat.

The play, final title of which is now Shooting Star, has been cast and rehearsals are due to start next week. Maybe if you come and visit us, you and I could go to a couple of rehearsals? I know you'd enjoy it. Try to come before the second week in March when my own little production is due!

Freddie and I are very happy. We are looking forward to the baby's arrival so much. And Steven and Freddie are revelling in the excitement of seeing their first show go into production. They have already started writing their next!

I know that Steven longs to make up his quarrel with you and have the chance to apologise for some of the things he said. His relationship with you is something very special that he has valued for a long time, but I'm sure you know that. Please – please try and come.
Again, with many apologies,
Much love from Clarissa

Carol read the letter twice more before slipping it back into the envelope and tucking it into her bag.

It was odd that Clarissa hadn't once mentioned her engagement. The invitation was tempting but she suspected that Clarissa was trying to heal the rift between Steven and Carol without telling him. She visualised the possible scenario. Clarissa was probably planning to get her up there, then invite Steven round and produce her like a conjurer's rabbit. She winced with embarrassment at the thought. It was too humiliating to contemplate. She would reply to Clarissa's letter, thanking her for the invitation but making an excuse not to go. After all, there were plenty of truthful reasons she could give.

She paused to ask herself if it might have been different if Steven himself had written to ask her. But he hadn't so the question didn't arise.

A few days later Carol was shopping for shoes in her lunch hour. Rose had grudgingly agreed that she was capable of choosing a suitable pair to go with her wedding dress by herself so she seized the opportunity before it was snatched away again. She went to her favourite shoe shop in Bridge Street where choosing the plain white satin shoes was a matter of minutes. She was just coming out of the shop with her purchase under her arm when a young man looking at a display of men's shoes in the window caught her attention.

There was something familiar about him but at first she couldn't place him. Then she saw that it was Paul Wilson. He had changed quite a lot in the years since she'd last seen him. He looked older and more mature. The Cliff Richard suit had been abandoned in favour of tight trousers and a suede blouson jacket. His hair was longer, in the current fashion, curling almost to his shoulders, and she guessed by the thick growth of stubble on his face that he was growing a beard. As soon as she realised who he was she turned away hurriedly, but not before he had spotted her.

'Carol! Hello.' He came towards her looking pleased and she realised it was too late to escape.

'Hello, Paul.'

'How are you?' He smiled. 'It seems like ages. You look great.'

'It is ages. I'm fine. You?'

'I'm okay, thanks. I saw your engagement announced in the *Independent*,' he said. 'So, when's the wedding?'

'May,' she told him. 'Ages yet.'

His smile faded. 'Saw your dad had died too. Sorry about that, Carol. Only met him the once but he seemed like a really nice bloke.'

'Yes, he was. Thanks.'

Paul shifted his weight from one foot to the other. 'Look – are you doing anything? I was just going to have some coffee and a snack. Keep me company?'

She was about to say no then changed her mind. It would be interesting to find out how much Paul knew about his father's activities. Had Eddie ever told him about the blood tie between them? Was he aware of his father's nefarious business deals? Surely if he had known that Eddie was blackmailing her father, Paul would have avoided her?

'All right, why not?' she said. 'I'm on my lunch break but I've got another half hour.'

In a nearby coffee bar they sat at a corner table. Carol looked at him speculatively as she stirred her coffee. 'You're still working for your father, are you?' she asked casually.

He shook his head. 'No. He and I fell out and parted company quite a while ago. I've been on the dole for a bit, but I've got a new job – trainee manager at Newfayre, a big new supermarket that's opened in Kettering. Start new week.' He grinned and rubbed his bristly chin.

'Have to have this lot off – gotta go back to being square again, but I reckon it'll be worth it. Real prospects there. Good money too. Not like with Dad.'

'I see. I suppose you'll be living there from now on?'

'I will as soon as I can find a flat. But I'm in digs at the moment – haven't been living at home with Dad for ages.'

'I see. So he's all alone now, is he?'

Paul nodded. 'No more than he deserves if you ask me. He led Mum a hell of a dance, you know. No wonder she left him. And my brothers had the sense to get out at the same time. I was the mug who stuck by him. And a fat lot of good it's done me! The times he held my wages back, fobbing me off with some cock and bull story. Just 'cause I was his son he thought he could treat me anyhow.' He looked at her. 'I expect you've heard that his business is on the skids?'

Carol looked up at him in surprise. 'No, I hadn't.'

He nodded. 'It's all these new supermarkets. He can't compete with the prices, see. Those places buy in massive bulk consignments. Little shops are closing in droves and that's where most of Dad's business was. Things go on like they are, he'll be back to working the markets before long.'

'Is that what you fell out over?' Carol asked.

'Not only that. He started encouraging me to get into deals that weren't strictly kosher. Stuff that fell off the back of lorries. Know what I mean?' He shook his head. 'That's a mug's game if you ask me. I told him straight: You might have made a pile out of shady dealings but I'm not starting it. If I can't make a decent living without making enemies and getting the wrong side of the old bill, I'll give up and sweep the streets instead.'

Carol looked at him with a new admiration. 'Good for you, Paul,' she said.

'Yeah.' He looked thoughtful. 'That wasn't all of it, though. I reckon he's up to something else iffy and I don't want to get involved.'

'Iffy? What, you mean besides the off-the-back-of-a-lorry stuff?'

He nodded. 'Dunno for sure, mind, but I reckon it was something seriously out of order.' He leaned forward and lowered his voice. 'There was this money coming in each month, see, and as far as I could figure there were no goods going out for it. It had been going on like that for ages.'

Carol frowned. 'How do you mean?'

He shook his head. 'Well – someone was paying him money for nothing. Now, I'm not the world's brightest businessman but I do know that no one pays out good lolly for nothing. Not these days.'

Her heart quickened. 'Didn't you see whose signature was on the cheques?'

'No. Cash was paid straight into the bank. All I saw were the monthly statements.' He frowned. 'Funny thing was that the amounts went down suddenly last autumn.'

She looked at him, her heart suddenly freezing. 'Stopped, you mean?'

He shook his head. 'No, went down – to less than half.'

'So didn't you ever ask him about it?'

'You're joking!' He laughed wryly. 'I knew better than that. Dad never took kindly to anyone poking their nose into his business methods. Not even me. Reckon his left hand don't even know what his right is up to!'

'But you drew your own conclusions?'

'Well . . .' Paul opened his mouth, then closed it again. 'I've got a pretty good idea what he was up to but I'd better say no more. Maybe I said more'n I should now.'

312

He smiled at her, obviously anxious to change the subject. 'What about you then? You given up your stage work now you're getting married?'

Carol shrugged. 'It's getting harder and harder to get a job. Things aren't easy in the theatre at the moment.'

'Like everything else, eh? You've gotta be in the know nowadays.' He tapped the side of his nose. 'Box clever and look after number one, right?' He sighed. 'Pity you and me couldn't have made a go of it, Carol,' he said wistfully. 'But there – I was never really in your league, was I? Trouble is, when you've got an old man like mine, people tend to tar you with the same brush. Couldn't really blame your folks. Reckon it is high time I put some distance between Dad and me.'

She was looking at him. there was nothing about his demeanour to suggest he knew they were half-brother and sister, and she decided it wasn't up to her to enlighten him. Much better to leave things as they were.

'I think you're doing the right thing, Paul. I admire you for sticking to your principles.' She looked at her watch. 'Look, I'm sorry but I'll have to get back to the shop now and give Mum a break. It's been really nice, seeing you again.'

'Yeah.' He stood up and held out his hand. 'Me too. Good luck then – with the wedding and all that.'

She shook his hand. 'Thanks, Paul. Good luck with the new job. I'm sure you'll do well.'

Walking back to the shop Carol's mind was spinning with what she had learned from her conversation with Paul. He had said that unaccounted-for money was still being paid into Eddie's account. It couldn't be anything to do with her family now. Eddie must be in possession of knowledge that a lot of people would pay to keep quiet. And if his business was in as much trouble as Paul indicated, he wouldn't hesitate to use that knowledge to supplement his income. Carol already knew there was nothing he wouldn't stoop to to save his skin, but that kind of thing must surely backfire one day. There would come a time when one of his victims would turn and strike back. It couldn't come soon enough for her!

March came in with rain and blustery winds that ripped the clouds into rags and washed the sky a clean blue. It was good to see the back of winter, but every week that passed reminded Carol that her wedding day was creeping closer. Not that she needed reminding. Rose was becoming quite frenetic with all her plans and arrangements, driving everyone mad with her constant 'brain waves' and endless lists. She and Eve were perpetually arguing about something or other.

In addition to the upheaval of the wedding preparations, the house in Sunnyside Crescent was now up for sale and after work each night there seemed to be an endless stream of hopeful couples touring the rooms and making critical comments. Carol began to feel as though she were living in a goldfish bowl. Her life seemed to be public property and there never seemed a moment she could call her own. So she was relieved to lift the telephone early one morning just as she and Eve had arrived at the shop and find Zelda at the other end of the line instead of her future mother-in-law.

'Zelda! How nice to hear your voice.'

'Well, as you never ring us these days we rather wondered if you'd slipped off the face of the earth, darling,' Zelda said pointedly. 'Now listen, I've got a telly commercial for you if you want it? The pay is quite good and it's for a good product. A chance to be *seen working* my angel. All right, I know you're not keen on the idea and you're up to your adorable neck in white satin and orange blossom, but I'm sure that at the very least

314

you'll be interested in making some extra cash. So what about it?'

Carol hesitated. 'When is it?'

'Tomorrow. One day's shooting. An early start, so you'd have to come up tonight, but your beloved will hardly notice you've gone.'

'Can I let you know?'

'Oh, come *on*, Carol. It's tomorrow, for God's sake. I have to let these people know. If you don't want it, I'll have to get on to someone else.'

Carol bit her lip. The prospect of getting away from Rose and the endless bickering for a few hours was too good to pass up on. 'All right, I'll do it,' she said breathlessly. 'Just tell me where and when.'

Eve wasn't too pleased to hear that Carol intended to go up to London that afternoon. 'Why do you want to do it?' she asked. 'You don't need the money that badly, surely?'

'Every little helps, Mum,' Carol told her. 'Janet will put me up for a night – two if necessary. Is it the shop? Are you afraid you won't be able to manage without me?'

'Of course not,' Eve said. 'I can manage perfectly well on my own. It's just that I don't see why you want to do it.'

'I thought it might be fun – make a break. And, as Zelda says, it's a chance to be seen working.'

'Seen working?' Eve frowned. 'But I thought you'd decided to give all that up?'

'I have – for the time being. But Mike doesn't mind if I want to go on with it later.'

Eve was shaking her head. 'Goodness knows what Rose will make of it.'

Carol, her nerves ragged, lashed out suddenly. 'Oh, *Mum*, for heaven's sake! What's got into you lately? You used to stand up to Aunt Rose but ever since Christmas you've let her boss you about as much as the rest of us! I don't give a *damn* what she thinks and she's going to have to learn that. She's going to have to understand that she can't run my life for me even if she is going to be my mother-in-law!'

'I don't think you realise how difficult it is for me,' her mother said. 'She and Ted are paying for the wedding. It's tricky.'

'I never wanted her to pay for anything, Mum. And I'll tell you this: Mike would like us to run off and get married on the quiet. He'd have done it long ago if I hadn't talked him out of it. And if Aunt Rose doesn't watch out, it might still happen!'

Eve gasped. 'Oh, no! Don't do that.'

'Then stand up for yourself and put her in her place,' Carol said. She went back to the phone to call Janet and ask for a bed for the night. By the time she'd spoken to her friend and arranged it she had calmed down. Slightly ashamed of her outburst, she rejoined Eve in the shop.

'Mum – I'm sorry. I shouldn't have blown my top like that. It's just that Aunt Rose is stretching everyone's nerves to breaking point with her overbearing manner.'

'I know.' Eve smiled. 'Never mind, love. It's just pre-wedding nerves making you edgy. Only a few weeks now and it will all be over. You and Michael will be happily married. Rose will leave you alone after that. I promise. Anyway, Elizabeth's babies are due soon. That should take her attention away from the wedding for a bit.'

Carol sighed. 'I hope so, Mum. I certainly hope so.'

Carol and Janet sat up late that night, gossiping. Carol heard all about the holiday Janet and Geoff had spent skiing in Switzerland and Carol made her friend laugh with some of her stories about Rose and the wedding preparations. Distance lent an air of unreality to it all and for the first time she found herself able to see the funny side of it all.

'If I were you, I'd do what Mike wants and elope,' Janet advised. 'This wedding sounds as though it's rapidly assuming the proportions of a Hollywood extravaganza! I reckon you'll be lucky to come through it with your sanity intact!'

'Don't!' Carol shuddered. 'Let's talk about something else.'

'I take it Mike knows you're here?'

'Yes. I rang him at the office before I left. He'll meet the train tomorrow and give me dinner.'

'Very supportive,' Janet said. 'Spoils you rotten by the sound of it. Look, I'm sorry for what I said last time you came up. I can see that for you wedding nerves began with your Aunt Rose ordering the invitations. Forget I said it, eh?'

Carol nodded. Actually she had almost decided to unburden herself to Janet. But maybe it was better to keep her misgivings to herself. After all, everyone said that brides-to-be felt like this.

Janet was in the kitchen when Carol got home from the studio late the following afternoon. When she heard the front door slam she looked out into the hall.

'Hi! Everything okay?'

Carol heaved a sigh and came through to collapse on to one of the kitchen chairs. 'Just you wait till I see Zelda,' she said between gritted teeth. 'I'll give her a *chance to be seen working*!'

Janet glanced round from the stove where she was preparing beans on toast. 'Oh, dear. Sounds ominous. Want to tell me about it?'

Carol sighed. 'I hardly know where to start. First, the *good product* Zelda mentioned was frozen chicken pies.'

317

'Right.' Janet pushed a plate towards her. 'So, what were you, the bright young housewife in the pretty pinny?'

'You're joking!' Grim-faced, Carol picked up her knife and fork. 'Would you believe I was the *chicken*? This utterly ridiculous, angelic chicken who saves the young mum's kids from starvation. I wore a big fluffy yellow costume complete with beak, wings *and* halo, and all I had to do was prance about on these great big yellow feet and flap my wings. There was even a voice-over for the squawks.'

Looking up, she saw to her annoyance that Janet was helpless with laughter. Her face was pink and tears were running down her cheeks.

'Oh – I'm sorry, love,' she spluttered. 'I'm really sorry, but I can't *wait* to see it.'

Carol's indignation began to dissolve and she felt a grin tugging at the corners of her mouth. 'Well, at least no one will be able to recognise me,' she conceded. 'That at least is a blessing. But as for being *seen working* . . .' Her resentment ebbed and she began to laugh with Janet, getting up after a moment to demonstrate the chicken dance, bringing the other girl to the point of hysteria all over again. They giggled until their sides ached and they fell about helplessly. The two young doctors who shared the house came down, putting their heads round the door and demanding to know what the joke was, but neither girl could find breath enough to tell them and eventually they went away, shrugging and shaking their heads at one another.

'Oh, Jan,' Carol said, managing to catch her breath at last. 'What *would* I do without you? You always put things into perspective for me.'

It was late when Carol arrived back in Northampton. She had telephoned Mike to let him know which train she was catching and he was there at the station to meet her. Back at the flat she described the day's filming and her own ludicrous part in it, chuckling reminiscently as she remembered Janet's response.

'The commercial was a complete fiasco but Jan helped me to see the funny side of it,' she told him. 'I haven't laughed so much for ages.'

Michael had been watching her animated face as she related her experience. When she had finished he said wistfully, 'The break has done you good, hasn't it?' He smiled at her ruefully. 'Does it really help so much to be away from me?'

'Oh, Mike.' She reached for his hand. 'I didn't mean to make it sound like that.'

'I know. That wasn't fair, was it? It's just that sometimes I wonder if you're having second thoughts. Mother is being a such a monumental pain in the neck, isn't she?'

'It's *you* I'm marrying though, isn't it?' She leaned across and kissed him.

He pulled her close, resting his chin on top of her head, and sighing. 'Do you have to go home tonight? Can you stay?' He drew back his head to look into her eyes. 'Or should I ask, do you *want* to stay?'

The look of raw, naked longing in his eyes hurt her and she wrapped her arms around him. 'Of course I want to stay, Mike. Mum isn't expecting me home so I don't need to phone.'

He smiled. 'Good. Shall we make it an early night then?'

Carol was still fast asleep when she heard the frantic ringing of the doorbell, as though someone was leaning on it. She was dimly aware of Mike getting out of bed and pulling on his dressing gown. It was only just getting light as she reached out for the bedside clock to squint at its face.

When she saw that it was half-past six she groaned and slid down the bed again, hoping that whoever it was wouldn't keep Mike too long. Outside in the hall she could hear voices, but, thinking it must be the postman or someone, she closed her eyes and allowed herself to drift towards sleep again. Then dimly through her drowsiness she recognised that it was Aunt Rose's voice she could hear and was instantly alert.

'A *boy and a girl*!' she was proclaiming, her voice shrill with excitement. 'I wanted you to be the first to know, after your dad of course. Went into hospital just after tea last night. I was there with her all the way through. Harold hadn't the stomach for it. Well, you men are all the same. I've rung your dad of course. Just wondered if you wouldn't mind running me home, love?'

Carol was sitting up now, her nerves taut as she listened with a kind of paralysed fascination to her future mother-in-law prattling away on the other side of the door. She heard Michael's quieter voice, gently trying to urge his mother to wait in the living room while he dressed, but she was having none of it.

'Just get into that bathroom and get shaved,' she ordered. 'I'll nip in and make your bed, then I'll put the kettle on for a nice cuppa. You can have breakfast with us when we get home.'

Carol was out of bed now, hurriedly pulling on her clothes, but in her heart she knew already that it was too late. A moment later the bedroom door burst open and she found herself looking into Aunt Rose's startled, outraged eyes.

'*Carol!*' she gasped, stopping in her tracks. 'What in God's name are *you* doing here?'

'Carol got home from London late last night so she

stayed here.' Mike stood behind his mother in the doorway. She turned and pushed him unceremoniously out of the room, slamming the door in his face and leaning her full weight against it. Her face white with fury, she faced Carol.

'*You dirty little slut!*' she hissed, eyes narrowed into angry slits. 'This isn't the first time either, I'll be bound. How many times have you stayed here, I'd like to know? Leading my poor boy on till you got your evil way! The morals of the gutter, you've got! Like your mother before you. A proper little alley cat she was and you've turning out to be just like her.'

She flung the door open to reveal Michael's white face. Before he could speak she had launched an offensive at him. 'How *could* you?' she demanded. 'Of all the nice girls you've known, how could you fall for *her* and her loose ways? Nothing but a tart, she is. Well if you marry that one you'll deserve all you'll get, believe me. Think she'll be satisfied with you – with just one man in her bed? Don't you kid yourself! Her sort never is. Soon's some other Flash Harry comes along and takes her fancy she'll up and leave you just like *that!*' She snapped her fingers under his nose. 'Kidding yourself she *loves* you, are you? Her sort doesn't know the meaning of the word. Sex and *lust* is all they know! Disgusting!'

Turning back to Carol she said, 'When I think of the work I've put in these past months – the money Ted and I have spent to give you a nice wedding. But don't you kid yourself it was for *you*, Carol Kenning. It was for my boy I did it. And to help my poor widowed sister. *I* never wanted you for a daughter-in-law. You with your flighty stage-struck airs and graces. Blood will out, I always say! Only to be expected from a girl with a whore for a mother and God knows who for a father!'

'*Stop it!*' Michael pushed past her into the room to

stand between his mother and Carol. 'That's quite enough, Mother. This is none of your business. Carol and I are adults. We're also engaged to be married. If you want to cancel the wedding, go ahead and do it. No one's going to give a damn. In fact, it'll be a relief. You've made everyone's life sheer bloody hell over the past months. Carol and I will get married quietly on our own.' He glared angrily at her. 'And now I'd like you to leave. I'll ring for a taxi for you. And if you don't mind, I'd rather you waited for it downstairs.'

'*Well!*' The word exploded sharply from Rose's mouth as her fury drained away to be replaced by surprise. Her eyes bulged and the colour drained from her face, leaving it white and livid. Temporarily speechless, her mouth opened and closed, making her look like a landed fish.

'I never thought I'd see the day when my only son would speak to me like that,' she said at last, glaring at Carol. 'This is all your doing, madam! My son never swore at me before he took up with you! I hope you're proud of yourself – splitting a family apart and ruining my poor Elizabeth's happy event.'

Carol found her voice at last. 'I'm sorry you feel the way you do, Aunt Rose,' she said. 'I don't believe I've split the family apart, or spoiled Elizabeth's happiness in any way. If we've shocked and offended you, I apologise, but you did arrive without warning. And it is only half-past six in the morning.'

Rose bridled. 'Oh, I *see*! I need to make an appointment to visit my son's flat now, do I? *Huh!*' She gave a dry, mirthless little snort of laughter. 'What about you? Do you make appointments to see him or do you just drop in whenever you feel like a quick roll in the hay?'

'*Mother!* You're making yourself sound ridiculous. Please stop now before you say something you'll regret.'

Michael took his mother's arm and steered her firmly out of the room with a look of mute appeal in Carol's direction.

Standing as though rooted to the spot, she heard him close the living-room door. She heard their voices, Mike's quiet and controlled, Rose's shrill as she continued her tirade, then, a moment later, she heard the tinkle of the telephone as he rang for a taxi.

Legs trembling with shock, Carol sank down on the bed and bit her lip hard. Being discovered in Mike's bedroom by Aunt Rose was the most humiliating, degrading thing that had ever happened to her. It was much worse even than coming face to face with Finn's wife that time in Bradwich. But, she told herself, she was entirely to blame. It served her right. She had deceived Mike just as surely as Finn had deceived his wife. She hadn't slept with him because she loved him, but to try and convince herself that she was doing the right thing. Rose's accusations weren't really all that far from the truth. She felt dirty and ashamed.

Still shivering, she rose slowly and pulled on the rest of her clothes, realising for the first time that while Rose had been haranguing her she had been wearing only her bra and panties. Rose would go straight to Eve, of course. There was nothing surer than that. By the time Carol arrived home her mother would be in full possession of every last detail, enhanced, no doubt, by Rose's lurid embellishments. Her heart sank at the prospect of the day to come.

She was fully dressed and wearing her outdoor clothes when the door opened and a grave-faced Michael came into the room.

'She's gone,' he said with relief. 'I've just put her into a taxi.' He sighed. 'I'm so sorry darling. What can I say?' He crossed the room and put his arms around her.

'Thanks for being so restrained with her. Most girls would have struck back after the things she said.'

'I'd better go home,' Carol said. 'You can bet she'll go straight to Mum. I'll have to straighten things out with her.'

'I'll come with you,' he offered.

'No. I'd rather keep it between Mum and me.'

'But you've always been completely truthful with her. She knew you spent the night here with me occasionally.'

'And you think that will help?' She raised an eyebrow at him. 'Can you imagine how Aunt Rose will feel when she knows Mum was aware of it all along?'

'I see what you mean.' He sighed. 'God! What a mess. Look, I'll get some clothes on and run you home.'

Eve was making herself a cup of tea in the kitchen when the front doorbell rang. Guessing it would be Rose, she hurried out into the hall to open the door to her.

'It's all right, I know,' she said with a smile. 'Ted has just rung me. Congratulations! How does it feel to be the grandmother of twins?'

But to her surprise Rose looked anything but pleased. Pushing past her, she walked through to the kitchen then turned to face Eve challengingly.

'Did you know that daughter of yours – *so called* – was sleeping with Michael?'

Eve caught her breath. 'Well, I . . .'

'I called in at his flat when I left the hospital just now to tell him the news and get him to run me home. And what do I find? That little slut in bed with my boy!'

'Now, just a minute,' Eve said. 'Who do you think you're calling a slut?'

'Your Carol. That's who! A fine daughter you've been nurturing. Poor Jack would turn in his grave if he knew what his little angel was really like.'

'It takes two, you know,' Eve reminded her grimly.

'And what's *that* supposed to mean?' Rose demanded. 'You're surely not suggesting it was Michael's idea?'

'He's a man, isn't he? A normal, red-blooded man. He and Carol are in love, and they are engaged to be married.'

Rose peered at her sister suspiciously. 'I must say you're taking this very calmly,' she said. 'I believe you knew what was going on between them?'

'What if I did? Carol has always been truthful with me. We understand each other. Which is more than can be said for you and your children!'

'Oh! Is that so?' Rose sucked in her breath sharply.

'Yes, it is. Elizabeth didn't confide in you about her pregnancy until she had to, did she? And while we're on the subject, I don't remember *her* being accused of seduction!'

'You're a fine one to criticise me as a mother!' Rose said, her face pink. 'Nice thanks I must say for laying out time and money on your Carol's wedding?'

'And whose idea was that? You were done out of having a showy wedding for Elizabeth so you made up your mind to commandeer all the credit for Carol's.'

'Well! Of all the ungrateful . . .' Rose stared at her sister for a moment, then narrowed her eyes and folded her mouth into a tight line of disapproval. 'I suppose I shouldn't really be surprised that you were in on her sleazy carry-on,' she said scathingly. 'I daresay you actually encouraged her. Come to think of it, you always stood up for that Sally Tyler, didn't you? Couldn't see that *she* was doing anything wrong either.' She folded her arms across her bosom. 'I can't help wondering if *you* were no better than you should've been when your Jack was away in that prison camp. Maybe she wasn't the only one giving home comforts to the Yanks . . .'

It was at that point that Eve's hand caught her full in the mouth, the blow sending her staggering back. There was a stunned silence as the sisters stared at each other, Rose's watering eyes filled with shock and disbelief.

'*How dare you*! Get out of my house, Rose Robson,' Eve said, trembling with rage. 'And you needn't bother coming back unless it's to apologise for what you just said. I've had just about enough of you and your nasty vicious tongue. You've always had a smutty mind and in my view the thought is as bad as the deed! These past few months you've made life unbearable for everyone around you. How those two young people have put up with it, I don't know. But *I* don't have to, and I've certainly got no intention of standing here letting you insult me in my own home.'

She took a step towards her sister who was standing as though dumbstruck, one hand clapped over her mouth. 'Well, what are you waiting for? Go on. Get out – before I throw you out!' She pursued Rose's retreating figure through the hall and slammed the front door shut behind her. Then she sank down on the bottom of the stairs and burst into tears.

When the tears had subsided she blew her nose and took a deep breath, suddenly realising with surprise that she felt better than she had for months. A sense of lightness and freedom made her feel as though a great weight had been lifted from her shoulders. In fact, now that she'd got all that off her chest and put Rose well and truly in her place, she felt absolutely wonderful!

Carol didn't let Mike drive her home. Mainly because she had decided not to go straight to Sunnyside Crescent. She had a lot of thinking to do and needed someone impartial to help her sort out her spinning mind.

It was still well before eight o'clock when she stood on

326

the step of the house in Chine Way, ringing the bell. Kitty opened the door in her dressing gown – a kimono of vivid blue silk embroidered with crimson lotus flowers. Her auburn hair tumbled about her shoulders and her face was innocent of its usual make-up, giving her a soft, almost childlike look.

'Carol! Darling, what's wrong? You look like a ghost!' Opening the door she reached out to draw the girl inside. 'You're shivering! Come down to the kitchen,' she said. 'It's warmer there. I'll make some tea.'

Typically, Kitty did not badger her with questions, knowing that she would open up when she was ready; though as she went about the business of making the tea her eyes kept straying towards the girl who sat huddled in the chair by the Aga, her face pale and eyes troubled.

At last they faced each other across mugs of strong tea at the kitchen table, still littered with the chaotic detritus of Kitty's business life.

'Now – tell me,' she said, sweeping a pile of paperwork aside with one arm. 'I know you wouldn't be here at this hour unless it was something bad.'

Carol wrapped both hands round the mug and took a long drink of her tea. 'Oh, Kitty. I've made such a mess of everything. Such a horrible mess!' she said, her shoulders slumping despairingly.

The older woman reached across to squeeze her arm. 'Tell me all about it,' she invited. 'Start at the beginning and take your time. We're all right. Gloria doesn't come in today and I haven't got a class till ten.'

It took Carol almost an hour to pour it all out. She told Kitty everything, from hiding her discovery that she was Eddie Wilson's daughter from her parents, to all the subsequent problems it had caused. She ended with her misgivings about her engagement to Mike, culminating in this morning's humiliating scene with Rose.

'I should have listened to Steven,' she said. 'He was so angry with me. We quarrelled because he said I was to blame for most of what happened. He said that marrying Mike would be wrong – just one more disastrous mistake. I suppose I knew then that he was right, deep inside.'

'Why did you get engaged Carol?' Kitty asked gently.

She shook her head. 'I don't really know. It was just that I couldn't see any way of going back to my career after Dad died. I wanted to make a new life – wanted to make some kind of sense of it all. Mike was – well he was *there*. He's always been there. He's kind and funny and gentle. And he said he loved me. He *does* love me, Kitty. And that makes it worse. Much worse.' She looked up. 'I tried to love him back like he deserves to be loved. I thought if we went to bed, if we became really close, it would all happen for me. But I was wrong. The more I tried, the worse it got. And the more poor Mike is going to get hurt.'

'All the same, you know you're going to have to end it, don't you darling?' Kitty said gently. 'Because you can't let this drift on Carol. Before you know it you'll be walking up the aisle with Mike simply because you can't face hurting him. You can't go through with it and the sooner you face that fact, the better.'

Carol swallowed hard. 'I know that now. Not just because of Aunt Rose and what happened this morning. All that did was show me what a sham I am. What a *fake*!'

'No. You're punishing yourself again.' Kitty refilled Carol's mug with more tea.

'Oh, Kitty. I've been so stupid!' Carol said. 'Steven was right when he said I should face up to who and what I am and come to terms with it. This morning Rose made me feel worthless and cheap. And she was right. I've played true to form as far as she's concerned. I've let everyone down, including myself.'

'You mustn't be so hard on yourself.' Kitty was shaking her head, her own eyes moist. 'Listen, Carol. Far be it from me to start giving advice. God only knows my own love life was enough of an emotional minefield! But I'm older now and I do have the benefit of hindsight. If I were you I'd make up my mind to put it all behind me and make a fresh start. Let poor Mike down as lightly as you can and start your career again. Get Zelda to find you something.'

Carol was shaking her head. 'Oh, Kitty, I don't know.'

Kitty leaned forward to look into her eyes. 'Carol – listen to me, darling. You've wasted too much time trying to make yourself into what other people want you to be,' she said earnestly. 'That's why you're so mixed up. You need time to find yourself. Take anything Zelda can get for you.' She smiled. 'Yes, even those ridiculous chicken adverts. At least they'll feed you and pay the rent till something better comes along. Stop hiding from yourself.'

'But what about Mum? She needs me.'

'Not nearly as much as you think. Look, Carol, I don't know your mother all that well, but I'm certain she wouldn't want you to sacrifice your life for her. Go somewhere where you can be the real Carol Kenning. The talented girl I know you to be. Believe me, darling, that's the only way you're ever going to feel free – to learn to like yourself.'

Kitty stood on the step, waving Carol out of sight, then sighed and went back inside to prepare for the coming day. 'Poor child,' she muttered to herself as she climbed the stairs. 'I wonder if Steven knows just how much in love with him she is?'

Carol went straight to the shop. She had guessed that Aunt Rose would have been to see her mother by now and the moment their eyes met across the counter she knew that her assumption had been right.

329

'You've seen Aunt Rose?' she said.

Eve nodded grimly. 'More than just seen her. I think I've put a stop to her ravings once and for all.'

'How?'

Eve's lips twitched. 'I gave her something she's been asking for for years – something Ted should have given her right at the start. A slap in the chops!'

'*Mum*!' Carol's eyes widened and she caught her lower lip between her teeth. 'Oh, Mum, I'm sorry if I caused a row.'

'Don't be!' Eve began ferociously rearranging a display of chocolate boxes. 'Our Rose has had things her own way far too long.' She perched the final box on top of the pyramid and glanced apologetically at Carol. 'The only thing is, I'm afraid I've probably put the lid on your wedding plans.'

'We're going to have to talk about that, Mum,' she said.

A customer came into the shop, putting an end to their conversation, and it wasn't until much later in the day that they had a chance to resume it.

'I can't marry Mike,' Carol said as they closed the shop for the night.

Eve, who had been pulling down the blinds, turned to stare at her in dismay. 'Is this because of Rose?'

Carol shook her head. 'No. It has nothing to do with Aunt Rose. She just brought things to a head. I should never have said I'd marry him in the first place. I think an awful lot of him but it isn't enough.'

Eve was clearly upset but didn't seem too surprised. 'Is it Steven?' she asked quietly. 'I know you've always liked him a lot. I thought it was hero worship and that you'd grow out of it.'

Carol looked at her mother. 'Last summer, before he went to New York, I thought he was marrying someone

330

else,' she said. 'It was all a misunderstanding. By the time he came home and I found out he wasn't getting married, I'd already got engaged to Mike.' She groaned. 'Oh, Mum, poor Mike. What have I done? How am I going to tell him?'

'Maybe he half knows already,' Eve said wisely. 'I've thought sometimes, the way he looks at you . . . It's as though he's never quite believed you were really his.' She looked thoughtfully at her daughter for a long moment, then said, 'You want to go back to the stage again, don't you?'

Carol looked up at her. 'Would you mind if I did, Mum? I know you've been hoping I'd stay here and settle – help you run the shop now that Dad – that you're on your own. But I need to get away. For a while at least. I need time to think, to find out who I really am.'

'Well . . .' Eve sighed. 'I can't really say that I understand. But if it's what you want, then of course you must go.'

'Mum.' Carol leaned forward urgently. 'I want you to understand this. It's important to me. I never knew my real mother, but people tell me she was flighty and promiscuous. Aunt Rose actually called her a whore this morning, and told me I was just like her. And the man who fathered me is mean and devious and crooked. Can you imagine how it feels to be the product of parents like that?'

For a moment the two of them stood looking into each other's eyes, then Eve said painfully, 'Carol, we – none of us know what we really are – what we're capable of till we face a crisis. *I know that*. I believe that what's in us doesn't only come from one set of parents. It can go back centuries. I *know* that for something that means a lot to us – for something we want, for someone we love desperately enough – we can actually kill.'

'Oh, *Mum*!' Her eyes full of tears, Carol threw her arms around her mother and hugged her tightly. 'You and Dad have always been marvellous. I owe you both everything, I'll never forget that. But I need to be by myself for a while. To be independent and find out if I've got any real talent. If I have anything to offer. If I'm *worth* anything!'

Eve held her daughter close, her heart filled with churning emotions. The moment had passed. Perhaps now she would never utter the devastating and traumatic confession she had been on the brink of making. Perhaps it was just as well.

Chapter Ten

Carol was wide awake. She could hear the sound of Janet's breathing in the next bed. Her friend never seemed to have any trouble getting to sleep. She always came home from her shift bone weary and questioning her sanity for ever wanting to become a doctor. But by morning she had usually recovered and was all enthusiasm once again. Janet knew exactly where she was going and what she wanted from life, Carol reflected wistfully. She had a clear conscience too and a comparatively uncomplicated life. Carol couldn't help envying her.

She knew by the sounds of the traffic out on Hackney Road that they were into the small hours. Between two and three a. m. there was usually a lull before the heavy lorries began, bringing their loads of fruit and fresh vegetables up from Kent to Covent Garden Market. Carol was used to the sound of London traffic by now. In a way the muted roar that penetrated the double glazing was strangely comforting.

It was May and she had been in London almost three months. Signs of spring were few here in the East End, but the softness in the air and the early-morning twittering of the sparrows in the sooty strip of back garden made her think, sometimes longingly, of home.

Eve had written that the house in Sunnyside Crescent was sold. The news had made Carol feel strangely bereft; somehow adrift, as though she no longer had a firm base. Eve seemed resigned to leaving, though. In fact there was a note of relief in her letter. She wrote that she had found a nice flat close to the town centre which would mean no more long bus journeys to the shop each morning. She had hurriedly added that it was quite spacious and there were two bedrooms so Carol wasn't to think there wouldn't be room for her to come home.

So far she hadn't been. Apart from the fact that there hadn't really been time, she was half afraid of the familiarity of it all. Of seeing people she knew and answering difficult questions. After all, there was as yet nothing tangible to show for her gesture of independence. Also, if she were truthful, she was half afraid of being tempted to take the easy option and letting herself be sucked back into the repressed environment she had escaped from.

Lying awake into the dawn as she often did, her thoughts inevitably drifted towards the people she'd left behind. Eve wrote that she'd seen Elizabeth and her twins when she was visiting Freda. They were beautiful babies, she said. And there was a new softness about Elizabeth since their birth. She and Harold seemed very happy, especially since Harold had got his promotion and they had found a nice bungalow at Spinney Hill, quite close to Ted and Rose. Then there were her grandparents. Carol had always been especially fond of Granny Freda and missed her.

Occasionally she thought of Paul Wilson, bravely struggling to make a new life for himself away from his father. And Eddie himself – scheming, devious Eddie. Was his business still afloat, or had he gone under as Paul had predicted? She could feel no sympathy for him after all he had done to her family. But most of all she thought of Mike. Dear Mike whom she had hurt so badly. Thinking of him always brought a lump to her throat.

He had been depressingly resigned when she had broken the news that she couldn't marry him. At first he had blamed his mother, but Carol had insisted that she alone was the one to blame. In the end he had admitted that in his heart of hearts he had never really believed the wedding would happen.

'It was always too good to be true,' he told her. 'I think maybe we were too close. We knew each other too well. There was never any real magic for you, was there?'

The look in his eyes had wounded her. All she could do was apologise over and over again, wishing there were some way she could explain properly – ease the disappointment and rejection that she knew she was inflicting on him.

'You deserve better than me, Mike,' she told him. 'You deserve the best. Someone who can give you all her heart.'

She remembered his rueful smile as he'd replied, 'But for me you'll always be the best, Carol. I'd have been willing to settle for whatever you could give. I'd happily have shared you with your career. But I know it wouldn't have worked unless you really loved me. And you didn't. At least, not enough. That's what it comes down to in the end.'

She still couldn't recall the wrench of their parting without it bringing a lump to her throat.

Janet had seemed unsurprised when she had telephoned with her news and asked to stay for a while. She had never actually said, 'I told you so,' but Carol was aware that her friend had never thought her engagement to Michael wise.

Sharing Janet's room was not ideal. It had been meant as a temporary measure, but so far Carol wasn't earning regularly enough to afford a room of her own. She had suggested that they look for a flat to share, but Janet had reservations about that. This house was conveniently close to the hospital. She couldn't face the thought of a long bus journey at the end of a gruelling night shift. And when her pre-registration year was through she was hoping to join Geoff anyway, wherever that might be. One plus was that they were hardly ever in at the same time. Both worked odd hours, so they didn't get in each other's way. And there was rarely any time for socialising, so, for the moment they were both content to let the arrangement stand.

So far Carol had had enough TV commercials to keep her busy and pay the bills, but as yet there had been no permanent offers. She had made it plain that the chicken pie commercial was not something she was eager to repeat and Zelda had promised to find her something better. Some of the commercial work she had done recently had actually been quite enjoyable. She had made one for a new brand of shampoo; there had been a series of toothpaste ads and she had made several short films for a well-known cosmetics firm, to be used for training their consultants. The same firm had recently contacted Zelda and asked Carol to model for their TV and glossy magazine advertisements. That was a possibility she was still considering.

She had had a tiny walk-on part in an episode of *Z-Cars* and another in *Emergency Ward Ten* – where, to her disappointment, she had played a heavily bandaged patient. 'Never mind, darling,' the eternally optimistic Zelda had said. 'If they haven't seen your face it means they can cast you again!' But so far that big break she had dreamed of – and which had slipped so frustratingly from her grasp the previous autumn – had failed to materialise. She wouldn't have minded another stint in rep, but nothing came up. Small provincial theatres were still closing at an alarming rate. Recently there had been a vacancy to play juvenile leads for a theatre group booked for a summer season in Cromer, but Carol had turned it down. It was only for six weeks and she didn't really want to be out of London, she told Zelda. Just in case.

As the sky began to lighten, she could pick out objects in the crowded room. Propped up on the mantelpiece she could dimly make out the small pale square of cardboard that had arrived in the post two days ago. Its elegant embossed gold script invited her to Her Majesty's Theatre on 27 May for the opening night of *Shooting Star*, words and music by Steven Manson and Freddie Manners.

Clearly it was to be a glittering occasion. Carol guessed that it would be heavily attended by the press and graced by many show business personalities, as any opening night of a production by the celebrated Graham Lang inevitably was.

The invitation had been sent on to her by her mother. On the back Steven had scrawled in his flowing hand: 'You'll probably still be on your honeymoon, but if you're back, bring your husband along. There's a party afterwards at the Cafe Royal. Do come if you can.'

Steven didn't know that her engagement to Mike was over. She hadn't contacted him or Clarissa since she'd been in London. When she went to say goodbye to Kitty she had sworn her to secrecy, promising to get in touch with Steven when she felt ready. She wanted to have found a job, something worthwhile, before she did, she explained. She didn't want him to feel he had to use his influence to help her. Deep down there was a deeper, much more complex reason for not contacting him. If she were completely honest with herself she was leaving her options open, unsure of whether she would make a success of things and not wanting to admit defeat if she didn't. And lately she had begun to wonder if it had been a good idea to leave home and try to start again. 'Finding herself' was proving as elusive as finding work. Up here in London she felt even less confident than she had at home. In fact lately she had been asking herself cynically whether looking for the 'real' Carol Kenning was just a euphemism for running away.

Clarissa had sent Carol a card announcing the birth of a baby daughter on 30 March. This too had been forwarded to her by Eve. Carol had sent a congratulations card and a small gift, promising herself she would go and see the baby and her proud parents some day soon. But somehow week followed week and so far she had done nothing about it. Receiving the invitation to the opening night of *Shooting Star* brought the decision to get in touch with Steven again into focus. Lying in the morning's first pale light, she thought about him. By now he would have moved so far out of her sphere as to be almost out of sight. She imagined herself at the opening night, standing on the fringe of press men, photographers and admirers, feeling shut out, like a wretched groupie or some hopeful hanger-on. Shuddering, she turned over and buried her face in the pillow, deciding she wasn't prepared to risk it.

Janet had been enormously impressed by the invitation when Carol had shown it to her.

'Wow!' she exclaimed. 'A West End first night! You'll go of course? It's just what you need to cheer you up.' When Carol had looked doubtful, she had thrown up her hands in exasperation. 'Oh! For heaven's sake, girl! You wouldn't catch me turning down an invitation to a glittering occasion like that! Not only should you go, you should treat yourself to a facial and swish hairdo. Go to that new place – what's it called, Vidal Monsoon?'

Carol laughed. '*Sass*oon, bird-brain!'

'That's the one! And buy yourself the most glamorous gown you can get your hands on.'

'Oh, yes? And what am I supposed to do for money?'

Janet pulled a face. 'Never mind the *money*! If you like I can chip in a few bob. Hire one. Everyone's doing that for special occasions. Don't you realise, with a bit of effort

338

you could have half the producers in London lining up for introductions? You'd be barking mad not to go!'

'Thanks for the vote of confidence, Jan,' Carol had laughed. 'But life's not quite like that. I wouldn't even be noticed in that kind of crowd. Girls who look like me are ten a penny.'

'Not with looks like yours *and* talent!' Janet shook her head. 'I don't know about you, I really don't. You used to have plenty of confidence when we were kids. Remember when we were in panto together? Everyone said you stood out from the rest of us with that bright-eyed vitality of yours. And you're getting more and more of the commercial work, aren't you? People keep asking for you so they must think you've got something.'

Although she tried not to show it, Janet had been worried about Carol since she'd come up to London. She seemed so withdrawn and sad. Janet could understand her regret at having hurt Michael, but she had tried to assure her that it was much better to have faced it now than left it until it was too late. Secretly she was convinced that the root of the trouble was that Carol had never stopped loving Steven Manson. She knew better than to say so, but sometimes she longed to give the man a piece of her mind.

Carol laughed. 'Just because someone happens to think that my face can sell toothpaste and shampoo, it doesn't mean I'm the next Deborah Kerr, you know.'

'Deborah Kerr?' Janet frowned, her head on one side. 'Is that how you see yourself? Funny, I'd say you were more Julie Christie. You know, she's that marvellous new actress we saw in *Billy Liar*.'

'Oh, yes? Chance'd be a fine thing!' Carol threw a pillow at her. She didn't add that it was more than lack of confidence that held her back from attending Steven's big night.

She must have fallen asleep. About half an hour later the alarm went off and she woke again to find sunlight streaming into the room and Janet flying round the room in her usual early-morning panic.

'Hi there, dozy!' she said, noticing Carol was awake. 'All right for some, I must say – lazing around in bed half the day.'

Carol got out of bed and hastily pulled on her dressing gown. 'I'll go down and make you some breakfast.'

'No time!' Janet grabbed her bag and coat. 'Go back to bed. I would if I were you.' She gave Carol a playful push. 'Go on, sleepy-head. I was only kidding. I'll get some breakfast later in the doctors' room.' She was halfway through the door when she added bossily, 'Don't forget to make an appointment to have your hair done for that first night. And get yourself a frock – how about something by Mary Quant? Slinky and the shorter the better. If I had legs like yours, I'd never stop showing them off.'

'Oh – *Jan*!'

'Better still, on my next day off I'll personally escort you up to the King's Road and we'll get you kitted out.' Janet wagged a warning finger at her. 'I shan't tell you again, girl. I'll have your guts for garters if you chicken out of this one! You can start looking for another roommate for a start!'

Carol lay back on her bed again, wondering idly where her friend picked up all those gruesome phrases. *Your guts for garters*! Young doctors seemed to have the most macabre sense of humour, she'd noticed. She dozed off to sleep again, to be wakened by the persistent ringing of the telephone. She lay sleepily listening to it for a moment, then, realising that there was probably no one but her in the house, she got up and went out on to the landing to answer it. Zelda was at the other end.

'Carol! At last! I was beginning to think you'd *died* or

something! Listen, darling, I've had a friend of yours on the phone. A Mrs Clarissa Manners. Ring a bell?'

'Clarissa. Yes. She used to be a friend of Steven's. She's married to his partner, Freddie.'

'Ah, *that* Manners. I thought the name was familiar.'

'What did she want?' Carol asked warily.

'Your address. Seems she rang your old telephone number in Northampton and discovered that someone else lived there. She wants to speak to you. It sounded quite important, but I thought I'd better check with you first.'

Carol swallowed. It looked as though her cover was about to be blown. 'Okay, I've got her number. I'll give her a ring,' she said. 'Any fabulous offers, Zelda?'

'Sorry, darling. Not a nibble at the moment. You really shouldn't have turned down that summer season. It's always foolish to turn down a chance to . . .'

'*Be seen working,*' Carol finished for her. 'I know, but who's going to see me working stuck out there on the Norfolk coast among the shrimping nets and buckets and spades?'

'You never know in this business. Still, the decision's yours. Why don't you let me tell Romaine Cosmetics you'll do that modelling job for them?'

Carol sighed. 'Oh, if you like. I've got to earn some money somehow.'

'Right. Leave it with me. I'll lay it on. Oh, by the way, are you going to Steven's opening night?'

'I might. I'll see.'

'Marty and I will be there. So will Kitty of course. She's coming up 'specially. I'm sure she's expecting you to go.'

'Yes, well . . .'

Zelda's audible sigh of exasperation at the other end of the line crackled in Carol's ear. 'Oh, well, you must do as you think of course, darling, but there'll be oodles of big names there. You'd be *awfully* silly to pass it up. Still, it's up to you of course. I'll get on to Romaine then. It'll only be a couple of days' work but the pay's not bad.'

'Thanks. Let me know when they want me. 'Bye, Zelda.'

Carol had a leisurely bath and got dressed before ringing Clarissa's number. It was nice to have peace to think while the house was quiet. No one thumping on the door just as you had stepped into the bath. Dressed and made up, she felt strong enough to speak to Clarissa. Vowing not to be railroaded into going to the opening night, she dialled the number and waited.

'Hello? Clarissa Manners.'

'Hello, Clarissa. It's Carol. Zelda rang and said you wanted to talk to me.'

'Carol! I'm so glad you rang. Your agent wouldn't give me your number. She sounded a bit cagey. Is everything all right?'

'Yes, of course. My mother has moved to a flat nearer the shop.'

'I see. So is that where you are?'

'No. As a matter of fact, I'm here in London. I'm sharing a room with my doctor friend, Janet, in Hackney. I'm trying to get back into my career now that my mother is over the shock of Dad's death.'

There was a stunned silence. 'You're actually *here* – in Town? I'd no idea. Why haven't you been to see us? Steven hasn't said a word.'

'Steven doesn't know.'

'Why not?'

'I haven't been in touch – with anyone.'

'You are all right, aren't you, Carol? I mean, tell me to mind my own business but I had the impression from Steven that you were engaged to be married.'

'Not any more. It's over.'

342

'Oh, I'm sorry.'

'There's no need. It wouldn't have worked. I decided not to contact anyone up here till I was more settled – didn't want people to feel obliged to give me a helping hand.'

'But why shouldn't they help? That's what friends are for.'

'I'd rather be independent.'

'Well, I can't tell you how nice it is to hear your voice again after such ages. Now, what I wanted to ask was, are you coming to the opening night of SS?'

'SS?'

Clarissa laughed. 'Sorry, it's our nickname for *Shooting Star*. Only the seats haven't been allocated yet and we'd like you to join our party. We'll be having a box. I was going to invite you to stay with us for the night, but you won't need to if you're already in London.' Into the pause that followed she asked, 'Carol – you did get an invitation, didn't you?'

'Oh, yes. From Steven. My mother sent it on to me. It arrived a couple of days ago.'

'That's fine. Then you'll join us?'

'Well, I don't want to intrude . . .'

'*Intrude*?' Clarissa sounded puzzled. 'Darling, there's nothing wrong, is there? You sound strange.'

Carol cleared her throat. 'It's just that it's a bit awkward. I'd hate to cause an atmosphere. You see, Steven and I haven't set eyes on each other since last Christmas, when . . .'

'Since that little spat you had. Is that it? Well, I can assure you he's forgotten all about that,' Clarissa assured her. 'You can imagine how frenetic life is at the moment for him and Freddie, what with an extra number to write for Madeleine Lindsay, the star, various frantic last-minute script rewrites and everything.'

In other words he's been too pre-occupied even to give me a thought, Carol wanted to say. Instead she asked, 'He doesn't know you're ringing me then?'

'Not exactly. But I can assure you he'll be more than delighted to see you. He and Freddie will be busy during the show of course. Steven is Musical Director and if I know Freddie he'll be panicking backstage for most of the first night. Kitty will be with us, though. She'll be staying the night at Steven's new flat. If you come too it'll be quite a family party. Oh, do come, Carol.'

'Well, if you're really sure . . .'

'Of course I am. Tell you what, I won't mention it to Steven. I'll keep it as a surprise.'

Carol swallowed hard. 'Are you sure that's wise?'

Clarissa laughed. '*Wise*? What's wise?'

'Well – all right.'

'That's *great*! Wait till I tell Freddie.'

'How is he? And the baby, of course?' Carol asked.

'Wonderful – both of them. Thanks for the sweet little teddy-bear you sent. I can't wait for you to see her. Once we get this opening night over you must come round for tea and get to know her.'

'Thanks, I will.'

' 'Bye, darling. Oh, give me your phone number so that I can get in touch about the arrangements. We'll come and pick you up, if you like?'

Carol replaced the receiver with a sigh. She had promised herself not to be railroaded into going – and then stood there and listened to herself giving in like a complete push-over. All the same, she couldn't help a stir of excited anticipation as she thumbed through the telephone directory to find the number of that West End hairdresser.

Eve's new flat, in a block on the corner of Derngate, seemed strange and unhomely to her. Although she had a fine view across The Meadow to the river from her fourth-floor windows and her own things around her, she still felt unsettled and transitory, as though she were living in a hotel.

She had brought her favourite things with her from Sunnyside Crescent; the three-piece suite and the television set, the best bedroom furniture that she and Jack had bought when they moved in. The contents of Carol's old room were in the smaller of the two bedrooms. Eve had made it look as homely and familiar as she could, in the hope that Carol would come home and use it as often as possible. All her surplus furniture had been sold.

Although she kept busy at the shop all day she could not get used to the silent loneliness of the empty flat when she got home from work in the evenings. She missed Jack and Carol more and more with each passing week. She missed Rose too, in spite of their acrimonious split. They had neither met nor spoken since their quarrel. Freda fretted about the breakup between her two daughters. She did her best to bring them together again, but so far had not succeeded. Eve could not forgive Rose for the vicious accusations she had made that morning or the hateful names she had called Carol. Rose in her turn was still incensed by her younger sister's violent response.

It was early in April when she had the first of her visits from Eddie Wilson. He arrived unheralded at the shop in the sly, familiar way that he had appeared so often in the past. When Eve spotted him, lingering against the newspaper stand that stood near the door, waiting for her to finish serving a customer, her heart sank. And when he sidled up to the counter with that deceptively humble smirk on his face she prayed that another customer would come in quickly and prevent the inescapable encounter. No one came.

'What do you want?' she asked him abruptly. 'Don't

tell me you haven't received my cheque. Don't pretend it bounced either because my statement says you've cashed it.'

Eddie held up his hands in mock surrender, his face a study in wounded pride. '*Eve*! Now, I ask you – what kind of welcome is that? I haven't seen you for ages. I was in the vicinity so I thought I'd pop in and make sure you were okay. Nothing wrong in that, is there?'

She looked at him suspiciously. 'Never known you to bother unless you wanted something?'

'Not this time.' He looked at his watch. 'Look – almost closing time, isn't it? Come and have a bite to eat with me.'

'No, thank you.'

'A drink then. Just a quick one. Come on, Eve. For old time's sake.'

She stared at him. '*Old times*? Are you mad?'

He sighed. 'Look, Eve, all that's water under the bridge now. Things have changed. *We've* changed, you and me. You've lost your Jack and Carol's flown the nest. I've lost my wife and boys. We're both in the same boat – on our tod.' He smiled at her ruefully. 'Not much fun, is it?'

'It certainly isn't. But I don't see . . .'

'Time me and you buried the hatchet, I reckon,' Eddie went on. 'Won't you at least talk about it?'

'You've got a nerve!' She leaned across the counter, eyes blazing. 'It may have slipped your mind, Eddie Wilson, but call it what you like, you're still blackmailing me. You probably shortened my poor Jack's life with your demands and threats. And all for nothing! Now you calmly turn up here asking me to bury the hatchet! Well, I know where *I'd* like to bury it!'

He grinned at her. 'That's what I like about you, Eve. Never lost your spirit. A woman after my own heart, you are. I really admire the way you've always coped.'

'Look, Eddie, I don't know what's on your mind, but I'd bet my life on it, it's nothing to *my* advantage. Just say what it is – get it off your chest and then go. But before you do, I'll tell you now. If it's more money you're after, you've had it. I can't afford any more.'

'No, *no*!' he sighed and shook his head. 'Oh, dear me. You've got me all wrong this time.' He looked round. There were two women looking at the magazine rack in the shop behind him. 'Can't talk in here, can we?' he whispered. 'How about if I come back at closing time? A quick drink, eh? Go on, Eve. After all, nothing for either of us to rush home for, is there?'

She hesitated. Knowing Eddie's persistence as she did, he'd only be back, pestering her again tomorrow if she refused now. Might as well get it over with. Find out what new dodge he'd dreamed up and try to forestall it. 'All right then, if you must,' she said. 'But just ten minutes, no more. And remember what I said.' She lowered her voice, 'It's no use expecting any more cash.'

He was there waiting when she closed the shop. As she locked the door for the night and pulled down the shop blinds, she saw him standing outside the florist's shop opposite. He waved to her and she ignored him. She'd already cashed up and put the takings into the bag ready for the night safe, which she passed on her way home. Putting on her coat she left the shop by the rear entrance, but when Eddie suddenly stepped out of the shadows as she was locking the door, she started violently.

'*Oh my God!* You frightened the life out of me, jumping out like that. I thought you were going to wait round at the front,' she said breathlessly.

'Sorry if I scared you,' he said contritely. 'I was afraid you might change your mind and nip off home the back way. That would have disappointed me.' He attempted to take her arm but she shook his hand off.

347

'I suppose people with devious minds like yours are up to tricks like that,' she said, still rattled. 'You should know by now that when I give my word, I keep it.'

'Not above turning to desperate measures to get what you want though, are you, Eve?'

She shot him a sharp look. 'I thought you said that was all water under the bridge?'

'It is, it is.'

She walked beside him in silence, pausing to slip the takings into the night safe as they passed the bank. Soon after that Eddie stopped at the entrance to a pub called The Mailcart.

'Shall we step in here?' he asked. 'It'll be quiet this early.' He ushered Eve through to the lounge bar, which was almost empty. Finding a seat in the corner, he raised an eyebrow at her. 'What'll you have?'

She shrugged. 'It's early. I'll just have a cup of coffee if they've got it.'

'Coffee?' He pulled a face. 'Okay. If you're sure.' He went off to the bar and came back a few minutes later with a coffee for her and a double whisky for himself. Taking a sip from his glass, he looked at her over the rim. 'How's Carol?' he asked.

Eve felt a stab of disquiet. 'She's fine. In London, catching up with her career. Why do you want to know?'

He shrugged. 'No reason, except that she's my daughter. Not that anyone'd know it. Only way I ever get news of her is through a third party.' He shook his head sadly. 'I've never worked out why she's so hostile towards me.'

'Then you've even less imagination than I thought,' Eve told him. 'Is that why we're here – to talk about Carol?'

Eddie ignored the question. 'Even my youngest has left me now, you know,' he told her. 'You remember young Paul, don't you? Well, you would – good reason to, eh?

348

Left for a job as trainee manager at a supermarket in Kettering. I told him he was making a mistake. Those Yankee places'll never take on over here. British housewives like the personal touch.'

'Well, I can't say I blame him for leaving.' Eve lifted her coffee cup. 'If you ask me, I'd say you're lucky he stuck you as long as he did.'

'That's not very friendly, is it?' He looked at her for a long moment, sipping his whisky then rubbing the back of his hand across his mouth. 'You're very bitter, aren't you, Eve? Look, fair enough. I've done a lot of rotten things in my time. Not least to you. Now I want to put all that behind me. I'm asking you to give me a chance to make amends.' He looked at her quizzically. 'I hope you're not going to make it hard for me?'

'Can you blame me for not trusting you?' she asked caustically.

'No. I daresay I deserve everything you think about me. But I'm like you now, Eve. I'm alone in the world. We've got that in common. We both know what it's like to sit looking at four walls every night – trying to struggle on alone. And it don't get any easier the older you get, does it?'

Eve shifted uncomfortably in her chair. 'Look, why don't you just say what you really want, Eddie?'

'Okay. But it's simple really. I just want you and me to be friends. And for starters you can drop those monthly payments.'

'Why? What's the catch?'

'No catch. I don't expect you to start trusting or even *liking* me all at once. All I ask is that you give me a chance to make it up to you – show you that I'm a reformed character.'

Deeply suspicious, Eve frowned. All this was so unlike the Eddie Wilson she had known since her youth. She had never felt easy in his company and sitting here now, having a drink with him, was slightly bizarre, like some kind of improbable fantasy. 'So you're saying I can stop the payments?' she said slowly. 'I take it your business is looking up?'

He looked surprised. 'Never better. What made you think different? Look, you've been a good mother to my girl. Better than poor Sally would ever have been. A hundred times better. She's a credit to us, is Carol.' Reaching across the table he laid a hand on hers. 'We've got our girl in common, haven't we, Eve? You and me, we're her mum and dad. Looking at it like that, we owe it to her to be mates, don't you think?'

Eve felt a shudder go through her as she withdrew her hand from under his. If he noticed he gave no sign.

'So – even if it's just for Carol's sake, why don't we meet up like this now and again? Just relax and chat over a drink or a meal – say once a week?' he went on. 'You can tell me your news and Carol's, and I can tell you mine. We can have a bit of a laugh together. It'll be something to look forward to. What d'you say then, eh?'

A bit of a laugh together! What a ludicrous thought. Eve took a long drink of her coffee, wondering why she had the feeling that this was merely some new form of blackmail. She was sure of only one thing. Whatever Eddie had in mind it was he who would benefit. Somehow or other she would still be paying. If she had the choice she would far rather keep sending him the monthly cheque than be trapped into meeting him like this on a regular basis.

'Oh, Carol, you look *gorgeous*!' Janet stood back to survey her friend as she stood ready to go to the opening night.

To Janet's delight Carol had agreed to the shopping

jaunt in the King's Road and to having her hair done at a West End salon. At Janet's suggestion she had had her thick blonde hair cut in the fashionable swinging jaw-length bob with a fringe. The dress Janet had urged her to buy was a vibrant shade of sapphire blue; a brief shift of delicately spangled chiffon over a silky underslip. Its simplicity suited her slender figure and shapely legs to perfection. There were plain satin shoes and a bag to go with it and, to complete the ensemble, Janet had begged the loan of a soft white fur stole from a colleague's wife at the hospital. Now she slipped this over Carol's shoulders as they waited on the steps for Clarissa to collect her in the car.

'You look fabulous, really you do,' she assured Carol. 'Like Dusty Springfield and Julie Christie rolled into one.' She touched Carol's hand and found she was trembling. 'You're cold!'

'No. Just nervous,' Carol said with a tremulous smile.

'Well, *don't* be. I've got a feeling about this evening. I can feel in my bones it's going to be special for you.' Janet hugged her. 'There's a hint of magic in the air.'

Carol laughed. 'You and your optimism. Thanks for everything, Janet. I don't think I'd have had the nerve to go if it hadn't been for you.'

'Rubbish, even someone as daft as you couldn't be barmy enough to pass up an occasion like this,' Janet said. 'Just don't forget to bring me a programme – and a doggie-bag. And spare a thought for your poor doctor friend slaving away in Casualty while you're living it up at the Cafe Royal.' She pulled a face. 'On second thoughts, I'm the barmy one. You get to go to glamorous opening nights while I'm sewing up broken heads and mopping up vomit? I need my head examining!'

Carol laughed. 'Go on, you know you wouldn't change places with anyone.'

351

As Clarissa's car drew into the kerb and hooted, Janet gave Carol a push.

'Go on, Cinders. There's your fairy coach. Have a ball! And if you dare come home before midnight, I'll never speak to you again!' She stood waving on the steps until the car had been swallowed up by the traffic, then went indoors to get ready for work.

'Have a lovely time, Carol,' she whispered. 'I've got my fingers crossed for you. If Steven doesn't think you're a complete knock-out tonight there must be something seriously wrong with his eyesight.'

Clarissa had already picked up Kitty, who sat in the back of the car bubbling with excitement. She was wearing a stunning evening dress of emerald green watered silk, shot with purple, and her luxuriant hair was an even more improbable shade of auburn than usual. She kissed Carol on both cheeks.

'You look lovely, darling. I want to hear all your news,' she said. 'I've seen you in the Romaine ad on TV, of course. And the one for Midnight shampoo. You look so glamorous. I'm very proud of you.'

Carol smiled. 'I wish there was something for you to be really proud of, Kitty. Anyone can do commercials.'

'Not a bit of it! Don't run yourself down so,' she admonished. 'You have to start somewhere. And as Zelda says, it's good to . . .'

'*Be seen working!*' Carol finished for her, and they both laughed.

'Dear Zelda,' Kitty said. 'She and Marty have had a new lease of life since they started that agency. They love it.'

The theatre foyer was buzzing with an atmosphere of excited anticipation when they arrived and while they waited for Clarissa to park the car Kitty and Carol studied the displays of stills. Madeleine Lindsay looked stunning in the leading part and Paul Slade was the perfect romantic leading man. From the costumes, Carol saw that it was set in the nineteen twenties.

'You know the story, I expect?' Kitty said. Carol shook her head and Kitty looked surprised. 'I'd have thought Steven would have told you. It's about a small-town girl who makes it to Hollywood in the silent film days. It's not just a romance, though. There are gangsters in it too and he tells me there's a hint of tragedy.' She gave an excited little giggle. 'Oh, I can't *wait* to see it, can you?'

Impresario Graham Lang was entertaining the invited guests with drinks in the Green Room before the show and as soon as Clarissa joined them they made their way up the stairs and through a pass door. There was still forty minutes till curtain-up and they were among the first to arrive. As they walked in Carol caught her breath. Standing at the bar was a tall, distinguished-looking man in evening dress whom Clarissa pointed out as Graham Lang himself. Standing on either side of him were Freddie and Steven.

Carol hung back a little, suddenly diffident. Steven looked handsome and slightly forbidding in his tails and white tie. He wore a new air of success about him like a glowing aura. How much had all this changed him? she wondered.

Clarissa took Carol's arm, with a gleeful smile. 'Come on. I can't wait to see Steven's face. I told him I had a surprise for him. Now he's going to find out that it's you!'

As they walked towards him Steven turned and looked straight into Carol's eyes. For a moment it was as though he didn't recognise her, then as realisation dawned a smile spread slowly over his face. His eyes lit up as he came towards her with his hands outstretched.

'*Carrie!*' He took both her hands, his eyes drinking in every inch of her. 'You look fantastic!'

Clarissa laughed. 'I told you I had a surprise for you.'

The breath caught in Carol's throat. He was suddenly the Steven she had always known.

He glanced over her shoulder. 'Where's – er – Michael?'

'Mike's not with me, Steven,' she said. 'He and I parted some months ago.'

'Oh, I'm sorry.'

'No, you were right. It wouldn't have worked.'

'Well, I'm glad you're here anyway.' For a moment there was a brief silence between them, then Steven said, 'What am I thinking of? You must meet everyone. Freddie you know, of course.' He turned to Graham Lang. 'Graham, I'd like you to meet Carol Kenning. My first ever girlfriend. One of my mother's most talented students, and a very promising actress.'

The silver-haired man turned to smile at her. 'How do you do, Miss Kenning?' he said. His voice was deep with only a hint of an American accent. 'I do hope you're going to enjoy this evening with us. I think it's going to be quite an occasion.'

The phrase, 'enjoy this evening' was the understatement of the century for Carol. The evening was sheer delight from the moment Steven stood in front of the orchestra and raised his baton for the overture, to the stunning finale. An explosion of talent. Splendid acting and wonderful singing. Colourful costumes and a brilliant storyline. But best of all was Steven's music. As she watched him conducting the orchestra from her seat in Clarissa's box, and listened to the sweeping melodies he had composed, Carol's heart swelled with pride and pleasure. With his musical genius he had recreated the atmosphere of twenties Hollywood so evocatively. All the emotion was there, from the hauntingly tender songs in the romantic scenes to the sinister undertones of the

354

darker moments. Freddie's lyrics were good too, sparkling with wit and inventiveness. But for Carol it was the music above all else that made the show. Throughout the evening she was enthralled by the joyous brilliance of it all.

As the final scene drew to its conclusion Kitty nudged her, pointing to the row of critics who, one by one, were now quietly leaving their seats, eager to reach the nearest telephone and ring their reviews through in time for the early editions of tomorrow morning's papers.

'I've been watching them,' she whispered. 'So much depends on these first reviews. But I've got a good feeling about them.' She felt for Carol's hand and squeezed it hard. 'I do believe Fred and Stevie have got a hit on their hands darling!'

It was a glittering throng that filled the large room at the Cafe Royal with their excited chatter. The cast of the show were all there, surrounded by admirers and well-wishers, all eager to offer their congratulations. There were other show business celebrities too, directors, producers and musicians. The press was represented by selected gossip columnists and journalists from show business magazines, all of whom had received invitations from Graham Lang's office. Every few seconds Carol saw the blink of flash bulbs as photographers captured intimate and exclusive shots of their favourite celebrities.

Kitty was enjoying herself enormously, sparkling like a woman half her age as she laughed and chatted animatedly. Someone put a glass of champagne in Carol's hand and somehow she found herself holding a plate of food for which she had no appetite. Then suddenly Steven was at her side.

'At last,' he said breathlessly. 'Well – what's the verdict?'

She saw that he had changed out of full evening dress into a black velvet dinner jacket. 'I'm sure you don't need to ask *me*.' She smiled. 'Everyone is saying how marvellous it was.'

'But you, Carrie – what do you say?'

He was looking at her as though it really mattered to him what she thought. Did he really mean it, or was this all part of the glossy new image that was Steven Manson, successful composer?

'I loved it, Steven. It was beautiful,' she said softly. She raised her glass. 'Here's to *Shooting Star*. May it run and run.'

'Thanks. Success to *Shooting Star*,' he echoed. Holding her eyes with his, he raised his own glass to his lips and drank. 'I've missed you, Carrie,' he said softly. 'I thought I'd probably never see you again. Rissa said she had a surprise for me this evening, but I never dreamed it would be something this good. It made the evening for me, knowing you were out there. How long are you staying in Town?'

'I've got a confession to make,' she said. 'I've been in London for the past three months. I've been trying to get my career started again.'

His eyes widened. 'And you didn't get in touch?'

She shook her head. 'I wasn't sure if . . .'

'Well, I hope you are now.' He raised an inquiring eyebrow. 'Aren't you?' The band began to play the theme song from the show, *My Shooting Star*, and he took her glass from her and put it on a nearby table. 'Dance with me, Carrie?' he invited. 'Make the evening complete.'

As they circled the small dance floor he said, 'I've seen you in that shampoo ad. The first time I saw it I could hardly believe my eyes. But it never occurred to me you were living in London. I thought by now you'd be in some cosy little suburban love nest with your new husband.'

'Don't, Steven,' she said, lowering her eyes.

He looked down at her. 'I'm sorry, darling. Was it painful, the parting?'

'Of course. I felt I'd let him down. And whatever else I feel, I'm still fond of Mike. I've known him all my life and he's a good man.'

He winced. 'I hope I never hear any woman describe me as a "good man".'

Carol frowned. 'There are worse descriptions.'

'Not when you want to be thought of as exciting and passionate.'

'Is that how you like to be seen?'

He laughed. 'Who doesn't?'

'Well, I'm sure you are,' she said coolly.

He made a wry face at her. 'You're still hurting, aren't you, Carol?'

She shook her head impatiently. 'There's more to it than just a broken engagement. It's a long story. One I've no intention of spoiling the evening with.'

'I want to hear it.'

'No. Not now. Maybe some other time. Tonight is for celebrating.'

The music came to an end and Zelda came hurrying towards them. She shot Steven an apologetic look. 'Excuse me for butting in, both of you, but there's someone over there who wants to say hello to Carol.' She grasped Carol's hand and before she could protest, began to draw her along. 'Hurry up, darling. He's over there talking to Marty.' Steven turned away to speak to someone else and was swallowed up by the crowd. Zelda led her to the other side of the room where Marty Waring was talking to a tall man who looked familiar. He turned and a moment later she found herself looking into the familiar craggy face of Gareth Dean. He smiled.

'How nice to see you again, Carol. Did you enjoy the show?'

She took the large hand he offered. 'I did, very much. I've known Steven since I was eight years old and I'm very proud of him tonight.'

'Justifiably. *Star* is one of the best musicals I've seen for a long time, on either side of the pond. Steven's music is so fresh and exciting. Wonderful! I'm sure he and Freddie Manners have a glittering future ahead of them.' Still holding her hand he asked, 'And what are you doing these days, Carol? Apart from the commercials, I mean.'

'Not very much. I was so disappointed not to be able to accept your offer of a part in *Dance With Angels* last autumn,' she said quietly.

'And I was disappointed not to get you,' he said. 'Especially as it's been so successful. But obviously you had no choice in the tragic circumstances.' He paused. 'So you're not under contract at the moment?'

'No.'

'I'm asking because I have a new project coming up shortly. Everything is still under wraps at the moment, but I can tell you that it's for television.' He smiled. 'Having seen how well you come across on the small screen, I feel confident that TV is a good medium for you. So would you be interested if I were to ask you to come for an audition?'

Carol heart leaped. 'Oh, yes. Thank you. I mean – if it happens.'

He laughed. 'Oh, it'll happen all right. It's just that we're still negotiating – thrashing out minor details and so on. I'll be in touch with Zelda then.' He patted her hand and dropped it. 'Enjoy your evening, Carol. I hope I'll be seeing you again soon.'

As he walked away to rejoin his party Zelda and Marty suddenly reappeared at her side. 'Well, what did he say?' she asked breathlessly.

Carol looked at her, feeling slightly dazed with

disbelief. 'He says he's about to get a new project off the ground,' she said. 'He didn't say what, but he asked me if I was willing and free to audition for a part in it.'

Zelda smiled with satisfaction. 'I've heard on the grapevine that it's to be a twice weekly serial for commercial TV,' she said. 'The kind of thing the Americans call a "soap opera". It could be the break you've been looking for.'

Marty frowned. 'Don't build the girl's hopes up too much, Zel,' he said. 'You know what these things are like. Could be a nine-days' wonder; nothing more than a couple of weeks' walk-ons. Who knows?'

'Don't be such an old Jonah!' Zelda tapped his arm reproachfully. 'I'm sure Carol's feet are firmly on the ground. She knows as well as we do that it's all in the laps of the gods in this game.' She slipped an arm round Carol's waist and gave her a squeeze. 'Just cross your fingers and hope for the best, sweetie. Gareth's certainly impressed with your work. Now perhaps you can see what I mean when I say it's good to be seen working!'

The evening passed in a whirl of music and champagne. Countless toasts were drunk to Freddie and Steven, wishing the show success and a long run. The band played for dancing and as often as he could Steven danced with Carol. As she circled the crowded floor in his arms, her head spinning with champagne and the heady elation of the evening, she wondered how on earth she would come down to earth tomorrow morning after all the excitement.

Clarissa came to find her soon after midnight and explained that she was going home because the baby would be needing a feed.

'I'm taking Kitty home with me,' she said. 'I've told Steven. She's looking rather tired. But of course Steven and Freddie must stay for the first editions of the papers.' She looked at Carol. 'You'll stay too, won't you?'

Carol nodded. 'If Steven wants me to.'

Clarissa smiled. 'Of course he does. Your being here has made the evening for him. Anyway, you can't possibly leave till the reviews come out.'

Breakfast was laid on at five for the revellers who had stuck it out and as they were finishing Harry Simmons, Graham Lang's personal assistant, went out for the papers. He had already scanned through the reviews on his way back in the taxi and when he breezed excitedly in it was plain to see that they were favourable. The three men read through them quickly, then Harry was given the task of reading them out aloud.

One after another, in varying degrees, the theatre critics praised *Shooting Star*, hailing it as a sure-fire hit. Harry picked out half a dozen at random, to be received with cheers and applause. Carol had only to look at the radiant faces of Steven and Freddie to know that for them tonight was a dream come true as well as the culmination of almost two years' hard work.

She left the table quietly and went in search of her wrap. She was at the top of the stairs on her way down when someone touched her arm. She turned and saw that it was Steven.

'What's this? You're not running out on me?'

She laughed. 'It's already tomorrow in case you hadn't noticed. You've got another show to do in a few hours' time. You should go home and get some sleep.'

'*Sleep?*' He shook his head. 'I couldn't sleep to save my life. At least, not yet. I'm still on too much of a high. Walk back to the flat with me, Carrie. I'll make you some coffee and we can wind down together.'

Outside the air was fresh and clean, a perfect spring morning. They stood for a moment, breathing it in. It was strange to see Piccadilly so empty of crowds, peaceful almost. Steven's new flat was only about ten minutes' walk away in Maddox Street. As they walked he took her hand.

'Oscar Wilde must have walked home from the Cafe Royal in the early morning like this after his first nights,' he said. 'Can't you imagine him and Lillie Langtry walking up Regent Street in all their finery – just like we are now?'

Carol laughed. 'I see what you mean about still being on a high.'

The flat was on the second floor above a solicitor's office. It was quite small but well appointed, a far cry from the scruffy little bed-sit he'd once had. In the kitchen they made coffee and toast together and, bit by bit, Carol revealed the humiliating and traumatic events that had led to the breaking of her engagement and her decision to leave home and come to London.

'Kitty talked me into it really. She said I needed enough time and space to find the real me. To work out who and what I am.'

Steven smiled. 'Wise old Kitty. I'm sure she was right.' He took her hand and turned her towards him. 'And I'm glad you're here and especially that you came to share tonight with me.'

'I'm glad too, Steven. It's been marvellous. I wouldn't have missed it for anything.'

'This has been the most magical night of my life.' He looked into her eyes. 'Made even more perfect by the fact that you were there.'

'Now you're teasing.' She turned away but he held on to her hand and pulled her to him, his eyes serious.

'I'm not teasing. Carol – surely you realise that I've always loved you?'

For a moment she thought she could not have heard him right. Her heart seemed to stop in her breast as she stood looking up at him, her wide with wonder. '*Me?* But I thought – there was always someone else.'

361

'Oh, I tried very hard not to,' he said with a wry smile. 'Everything seemed to point to the fact that it wasn't on. You were so much younger. It wouldn't have been fair, before you'd grown up – tried your wings. Before – as Kitty said – you knew who and what you really were.'

'I'm grown up now,' she whispered.

He smiled. 'I've noticed.'

'I've been grown up for a long time. And anyway, you're not that much older.'

'Perhaps not now. It was different when you were fourteen and I was twenty-two.'

'You're still on that high,' she warned him. 'When you come down to earth again you'll wish you hadn't said any of this.'

'Oh no I won't.' His arms went round her, pulling her close. 'The only regret I'd have now would be letting you slip through my fingers again.'

Outside the window the sunbeams danced on the dew-wet rooftops as their lips met in the kind of kiss Carol had known only in her dreams. When they drew apart they were both breathless and trembling.

'Can you imagine how I felt last Christmas when you told me you were engaged?' he whispered.

'Why didn't you say anything? Why didn't you tell me then?'

He shook his head. 'God only knows I wanted to. Everything in me screamed out to beg you not to marry Mike – to tell you how I felt. But you seemed so sure about it. For all I knew you really did love him. Who was I to stand in your way?'

' 'How do you think I felt, seeing you with Clarissa – knowing you and she were living together – seeing the places and the things you shared? It hurt so much, Steven. And being young didn't make it any easier.'

'I'm sorry, darling.' He held her close for a moment.

'Oddly enough it was Rissa who made me face up to the truth in the end,' he told her. 'She always knew things weren't right between us – that deep inside I belonged to someone else. Eventually she worked out that it was you. Only by then it seemed I'd left it too late.' He looked into her eyes. 'Carrie, when you grew up, did you put me aside with other childish things?'

'I often wished I could.' She smiled wryly. 'But I could never put you aside, however hard I tried. What I've always felt for you hasn't changed. It's as much a part of me as breathing.'

He kissed her again. 'You don't have to go yet, do you?'

'No, but . . .' Carol's heart began to quicken as he led her gently through to the hallway. 'Kitty . . .

'It was no accident that Rissa took Kitty home with her.' Steven smiled. 'I've arranged to go and pick her up later. We have the day to ourselves, Carrie. Please stay.'

The bedroom was spacious and dim, with the curtains drawn against the rest of the world. The sheets felt smooth and warm against Carol's skin as she lay drowsily relaxed in Steven's arms, watching a sunbeam that had found its way through a chink in the curtains to dance on the floor. Its light caught the blue dress that lay by the bed where she had stepped out of it, turning it into a shimmering pool.

No two people have ever been closer than this, she told herself sleepily, her face buried against Steven's shoulder; fused and melted into one by the fulfilment of the love they had each longed for and wanted for so long.

When the storm of their passion was spent they had slept briefly, but now they lay drowsily entwined, drugged with the languor of love, too heavy to move until Steven stirred and kissed her forehead.

'Tell me what you're thinking?' he asked.

She looked up at him. 'I was thinking that if I were to die right now it wouldn't matter,' she told him. 'My life – everything that's happened in it – would not have been in vain. Because nothing else could ever be as beautiful as this moment, here and now.'

He cupped her face in his hands. 'Don't say that. You make it sound as though this is all there is. From here on life is going to get better and better. We're together now. The future is wonderful and it's all there, pristine and untouched, waiting to be lived.' He kissed her. 'Oh, Carrie, I feel twelve foot tall. Now I've got everything. There isn't anything I couldn't do. I could go out and . . . and . . .'

'And kill dragons?' She raised herself on her elbow to smile down at him.

He laughed and pulled her close. 'Yes, dragons. The biggest, the fiercest, the *fieriest* ones you can find!'

'There are no more dragons to kill,' she whispered. 'Not any more. I'm free now. I can even think about Eddie Wilson's being my father without shuddering. None of that seems to matter any more.' She laid a finger against his lips. 'But even though I'd like this moment to last forever, I think I'm going to have to go home. Because you absolutely *must* get some sleep, my darling.'

As she made to get up he caught her hand. 'No. Don't go. Stay with me, just a little longer. Later we'll get up and eat, then you can be with me until I have to go to the theatre.'

'No!' She laughed and shook her head. 'One of us has to be practical. If I stay you won't sleep and there'll be no *Shooting Star* tonight. And that would be a disaster, now that the whole of London will be talking about it. Even now they're probably queuing up to buy tickets.'

She slipped out of bed and wrapped herself in Steven's

dressing gown. 'I'll set your alarm clock for you then I'll ring for a minicab.'

She showered and dressed, then ordered her taxi. When she came back to say goodbye Steven lay on his back, fast asleep, an ecstatic smile on his lips. One arm was spread across the warm hollow left by her body. She scribbled a note for him, including her telephone number, then tucked the blankets gently round him and bent to kiss his cheek.

'Sleep tight, darling,' she whispered. 'Sweet dreams. See you tomorrow.'

Chapter Eleven

Eve picked up the handful of envelopes from the mat and smiled as she caught sight of the one with Carol's handwriting. She looked forward to her letters eagerly. Since the girl had left home for London, Eve had been feeling more and more isolated. She still missed Jack, of course, but was resigned to that, knowing that she would miss him for the rest of her life.

She missed her family too. Because she and Rose were still not speaking she felt cut off from the rest of her relatives. Knowing that Freda loved to see her great-grandchildren and that Rose would encourage Elizabeth to stay away if she thought Eve would be there, she thought up fresh excuses every week not to join them for the usual family Sunday tea at her mother's house. She would claim that there was paperwork to catch up on for the shop or letters to write. She would say she was tired – had a cold she didn't want to pass on to the babies. It was all a façade of course. Freda knew quite well that her daughters were stubbornly refusing to make up their quarrel but, caught in the middle, she took the line of least resistance, seeing Eve as often as she could and putting in the odd soothing word to both daughters in the hope that things would eventually get better.

Eve carried her letters back to the kitchen where she had just brewed her morning pot of tea. Pouring herself a cup, she opened them one by one, leaving Carol's till last. There were two bills and the rest were birthday cards, one from her mother and father and one each from Michael and Elizabeth. There was one from Jack's mother too, none from Rose. But then, she had hardly expected one.

Finally she opened Carol's. There was a lovely card with a glossy picture of roses and, tucked inside, a long letter. She sounded happy and excited; full of the opening night of Steven's musical play and the grand party that had followed at a smart London restaurant. Eve already knew that the play had been a great success. There had been write-ups and interviews in many of the papers. Now, reading between the lines of Carol's letter, it seemed that she and Steven were seeing a lot of each other.

Eve laid down the letter and sipped at her tea thoughtfully. She could not deny that she had been upset and disappointed when Carol had broken off her engagement to Michael. She had been so sure they were made for each other, and his future was stable and assured. Carol would have wanted for nothing as his wife. Eve had looked forward to seeing her daughter settled and happy, with a loving husband and children and no money worries.

Steven was a nice enough young man, of course. Eve had no fault to find with him as a person. But from what she could see, life in the theatre world was insecure and precarious. No such thing as a steady job with prospects. It seemed to be either fame and fortune or a hand-to-mouth existence of poverty and struggle. Living out of a suitcase and never having a place to call home. A gypsy's life. Show business marriages seemed doomed too, if what you read in the papers was anything to go by. And the more successful the partners, the more chance there seemed to be of its not lasting. Kitty Manson was living proof of that, and Steven was her son after all. He'd been brought up to it and had known no different.

She sighed, acknowledging that there was nothing she could do about it any more. She herself had encouraged

367

Carol to take up drama and dancing as a child. It had been because she'd so badly wanted her to shine at something. She had never envisaged the child going on to make a career out of it. Appearing in Kitty's concerts was fine. Something to show off about a little if she were truthful. But taking it up professionally . . . Still, Carol was a grown woman. She must make her own decisions, choose the kind of life she wanted. True she'd had some success appearing in those TV commercials, but to Eve it didn't seem much of a job. When customers came into the shop and mentioned that they'd seen Carol the previous night on television, she felt slightly embarrassed. Having the world and his wife seeing your daughter scrubbing her teeth in their living rooms seemed slightly demeaning to her. But she smiled and put up with the well-meaning jokes, hoping that one day Carol would grow tired of it all; give up the idea of being a famous actress and come home.

Eve couldn't help thinking that when she was young life had been so much simpler. As often as not the man you married was someone you had known all your life. You walked out together, worked hard, saved up, got married and had your family, in that order. But since the war everything had changed. There had been so much turmoil. She thought of all those GI brides and the culture shock and disillusionment many of them had faced going out to a new life in America. And now there was all this talk of women's liberation. Equality, they called it. And this newly invented contraceptive pill that meant women could make their own choices about sex and pregnancy. Couples nowadays seemed to feel there was no need for a marriage certificate as often as not. It would all end in tears, Eve prophesied. As long as women were the ones who gave birth there could be no equality; no easy way out for them. Women were just plain

368

different and there was no getting away from the fact.

As she washed the dishes from her solitary breakfast she was already composing the letter she would write Carol in reply. It was becoming increasingly difficult to sound enthusiastic or to think of interesting items of news. Life was lonely and tedious, and recently even telling the truth was becoming a problem. She didn't want the girl worrying about her loneliness or her alienation from the family. Or about the other problem in her life that seemed to loom larger with every week.

Since Eddie's first unexpected visit she had received several more. He would arrive without warning at closing time, trapping her into going for a drink with him on the way home. He insisted that he was trying to make amends for the pain he had caused her in the past. Sometimes he was so convincing that she almost believed he was the reformed character he made himself out to be. His last visit had been two days ago, when he had informed her that he was booking a table for dinner for Friday evening.

'Come on, Eve,' he'd said. 'I know it's your birthday on Friday.'

'Who says it's my birthday?' she asked him, trying to hide her dismay.

He grinned delightedly. 'It's all right. I'm not going to ask which one.' He looked at her. 'Well, isn't it?' Her silence confirmed it. 'And are you telling me you're just going home after work to an empty flat?'

'What if I am?' she said. 'It'll be nothing unusual. Anyway I don't need a reminder of how old I am. Not at my age.'

'Get along with you,' he said. 'You're as old as you feel. That's what I always say.' His eyes glinted at her persuasively. 'And as old as you *look*. And you look younger than ever. Come on, girl, be a devil. Let's live it up a bit. I'll give you a good night out. Trust me, eh?'

Trust me! The phrase was ironic. Reluctantly, Eve told him she'd think about it and he had to be content with that. But she knew he'd go ahead and book the table anyhow. She also knew that he'd probably wear her down in the end. She'd go just to get rid of him. Though even Eve knew that as far as Eddie was concerned, giving in wasn't the answer.

Halfway through the morning a boy arrived with a huge bouquet of pink roses. Nestling among the cellophane paper and ribbon was a card. *From Carol, with love and best wishes for a happy birthday*. The shop was empty and Eve hurried into the back room to put the flowers in water. She was just unwrapping them when the telephone rang.

'Hello? Kenning's newsagents.'

'Mum! Happy birthday. Did you get my card?'

'I did, love. And the beautiful roses. They've just this minute arrived. I was just putting them . . .'

'Mum! Listen, I've got an audition. It's for a part in a television serial. I think I told you in my letter that I'd met Gareth Dean again?'

'Yes, you did. That was the man who offered you a part the day that your dad . . . ?'

'Yes. It's this afternoon, Mum. Oh, wish me luck.'

'I do, of course. You'll let me know?'

'I will. As soon as I know myself.' There was a pause. 'Mum – there's something else. You've probably gathered that Steven and I have been seeing each other?'

'Yes.' Eve held her breath. Surely they weren't planning to get married yet?

'Well, I – I just wanted you to know that I've moved into his flat. So when you write the address will be . . .'

'Oh, *Carol*!'

'It's all right, Mum. I love him. We love each other. We always have. That's why I couldn't marry Mike. Deep down I always knew it wouldn't work. Oh, *please* be happy for me, Mum.'

'If you say so.' Eve's heart was heavy as she carefully wrote down the address that Carol gave her. No good would come of all this, she told herself gloomily.

'I'll try and come home soon, Mum,' Carol said. 'Steven too. It all depends on what happens really.'

'Yes. Yes, I see.'

'I wish I could be with you for your birthday, Mum. Are you going out – doing anything special?'

'As a matter of fact, I'm being taken out to dinner,' Eve heard herself say.

'Dinner, eh? Sounds intriguing. Who with?'

Eve hesitated, wondering why she'd said it. If Carol knew who her dinner companion was to be she'd be horrified. 'Oh, no one special,' she said. 'Just a friend.'

'Well, have a lovely evening. I'll be in touch again soon. 'Bye, Mum.'

Carol's news put a cloud over the rest of the day for Eve. She'd almost forgotten about Eddie when he came sauntering into the shop at closing time.

'For the birthday girl,' he said, producing an orchid in a transparent box from behind his back.

Eve looked at the exotic flower with something approaching revulsion. 'Oh, my God! Whatever possessed you to bring me a thing like that?'

His eyebrows rose. 'I thought all ladies liked orchids?' he said. 'I wanted you to have something nice to wear to the restaurant.'

Eve looked down at her plain navy and white Crimpelene dress and jacket, then back at the showy purple bloom. 'I can't wear that. It'll make me look like a floozy,' she said uncomfortably.

Eddie sniggered. 'As if you could ever look like a floozy!'

371

She shook her head. 'I'm sorry, Eddie, I'm just not the orchid type. It's lovely, though. Do you mind if I just take it home and put it in water?'

'Course not,' he said. 'Do whatever you want. Come on. Table's booked for seven and I've got the car waiting.'

When Eve saw that Eddie had booked a table at the most expensive restaurant in town she almost refused to go in. But once inside, the luxurious ambience of the place intimidated her into silence. A waiter ushered them to their table, pulled out Eve's chair for her and gave them each a tasselled menu. When he had gone Eddie looked at her over the top of his.

'Go on. Anything you fancy,' he said. 'And don't look at the prices. This is my birthday treat.'

Eve scanned the menu and conservatively ordered soup, followed by a steak. Eddie followed suit. He also ordered a bottle of wine and insisted that Eve drink to her birthday and the 'renewal of their friendship', a phrase that made her distinctly uncomfortable. As she remembered it there'd been never been anything remotely approaching a friendship between them in the first place.

The food and wine were good and she gradually felt herself relaxing as the evening wore on. Perhaps Eddie really did feel remorseful about what he had done? They lingered over coffee and he lit a cigar and sat back to enjoy it. It was almost ten o'clock when he looked at his watch. 'How about a brandy or liqueur?'

Eve shook her head. 'I've had far more to drink tonight than I'm used to. It's all been very nice.'

'Want to go then?'

She nodded.

Eddie drove into the underground car park at the flats and turned to her as he switched off the engine. 'Eve – there's something I'd like to discuss with you. I reckon this is as good a moment as any, don't you?'

She shrugged. 'I can think of better places than in a dark car park,' she said dryly.

'Exactly.' He smiled. 'So shall we go up to your flat for a nightcap?'

She bit her lip, realising she had walked neatly into his carefully laid snare. 'What is it you want to discuss?' she asked. 'It's getting late and . . .'

'It won't take long,' he told her. 'In fact, what I've got to say can be said in a few words. But if I'm not welcome . . .' He looked suddenly crestfallen and she hesitated.

'Well . . .'

'Oh, come on, Eve,' he wheedled. 'I've got to talk to someone or I'll go round the twist. There's no one but you who understands. All my family have gone now – like yours. You know what it's like when you've got a really pressing problem and no one to talk it over with.'

Eve sighed. He had just bought her an expensive meal, whether she had wanted him to or not. It would be mean to walk away now. She began to get out of the car. 'All right then, if you promise it really won't take long.'

In the flat she put the kettle on for coffee and switched on the electric fire. Eddie stretched out in her favourite chair. 'This is nice, Eve,' he remarked, looking round. 'A little place like this is all you need when you're on your own and out working all week. Did I tell you I'd put my place on the market?'

'No.' She sat down on the settee opposite him. 'Too big for you now, is it?'

'It's true I rattle around in the place.' He sat up to lean his elbows on his knees, his face grave. 'But it's more a case of having to sell up. Business is on the skids, Eve,' he said, shaking his head. 'I've been trying to pull things together for months now, but it's no go. Fact is, I've got to find some cash from somewhere to pay my creditors. It's either that or declare myself bankrupt.'

'Oh, dear.' Eve looked at him. 'I'd no idea things were as bad as that.'

'Trouble is, if I go bankrupt I've had it as far as business is concerned,' he told her. 'Never be allowed to trade again. Then what'll I do?'

'Isn't there some way you can save the business?' she asked.

He shook his head. 'Not that I haven't tried. The small shops I've always supplied are going to the wall. It's these bloody supermarkets. There are still the corner shops, of course, but now these new national conglomerates have taken over them. They've banded together and formed a company, to buy in bulk and supply the little shops cheaper. The competition's too fierce.' He swallowed hard. 'I'm finished, Eve, done for. On the scrapheap at fifty. Fifteen good working years in me yet – more even.'

'I'm sorry to hear this, Eddie,' she said uncomfortably.

'Yeah, well . . .' He pulled out his cigarette case and went through the ritual of lighting a cigarette. Blowing out a cloud of smoke, he peered at her. 'There is just one last chance – one way out for me. But that would involve throwing myself on your mercy.'

Eve could hear the kettle boiling and stood up. Something about Eddie's servile manner and the way he was looking at her was ringing all her alarm bells. She was pretty sure she was about to be presented with a problem she could do without.

'No, don't go, Eve. Sit down,' he said, his voice suddenly urgent. 'Never mind the coffee. I'm not thirsty anyway.' He reached for her hand and jerked her off balance so that she sat down again. 'Listen . . .' He got up and quickly joined her on the settee, so close that she could feel his thigh pressed against hers and his breath on her cheek when he spoke.

'You 'n' me could be partners,' he said with breathless

urgency. 'We're two of a kind, Eve. Even if you don't think so now, I could prove it to you. I've got a bloody good business head on me. I could make that newsagent's of yours into a little gold mine.'

'It's all right as it is. I don't need a partner,' she said. 'The business wouldn't run to it.'

'Rubbish! It kept you and your Jack, didn't it?'

'Yes, but . . .'

'Why don't you admit it, Eve?' he said. 'You're lonely. You must miss him – miss having a man in your life. Someone to make the decisions for you, take the strain.' His hand reached for hers. 'Someone to give you a bit of a cuddle when you're down, eh?'

'*No!*' Eve sprang up from the settee, suddenly alarmed. 'I think you'd better go, Eddie,' she said. 'Look, I don't need a partner – business or otherwise. And more especially I don't need *you*. I've been a fool to put up with your unwanted visits all these weeks, especially after the trouble you've caused in the past. I might have known you'd have some ulterior motive.'

'*Put up with my visits?*' Eddie too was on his feet now. 'Don't make me laugh! I'll tell you why you *put up* with my visits.' His face was red, his pale eyes narrowed and glinting. 'You couldn't afford not to, that's why. And you bloody well know it too. You know that I could have you in jail so fast your feet wouldn't touch the ground if I chose to. Yes, even after all these years. Getting rid is still called murder, you know. Even last week I read in the paper where they put away a man who bumped his wife off thirty years ago. How would you like to go down for life? How'd you like your Carol to know her loving mum is a killer, eh?'

Eve's heart leaped into her throat. She could hardly breathe and her knees felt as though they could barely support her, but she stood her ground. Something told her that if she showed the slightest sign of weakness now he would close in for the kill and she would be finished. The time had come to face up to Eddie once and for all. To play him at his own game: the game of bluff.

'What happened to Sally was an accident,' she said, surprising herself with the cool strength of her voice. 'But if you think you have enough evidence to prove otherwise, then you go ahead. God knows I've paid for what happened in worry, remorse and grief since; paid for it over and over again. But I know one thing, Eddie. If there's still a price to be paid, I don't owe it to you. So go on, you do your worst, but don't think you can threaten your way into my business. It didn't work before and it won't now!' She walked to the door, trying to conceal the trembling of her hand as she reached for the handle.

'Now, get out,' she said, holding the door open. 'And if you show your face here or in my shop again, I'll send for the police.'

For a moment he stared at her, pale eyes fiery with hate – and also with something close to desperation. He took a step towards her, opening his mouth as if about to say something more. Then he turned on his heel and walked out.

Eve slammed the door behind him, shot the bolt and put on the chain. For a long moment she stood motionless and trembling, half expecting him to return and start banging on the door, making a scene. She wondered briefly what she would do if he did. But after the minutes had ticked by she let out slowly her breath, reassured that he had gone. As she turned she caught sight of herself in the hall mirror and stopped to study her face.

'You're a fool, Eve Kenning,' she told herself. 'How could you ever have trusted a man like Eddie Wilson? The day *he* behaves decently to anyone is the day hell will freeze over!

She traced the fine lines around her eyes and mouth with one fingertip. If she hadn't been so lonely, if she and Rose hadn't fallen out so badly, none of this would have happened. You're fifty-one today,' she reminded herself brutally. 'You're *old* and *gullible*. You're vulnerable. *Pathetically* vulnerable, but you should have known better, you stupid old bitch!' Tears welled up in her eyes. Tears of self-pity and shock. Suddenly she needed to sit down. Fumbling for her handkerchief, she dabbed at her eyes.

Was there really anything Eddie could do? Had he really seen anything that night? Could he prove it if he had? Common sense told her that he couldn't. Looking at it sensibly, there wasn't a thing he could do to harm her. She had done the right thing, sending him packing. But it didn't stop her from feeling like a common criminal with a guilty secret to hide. It didn't stop her despising herself.

It was almost six weeks now since the opening night of *Shooting Star*; a month since Carol had moved into Steven's flat. She had never been happier in her life. So happy in fact that she had hardly noticed the weeks flying past. The show, which had received excellent reviews, had been playing each night to packed houses. According to the box office they were booked solid for weeks ahead. It was only when the first month was up and Graham Lang threw a party to celebrate that she realised she had heard no more from Gareth Dean about the audition he had mentioned at the opening night party.

She hadn't been short of work. There had been several more TV commercials to do and she was booked to do the Romaine Cosmetics magazine spread. With that and keeping the flat neat and clean Carol had been occupied and contented, so that when Zelda rang one morning and told her she was invited to audition for Gareth Dean she was slightly taken aback.

'Oh. I thought that must be over by now,' she said. 'All cast and done with.'

'Heavens, no,' Zelda said. 'You know how long these things take. They definitely want you. It's at two next Friday. Out at Teddington. I think there are about half a dozen girls up for the part. Good luck darling.'

Carol was at the studio in good time and was third to read for the part in the new serial that was to be called *Queen's Square*. It was a small part but interesting, and she thought it had gone quite well. When everyone had read they were told they'd be notified by their agents in the usual way, thanked and dismissed.

Carol walked down the road towards the Underground station, deep in thought about the part she had auditioned for. Harriet, the character she had read, was fascinating. Much deeper than the few simple lines in the script. As she walked, Carol fleshed out the character in her mind, thinking up a background for her and a deeply hidden disposition, full of secret longings and ambitions.

Passing a small cafe, she decided to drop in for a cup of tea before catching her train back to the West End. She had just ordered when someone came to stand beside her.

'It's Miss Kenning, isn't it? Carol.'

She looked up to find Gareth Dean standing by the table. 'Oh, Mr Dean. Hello.'

'May I join you? I often pop in here after a day's filming. They make a proper cup of tea and the buns are home-made. Better than the canteen.' He pulled out the chair opposite and arranged his long legs under the small table. 'I liked the way you handled the scene,' he told her. 'Very sensitively. I believe you really saw beyond the mere words.'

Carol hid her blushes in her teacup, murmuring, 'Oh, well, I tried.'

The waitress came, greeting Gareth like an old friend.

He gave her his order, flirting with her a little. When she had gone he looked across the table at Carol, his expression serious.

'Tell me, do you really want this part?'

She bit her lip, suddenly realising just how important it was to her. 'Yes. Oh, yes, I do. Very much. I wouldn't have auditioned for it otherwise, would I?'

He smiled wryly. 'Some do, you know. To some young actors and actresses, going for auditions is no more than experience. Keeping your hand in, as they say. I can usually tell those a mile off.' His tea and bun arrived and he leaned across the table. 'Have you given much thought to the character?' he asked. 'How do you feel about Harriet? Do you like her – *feel* for her?'

'Yes, I believe I do.'

'Tell me something about her. In your own words.'

Carol paused, slightly taken aback. 'Well, she seems very sophisticated – quite brittle on the surface. But I feel that she's very soft and vulnerable underneath. Occasionally someone will get through her tough shell and touch that tender place and she won't be able to help revealing it.' She paused to glance up at him. He was still waiting. 'It's silly, I know – and I don't know why – but I get the feeling that she's adopted,' she said. 'It's something that's always made her feel slightly insecure in her relationship with her mother.'

His eyebrows rose. 'Really? Anything else?'

'Yes. I think there is someone she loves very deeply but can't have. Because of this she goes from one love to another, like a butterfly, trying to escape from the grip of that other love. None of her relationships work because her heart is elsewhere. There's a lot of wistfulness about her. Sadness too, even though she hides it.'

'And why can't she and this love of hers be together, do you think?' Gareth was looking at her intently.

She shrugged. 'Perhaps he's married. Maybe his wife is ill and needs him. He loves Harriet but can't leave.'

Gareth sat nodding thoughtfully as he finished the last of his bun. 'Mmm, I like that,' he said at last. 'It'll be interesting to see if that's what the scriptwriter had in mind.'

There was a long pause. Carol looked at her watch. 'Well – I suppose I'd better go,' she said. As she gathered her bag and gloves together, she looked at him. 'I enjoyed the audition, Mr Dean. Thank you for asking me. I'll wait to hear from Zelda.'

'Don't *thank* me,' he said quite sharply. 'I don't waste other people's time any more than I waste my own. You were the only person I asked for personally. I asked because I thought you'd be perfect for the part. After I heard you read, I was sure. Now you've proved me right. I've already spoken to the casting director and he agrees with me. The part is yours if you want it, Carol.' He looked at her. 'Well – *do* you?'

She sat down again suddenly, the shock taking all the strength from her legs. 'Do I want it! Oh, if you only knew how much.'

He gave her his wry lopsided smile. 'Take a tip from me, Carol. Don't show that kind of eagerness unless you want to be ripped off. Be cool – like your character in *Queen's Square*.'

Her eyes were round as she looked at him. *Her character in Queen's Square*. It sounded so wonderful. She could hardly believe she wasn't dreaming.

Gareth stood up. 'Right. No time like the present. We might as well go back to the office now and get Zelda on the phone – start negotiating your salary.' He looked at her. 'That is, if you have time?'

'Oh, I've got time,' she told him with a smile.

He took her arm, looking down into her face. 'What I

said earlier about not showing all that youthful enthusiasm,' he said. 'Apart from business deals, forget it. I think it's quite delightful. It's not every day I get to be the cause of this much radiance.'

Carol put the finishing touches to the table. On the way home she'd stopped off to buy fillet steaks, Steven's favourite, a bottle of champagne, flowers for the table and two red candles. Lighting a match, she watched the twin flames flicker and spring to life. Like us, she told herself. Steven and me. Two flames, strong and bright, glowing together.

She heard his key in the lock and hurried into the hall to meet him.

'Darling – guess what . . .'

His face was aglow as he turned to look at her. 'No. *You* guess what. Graham Lang has booked the show for a season – wait for it . . .' He reached out to take both her hands. 'On *Broadway*! But that's not all. He wants Madeleine Lindsay and Paul Slade, naturally – and *he's asked me* to go as MD, to get the thing off the ground!'

Carol was beginning to get a chilly feeling in the pit of her stomach. 'I see.'

He laughed. 'Is that all – *I see*?'

'No. It's wonderful, of course. So you'll be away. Do you know for how long?'

'Six months. Could be a year.'

'Oh.'

Suddenly he threw his arms round her and lifted her off her feet. 'Don't look like that darling. I really shouldn't tease you. Listen. I've got a marvellous surprise. The girl who's understudying Madeleine has other commitments and doesn't want to leave the country. Her job is yours.' He reached for his briefcase and drew out a script. 'Look, I've even brought you this so you can begin studying.

And we can rehearse the numbers together. You do see what this means, don't you? We can *both* go to New York. We needn't be apart at all.'

Carol's heart sank. 'Perhaps at this point I should tell you my news?'

'What's the matter?' He looked crestfallen. 'Aren't you excited?'

'Steven, if you remember, I went for an audition this afternoon. I got the job. I begin rehearsing the week after next.'

There was a stunned silence between them that seemed to last forever, then he said, 'You're not talking about this soap opera thing, are you?'

'Yes.'

'Well, there's no problem. Just ring them and say you've changed your mind.'

'No, I can't do that, Steven.'

'*Can't?*'

'I suppose what I'm saying is – I won't.'

'Just a minute. Are you telling me you actually want this job? A *minor part* in a soap opera? I can't believe you'd even *think* of taking something like that in preference to what I've just offered. What's the point?'

'I got it by myself, Steven,' she said painfully. 'That's the point. I've always told you I wanted to get there on my own merits – didn't want any hand-ups.'

'Don't you want us to be together?'

'Of *course* I do.' Her eyes filled with tears. 'It's all I've ever wanted, ever since I can remember.'

He threw up his hands in an exasperated gesture. 'Then what's the problem, for God's sake?'

'I don't want to understudy,' she said. 'I don't want to sit in the theatre every night wearing the costume and make-up just on the off-chance that Madeleine Lindsay might break an ankle or something. Never being seen.

Besides. I haven't got the voice for a part like that and you know it.'

'I could coach you. You'd be fine. As for the other, you wouldn't sit in the theatre doing nothing. You'd be part of the chorus.'

'Steven. I said no.'

He frowned at her, running a hand through his hair. 'How much are they paying you for this rubbish?' he asked. When she told him he gave a dry laugh. 'Peanuts! Lang would give you three times that.'

'It's not about money, Steven.'

'Then what is it about?' He walked into the living room and poured himself a stiff whisky. 'How long have you signed up for?' he asked, squirting soda into his glass.

'I haven't signed up for anything yet. I'm going to Zelda's office in the morning. But it will be three months to begin with.'

He swung round to face her. 'So – you're turning down a chance to appear on Broadway for a mere three-month contract with a tuppenny-ha'penny TV soap opera that'll probably only last a month at most?'

'If that happens, I'll know you were right,' she said. 'I can fly out to join you then.'

'Why not now?'

'Because I have this feeling,' she told him. 'I just know it's going to be good. I've read the script and I *know*. Besides, Gareth Dean wouldn't have taken on the job of director if he didn't have faith in it.' She watched as he sprawled in the chair taking gulps of whisky. 'Oh, Steven, don't be like this. I was so happy! I've even cooked a special meal for us, bought champagne to celebrate. Please try to understand?'

'I understand all right,' he said bitterly. 'You set more store by this piffling little part you've landed than by coming to New York with me.' He put his empty glass down on the table and got to his feet to walk to the window. 'Good God! It isn't as if I've asked you to give up your career. I've even got you a new chance.'

'To be in the chorus?'

'Well, it's something you'd never have landed on your own.'

'Of course I wouldn't,' she said, going to him. 'Because I'd never even have applied for a job like that. It's not my kind of thing.' She laid a hand on his arm but he shrugged her off. 'Steven, please listen – we've had this conversation before, when I told you I was engaged to Mike, remember?'

'Exactly! And you have to admit that I was right about that. You made a mistake. Well, now you're about to make another. Why can't you face up to it, Carrie?'

'It's not a mistake. Not this time.' For a moment she stood staring at him helplessly, biting her lip until it hurt. Why didn't he understand? Why couldn't she make him *see*? 'Look, Steven – all my life I seem to have been waiting. Waiting for things I might never have – a life of my own – a real stage career – *you*! Other things – other people have always come between what I really want. I've always felt bound to put other people's needs before my own. I had to give up a wonderful opportunity when Dad died. I didn't regret it but I was disappointed. Crushingly disappointed. Well, now I have a real chance to show what I can do. *Me*. Alone and without any help. I can't just throw it away. All I want is this one chance to prove that I can make it on my own.'

'I see. Well, now you'll have ample opportunity for that, won't you?'

As she watched him get up and begin to walk towards the door every human emotion seemed to boil up inside her. Frustration, anger, love and resentment seethed away until she felt she was on fire.

'You just can't *see* it, can you, Steven?' she demanded. 'It's all what *you* want! What did you ever really care about me all these years? Did you give a damn how much it hurt me when you flaunted Fern in front of me, then Clarissa? God knows how many more there have been. How do I know that I'm not just another of your passing fancies? This time next year there might be some American beauty sharing your life. Where will I be then?'

He turned and the look of anger on his face made her take a step backwards. 'How dare you say that to me?' he growled. 'It's always been you, Carrie. And if you don't know that now, then you never will. Fern, Rissa and all the others . . . yes, you were right, there have been others. Lots of them. They were attempts at trying to live normally. Stop myself from longing for something that might never be. I enjoyed their company, enjoyed having relationships with them, of course I did. I'm a man, with the same feelings every man has. But I'm no philanderer. Deep inside there has only ever been one woman for me. Do I need to tell you who that is?' He grasped her shoulders so tightly that she had to grit her teeth to stop from crying out. 'Do I *really* have to put it into words?'

Painfully she shook her head.

'There were others for you too,' he said huskily. 'Paul Wilson. And Michael. You almost married him.'

'I was fooling myself,' she said. 'Deep down I always knew I couldn't go through with it.'

Putting a finger under her chin, he raised her face to his. 'I love you, Carrie. That's the truth. Believe me, it was my only motive for doing what I did. I never meant to patronise you.'

'I know.' She turned away.

'So what are you saying – that you don't love me after all? That you want to be free now?'

Tears ran down her face as she said, 'Of course I love

you. I've always loved you. I've never been free and I never want to be.'

'Then come with me to New York?'

She swallowed hard. 'I suppose it's no use asking you to stay here?'

He stared at her incredulously. 'Is that what you're asking? That I give up the chance to take the show to Broadway, so that you can be in this wretched soap?'

'What about Freddie? You and he are halfway through another show.'

'Freddie could come too – if he wanted.'

'Have you asked him?'

He turned away. 'Yes.'

'And . . . ?'

'He doesn't want to go.'

'You mean, he doesn't want to leave Clarissa and the baby?'

Steven shrugged. 'I suppose – something like that.'

'I see.'

The two small words carried a wealth of meaning and there was a long silence between them.

'So what about the new show?' she asked at last.

'The storyline and book are ready and most of the music is written. Freddie can get on with the lyrics without me. Besides, there's always the telephone and the post.' He turned to her impatiently. 'For Christ's sake, Carrie, this has nothing to do with you and me. It's a whole different setup. For the last time – will you come with me?'

She turned away, trying to swallow the lump in her throat. 'No, Steven. I'm sorry, but the answer has to be no.'

Chapter Twelve

Carol found her new working routine hard and unfamiliar. Her first few appearances in *Queen's Square* were minimal, scarcely more than walk-ons with one or two brief lines. The character of Harriet was a girl who ran a cafe in the community that made up a small square in a run-down part of London. So far there had been so little for her to do that Carol began to doubt the wisdom of her decision. She had given up so much for this part. More than anyone would ever realise and now, as far as she could tell, the character was so irrelevant that she could easily be cut without anyone noticing. Had she made a terrible, tragic mistake?

After she had left Steven's flat on the night they had quarrelled she had moved back in with Janet. Her friend had tactfully suppressed her own views on the matter. However she could not resist telling Carol that she thought she had been too hasty; that in her opinion she should have stayed and at least tried to come up with some kind of compromise.

During the two weeks before rehearsals began Carol searched hard for a flat and eventually was lucky enough to find one in Chiswick. It was scarcely more than a bedsit and expensive for what it was. But at least it was closer to Teddington. The journey from Hackney would have taken hours each day. Besides which, if she were honest with herself, she was relieved to escape Janet's tacit disapproval.

There had been several phone calls from Clarissa while

she was at Hackney. Guessing that Carol would be staying with Janet she had telephoned, trying to persuade Carol to go and see Steven and make up their quarrel.

'If he really wants to make up and think of some kind of compromise, why doesn't he ring me himself?' Carol had asked.

'You know Steven,' Clarissa answered defensively. 'He's always been stubborn. But he's really upset at your attitude over this. It isn't as if he was asking you to abandon your career. You would have been working together. And surely no job is worth giving up what you and he had?'

Deeply resentful of Clarissa's interference, Carol had had to bite her lip hard before answering. 'There's nothing to stop him picking up the phone if he wants to talk,' she said.

'Why don't *you* pick up the phone, Carol?' Clarissa had demanded crisply. 'You're the one who walked out.'

They were all on Steven's side, she told herself. Even Janet, her best friend, didn't seem to understand how much it meant to her to make a success of this part she had found for herself. All she wanted was this one chance to prove herself. When she tried to make Janet appreciate this the other girl had horrified her by answering, 'What you're saying is that if you don't succeed in your career, you'll fall back on Steven as some sort of consolation prize. Can't you see how that looks? You're making him feel like second best – a last resort! No man is going to feel happy about that.'

Carol gave up trying to make them see. Steven could never be second best. Their quarrel wasn't about who or what came first. It was about respecting the other person's right to an independent life, as she tried to point out.

'It's a good job I'm not as inflexible as you,' Janet said.

'I could have gone on to specialise in obstetrics, but I decided to compromise and let Geoff be the one to carry on studying.'

'But that was a *joint* decision,' Carol argued. 'You and Geoff discussed it like equals and worked it out between you. Besides, at least you're qualified. You've proved yourself.'

'I don't understand what's so important about *proving* yourself,' Janet said. 'You seem almost obsessed with it.'

'Maybe I should tell you some things you don't know about me, Jan,' Carol said slowly. 'Fill in some of the gaps. Maybe then you'll see.'

She went on to tell Janet about her origins and shaky background, finishing with the angry taunting of her Aunt Rose on the morning when she had caught her at Michael's flat. 'So, you see, I have to prove to myself and everyone that I'm not the worthless product of a promiscuous woman and a small-time villain,' she said. 'What's more, I have to do it by myself, without any help from anyone.'

Janet relented. 'Of course you do. I can understand how you feel, especially now that you've told me all this. But surely if you really love Steven there has to be *some* way the two of you can work it out?'

But Carol couldn't think of one. As each day went by she missed Steven more. No one could possibly have guessed how deeply she felt, how much she ached to see him and hear his voice. She regretted the things they had said to each other that night and wished with all her heart that she could have succeeded in making him see how strongly she felt about her own work.

One day, when she was alone in the house, she had actually given in to the temptation and dialled his number. There had been no reply and she had taken it as a sign that it was not to be.

When she had announced her intention of moving out right away that night, and gone to the bedroom to begin packing, he had grown very angry and they had quarrelled bitterly. Her decision to leave so abruptly had not been made out of pique, but from sheer desperation. She knew quite well that once they made their quarrel up, once they went to bed and made love, she would give in. With Steven's arms around her and his lips on hers she would have had no defence – would have weakly agreed to anything he asked.

'All I'm asking is that you just let me take this one chance,' she had begged him. 'If I fail, I promise I'll be the first to say I was wrong.' He said nothing and she felt exasperation tighten her throat. 'Oh, Steven, for God's sake! How can you be so selfish? You're expecting me to pass up an opportunity like this for the sake of a few months . . .'

'A few months *with me*?' he rounded on her. 'Yes, I was as a matter of fact. I was foolish enough to imagine you'd be as excited as I am!'

'If this TV thing flops, as you seem so sure it will, I'll take the first plane out to join you.'

'Really? That's good of you! Very kind. Thank you,' he said bitterly. 'I'm sorry, Carrie, but if you leave now it's for good.' His voice was hard and unyielding. 'It's your choice. Just remember that.'

His face was strained and white with anger. She had never seen him like that before. Half of her wanted to throw herself into his arms and beg forgiveness, say she would go with him and to hell with her job. But the other, more stubborn part of her insisted that there was no reason why she should give up everything. She had a right to her career too. The way he was reacting astounded her. She could not believe he was being so uncompromising. But her own feelings shocked her too. There had been a time when she had believed that for the sake of Steven's love she would go anywhere, do anything just to be with him. Could it be that she had inherited some of her mother's wilful, selfish ways after all, just as Rose had claimed? Was this new uncompromising person the 'real' Carol Kenning she had been searching for? And now that she'd found her, did she really like what she had uncovered?

Once she had moved into the new flat and rehearsals began things were slightly easier. There was a lot to assimilate and that gave her less time to think. Although her part was relatively small, the schedule was heavy – each day routinely planned from the video filming on location on Monday mornings and the initial walk-through in the afternoon, to the final dress rehearsal complete with costumes, scenery and props before the live episode went out the following week.

In spite of the help and generosity of her fellow cast members it came hard to Carol, who was unused to things like camera and lighting rehearsals. The function of sound and technical supervisors was new to her too, and having script writers on hand was also something she had not encountered before. She found it disconcerting to have lines changed or phrases switched at the last minute. Television techniques were so different from the way things had been done in the live theatre. There were new things to learn every day. But she found it all fascinating and enjoyed every moment.

They had been working for three weeks when she ran into Gareth Dean in the corridor one afternoon.

'Carol. We haven't had the chance to talk since you began. How are you coping?'

'Fine, thank you,' she said politely. 'It's all still a bit strange, but everyone's very friendly and helpful and I'm getting used to it.'

'Come and have a coffee,' he suggested. 'There's something I'd like to talk to you about.'

As they sat opposite each other at a table in the Green Room, Gareth looked at her. 'I've been giving some thought to what you said on the day of your audition,' he said. 'You've obviously given a lot of thought to your character and your interpretation in the scenes you've appeared in so far is very different from the way the character was originally seen.'

'Oh.' Carol looked at him apprehensively. 'Does that mean I've got it all wrong?'

He laughed. 'Far from it! I've been talking to the director and the writers about your ideas and they've suggested a meeting. Is that all right with you?'

Carol felt her cheeks colour. 'With *me*?'

He laughed. 'Of course. Why not? It's your character we're talking about.'

'But why me? I mean, how could I help? I'm not even used to this medium yet.'

'It's simple. We'd like to build up your part,' Gareth said. 'I've already talked to the directors and the writers and we can all see great potential in Harriet as you envisage her. Because she's had problems of her own and she is in contact with all the other residents of the square through the cafe she could become a kind of agony aunt, a young woman wise beyond her years. A sympathetic figure in whom people confide their hopes and fears – their secrets. Yet in all this she has her own hidden secrets and traumas. I believe one of the writers has already dreamed up a fantastic storyline for her.' He looked at her inquiringly. 'So – what do you say?'

Carol's heart was beating fast with excitement. 'It sounds wonderful. If you really think I could do it?'

'Of course I think you can do it,' he said. 'We wouldn't be sitting here like this if I didn't. You have just the right

392

look for the part. Attractive and confident on the surface, but with just that trace of wistfulness that keeps people guessing.' He smiled at her. 'There's the question of style too. That's something you might like to give some thought to in the meantime. I'd appreciate your ideas about the way you feel she'd dress and wear her hair. That kind of thing.'

The script conference was arranged for the following lunchtime and Carol stayed up that night until the small hours, working on ideas and building on the way she saw her character. She put these forward at the conference and, to her surprised delight, everyone seemed enthusiastic about them.

'What we need is a really gripping storyline for Harriet,' Gareth said. 'I see her as a character who will act as a catalyst; someone who will draw the whole thing together. I thought we could start with the idea Carol herself thought up – the adoption thing. Maybe she's looking for her real mother and when she finds her the woman turns out to be a walking disaster!' The writers seized on this idea, scribbling down numerous notes to which Carol contributed. By the end of the session they had roughly worked out a strong storyline between them.

It was almost two o'clock when they dispersed. Gareth looked at Carol. 'Well, I think that went rather well, don't you?'

She nodded, her eyes bright with excitement. 'It all sounds terrific. I can't wait to begin.'

'You've missed your lunch. Are you hungry?'

She shook her head. 'I'm much too excited.'

He looked at his watch. 'Better run along and get yourself a sandwich just the same. Can't have you rehearsing on an empty stomach, can we?'

On the notice board in the Green Room there was a message for Carol to ring Clarissa. She stood looking at it for some minutes, wondering what to do. Should she ignore it? All manner of thoughts went through her head. Was Steven all right? Suppose he had an accident – decided not to go to New York after all? Finally she made up her mind and went to the pay-phone in the corridor, dialling the number. Clarissa answered.

'Oh, Carol! I'd almost given you up. Look, I thought you might like to know that Steven flies out tomorrow afternoon from Heathrow. He's booked on the four-thirty flight. I'm not making any suggestions. I just thought you might like to know.'

'Thanks, Clarissa.'

'Everything all right?' she asked after a pause.

'Fine, thanks. You and Freddie?'

'We're fine too.'

'And the baby?'

'Look, Carol, why don't you just come right out and ask how Steven is?' Clarissa's voice was brisk and hard. 'I'm sure you want to know.'

'Of course. How is he?' Carol whispered.

'Depressed,' Clarissa told her. 'As a matter of fact Freddie is going out to New York with him. Just for the first couple of weeks. We discussed it and decided that it wouldn't be a good idea for him to spend too much time on his own.'

'I would have thought he'd be busy . . .'

'Would you? Have you really given it any thought at all, Carol, or have you been too preoccupied with your own affairs?'

'That's not fair, Clarissa.'

'I know. I'm sorry. Of course there'll be a new cast to rehearse, and a new orchestra. The days will be full. It was the evenings that worried us. Steven, in some impersonal hotel room, alone with his thoughts. He and Freddie still have one or two numbers for the new show to knock into shape. It seemed a good idea for Freddie to go along for a couple of weeks so that they could work on them.'

'I thought Freddie didn't want to go.'

'He didn't. I didn't want him to go either. But someone has to make sacrifices. That's what friends are for,' she said meaningfully.

'I wish I could make you understand . . .'

'It's none of my business,' Clarissa interrupted. 'I'm sorry. I didn't mean to preach. All I meant to do was tell you what flight he'll be on tomorrow. The rest is up to you. Goodbye, Carol.'

Tuesday's rehearsals went on at length. They broke only briefly for lunch, then began again. Carol's only scene was right at the end of the episode and she found herself waiting around while two of the main characters argued with the script writer and the director. As this had to be done through the floor manager it took time. She found herself surreptitiously looking at her watch as the afternoon crept on. Even if she got a taxi it would take her at least half an hour to get to Heathrow.

By the time they had reached her entrance it was three o'clock. She was nervous and fluffed her lines and the scene had to be taken again from the top.

At last they were finished. Holding her breath as she peered at her watch, she saw that it was four o'clock. She waited, desperately afraid that the director would require them to run through any scenes again, but to her enormous relief he dismissed them.

Out in the street all the taxis seemed to be occupied and sped past her with their red lights switched off. But at last an empty one responded to her frantic waving and drew into the kerb beside her.

The traffic was heavy and the minutes ticked past while they sat in jams and at seemingly interminable traffic lights. Carol seethed with frustration and the taxi driver caught her anxious expression as he peered at her through his mirror.

'Got a plane to catch, love?' he asked sympathetically.

'No.' She sighed, almost resigned. 'But I was desperately hoping to catch a friend who has.'

'Which flight is he on?'

'The four-thirty for New York.'

'Right, hold on to your hat, duck. I'll get you there if I can.' The driver executed a nifty U-turn and sped down a side street. Weaving in and out of a series of narrow streets and alleyways, he eventually arrived at the airport in record time.

'This is it, love. Hope you're in time.'

'Thanks.' Carol tipped him with all the loose change in her purse. Looking at her watch she saw that it was already twenty to five and her heart sank.

'Good luck!' the driver called as he drove away.

'Thanks. I'll need it,' she muttered dejectedly.

To her amazement she was in luck. Looking at the monitor she saw to her relief that Steven's flight for New York was delayed. Hurrying, she made for the coffee lounge in the hope that she might find Steven and Freddie passing the time there.

She saw them as soon as she walked in. Steven had his back to her but Freddie was facing in her direction and spotted her almost at once. Bending towards Steven, he said something then stood up and walked tactfully away in the direction of the newsagent's.

Carol walked slowly towards him.

'Steven.'

'Carrie! Why are you here?'

'I came to see you off – to say goodbye.'

'I thought you'd already said that. Anyway, how did you know when I'd be leaving?' He smiled wryly. 'Don't bother to answer that. I can guess.'

'I couldn't let you go without seeing you again. I thought I was going to miss you. Rehearsals went on and on.' She sat down in the chair opposite. 'Steven – I'm sorry. I wish I could make you understand how I feel.'

He shrugged, avoiding her eyes. 'There's no need to be sorry. I think you've made it pretty plain. Your job comes first.'

'It isn't *like* that,' she told him. 'It's important to me, yes, but nothing is more important to me than you are.'

'No?' He gave a dry laugh. 'You could have fooled me!'

'Please don't be like this. I love you, Steven.' Tears thickened her voice and stung her eyes. 'If you had any idea what I've gone through these past weeks.'

For the first time he looked into her eyes. 'If you really mean that, the answer is simple. Get yourself a visa and come over to join me as soon as you can.'

Carol bit her lip. 'I *can't*, Steven.'

'What's stopping you?'

She swallowed hard. 'To begin with, you know I'm under contract. And now it's going to be a better job than I originally thought. They're building my part up – a special storyline has been written in for me. We've already started.'

'Oh, I see. You're indispensable!' His voice was hard. 'Good for you. There's nothing more to be said really then, is there?'

His tone was sarcastic and bitter and Carol's heart sank as they stared at each other. Obviously he was not prepared to make the smallest compromise. Suddenly she felt that in spite of all the years she didn't know him at all. His face was like a stranger's, hard as granite, his mouth set and his eyes devoid of expression. Her heart sank as she saw Freddie walking back towards them across the lounge, a bundle of magazines and papers under his arm. There was so much she wanted to say, yet in a few short

397

minutes there would be no more time left in which to say it. Then, as Freddie reached the table, their flight was called over the public address system.

Steven stood up and hoisted the strap of his flight bag on to his shoulder. 'This is goodbye then, Carrie,' he said, looking down at her. 'It was good of you to spare the time to come and see me off.'

Her mouth was dry as she fumbled in her handbag and pushed a piece of paper into his hand. 'This is my new address,' she said. 'Please, you will write to me, won't you, Steven?'

He took the paper and pushed it into his pocket without looking at it. 'I'm not much good at letter writing. You know that.'

'But it's only for a few months. The time will pass quickly. Say you understand? Say . . .' She broke off, unable to hold back the tears that constricted her throat and ran down her cheeks.

'Yes, okay. I'll write.' He began to walk away. For a moment she stood staring after him, then, abandoning the last shreds of pride and dignity, she ran after the two retreating figures.

'Steven! Please don't leave like this.' She didn't care now that the tears were making her mascara run down her cheeks, that people were staring at her, some with sympathy, some openly amused.

He turned and for a moment stood looking at her, then he dropped his flight bag on the floor and pulled her into his arms. Neither of them spoke as they clung to each other. Carol raised her face to his and he kissed her hard.

'Oh, God, Carrie, these past weeks have been hell,' he said huskily. 'I've hated your guts one minute and the next I've missed you so much it was like a physical bloody pain.'

'I know. Me too. I love you, Steven. I really do.'

They stood clinging to each other as people stepped aside to avoid them, till at last Freddie cleared his throat and tapped Steven's shoulder. 'Steve – look, sorry, old man, but they've just called the flight for the last time. We really will have to get a move on.'

Steven looked at her. 'You're sure – that you can't come, I mean? If there's any way . . .' He stopped as she shook her head. 'Is it always going to be like this?' he asked dully. 'Will we ever find ourselves going in the same direction at the same time?'

'Of course we will. It's just that at the moment I'm – committed.'

'Committed.' He nodded. 'Of course. But not to me.'

As he walked away from her she watched with a full heart. He turned once and raised his hand. She waved back. And then he was gone.

In the weeks that followed Carol threw herself wholeheartedly into her work. Her contract was renegotiated and Zelda got her a substantial salary increase. At Carol's suggestion a whole new wardrobe of costumes was acquired for Harriet, and what had originally been a minor character began to emerge as one of the principal roles. Gareth was pleased and after the first week's showing of the new storyline had gone out he invited her to lunch.

'In case you're wondering, I always do this when any new star I'm grooming begins to rise,' he said with a wry smile.

She coloured at the word 'star'. 'Is that really what I am?'

He shrugged. 'The ratings and tomorrow's reviews will tell us that,' he said. 'But if I'm any judge that's certainly what you'll be before long.' He leaned towards her across the table. 'You've come a long way since I awarded you that drama medal,' he said. 'That wistful air of yours and your sincerity really stirred a chord in me that day. I think I knew then that we'd work together some day.' He raised his glass. 'Here's to Harriet Jameson, future queen of the square.'

Carol raised her own glass. 'To Harriet,' she echoed.

Eve had watched *Queen's Square* ever since it had begun. She'd always liked serials. They gave her something to look forward to at the end of a long day. And this new one, with two episodes every week, on Tuesdays and Thursdays, was a special treat. The characters were everyday people with whom she could identify, and when she'd heard that Carol was to be in it she'd had an extra incentive for looking forward to it.

Still isolated by her unresolved feud with Rose, Eve was finding life lonely and tedious. The television was her only source of entertainment and her daily routine seemed to consist of little else but work and sleep, though even her sleep was troubled. Since the night of her birthday and the confrontation with Eddie Wilson she hadn't seen or heard from him. She wished she could believe she had heard the last of him but, knowing him as she did, she wasn't that naive.

Every time she thought about the partnership he had suggested that night, she shuddered. She was certain that if she had agreed it would have been merely a matter of time before she found herself edged out altogether. Grateful as she was for Eddie's silence, she didn't trust it. It was totally unlike him to give up so easily. Besides, while he was in possession of the secret that had haunted her down the years he still had a hold over her, and a niggling voice at the back of her mind warned her that it wouldn't be long before he dreamed up some devilish new scheme to torment her with.

Carol kept in touch, of course. She had written an excited letter to her mother about the building up of her part in *Queen's Square* and her own involvement in it. She didn't write much about her personal life. All Eve knew was that Steven had gone to America and Carol had moved out of his flat. In some ways she couldn't help feeling relieved and hoping that the relationship would fizzle out. Carol was making a success of her life now. It would be a shame to throw it all away.

On the night that Carol's new storyline was to begin Eve washed up the dishes from her evening meal in good time and brewed a fresh pot of tea. Then she switched on her TV set and settled down eagerly to watch. At the end of the programme she was pleasantly surprised. She'd had no idea that Carol was so talented. She had played the part of the girl in the cafe with such conviction that Eve had almost forgotten it was her own daughter she was watching.

The final credits had hardly finished rolling when the telephone rang. It was her mother. Freda too had been looking forward to seeing her granddaughter on TV and was bubbling over with enthusiasm.

'Wasn't she *good*?' she said. 'Just fancy, our little Carol on telly. I always knew she'd make a name for herself one day. Your dad and I were so proud!'

As Carol's role in *Queen's Square* became more prominent the television pages in all the papers were full of praise. The gripping new storyline about the girl searching for her real mother had everyone looking forward eagerly to the next episode and the ratings soared. *Queen's Square* was rapidly climbing to a top position. For the first time in her life Carol began to be recognised in the street. She even received fan mail.

At the end of November she bought a car, to make

travelling to the studios easier, and at the beginning of December moved into a new flat in Richmond. To celebrate she invited Janet to come and stay for a weekend.

Her friend was nearing the end of her pre-registration year at St Gregory's and was planning to join Geoff in Edinburgh soon after Christmas. She was impressed with the flat, which was spacious and airy with views of the river, and during the two days and nights the girls spent together they talked incessantly, catching up on all their news.

'So, you're really happy with the new job then?' Janet asked as they shared a late supper on the Saturday evening.

'Oh, yes. Everything has worked out so much better than I ever dreamed.'

'And Steven?' Janet looked at her friend, her head on one side. 'No regrets there?'

'I hear from him,' Carol said. 'We write regularly. He seems to be enjoying himself over there.' She didn't tell Janet that Steven's communications were more often than not merely postcards, hasty and unforthcoming.

'You sorted things out before he left then?'

'I went to the airport to see him off,' Carol told her. 'I suppose you could say that we agreed to compromise. He's excited about the show. They open in the new year.'

'I see. When will he be home?'

Carol shook her head. 'It's hard to say. He's signed up for six months, but he may stay longer.'

'And how do you feel about that?'

'How do you think?' Carol said. 'I miss him terribly. I wish he hadn't had to go. But there's nothing either of us can do about it.'

'You could go over and spend Christmas together.'

Carol sighed. 'If only I could. We just get a normal

weekend off with Christmas Day falling on Friday. I've promised Mum I'll go home. It's only for a couple of days, and with the car it'll be easier than catching trains.'

Janet said nothing but her expression made her feelings on the subject plain.

'It's not as simple as you seem to think,' Carol said defensively. 'Anyone who works in our business will tell you. You have to be prepared for partings. You need to have a very strong relationship – to be very under-standing.'

'Well, I'm sure you and Steven have all that and that you'll be the better for it,' Janet said. Then she said: 'I gather you've been seeing quite a lot of this – what is his name – Gavin Dean?'

'Gareth?' Carol shrugged. 'Of course I see a lot of him. He's our producer.'

'I think I remember your mentioning that you went to a play at the National Theatre together?'

'Oh, you mean *Othello*?' Carol said. 'I'd never seen it before and when Gareth heard he offered to take me. Laurence Olivier and Maggie Smith were in it. It was wonderful.' She looked at Janet's sceptical expression. 'You needn't read anything into it, Jan.'

'I'm not. It's just that you want to be careful. An attractive, older man, and your producer too. It must be very – well, flattering.'

'I'm not a schoolgirl! Besides, he's old enough to be my father.'

'Okay, okay! It's just that these things get around. Gossip spreads like wildfire. You're getting pretty well known nowadays, you see. There are eyes and ears everywhere.'

But Carol dismissed Janet's warning as nonsense. Everyone who knew her knew that she was totally committed to Steven. And surely gossip, true or untrue, couldn't spread as far as New York!

She drove up to Northampton on Christmas Eve after the Thursday episode of *Queen's Square* had gone out. There were rumours that they would soon be video-taping in advance instead of going out live. Everyone was excited about it. It would mean more chance of proper breaks and fewer anxieties about making mistakes. Anything that was less than perfect could be edited out. Not that Gareth would ever be satisfied with work that was sloppy. As an experienced producer-director he was a perfectionist and demanded a very high standard from his actors and directors. All the same, it would be quite luxurious to be able to film well in advance.

Eve was disappointed to hear that Carol would only be able to stay until Sunday evening. Her feud with Rose made things especially difficult at this time of year. The usual family Christmas Day at Freda's was out of the question. Eve had persuaded her mother that it would only make an atmosphere if she and Rose were to be together. Instead she had invited her parents and Jack's mother round for lunch on Boxing Day, knowing that Rose and Ted would be spending that day with Elizabeth, Harold and the twins. However, she did have one surprise up her sleeve for Carol.

'Guess who's coming to have Christmas dinner with us?' she challenged as soon as Carol had unpacked her small case.

Carol shook her head. 'I couldn't possibly.'

'Kitty Manson,' Eve told her. 'I knew she'd be on her own with Steven away so I rang and invited her. I told her you'd be home. She sounded really pleased.'

'That was nice of you, Mum,' Carol said. But privately she was a little apprehensive. Would Kitty share the views of everyone else that she had let Steven down? On Christmas morning after they had opened their presents, Carol suggested she should go and meet Kitty. Eve agreed, saying it would give her time to organise the meal and lay the table.

It was only a short walk from Derngate to Chine Way. Standing on the doorstep, Carol was suddenly overcome with nostalgia, remembering all the times she had stood here in the past. Gazing out over the green sweep of The Meadow she thought about Steven: the times they had walked down to the river together, the times she had confided all her hopes and fears in him, and the way he had always managed to make things seem better. Until recently, that was. She remembered the row they had had about her engagement to Michael just a year ago that had made her so miserable. There had been so many misunderstandings. So much confusion – so many partings. Steven – going off to do his National Service – going to music college – leaving to work for P&O. Steven with Fern – with Clarissa. Always just out of reach. And now, just when she had been so sure they had found each other . . .

'Carol, *darling*! How lovely.' The door opened and Kitty stood framed in the doorway, a broad smile on her face. Carol's heart warmed at the sight of the dear familiar Kitty she had always known, flamboyant and gaudy as a butterfly in her emerald green dress, her red hair tumbling loose.

'Welcome home, darling!' Kindness and generosity beamed unconditionally from the kindly green eyes as Kitty reached out to hug Carol. Clearly here was one person who didn't blame her even though she was Steven's mother. Greatly relieved, Carol threw herself into her arms.

'Oh, Kitty, it's *so* good to see you!'

Kitty kissed her, then, dismayed by the tears she saw welling up in the girl's eyes, drew her inside. 'Come in, darling,' she said. 'Tell you what, we'll go downstairs and have a sherry to warm us up before we walk back.'

The big warm basement kitchen was as cluttered as ever. In spite of the fact that she was to be alone for Christmas, Kitty had unearthed the well worn decorations and hung them up. There was even a tree in the corner, its coloured lights blinking bravely.

'You must be missing Steven,' Carol said as she watched Kitty pour the sherry.

'Well, of course I am darling,' she said, sipping her drink. 'But who am I to stand in his way? He's done fantastically well and I'm enormously proud of him. That's what it's all about after all, isn't it?' She handed Carol a glass and looked at her searchingly. 'Sit down and tell me all your news,' she invited. 'I'm so proud of you too, you know. I tell everyone you were my protégé. I never miss an episode of *Queen's Square*.'

Carol sighed. 'I expect you know that Steven wanted me to go with him?'

Kitty nodded. 'Foolish boy! I told him not to be so selfish.'

'It was awful. It all happened on the very day I got the part in *Queen's*,' Carol said. 'I thought we were going to have such a celebration. I'd bought champagne and everything. Then he told me his news about going to New York and completely took the wind out of my sails.' She paused to take another sip of her sherry. 'He'd arranged a place in the chorus for me, and to understudy Madeleine Lindsay, so that we could both go. He couldn't have known, of course, that I'd be offered the part in *Queen's Square*. But I couldn't believe it when he actually expected me to give up the part I'd just landed. I just couldn't make him understand why it was so important to me.'

'I can imagine. But you were quite right to stick by your decision.'

'Really? You really believe that?' Carol asked.

'Of course I do. You have the same right to your career as he has.' Kitty shook her head. 'Men are so selfish. They think we should allow them to manipulate us; that the world revolves around them. I told Steven so. No use moaning at me, I said. Carol's right and you should respect her for it. And now you've proved that you made the right decision, accepting the part you were offered.'

'But I love him,' Carol whispered. 'I miss him dreadfully. We had such a short time together. Suppose he finds someone else over there? Suppose I lose him because of this? In the end, will it have been worth it?'

Kitty smiled ruefully. Reaching out she took Carol's hand and squeezed it. 'Only you know the answer to that, darling.'

'We've said so many goodbyes. We've been like two people on different trains. There have been other people too – in both our lives. This time it felt so *right*. We were so happy. This time it was meant to be forever.' She raised her eyes to look at Kitty. 'Have I ruined it all? Have I spoiled everything?'

'Why should it always be you? Why are you taking all the blame?'

'I could have given up my part,' Carol said. 'Steven couldn't refuse to go to New York, I knew that. If anyone was going to give way it had to be me. And – and I wouldn't.'

'Listen, love, all relationships in our business are hazardous,' Kitty said. 'Show business marriages have to withstand far more strains than any ordinary marriage: partings, jealousies, rumours. So the bond between you has to be especially strong. And it isn't a good idea to start off with one person doing all the giving in. To be

407

fair, Steven only asked you to give up the part because he was afraid of losing you. But you were right to make your stand, and, like it or not, if he's got any sense he'll have realised that by now.'

'Yes, but will it have made him stop loving me?'

Kitty smiled gently. 'Somehow I don't think anything could do that. I've a feeling that nothing will keep you two apart for long. Steven is my son and I watched him falling in love with you long before he realised it himself. He may be disappointed with you at the moment, angry even, but if I'm any judge, hell will freeze over before he stops loving you.'

Carol stood up and hugged her. 'Oh, thanks, Kitty. You've made me feel so much better. Now we'd better go before that turkey is burned to a crisp.'

The two days at home made a pleasant break. Carol enjoyed seeing her grandparents on Boxing Day, but over the short holiday she became increasingly aware of her mother's tension and weariness. They had Sunday to themselves until it was time for Carol to leave later in the afternoon and as they were sharing a late breakfast she tactfully broached the subject.

'Mum, you're not doing too much, are you? You're looking very tired.'

Eve shook her head. 'No, I'm fine. I expect it's just the Christmas rush. Things will be quieter after the holiday. I'm thinking of taking on a young girl to help out.'

'Mum, who took you out to dinner on your birthday? I got the impression you might have met someone. I've been waiting for you to tell me.'

Eve flushed and lowered her eyes. 'Good heavens, no! There's no one.'

'But you told me someone was taking you out. Who was it?'

Eve sighed. It would be a relief in a way to tell someone

about her foolishness. When she haltingly recounted the way Eddie had insinuated himself into her life again and eventually put the proposal to her that they should share the business, Carol was angry.

'*Eddie?* Of all people! How could you, Mum?' she said accusingly. 'When you knew what kind of man he was. Fancy actually going out for drinks, eating with him, after all the things he's done to us in the past!'

'Do you think I don't feel badly enough about it?' her mother said hotly. 'Do you think I haven't reproached myself time and again for the way I let myself be taken in? I've lain awake at nights, telling myself what a fool I was.'

'Then why . . . ?' Carol broke off at the look in her mother's eyes.

'Loneliness! That's why.' Eve's voice trembled with emotion. 'Do you think I'd have let him within a mile of me if I hadn't been so lonely?'

'Oh, Mum.' Immediately relenting, Carol reached out to take her mother's hand. 'I'm sorry.'

'Since I fell out with your Aunt Rose life has been difficult, what with you living away from home too. I don't feel free to go round to your Gran's any more in case Rose might be there. Sundays are endless. I spend them here in the flat, alone. Sometimes it feels like a treadmill, all work and sleep and not a lot to look forward to.' Eve took a long breath. 'It was stupid of me, I know, but Eddie really seemed different. I thought that maybe with his family gone too, he felt the same as me – that he'd mellowed.'

'Have you heard from him since?'

'No, and I don't want to. But I can't help feeling I haven't heard the last of him.'

'Why should you hear from you again? He can't make you do anything you don't want to,' Carol said. 'If he starts pestering you again, just tell the police.'

Eve nodded silently, unable to tell Carol just how much she feared Eddie, or what trouble he could still make for her if he chose. She looked up to see Carol studying her.

'Did you hear me, Mum? You will tell the police if he comes round here again, won't you? Promise me?'

'Yes, I'll tell them,' Eve muttered. 'I promise. Don't worry. I gave Eddie a good telling off last time he was here. I don't think he'll be back for more of the same.'

After Christmas there was a lot to do. Now that Carol's part in *Queen's Square* was more important there were more lines to learn and rehearsals were more intensive. The storyline had reached the stage where Harriet had found her real mother. The woman had turned out to be an alcoholic and was badgering her for money, using emotional blackmail to get what she wanted. Harriet's boyfriend was about to desert her and business at the cafe was falling off because her mother kept turning up and making scenes.

Rehearsals were just finishing for the day and Carol was heading for the Green Room and a much needed cup of tea when she received a message to see Maxine Hadham, the PRO.

'We've had a request for you to be interviewed by Josephine Greaves,' she told Carol. 'It's for one of the popular Sunday supplements.'

'Really? That's great.'

Maxine pulled a face. 'Maybe we should prepare a press hand-out for you, but it's okay with us if you really want to do it. I warn you though, Jose is hot stuff, she won't be satisfied with anything superficial. She'll want an in-depth interview.'

'What do you mean by in-depth?' Carol asked.

'She'll ask all kinds of intimate questions. Better think carefully before you answer, unless you want all your secrets laid bare for all to see.'

Carol laughed. 'I haven't got any secrets,' she said. 'At least none that Sunday newspaper readers would find interesting.'

'Want to bet?' Maxine raised her eyebrows. 'You'd be surprised what they can make of the smallest remark. As I said, better be on your guard. Are you really sure you want to do it then?'

'I'd love to,' Carol said. ' 'Specially if it would be good for the show.'

'Any publicity is good for the show,' Maxine said. 'Even bad publicity.' She grinned ironically. 'Perhaps I should say *especially* bad publicity!' She made a note on her pad. 'Right, I'll let them know. You can expect a phone call.'

The call came next day and an arrangement was made for the journalist to bring along a photographer and interview Carol at home the following Saturday.

Josephine Greaves wrote a weekly column in a popular newspaper and freelanced for other publications. She was well known for her gritty, no-nonsense approach and her talent for getting to the heart of her subjects. Carol was a little apprehensive as the time drew near for the interview, but when she answered the ring at the doorbell she was surprised to find not the large bespectacled ogre she had envisaged, but a small slender woman with neat blonde hair. Josephine Greaves was dressed simply in a blue suit and carried a briefcase under her arm. She smiled and held out her hand.

'Hello, Carol. How nice to meet you. I'm Josephine Greaves.' As she stepped inside she added, 'My photographer will be along later. I always like to get the interview done first.'

Carol already had coffee percolating and a tray laid with cups and saucers. She led the way through to the living room, of which she was especially proud. Josephine looked out of the large window and exclaimed delightedly at the view.

'I always think moving water is so relaxing, don't you?' she said. 'And the willows are so pretty at this time of year with the leaves just beginning to show.' She looked round her. 'This is such a lovely room.' She seated herself comfortably on the settee, unzipped her briefcase and took out a small tape recorder. 'I wonder, do you have any objection to having this switched on while we talk?'

Carol shook her head. 'Of course not.'

'It's so much better than taking notes.' Josephine laughed. 'Not to mention more accurate. I'll let you into a secret – my shorthand is garbage. More often than not I can't read my notes when I get back to the office. In my early days I was often reduced to making up half the interview.' She clapped a hand over her mouth. 'Heavens! What am I saying? You won't tell anyone I said that, will you?'

'Of course not.' Carol poured coffee for them both and found herself beginning to relax. The woman wasn't anything like as frightening as Maxine had led her to believe. In fact, as the interview progressed it seemed to Carol that she was learning as much about the interviewer as she was telling about herself.

'I have to admit to being a fan of *Queen's Square*. I never miss an episode if I can help it,' Josephine said. 'And I'm very much enjoying the present storyline. You play the part of an adoptive daughter so convincingly that I'm tempted to ask you if you yourself are adopted?'

'I am, as a matter of fact.'

'Well! Isn't that a coincidence? So am I! In fact only last year I met my real mother for the first time.' The journalist laughed. 'Thank God she wasn't at all like the mother in *Queen's*. She's rather a poppet actually and we've become quite good friends.' She glanced at Carol. 'Have you ever tried to get in touch with yours?'

412

'She's dead, I'm afraid.'

'Oh, I'm sorry.'

'She was killed in an air raid when I was a baby. I don't remember her at all.'

'And your father?' Josephine asked. 'I expect he was in the services.'

For the first time Carol was on her guard. Suddenly a picture of Eddie flashed into her mind. Eddie on that awful morning in the shop when he had told her with such gleeful relish that he was her father. It took an effort to stop herself from shuddering. 'My father?' she muttered. 'In the services? Yes, the Navy. I believe the ship he was on was torpedoed. It – it was before I was born.'

'Aah.' Josephine nodded sympathetically. 'So you were orphaned while you were still a babe in arms? A war baby? How sad. And you were what – placed in an orphanage and put up for adoption?'

'Oh, no. My mother – I mean Eve Kenning, my adoptive mother, had looked after me from birth anyway. She and my real mother were both service wives and shared a house. Eve couldn't have any children of her own, so I suppose it followed naturally that she would be the one to bring me up. When her husband came home from the war they adopted me legally and I had a very happy childhood.' Carol frowned, suddenly recalling little Wendy, the baby Eve had lost, and the impact the loss had had on the family. She hadn't thought of that traumatic, unhappy period of her childhood for years and suddenly, for some inexplicable reason, she felt guilty. She looked at Josephine. 'But don't you want to hear more about my acting experience?'

Josephine chuckled. 'All in good time, dear. If you read my column as I'm sure you do, you'll remember that I specialise in the human angle.' She peered at the tray. 'Would there be any more coffee in that pot?' She

413

watched Carol refill her cup thoughtfully. 'A little bird tells me that you have a long-standing relationship with Steven Manson, the rising young composer of *Shooting Star*,' she said.

Grateful for a change of subject, Carol smiled. 'Steven and I have known each other almost all our lives,' she said. 'His mother ran the stage school I attended as a child.'

'I see. And he's in New York at the moment, getting the Broadway production off the ground. You must be missing him.'

'I am, of course.'

'And of course you'll be laughing off all those stories about his being seen at smart nightspots with Karen Livesey, one of the gorgeous young supporting actresses from the show?'

Carol felt the colour leave her face, but kept the smile firmly glued in place. She swallowed hard. 'It doesn't do to pay any attention to show business gossip,' she said lightly.

Josephine nodded and took a sip of her coffee. 'Oh, very wise. No doubt he will feel the same about the warm rapport you clearly have with your producer, Gareth Dean?'

'Warm rapport?'

'Well, you have been seen together: at the theatre . . . dining . . .'

'I've known Gareth ever since he judged a drama exam I took years ago as a student,' Carol said crisply. 'He's always been very kind to me.'

'*Kind*, eh?' Josephine's finely arched eyebrows rose suggestively.

'But I still had to audition for the part of Harriet along with all the others,' Carol went on quickly. 'I was offered a part in a play he was directing once before, Carl

Gibson's *Dance With Angels*. But I had to turn it down at the last minute because my father died suddenly.'

'How disappointing for you both.' Josephine smiled. 'Obviously Gareth was determined that you and he should work together eventually.'

'Perhaps. But it *is* just a friendship,' Carol said. 'A working relationship.'

Josephine smiled enigmatically. 'But of course.'

The interview went on, Josephine employing her gentle probing technique to worm out the details of Carol's childhood and education, whilst at the same time Carol grew increasingly aware that this friendly approach was designed to lull her into a false sense of security in the hope that she would let fall some indiscretion. When the photographer arrived and Josephine switched off her tape recorder, declaring that the interview was at an end, Carol drew a sigh of relief.

'It'll be in next Sunday's edition,' the reporter told her when the photographer had finished. 'I think it's going to make a very nice article indeed. One that the viewers will lap up.' She zipped up her briefcase and took her leave.

As Carol closed the door behind her she tried to remember just what she had actually said. If only she could listen to that tape herself and edit out the bits she wished unsaid. What was it Josephine had said about Steven – that he'd been seen at smart New York nightspots with one of the young actresses from the show? Where had that information come from? Carol had little time to read the papers or show business magazines these days. Steven's letters were few and far between and there was very little news in them. It was probably just some journalist making something out of nothing. All the same, the seeds of doubt had been sown and, try as she would, she could not get the image of Steven sharing an intimate evening with some glamorous young starlet out of her mind.

True to Josephine's word, the profile of Carol came out in the supplement of the *Sunday Clarion* the following weekend. The title in large letters read: THE PRINCESS OF QUEEN'S SQUARE and it held pride of place in the centre pages of the magazine. The photographs, three of them, took up almost the whole of one page. *Lovely Carol Kenning relaxing at home*, was the caption under the largest of the three. The others were of Carol making coffee in her small kitchen and then wistfully watching the river from her living-room window. She began to relax. At least the photographs weren't bad. She turned the page and began to read.

Josephine described her childhood in the flat above a corner shop in the industrial Midlands fairly accurately as Carol had told it to her. She went on to outline her early achievements at Kitty Manson's stage school. Then came the bit about her adoption.

Carol's own life bears a striking resemblance to that of her fictional character. Carol was a war baby. Her mother was tragically killed in an air raid while her sailor father went down with his ship before she was born.

Carol bit her lip. It wasn't quite true, but it was the closest she was prepared to disclose. The next section sketched in her theatrical experience, but it was what followed that made her catch her breath.

Carol's long standing friendship with Steven Manson, talented young composer of the hit musical, Shooting Star, has been under strain lately. Presently in New York, tall, good looking Manson has been seen on several

*occasions squiring gorgeous young up-and-coming ac-
tress Karen Livesey around some of the Big Apple's more
exotic nightspots. Spotted sharing an intimate dinner or
dancing into the small hours, it would appear that the
couple have eyes only for each other.*

*However, Carol seems untroubled by it all, insisting
that she never pays any attention to showbiz gossip. She
certainly does not give the impression that she is losing
any sleep over Manson's faithlessness, consoling herself –
if that is the right word – with admirers of her own, most
notably the handsome, mature producer of Queen's
Square, Gareth Dean, who, Carol tells me, has for some
time past been a 'kind friend'. It seems that Gareth has
been determined to work with her since they first met in
her student days. And although, she hastened to tell me,
she had to audition for the part of Harriet just like
everyone else, one can't help wondering if – perish the
thought – Gareth might already have made up his mind to
cast Carol in the part. In any event, one cannot deny that
the advent of mystery woman Harriet Jameson in the
twice-weekly 'soap' has sent the show's ratings soaring
and looks certain to make a star of talented, attractive
Carol Kenning.*

Numbed into apathy Carol sat with the magazine on
her lap, wondering what she could do to put right the
damage. The woman had twisted her words in the most
malicious way. Why had she made so much of her
friendship with Gareth? She made it sound as though
she had *slept* her way into the part of Harriet? Carol
shuddered with horror at the effect the insinuation
might have on him. How would she face him
tomorrow? It would be so embarrassing. And how
would she stand with the other members of the cast
after this?

417

Stirred into action, she went into the hall and searched in the telephone directory for Gareth's home number. She dialled, hands trembling and heart beating fast as she waited for him to answer.

'Hello? Gareth Dean.'

'Hi, Gareth, it's Carol.' She swallowed, her mouth dry. 'Have – have you seen the article about me in the *Sunday Clarion's* supplement?'

She heard his deep chuckle at the other end of the line. 'I've just finished reading it and I must say I'm deeply flattered.'

'Please don't joke. Look, I don't know what to say, except to promise you that I never said any of that. That woman – Josephine Greaves – she twisted what I said, put words into my mouth. I'm so sorry, Gareth.'

'*Carol!* For heaven's sake, don't apologise. There's no need to take it so seriously. This kind of thing is an occupational hazard, I'm afraid. Anyway, at my age it does my ego no harm at all to have my name linked with that of a beautiful young actress.'

'It's good of you to take it like this. What will the others say though?'

'Don't be silly. They're used to this kind of thing. Everyone's suffered from the over-attention of the press at one time or another. It's when they *don't* write about you that you have to worry!' He paused. 'You're not upset about it, are you?'

'Well . . .'

'Right. Then I insist on taking you out to lunch,' he said decisively. 'Call it compensation, or a gesture of good will. Anything you like to stop you sitting there worrying. What do you say?'

Carol's mind was on the rest of the article. The part about Steven and this Karen Livesey girl. She wondered if that was exaggerated too. Gareth was right, she didn't fancy spending the day agonising about it. His invitation was tempting.

'Carol – are you still there?' he asked at the other end of the line.

'Yes, Gareth. And I'd love to go out for lunch,' she told him.

They went to a restaurant on the river where they could watch the ducks and other waterfowl as well as the occasional boat going by. Gareth didn't seem at all perturbed about the contents of the article in the *Clarion*, but as they were drinking their coffee he looked at her inquiringly.

'That article – you're worried about more than just your alleged relationship with me, right?'

She knew he meant the reference to Steven and sighed. 'Gossip,' she said noncommittally. 'I daresay it's something and nothing.'

He looked at her thoughtfully. 'Was . . . is it serious, between Manson and you?'

Carol lowered her eyes. 'Yes. At least, it was, but we didn't part on the best of terms. You see, Steven wanted me to go to New York with him.'

'And you didn't want to go?'

She looked up at him. 'I'd just got my part in *Queen's*. It was the very same day. It was important to me. It meant a lot.'

'So – you didn't love him enough to give it up?'

'It wasn't that! He was only going to be away for a few months. I just couldn't make him see.' She shook her head, weary of trying to explain the way she felt.

'You wanted both,' Gareth said gently. 'You wanted to have it all.' He shook his head. 'We all want that at one time or another, Carol,' he told her. 'Realistically most of us have to settle for what we can get.'

'Or lose everything? Is that what you're saying?'

'It is a risk. If we're very unlucky that can happen, yes.' Reaching across the table he covered her hand with his own. 'Are you very much in love with him, Carol?'

She felt her throat tighten and willed the tears not to start. She had suffered enough humiliation for one day. 'I've loved Steven for almost as long as I can remember,' she said softly. 'I don't know how to stop. I wish I did.' She sighed. 'But it looks as though he's found a way.'

'Don't you think he might just be paying you back for not going with him?'

'Perhaps. Steven has always enjoyed the company of pretty girls.'

'Haven't we all? You don't have to read anything into it, though. Unless you're a Josephine Greaves, of course.'

Something about his tone of voice made Carol look up at him. His dark eyes were dancing with that sudden quick smile of his and suddenly her heart lifted. He'd made his point. 'You're right,' she said, shaking her head. 'I am taking it all too seriously. You must think me really silly and naive.'

'No. I think you're a dedicated, talented actress and a delightful person.' He shrugged. 'But then, what do I know?' He laughed and Carol joined in.

'I see this parting between Steven and me as a kind of test,' she said. 'If we get through this we can get through anything. Wouldn't you think?'

He nodded. 'That's the spirit!' He beckoned the waiter and asked for the bill. 'Right,' he said, looking at her. 'What shall we do with the rest of the afternoon?'

'Well, I've got my lines to learn,' she said.

'You can't learn lines after a lunch like that,' he told her. 'Besides spring's definitely in the air today. The sun's coming out and everything's bursting into bloom. How about a walk along the river to blow away the cobwebs?'

'All right then. That would be lovely.'

As they walked Carol glanced at him. She'd never thought about his personal life before but now she found herself becoming curious about him.

'Have you any family, Gareth?' she asked.

He smiled. 'Two daughters and a son. My wife and I divorced when they were all quite young, so I don't see as much of them as I'd like. The younger girl, Moira, is at university and Tim, my son, is still at boarding school. My elder daughter, Fiona, got married last summer. I gave her away. That was a happy occasion.'

'So you're still on good terms?'

He lifted his shoulders. 'Not bad. Helen, my ex-wife, is married again. We're all very civilised.' He dropped an arm across her shoulders and smiled down at her wryly. 'You know, it's just occurred to me that you are one year younger than my elder daughter. If you'd known that you could have dropped it into your interview with the formidable Miss Greaves.'

Carol laughed. 'I think it would only have whetted her appetite,' she said. She thought about what he'd said earlier, about trying to have it all and sometimes losing everything. And she guessed that he was probably speaking from experience.

When the sun went down it grew chilly and they made their way back to Carol's flat where Gareth had left his car.

'Come up for some tea before you go,' she invited.

He hesitated. 'What about those lines you were going to learn?'

She laughed. 'Tea won't take long. I still have all evening. Which reminds me, I'll have to ring my mother to explain that article to her.'

They had tea by the big window that overlooked the river, sitting there until the light faded and Carol had to switch on the table lamp. She talked about her childhood and her training at Kitty's; the fun she and Janet had had appearing in the concerts and pantomimes. She told him about Kitty, her endearing flamboyance and worldly wisdom. She missed out the insecurity she had suffered when baby Wendy had died and the traumatic shock later when Eddie had revealed to her that he was her true father, preferring to recall only the happy times. Gareth listened to it all, occasionally putting in a word of his own.

'I had a happy childhood too,' he told her. 'We lived in Wales and my father was the local vet. My parents are both dead now, but I do still have some cousins there.'

'Do you go back?'

He shook his head. 'We keep in touch, Christmas cards and so on, but I think it's a mistake to go back – to try to recapture the past. At best it's painfully nostalgic, at worst it's a torture of reminiscences and regrets. There are some parts of one's life that it's best to leave behind; close the door on.' He looked at his watch and sighed. 'Oh dear. I must go and let you get on with those lines.'

Carol got up and fetched his coat. 'Thanks for today, Gareth,' she said. 'If you hadn't come and rescued me, I might have sat and worried about that wretched article all day.'

He smiled. 'Any time you want rescuing again, just let me know.' At the door he turned and put his hands on her shoulders. 'Goodnight, Carol. I've enjoyed today. And don't worry about what the rest of the cast are thinking tomorrow. After all, it's really none of their business what you choose to do with your life, is it?'

'I don't want them to think I'm getting special attention from you.'

'And why shouldn't you get special attention from me?' For a moment there was a teasing expression in his eyes as

422

they held hers, then the teasing vanished to be replaced by something else. His hands still on her shoulders, he drew her to him, bent his head and kissed her.

It was a firm, undemanding kiss, yet it took her breath away with its unexpectedness.

'I'll tell you a secret,' he whispered against the corner of her mouth. 'It's a long time since a woman made me feel as I have today. A very long time.' His lips lingered on hers and his hands cupped her face gently. 'I should be the one thanking you, Carol,' he said, looking into her eyes. Then he stood back and smiled his quick, sudden smile. The brief, intimate moment was over.

'Well, I must go,' he said briskly. 'Or I'll have no excuse to shout at you when you don't know your lines tomorrow.'

He looked at her once more as he walked through the door and what Carol saw in his eyes both moved and shocked her.

To her consternation she realised that Gareth was falling in love with her.

Chapter Thirteen

Madge Blakely was fifty-two and had been out of work for almost a year when her agent had got her the part of Kate Jones, Harriet Jameson's true mother in *Queen's Square*. It was a meaty character part, the kind she liked best and, although she had been resigned to the decline in her career, she had jumped at the chance of this part when it was offered. Since she and Carol had been working together they had become good friends. When Carol came into the studios early on Monday morning, she was surprised to find Madge sitting in a corner of the Green Room, slaving over her lines.

'Oh, hello. You're early. I thought I'd be first.'

The older woman looked up over the top of her reading glasses. 'Been here for the past hour,' she said glumly. 'Haven't had a minute's peace all weekend. My daughter dumped the grandchildren on me on Saturday morning. It was their dad's weekend but he couldn't have them and Susan had agreed to work all weekend. Little devils had me on the go right up till their mum collected them last night. By then I was too damned exhausted to study. That's why I came in early.'

'Well, we don't have to be word perfect by Monday morning,' Carol told her, plugging in the kettle for coffee.

Madge sighed. '*I* do. When you get to my age and you've been out of work for a year it's hard enough remembering one thing, let alone two. At least if I get the words under my belt I can concentrate on moves.'

As Carol busied herself making coffee she watched

Madge out of the corner of her eye. The older actress was a picture of concentration, eyes tightly shut and lips moving as she struggled to memorise the script. When the cup of coffee was put down in front of her she opened her eyes and smiled up at Carol gratefully.

'Oh, thanks, lovie. I need this.'

Carol looked thoughtfully at Madge over the rim of the cup as she sipped her coffee. 'If you've been busy all weekend, I don't suppose you've had time to read the papers?' she said cautiously.

Madge pulled a face. 'You can say that again! If those two little monsters had had their bums well and truly tanned they'd have learned some manners by now. My Susan is as daft as a brush with them.' She shrugged. 'Comes from being divorced, I suppose.'

'So you won't have seen this?' Carol pulled the folded magazine from her handbag, opened it at the centre pages and passed it across the table. Madge pushed her glasses on to the bridge of her nose and read swiftly. When she came to the end she glanced at the photographs.

'Nice piccies dear,' she said coolly.

'Yes, but what about the article? It's not true, you know – the bit about Gareth and me.'

'Isn't it?' Madge looked up innocently. 'I could see he was sweet on you. I imagine everyone else could too. You mean it isn't reciprocated?'

'I mean there's nothing *going on*,' Carol said. 'Gareth knows my work. He's been kind enough to think of me a couple of times when he's been casting. But that's all there is to it. I didn't get the part because I – because he . . .'

''Course you didn't, lovie . . .' There was more than a hint of scepticism in Madge's smile as she added '. . . if you say so. But why get upset about it? Gareth's a bit of all right if you ask me! Anyway, everyone knows that these journalists have to have a story, a bit of human

425

interest to spice things up. I expect that applies to the bit about your boyfriend too. All hype as they call it nowadays.' She chuckled. 'I only wish they'd dream up a romance for me. Past all that now, more's the pity.' She leaned across the table to pat Carol's arm. 'As for that boyfriend of yours, it never does these fellers any harm to show them they're not the only pebble, you know.' She winked broadly and although Carol smiled back she was still only half convinced.

'Well, I just hope the others feel as you do,' she said. 'I'd hate to have to work in a hostile atmosphere.'

Madge pulled down the corners of her mouth. 'Can't avoid the occasional spat in our business dear,' she said. 'There might be the odd flicker of jealousy, but that'll be more to do with your talent than anything printed in the papers. Just ignore it and it'll pass. For my part, anything that takes the director's mind off my shortcomings is a bonus!'

Carol was content to believe what Madge said. She had learned a lot from the older actress. She was a pro to her fingertips and the 'shortcomings' she spoke of were pure fabrication, designed to reassure Carol.

'You're not the first member of the cast to get an article written about you, you know,' Madge went on. 'Remember, the custom is to pin it up on the notice board,' she added, eyes glinting with mischief.

'Pin it up for everyone to see?' Carol stared at her. 'I couldn't do that!'

'Why not? Bring it out into the open and laugh it off,' Madge said. 'Show them you've nothing to hide.'

Eve was in the kitchen preparing her supper when her doorbell rang. She paused to take off her apron, wondering who could be calling on her, then she remembered her mother saying that she'd drop in a

426

knitting pattern on her way home from town. Going into the hall she opened the front door, a smile of welcome on her face. But the smile froze when she found not her mother standing outside, but Eddie Wilson.

'Hello, Eve,' he said coolly. 'Seen this, have you?' He held up a copy of the *Sunday Clarion's* supplement folded back at the centre pages to show Carol's photograph.

'Of course I've seen it.'

'And have you read what the lying little trollop said?'

'Don't speak like that about . . .'

'About who?' Eddie took a step forward as Eve tried to close the door. 'About *my daughter*? Is that what you were going to say?' He gave a snort of laughter and thrust his foot firmly in the doorway. 'I think you'd better ask me in, don't you, Eve? Unless you want all your neighbours to hear what I've got to say. I'm sure they'd be interested!'

With great reluctance she opened the door and allowed him to step into the hall. 'All right,' she said, closing the door. 'This is as far as you're going to get. Say what you've come to say and then go.'

He looked at her reproachfully. 'Now is that nice? Is that the way to treat the father of your daughter? Especially when he's all upset. I think I'd like to sit down somewhere comfy, Eve. If I were you I'd be nice to me.'

She turned and led the way into the living room where Eddie made himself comfortable on the settee, putting his feet up on her glasstopped coffee table.

'What do you want?' she asked edgily from the doorway.

He took out his cigarettes and lit one slowly, flicking the match in the direction of the fireplace. 'If you've read this junk . . .' he held up the magazine '. . . you'll know that she's told them her father was Sally's husband, the poor sap who got himself torpedoed. What right has she got to tell lies about it?'

'Carol rang me on the night the article came out,' Eve told him. 'The journalist who interviewed her just assumed that her father was in the services and Carol let her go on thinking it.'

'And what's wrong with telling the truth?' he demanded. 'Carol's her mother's daughter all right. Sally was the same. She wouldn't have known the truth if it had jumped up and bitten her! Seems Carol's like her in other ways too. No wonder she's made a success of her acting career. She knows who to sleep with, it seems!'

'That part isn't true either,' Eve protested.

Eddie laughed. 'No? Well, you would say that, wouldn't you? No one likes the idea that the kid they brought up has turned out to be a lying little whore.'

'*Get out!* How dare you say that to me?' Eve took a step towards Eddie who lifted his feet off the table and sat up.

'Okay, okay! Keep your hair on. No need to get your rag out just because you're hearing the truth for once. I'll make a deal with you.'

'What kind of deal? Why should I make deals with you?'

'Because I don't think you'd like to see my picture in the papers next to one of your beloved Carol,' he said, pale eyes glinting maliciously. 'Or read the real story of her birth.' He laughed. 'That'd be something for the viewers to gloat over, wouldn't it? That ought to get the fans going! Carol Kenning disowns the father who's bankrupt and living on benefits in a council flat. Make a good story, that would.'

Eve gritted her teeth, determined not to be intimidated by him. If she kept her head and thought this through she might still outwit him. 'You can't prove you're Carol's father,' she said. 'Your name isn't on her birth certificate. You denied it at the time. You deserted her.'

'Only to begin with. It was a shock. I had a wife and kids of my own.'

'But you've said yourself that Sally was a liar. She was promiscuous too. As you told her at the time, her baby could have been fathered by anyone.'

Eddie shrugged. 'I told you, I was taken off my guard. My kids needed me at that time. I did try to make it up to her later, though.' He regarded her through narrowed eyes. 'At least, I would have if you hadn't bumped her off.'

Eve felt the blood chill in her veins but she kept her voice steady as she said, 'No newspaper is going to take any notice of you without proof.'

'No? Perhaps I should ask Carol if she believes it?' he said slyly.

Eve's heart quickened. 'You're not to worry Carol with this. Leave her alone!' Too late she realised she had let her guard slip, given Eddie the opportunity he was looking for. He was quick to seize it.

'Why should I leave her alone? She must be making a packet and here am I, her own flesh and blood, on the breadline, hardly able to make ends meet. She's always been a snooty little bitch to me. I think it's time I called in the debt she owes me.'

'Carol owes you nothing!'

'She owes me her life! Her very existence,' he insisted. 'And she's mine all right, I know that for sure. I always did.'

'How can you know?'

He stepped closer, his eyes glinting unpleasantly. 'Because when Sal and I were together there was only me, I knew that. She never had time to see anyone else. We were together every night and she couldn't get enough of me. I was pretty virile in those days but even I couldn't satisfy her. That kid was conceived in your house, Eve. While you were working on the night shift.'

'Stop it!' She turned away in disgust. 'I don't want to hear about it.'

'Well, you asked so you can bloody well hear it whether you like it or not,' he snapped. 'It's true. Everything worked out – dates and everything. Carol can have the details too if she doesn't believe me.' He leaned forward and stubbed out his cigarette on the glass top of the coffee table. Looking up at her defiantly, he said. 'Well – want to hear the deal now?'

Eve swallowed the lump in her throat. 'You want to come into the business?' she said quietly.

'Oh, no! I offered you that and you turned it down.' He sat back and examined his fingernails. 'No, I've worked hard all my life. I reckon I deserve to put my feet up and take it easy for a change.'

She frowned. 'What then? What do you want?'

'Half your takings each week.'

She stared at him in shock. '*Half?*'

'Either that or I go to the press.'

'I still say they wouldn't be interested,' she said, bravely attempting to call his bluff.

'You reckon?' He leaned forward. 'I'll tell you something, Eve. It doesn't matter how long ago you committed it, murder is still murder and the law can nail you for it. If you don't believe me just ask any copper.'

'Not without proof,' she said, clinging desperately to her composure. 'There's such a thing as the law of libel. Papers have to be careful of that.'

'In that case maybe Carol would be interested to hear how her mother really died.' In the stunned silence that followed Eddie lit another cigarette. 'That'd make an interesting story, wouldn't it? Give Carol something to think about. It might even give her a taste for the truth – get her asking a few searching questions.' He smiled up at her. 'Some you might find a bit dodgy to answer, eh, Eve?'

430

'I can't give you half my takings,' she said shakily. 'I have my overheads to pay: the rent of the shop, this flat. I have to live.'

'That's your problem. That's the deal. You know the alternative,' he said brutally and got to his feet. 'It's up to you how you manage it, Eve. Why don't you ask Carol for some cash? I'm sure she'd like to help her mum, and God knows she can afford it. I'll call round for my share every Friday night. Seven on the dot. Okay?'

She watched as he walked towards the door, panic rising suffocatingly in her chest. There was large vase on the hall table and for one blinding second she wanted to pick it up and smash it down on his head. Her hands clenched into fists at her sides and her voice trembled with emotion as she said, 'I – I'll go to the police.'

He turned and looked at her with a pitying smile. 'No, you won't, Eve,' he said softly. 'You can't fool me, so stop fooling yourself. Give in. It's the only way.'

'All right, lovie? You're looking a bit pensive.' Madge squeezed Carol's arm as they came off the set. 'What's up? Not happy with your script?'

It was Wednesday and they had reached a more intensive stage of rehearsal. Normally word-perfect by this time, Carol had needed several prompts during the morning's rehearsal. Preoccupied with the contents of the letter she had received in that morning's post, she had found it hard to concentrate.

Now that the morning stint was done Gareth would be conferring with the lighting director and the sound supervisor ready for the afternoon's technical run-through. Carol was glad of the break. She needed time to think.

She smiled at Madge. 'No, I'm all right. It's just that I had a letter from my mother this morning and I'm a bit worried about her.'

Madge looked sympathetic. 'There comes a time when mothers are as much of a worry as teenage kids,' she said. 'What she been up to? Not getting married again, is she?'

Carol shook her head. 'No. She's talking about moving out of her nice flat though – going to live with my grandparents.'

'Is that all?' Madge lifted her shoulders. 'I shouldn't worry too much about that, dear. I expect she's got her reasons. Look, I've got to go. Have to look in on wardrobe.'

When she'd gone Carol found herself a quiet corner and took out Eve's letter again. It was a month now since the article in the *Sunday Clarion*. As Madge had predicted the rest of the cast had been only mildly interested in it. The younger members seemed to admire the way she'd made light of it and the older ones, like Madge, were all too familiar with the ways of the press to be bothered one way or the other.

Eve, however, had been a little more disturbed. When Carol had rung her on the Sunday evening that the article had appeared she had seemed afraid that the article's disclosures might affect Carol's part in *Queen's Square*, and it had taken all Carol's powers of persuasion to convince her that she had not in fact said those things and that Gareth wasn't in the least annoyed with her.

'We've been out for lunch today,' Carol reassured her mother. 'I rang him as soon as I read the article. He's been very kind and understanding.'

'Oh! You mean it's true then – about you and him?'

'No, Mum. He's a friend, but he's also the producer. My boss, if you like.'

'So – you're not upset about Steven seeing another girl then? It's all over between you.'

The note of blatant relief in her voice had irritated Carol intensely. 'Of course I'm upset, Mum,' she had

432

snapped. 'Unlike you! I suppose you were hoping for something like this to happen?'

'No. Not if it makes you unhappy. It's just that you don't sound too upset.'

'Only because I'm hoping it's another exaggeration dreamed up by the press,' Carol told her. 'I can't do anything about it until Steven comes home. Frankly, Mum, I just don't know how we stand at the moment.'

'Well, I've never thought you were right for each other,' Eve said. 'If only you and Michael hadn't broken it off. I wish . . .'

'I'm sorry, Mum, I'll have to go. There's someone at the door. Take care. Goodbye.' Carol rang off abruptly, knowing that if they got into an argument about Michael one of them would say something they would regret. Since that night she hadn't rung home at all. This morning she'd received this letter which made her feel puzzled and not a little guilty. Taking it out of its envelope she read it through again carefully, hoping to pick up some clue that she might have missed the first time.

Dear Carol
This is just to tell you that I'm planning to move out of the flat and in with your Granny Freda and Grandad. It makes sense as they are both getting on in years and have that house all to themselves and it will be better if I can keep an eye on them. We shall also be able to share the expenses which will help us all. Don't worry about any of us. We're all fine. And if you want to come home any time there is still plenty of room for you.

Write soon. We all enjoy seeing you on Queen's Square and we are so proud of you.
Your loving Mum

Carol folded the letter and slipped it back into the envelope. She was still no wiser. Why would Mum give up her independence, leave the flat – so convenient for the shop – and move in with Granny and Granddad? They were in their seventies, it was true, but they were both active and in good health, as far as she knew. There had been no mention of the house getting too much for Gran or that they were finding it hard to manage. Was Eve keeping something from her?

After a snack lunch Carol found a quiet phone booth and dialled her grandparents' number. Freda answered and seemed delighted to hear her granddaughter's voice.

'Carol! What a surprise. Nothing wrong, is there?'

'No, Gran. It's just that I've had this strange letter from Mum. She says she's coming to live with you. Is that right?'

'Yes, love. As soon as she can sell the flat.'

'But why?'

'To tell you the truth, your granddad and I were surprised too when she suggested it,' Freda confided. 'Between ourselves she hasn't looked at all well lately. She seems all nerves. I wish she'd sell the business and take things easy, but she says she can't afford to.'

Carol bit her lip. Surely her mother couldn't be that hard up? Why hadn't she said anything? She made up her mind. 'I'm coming home this weekend, Gran,' she said. 'I haven't been home since Christmas and I've got a week off. I think it's time Mum and I had a talk. If it's money that's worrying her, I'm earning enough now to make her an allowance without missing it.'

'Well, I don't think I'll mention that to her,' Freda said doubtfully. 'You'll have to talk to her yourself about it. You know how independent she is.'

'I certainly do! I'll have to think of a way round it. I'll

434

ring her at home this evening. See you at the weekend, Gran. 'Bye.'

The rest of the day was hectic. The technical run through always made Carol feel like a chess piece on a board. This time the important people were the cameramen, lighting and sound technicians. The writers were allowed to have their say too at this stage; mainly to complain about the cutting of their much-prized lines, or what they considered to be the wrong interpretation of them.

Carol was tired as she crossed the car park later. Her only thought was of getting home to the flat and soaking in a hot bath. She was just unlocking the car when she heard someone call her name and turned to see Gareth hurrying after her.

'Hi there! I've been trying to get a word with you all day,' he said. 'You're not going to be around next week and I wondered if we might have dinner? Are you free at the weekend?'

'No, I've got to go home,' she told him. 'There's a family problem I need to sort out and I want to set off as soon as we've finished shooting tomorrow evening.'

'Oh, that's a pity. I did rather want to talk to you.' His face brightened. 'Look, I've got a meeting with the scenic designer and the lighting director later this evening. There's a problem with one of the new sets. But I've got a couple of hours. We could go somewhere now and eat if you like?' When she looked doubtful he added, 'If not I won't see you till you come back the week after next.'

She looked at his hopeful face and gave in. 'All right. But I warn you, I'll probably fall asleep.'

He laughed. 'Oh, thanks!'

'I just meant I'm tired. It's been a long day.'

'In that case, leave the car here and let me drive. We'll go to a pub I know. It's off the beaten track. We can have an hour's peace and quiet.'

As they drove Carol found herself wondering apprehensively what he had to say to her that needed peace and quiet and couldn't wait until the week after next.

It was a warm evening and they had a pre-dinner drink on a terrace overlooking the river. Gareth smiled at her across the table. 'It's almost a year since you joined the cast of *Queen's*, Carol.'

'I know. I can hardly believe it. It's gone so quickly.'

'The show's come a long way since then,' he said. 'And that's largely down to you. I don't think there's a member of the cast who wouldn't agree that you've made Harriet one of the most popular characters in the show.'

Slightly embarrassed, Carol took a sip of her drink. 'I owe you so much, Gareth.'

'Nonsense. I merely cast you. You did the rest. You've brought so much of yourself to the part.' He drew a deep breath. 'The thing is, have you thought about the future?'

'No.' She looked at him. 'Not really. Why?'

He leaned back in his chair, stretching out his long legs in front of him. 'I've been in the business for a long time. Far longer than I like to admit,' he said. 'And lately I've begun to worry about you.'

'About me – why?'

'It's all very well, starring in a soap opera; being famous. But you're still very young, Carol. You have a whole career ahead of you. I know it must be nice, getting fan mail, being recognised in the street, asked for your autograph. But soon you're going to have to make that big decision whether to stay with *Queen's* or break out and make your name as something other than a soap opera star.'

She frowned. 'Gareth, is this your way of letting me down lightly? Are you trying to tell me something?'

He shook his head. 'Far from it. We're riding high in the ratings. *Queen's* looks set to run and run. Your contract is up for renewal and you can take it from me, you'll be asked to sign up for longer this time, probably be offered a substantial salary increase. Harriet Jameson is a firm favourite. I'm sure that the viewers will keep tuning in to *Queen's Square* for as long as she stays. The time isn't far distant when you'll be able to write your own cheque.'

'Oh!' Pink-cheeked, Carol tried to protest. 'Surely not.'

'It's true. I'm not just flattering you, Carol. All that is very tempting to any young actress and if you want to stay, I understand. The problem will be shaking the character off. The longer you play Harriet, the harder it will be for the public to see you as anyone else.'

'You mean, I'd be typecast?'

'Oh, it's more than that. Much more. Carol Kenning herself would eventually become totally submerged. No one, producers and casting directors included, would be able to see you as a versatile actress any longer. You'd be stamped "Harriet Jameson" all the way through like Blackpool rock. It's a trap, Carol. A comfortable trap, but a trap nevertheless. And the longer you let yourself stay in it, the harder it is to get out.'

'Why are you telling me this, Gareth?'

'Because I feel responsible. When I agreed to produce *Queen's* we thought it might run for a few weeks – maybe months. A year at the most. Now it looks as though it's becoming something of an institution.'

'So – what do you suggest I do about it?'

'I'm not suggesting anything. It's up to you. I'm only warning you.' He looked at her for a long moment. 'Look, this is just between the two of us. I've got a new venture in the offing. It's theatrical. Nothing's settled yet, but it's on the cards that I'll be bowing out of TV in a few months' time. It's highly likely there'll be something worthwhile for you there – if you do decide to leave *Queen's*, that is.'

'I'll need time to think about it, Gareth.'

'You wouldn't be earning as much,' he warned. 'Your standard of living might have to go down and for a while you'd be just another face in the crowd. And there's always the chance that it might come to nothing. Like everything else in this business, it'd be a gamble so it's not a decision to be taken on impulse. And, for God's sake, don't breathe a word of this to anyone else. If the powers that be heard I'd been talking to you like this they'd probably sue me for trying to influence you. At the moment you're very valuable to them.'

Carol laughed. 'Perhaps I'd better just forget all about it?'

They talked of other subjects over their meal, carefully avoiding anything to do with work. But Carol found it hard to concentrate. She found what Gareth had said earlier very thought-provoking – disturbing even.

When they'd eaten he drove her back to the studios to pick up her car. In the car park he switched off the engine and turned to her.

'Have you thought at all about what I said earlier?'

'Yes, but not enough. Not yet. You see, I've always thought myself a fairly lightweight actress anyway. I could hardly believe my luck when I landed the part of Harriet.'

'You're not lightweight, Carol,' he said. 'You have depths you don't even know about yet. You're still developing as an actress. That's what I mean when I say you're too young to get stuck with *Queen's Square*. Look . . .' He turned in his seat to look at her earnestly. 'Suppose *Queen's* runs for – say – ten years. Then suddenly it's taken off. It happens, you know. You'd still be young, but where do you think your career would go after that?'

She nodded. 'I see.'

'You could do anything with the right direction, Carol, believe me. The classics, Shakespeare . . . Remember Maggie Smith in *Othello*?'

'What, *me*?' she laughed.

'Don't laugh. It's more than possible in a few years' time. You must learn to know your strengths, Carol.'

She couldn't meet his eyes as she said, 'Gareth, I appreciate what you're saying. You've always been very kind to me. I'm so grateful, but . . .'

'All right.' He pulled a face. 'You've already guessed that my motives aren't totally altruistic.'

'No, don't say any more. I . . .'

'You were probably well aware of the fact that I'd fallen in love with you even before I was myself,' he interrupted. 'Women have an instinct for that kind of thing.' He held up his hand, forestalling her protest. 'No. There's no need to say anything. I'm happy to hold my hand up to that, but it has nothing to do with my belief in your ability.'

'Thank you, Gareth.'

He looked at her. 'I didn't mean to embarrass you, Carol. I know you're still in love with Manson, though God knows he doesn't deserve you. I also know I'm old enough to be your father and that at this moment I'm making a monumental fool of myself. But all that aside, I sincerely believe you have a lot of talent and I want you to know that you can go much further than *Queen's* – if you want to. And I hope that if you do, you'll let me help.' He smiled wryly. 'Without any strings attached, I should add.'

There was a lump in her throat as she looked at him, knowing what it must have cost a man of his age to bare his soul as he had just done. 'Thank you, Gareth,' she said huskily. 'I really do appreciate everything you've done for me and, for what it's worth, I – I love you too, though not . . .'

'Not in the same way,' he finished for her. 'Don't expand on that, please, darling. I know you're trying to be sweet and kind but I don't think I could take being told you see me as a dear old uncle or even a big brother.'

She smiled in spite of herself. 'I wasn't going to say anything like that. In fact – if it wasn't for Steven . . .'

'Yes, yes, I know.' He lifted her hand and pressed a kiss into the palm. 'I'm not being fair to either of us, am I, darling? I think that after this evening we'd better not see each other again. Out of working hours, I mean. But I do want you to promise me you'll give a lot of thought to what I said?'

'Of course I will, Gareth.' She put her arms round his neck. 'And thanks again for being so wonderful to me. I'll never forget it.' She kissed him and for a moment he held her close, then he took her arms gently from his neck and smiled wistfully at her.

'Off you go then. Because of you I'm going to be late for my meeting. You'll be all right?'

'Of course.' She looked at him. 'Gareth . . .'

'Yes?'

'I'm sorry.'

'Don't say that,' he said almost harshly. 'You've nothing to apologise for.' He leaned forward and kissed her forehead. 'Off you go now. Enjoy your break. See you the week after next.'

Carol had a lot to think about on the drive up to Northampton. What Gareth had said to her was deeply disturbing. Regular work, an increase in salary and star status were achievements all young actresses dreamed of. The prospect of a long-term contract was too tempting even to contemplate turning down. On the other hand, what might she achieve if she spread her wings a little? Was Gareth right when he said she could go further? She decided to go and see Kitty while she was at home, if she had time. Kitty had such a clear way of thinking. She would see things in perspective, unclouded by emotion.

Carol's mind was filled with anxiety about Eve too. When she had telephoned to say she was coming home for a few days her mother had seemed almost discouraging. There was something distinctly odd about her manner. She'd seemed vague and preoccupied.

'I was going to suggest I came up to spend a few days with you,' she'd said surprisingly.

'How could you do that when you have the shop, Mum?'

'I do take holidays sometimes,' Eve told her. 'I know I can't ask Rose to stand in for me any more, but I could always advertise for someone.'

'But you hate London,' Carol insisted. 'You always prefer me to come home. Besides, I'd like to see Granny and Granddad and look in on Kitty.'

There was an audible sigh at the other end of the line. 'Yes, all right then,' Eve said wearily. 'When do you want to come?'

'I thought I'd come tomorrow. I'll drive up in the evening after the programme goes out. I might be late, though. Don't make any preparations. I'll make up my own bed and everything.'

'When have I ever let you do *that*?' Eve snapped.

'I know. I just thought it might help.'

'Yes, well, you'll have to take me as you find me. I've already started packing to move.'

Carol had been about to mention the move, but thought better of it. Eve sounded unwilling to discuss it. Better to wait until they were face to face.

She arrived at about half-past ten, parked the car and went up in the lift to the flat. When Eve opened the door Carol was shocked by her appearance. There were dark

441

circles under her eyes and she'd clearly lost weight since they'd last seen each other.

'Sorry I'm so late, Mum, but I didn't want to wait until tomorrow.'

Eve kissed her briefly and led the way through to the living room. 'I'll make you some tea. Have you eaten?' Her voice was flat and dull. She sounded like an automaton. Carol put out a hand to stop her.

'Mum, sit down. The tea can wait. What's wrong? You look terrible.'

Eve held up her hand. 'Don't start, Carol. I'm tired and . . .'

'I can see that. You look positively ill. Mum, something is very wrong. I could tell on the phone. And there was your letter – about the move. That's why I came tonight. You have to tell me about it – now.'

Eve sighed. 'It's nothing. I've told you, I'm tired. I'm not as young as I was, Carol, and I work a long day in the shop without any help.'

'You were talking of getting a girl to help.'

'No, I couldn't afford to pay anyone.'

'But, surely, just part-time?'

Eve rounded on her. 'Look, Carol, do I tell you how to do your job? Just – just mind your own business, can't you?'

'*Mum!*'

Eve looked at Carol's shocked expression and her face seemed to crumple. She struggled for control but the tears welled up, spilling over to slip helplessly down her cheeks. 'Oh – why did you have to come home?' she asked brokenly, fishing for a handkerchief in her pocket. 'I was all right till you started going on at me.'

Carol went to her and put her arms around her. 'Mum, what's wrong? You have to tell me. Are you ill? Gran's worried about you too. Look, we've got to talk.' She held her mother away from her and looked into her stricken face. Then a sudden chilling suspicion struck her. 'Mum – it isn't Eddie again, is it?' Eve made no reply and Carol shook her gently. 'Oh God, it *is*, isn't it? What's he done this time?' She led Eve to the settee and pressed her down on to it. Eve found her handkerchief and dried her eyes.

'It was that article of yours,' she said. 'He came round here, angry because you said that Sally's sailor husband was your father.'

'Oh, no!' Carol shook her head. 'I never actually *said* that. They just assumed he was my father and I let them. They got a lot of things wrong and that was just one of them.'

'He felt slighted,' Eve said, blowing her nose. 'He said some terrible things – threatened to contact the papers and say that you'd abandoned him. Tell them some pathetic tale about how he lived in poverty in a council flat with no income while you were rolling in luxury.'

'Are you telling me that he's blackmailing you again, over that?' When Eve nodded Carol got up angrily. 'Is this why you're having to give up the flat? This is ridiculous, Mum! Why didn't you tell me? You promised me you'd go to the police if he bothered you again. Why do you keep giving in to him, Mum?'

'I couldn't let him ruin your career.'

'But he couldn't! There's no way he could prove that he's my father. If he wants to go to the papers, let him. I'll just deny it. It's not worth putting yourself through all this!'

When Eve was silent Carol bent to look at her. 'There's more to this, isn't there? What is it, Mum? Look, this can't go on. I insist you tell me – *now*.' When Eve remained silent she said firmly, 'Until you do, neither of us is leaving this room. Are you listening, Mum?'

Eve looked up in surprise. She had never known Carol

to be so forceful before. Was this new self-assured young woman really the quiet, dreamy little girl she had brought up? Suddenly she felt as though their positions were reversed. She felt like the fearful, erring child, Carol the mother. Instantly her stoic reserve collapsed. She knew the time had come. She had to confess. The burden was too heavy to bear. She knew that by telling Carol what happened all those years ago she risked losing her love. But if she carried her guilt alone a moment longer she would break under the strain.

'Eddie knows something terrible about me,' she whispered, her voice so quiet that Carol had to bend close to hear. 'Something that happened a long time ago, during the war – when you were still a baby.' She swallowed hard. 'He's been holding it over me for years.'

'And he's threatened to tell me?' Carol prompted. 'The answer's easy then, isn't it? Just tell me yourself. Tell me now and take away the hold he has over you once and for all.'

Eve sighed. 'If only it were that simple. He's threatened to go to the police.' She looked up fearfully into Carol's eyes. 'Yes, it's as bad as that, and when you know what I did you might not want to call me Mum any more.'

As Carol looked at her mother she felt her blood chill. Eve had always been a loving, caring mother; a gentle person. What could she possibly have done that was so terrible? She went to the sideboard and found the bottle of brandy Eve had always kept for emergencies. Pouring a generous measure into a glass, she pressed it into Eve's hand and sat down beside her.

'Drink this,' she said. 'Take your time and then tell me. I want to hear it all, Mum – everything. I'll always be your daughter, no matter what. I'm not going to judge you, whatever it is. I can't believe you can possibly have done anything as bad as all that.'

'I did, though.' Eve spluttered over the strong drink as it seared her throat. Then she took a deep breath and looked at Carol.

'I killed her,' she said slowly. 'Sally – your mother. I killed her.'

Carol's heart missed a beat and she felt the colour drain from her face. 'No,' she said. 'You can't have. You couldn't.'

'But I did! That night when she left – I followed her. She'd taken you, you see. It was a terrible night. It was snowing and you were poorly.' Eve's hands twisted and wrung the damp handkerchief. 'She hadn't got a clue how to look after you – hadn't even taken a bottle for you and only – only one nappy.' Her voice faltered and she picked up the glass and took another sip of the brandy before continuing. The spirit seemed to steady her a little and she went on. 'There was an air raid. I caught up with her on the old railway bridge. You won't remember it, it's not there any more. She wouldn't give you to me. We quarrelled – called each other horrible names. You started to cry. You were so tiny and helpless. You had such a bad cough and – and I couldn't bear the thought of you being cold and poorly. I tried to snatch you from her and she gripped you so hard she made you cry out. She didn't care, you see. She didn't really want you. Not really. All she wanted was to take you away from me. That – that was when I lost my temper and – hit her.' Eve's lip trembled and she put up her hand to cover her mouth. 'Oh, dear God, forgive me. I never meant to do it, Carol. I never meant to harm her. Not really. Not like that.'

Carol took both her mother's hands in hers. They were like marble, stiff and icy cold. Her own heart was pumping hard in her chest but she forced herself to stay calm. 'Go on, Mum,' she prompted. 'I'm listening. What happened next?'

Eve shook her head. 'I – I never really knew. She – she just seemed to slip and fall. The ground was icy, you see. She stumbled backwards and suddenly she'd gone – toppled over the parapet. I heard her scream and then the sickening thump as she hit the track underneath. Then the bomb fell and all at once it was like hell breaking loose. Broken glass and bricks and rubble. All I could think of was getting you home safely as fast as I could.' She paused to swallow, pressing her handkerchief to her lips.

'Later they found her under the rubble. When the bomb fell on the station the old bridge collapsed. It was your grandad who identified her. Gran came to tell me next morning. Everyone assumed that she was killed in the raid, but . . .' Eve's eyes were wide and bleak with remembered horror. 'But it was only me who knew the truth, and me who had to live with it,' she whispered. 'I never told anyone. It wasn't till years later that I found out that someone else was there that night and that he knew too.'

'Eddie?'

Eve nodded. 'He told me that Sally never intended to go back to her husband, that they were planning to run away together. He was waiting for her in his car on the far side of the bridge and he – saw everything.'

Eve began to weep. 'Don't you understand, Carol? It's your *mother* I'm talking about. I took you away from her and then I . . . Oh, how can you ever forgive me for what I did?'

Carol swallowed hard and stared at Eve. What she was hearing was so bizarre – like a bad dream. Eve, the only mother she had ever known, was actually telling her she had killed someone. And not just anyone, but the woman who had given birth to her. It was so hard to take in. It was going to take some coming to terms with. She blinked and shook her head, half turning away.

446

Eve broke into loud heartbroken sobs. 'I knew it! I can't expect forgiveness from you. How can I when I killed your mother?'

Moved to compassion Carol reached out and put her arms round her. 'Mum – don't. *You're* my mother. I've never known any other. It's just so unbelievable. I – I just *wish* you'd told me before.'

'I wanted to. I longed to tell someone,' she said. 'I wanted to make amends, to pay my debt in some way. When little Wendy died I thought it was my punishment. I never told your dad.' She buried her head against Carol's shoulder. 'All those years, I never told him what I did. And then I lost him too. I knew then that even losing Wendy wasn't enough to pay for what I did.'

Carol held her mother close. She was remembering how Eddie had blackmailed Jack, draining away all her parents' savings. Had he acquainted him with more than the fact that he was her father? Her blood ran cold and she promised herself that was something Eve must never suspect. At least she could save her that. Suddenly so many things were falling into place. She understood now about that bleak period of her childhood after Wendy died, when she had felt so alone and unwanted. She also remembered another occasion not so long ago when Eve had been close to confessing to her. The words echoed clearly in her mind. *For something we want – someone we love desperately enough – we can actually kill.*

After a while Eve composed herself enough to help Carol prepare supper and they sat down to share it, though neither had much appetite.

Carol lay awake into the small hours of the morning, trying to come to terms with what she had learned that evening. It was so hard to believe that Eve, the gentle woman she had known all her life, was actually capable of causing the death of another human being. She tried to put herself into Eve's situation on the night that it had happened. She had never meant to kill, she had said so and Carol believed her. Her guilt had grown to overwhelming levels over the years from keeping it bottled up. There were the circumstances too. The war, the air raid, the severity of the weather. Had it not been for those factors the whole thing would have been discovered, reported and cleared up years ago. Above all, it was for her, Carol, that Eve had done it. What would have happened to Carol if Eve had not intervened that night – even had she survived? And surely over the years Eve had paid a terrible price for what she saw as her crime?

Finally, as the first light began to lift the darkness, Carol made up her mind. She owed it to Eve to do all she could to help her put things right. To begin with, Eddie must be stopped. He must be prevented from any further intimidation; stopped once and for all. And as far as she knew there was only one person who could help her.

Next morning at breakfast it was clear from her pale face that Eve hadn't slept much either. She was quiet, darting occasional looks at Carol. Determined to say nothing till she had had advice, Carol suggested that she take the day off and try to get some rest, offering to go to the shop herself, but Eve would have none of it. There was a rep due in today, she said. Someone who needed her personal attention.

As soon as she had left the flat Carol lifted the telephone and dialled. A girl's voice answered.

'Good morning. Webb and Mather's. Can I help you?'

'Can I speak to Mr Robson, please?'

'Hold on, I'll just see if he's in yet. Who's calling, please?'

'It's his cousin, Carol.'

There was a click and a moment later Mike's surprised voice said. '*Carol*? Is it really you?'

'Yes, it's me, Mike. How are you?'

'I'm fine. What can I do for you?'

'I've got a problem. It's a tough one and I'd like your advice.'

'Of course. Are you staying at Aunt Eve's flat? I'll pop round this evening.'

'No. I want to come and see you professionally, Mike.'

'There's no need for that.' He sounded slightly hurt. 'You know I'll be happy to help in any way I can.'

'I know you will, Mike. But it's your professional advice I'm after. It's quite serious, I'd rather do it officially. You'll know why when I explain.'

'Of course, if you say so.'

'I'm only home for a few days and this needs urgent attention. So could we make it soon?'

'Right. How about a working lunch today – here in the office? I'll send out for some sandwiches.'

'Thanks, Mike. I appreciate that. One o'clock?'

'Fine. See you then.'

When she walked into the office the young receptionist stared at her open-mouthed.

'I have an appointment with Mr Robson at one o'clock.'

'Oh! Are *you* his cousin Carol?'

'That's right.'

The girl blushed. 'He never said you were a TV star. Excuse me, but you're Carol Kenning, aren't you? From *Queen's Square*?'

Carol smiled. 'It's clever of you to recognise me. But I'm not sure about the star part.'

'Oh, you *are*,' the girl insisted. 'We all watch every Tuesday and Thursday and we can't *wait* to see what happens next. What about that horrible mother of yours then? She's a proper old cow!' She stopped. 'Oh! *Sorry*.' She giggled, one hand to her mouth. 'We get carried away

449

sometimes. It's all so real. My youngest sister even tries to do her hair like yours.' She turned and grabbed a piece of paper from her desk. 'Here – you wouldn't autograph this for her, would you? She'll be dead chuffed when I tell her I've met you.'

'Of course.' Carol signed her name on the scrap of paper.

'Patsy, isn't it time you went for your lunch break?' Michael stood in the doorway of his office. The girl spun round, her cheeks colouring.

'Oh! Sorry, Mr Robson. I was just going when Miss Kenning – er – when your cousin arrived.'

The girl pushed the autographed slip of paper into her bag, grabbed her coat and bustled out.

'Sorry about that, Carol. I purposely didn't give your name in the hope that you'd get in without anyone bothering you.' He smiled. 'I'm not quite used to having a celebrity in the family yet.' He took both her hands and smiled warmly at her. 'You're looking fabulous. Come and have some coffee and sandwiches and then we can talk about this problem of yours.'

'It's a pity about the row our mothers had,' he said. Gran seems to think they're regretting it. But you know how stubborn they can both be. Neither will want to be the one to give in.'

'At the moment Mum has more than the row with Aunt Rose to worry her,' Carol told him.

'Ah, I see.' He raised an eyebrow. 'Is that why you're here?'

'Yes. Mike, do you remember my telling you some time ago about Eddie Wilson?'

He nodded. 'The man who says he's your biological father?'

Carol relaxed. He couldn't possibly know what a comfort the word 'biological' was.'

450

'He was blackmailing Uncle Jack, wasn't he?' Mike went on. 'The little rat was obtaining money under threat of telling you – when you already knew anyway.'

'That's what I thought at the time,' she said. 'Now I know there was more to it than that. Last night Mum told me about something she's been hiding for years. Something she believes herself guilty of. Only one other person knows this secret.'

Mike leaned back in his chair with a sigh. 'Wilson? And he's blackmailing her.'

'I think he has been for some time,' Carol said. 'Soon after Dad died I met Eddie's son, Paul. He told me he'd finished with his father because of his devious business methods. He mentioned that he thought he was still getting some shady money from somewhere. I didn't connect it with Mum at the time, but after what she told me last night . . . apparently he made an effort to win her over a few months ago, even let her off the payments. But it turned out he was only after a partnership in the business because his was almost bankrupt. Now it seems he's turning the screw even tighter. He's been getting at her through me again, threatening to go to the press – wreck my career if she doesn't give him half her takings from the business. And to protect me, she's been letting him do it. I might never have found out if I hadn't come home. He's got to be stopped, Mike. It's making Mum ill. Is there anything we can do?'

'Do you mind if I ask you what this thing is that Aunt Eve is so afraid of people knowing?' Mike looked at her closely. 'It will be in complete confidence of course. I can't really be much help unless I know.'

'No, of course.' Carol hesitated. Her mother had confided her secret in complete trust. Telling Mike would feel like a betrayal. And yet she must be open with him if she wanted his help. Slowly and carefully, word for word,

451

she recounted what Eve had confessed to her the previous evening.

When she had finished Michael shook his head. 'Clearly it was a tragic accident.'

Carol's heart lifted with relief. 'That's exactly what I thought.'

'It sounds to me as though the guilt of wanting the other woman's child became distorted into guilt of a deeper kind. In the confusion of the raid and the heat of the violent quarrel she imagined she'd caused the girl's death.'

'But she's convinced herself that she killed Sally,' Carol told him. 'She's built it up and suffered so much for it all these years. Whatever actually happened Mum's paid well over the odds for it.' She looked at him. 'Is it true that one can be brought to trial for a murder even after many years have passed?'

Michael nodded. 'It is, though in most cases it's very hard to get enough evidence for a conviction.' He looked thoughtful. 'You say that Wilson was a witness to the incident?'

'So he says. He was waiting for Sally in his car on the other side of the bridge. It seems that she wasn't going to Portsmouth to see her husband as she'd said. She and Eddie had arranged to run away together.'

'Wait a minute.' Mike was frowning. 'You say that Wilson was waiting in his car on the *far side* of the bridge?'

'That's what he claims.'

'I can just remember that bridge,' he said. 'When I first went to school my mother used to meet me there when we came out in the afternoons. I can remember being worried sick in case she wasn't there because you couldn't see the road from the centre of the bridge. It wasn't visible until you were about three-quarters of the way across. A big lamp standard stood in the way.'

'Are you sure?'

'Positive.' He grinned. 'As a five year old I used to panic regularly.'

'A lamp standard, you say? If he'd got out of the car and come on to the bridge, could he have seen by the light of that?'

'Not in the blackout! It's wartime we're talking about, remember.'

'Of *course*. It would have been pitch dark. I hadn't thought of that.'

'Let's think this through, replay the scene. Wilson sat waiting in his car – and Sally never came.'

'He might have heard them, though,' Carol put in. 'Mum says they were shouting. And I was crying too. He must have heard a baby's cry.'

'So – he got out of the car and walked on to the bridge to see what was going on. But by that time it would have been over. Maybe he saw Aunt Eve running off with you in her arms. He might even have looked over the bridge and seen Sally lying there.'

'Then the bomb fell on the station and he would have run for cover. So he never actually *saw* anything,' Carol concluded. 'He just put two and two together, and later, when he made threats and Mum responded guiltily . . .'

'*Exactly*. Aunt Eve's terrible feelings of guilt made her an easy target.'

For several moments they just sat there, looking at each other, then Carol said. 'But it's still his word against Mum's, isn't it? Is there anything we can do, Mike?'

'There certainly is. Blackmail is still blackmail. I'll write him an official letter – make it as stiff and formal as I can. That should silence him.' Noticing her anxious expression he added, 'It'll be on the firm's headed paper but I'll do it personally, Carol. No one else will see it, I promise you. Don't worry.'

'Thank you, Mike. Are you sure it will work?'

'Positive. I'll put the fear of God into him, threaten to have an injunction served forbidding him to go anywhere near Aunt Eve on pain of being arrested and charged with blackmail and demanding money with menaces. I'll remind him of the minimum sentence for those offences. Throw the book at him.'

Carol sighed. 'You're right. He'll surely have to take notice of that.' She opened her handbag and took out a card. 'Now, I meant it when I said I wanted to do this professionally, Mike. Please send the bill to me at this address.' She put the card on his desk.

'There's no need. You know I'm happy to do this for you, Carol. And after all, Aunt Eve is family.'

'I know, but all the same . . .'

He smiled and picked up the card. 'Very well then, if it'll make you feel better. Now, help me finish this coffee and tell me all your news? We all watch you in *Queen's Square* every week. You're very good. Mother and Liz wouldn't miss it for anything. And just between you and me, they boast unashamedly about your being a relative.'

Carol smiled wryly. 'There was a time when they wouldn't own me as one.'

'Mother is sincerely sorry about what happened that morning, you know,' Mike said quietly. 'She was always too hasty. Speak first, think later, that's Rose Robson. I think she feels she ruined things for me.'

'In a way she did you a favour,' Carol said. 'I think we both knew all along that it would never have worked out, didn't we?'

He nodded resignedly. 'Not for the want of trying.'

'No. I believe we both wanted it to succeed. It just – wasn't on the cards. I wouldn't have made a good solicitor's wife. I wouldn't have made you happy, Mike.'

'Well – maybe. What about you, Carol? You've done

454

well. Are you happy? Have you got what you wanted now?'

'I'm not sure,' she said. 'Do we ever really get what we want?' She looked at him. 'Have you met anyone else?'

He shrugged. 'There is someone. We get along. But it's early days yet. I'm not going to hurry things. What about you? Are you and Steven Manson together again?'

She shrugged. 'He went to America without me.'

'I know. I read the article in the *Sunday Clarion*.'

'I could have gone too. I chose this job instead.'

'Which proves how dedicated you are.'

'Or how stupid!' She felt her throat thicken as she looked at him. 'I made a stand. I stuck out for what I wanted. I thought that Steven of all people would understand. I thought we had the kind of love that would stand the test. I told myself that however angry he was with me he'd come back. But now, as you've no doubt read, the gossip columns are full of his romance with some starlet over there, so it looks as if I was wrong.'

'You regret letting him go – taking the job?'

'No. It's not that so much. What I do regret is that I can't stop loving him, Mike. I only wish I could.'

He nodded slowly. 'It isn't easy to stop loving someone. That's the one thing we aren't in control of. I know that.'

The implication was all too plain. 'Oh, Mike.' She looked at him. 'Did I really cause you so much pain?'

He laughed and pushed the almost empty plate towards her. ' 'Course not! Come on, I think we've had enough guilt for one lunchtime. We're in danger of becoming maudlin. Here, have this last sandwich, and for heaven's sake let's change the subject.' His voice softened as he watched her struggling for control. 'Steven will be back for you, Carol. He's got to have at least that much sense. You might have dented his ego a fraction but it won't have done him any harm.' He looked at his watch. 'Now,

I'll get that letter done right away, before Patsy gets back, and put it in the post on my way home this evening. You can tell Aunt Eve to rest assured she won't be hearing from Wilson again.'

Carol felt her heart lift as she walked out of the offices of Webb and Mather. It was a warm afternoon and she found her feet taking her in the direction of Chine Way. Kitty would not have started her afternoon class yet. There might be time for a cup of tea and a chat. Gloria answered her ring at the bell and told her to go right on downstairs where, as she put it, Mrs Manson was having a tussle with her books.

Carol tapped on the kitchen door before putting her head round it. Kitty sat at the table, her red hair piled untidily on top of her head and her reading glasses perched on the end of her nose. The table was littered with bills and receipts, invoices and bank statements, either loose or speared on the various spikes that Kitty referred to as her 'filing system'. She looked up and beamed with delight when she caught sight of Carol.

'Darling! What a sight for sore eyes!' she said, pulling off her glasses. 'And just the excuse I need to take a break from all this.'

'Maybe I should come back later, let you get on with it?' Carol said doubtfully. 'I can make it tomorrow if you like? I'm home for a few days.'

'Don't you dare go away!' Kitty swept the pile of paperwork to one side and stood up. 'Come over here and let me have a look at you.' She reached out and took Carol's hands, eyeing her critically. 'Mmm. A bit on the skinny side. Long rehearsals and short lunch breaks, eh?' She laughed. 'Ah, happy days. Brings back memories of when I had a waistline. Never mind, plenty of time to develop middle-aged spread later. Now, come and sit down and tell me all about it.'

Carol told her about the show and the others in the cast. Kitty told her that she had once met Madge when they toured together with an Agatha Christie play. Carol promised to pass on Kitty's good wishes and an open invitation to come and visit. She finished by telling her about Gareth's disturbing advice.

'Tell me honestly, what would you do if you'd been in my position, at my age?'

Kitty laughed and raised her eyes to the ceiling. 'To begin with I'd have given my eye teeth, an arm and a leg for that kind of problem! Dilemmas like that just didn't exist in my day. But seriously, there's a lot of sense in what he says. It's true you can get stuck in a rut, even in a West End run. And TV gives you a much wider audience. Suppose *Queen's Square* ran for five years? You'd still be under thirty, but might well find it hard to be cast in anything else. They'd take one look at you at auditions and be unable to see past Harriet Jameson.' She looked at Carol. 'I'm afraid that if your contract is up for renewal, darling, now is certainly the time to make up your mind. Before you, or rather *she*, gets too firmly stuck in the public's affection.'

Carol sighed. 'So basically you agree with Gareth? You really think I should get out now?'

Kitty smiled sympathetically. 'It's hard, isn't it, darling? This business is so much of a gamble. I know damned well that at your age I'd probably have taken the new contract. Snatched it with both hands while it was still hot, and be damned to everyone's advice.'

'It's so tempting,' Carol said wistfully. 'I might never get another chance as good. Yet if I don't try I'll never know. I thought that if . . .' She broke off, frowning as she heard footsteps on the basement stairs. 'Oh, I think someone's coming . . .' Her voice trailed off as the door opened and she found herself face to face with an equally astonished Steven.

For a moment the breath stopped in her throat. Her mouth dried and all she could do was stare at him. For a few seconds that felt like a lifetime it was as though the three of them were frozen into a tableau.

Then Kitty cleared her throat and said, 'Oh – didn't you know that Steven was home, Carol?'

'No.' She swallowed. 'I had no idea he was back in England.'

'I got in yesterday afternoon,' Steven said, coming into the room and closing the door. 'Actually I rang your flat but there was no reply so I picked up the car and drove straight home. I've been a bit jet-lagged, I'm afraid – couldn't stay awake.' He rubbed a hand over his chin. 'If I'd known you were going to be here, I'd have shaved.'

'I told him how silly it was to drive up here straight after the flight,' Kitty said. 'He drove me barmy, nodding off over breakfast when I wanted to talk to him. No use to man nor beast in that state so I sent him back up to bed again.' She got up and began to bundle all her paperwork together into a tattered folder. 'I'll finish this lot later,' she said, taking it across to her overflowing bureau. 'Well, time I got ready for the afternoon class.' She looked from one to the other. 'Sorry, darlings, but I'll have to love you and leave you.'

When she'd gone the room seemed unbearably silent. Carol stood up and looked at her watch. 'I suppose I should . . .'

'Why don't you . . . ?'

They spoke in unison and both laughed nervously.

'You first,' Carol said.

'No, you.'

He crossed the room and pulled out a chair. 'Please –

come and sit down again. How have you been, Carrie? You look great.'

Hearing him call her 'Carrie', the name that only he had ever used, made her stomach lurch. She tried in vain to swallow the lump in her throat, hoping that her voice would sound normal as she said, 'So do you. I – I'm fine.'

'I caught your show on TV last night,' he said. 'Thought you were very good.'

'Really? Thanks.'

The silence set in again and they both looked anywhere but at each other. Then Carol asked casually, 'So – are you home for a break or for good?'

'For good,' he said. 'Or at least till next time I'm asked to go over there. Freddie and I want to get the new show polished. We're scheduled to open in late autumn. We're going straight into the New Theatre.'

'Oh? That's good.' There was a pause, then she asked, 'I suppose Karen is with you.'

'Karen?' He looked puzzled. 'Karen who?'

There was a sharp edge to Carol's voice as she said, 'Don't pretend you don't know who I mean, Steven! Karen Livesey, of course.'

He laughed. 'Oh, *that* Karen! Good heavens, no. What on earth makes you think she'd want to come home with me?'

'According to the gossip columnists you and she are practically engaged,' Carol said smartly.

Steven grinned. 'That's precisely what they were supposed to think. Obviously it worked. Karen is a very ambitious young woman. She wanted to get on and she asked me to help her. If she's seen with enough eligible show business bachelors she's bound to get her photograph in the right magazines.'

'Really?'

'She's a very beautiful girl but short on talent, you see. Still, she'll make it for two good reason.'

'And what would they be?'

'Because she also knows how to get herself noticed. But, more importantly, she knows her limitations.'

'I see.' Carol paused. 'So that's what you are nowadays – an eligible show business bachelor!'

He shrugged. 'In the eyes of the gossip columnists.' He was looking at her closely. 'You'd know about eligible show business bachelors though, wouldn't you, Carol?'

'I don't know what you mean.'

'Gareth Dean, for instance. It appears he's your constant companion from what I hear on the grapevine.'

'The grapevine being Clarissa, I take it.'

'You don't need that kind of help, Carol,' he said, ignoring the accusation.

'No, I don't!' She felt her cheeks turning pink. 'And Gareth is *not* my constant companion. Far from it. None of the rumours you might have heard are true. For your information he's more of a – a mentor than anything else.'

'*Mentor?*' Steven laughed. 'Ten out of ten for originality! I've never heard it called that before.'

Carol picked up her handbag and turned towards the door. 'I think I'll go now. Your visit to New York seems to have turned you into a cynic.'

'Carol – *don't*.' He placed himself between her and the door. 'Look, we're getting off on the wrong foot. I'm sorry. I didn't mean to snipe. I'm sure you didn't either. Can we start again?'

'Is there any – any point?' To her horror she found she was close to tears as was only too obvious by the wavering of her voice. 'I'll be honest with you, Steven. If I'd known you were going to be here today, I'd have stayed away. We have nothing to say to each other any more.'

'That's not true and you know it. We have a great deal to say to each other,' he said quietly. 'And the sooner we get it out of the way, the better.' He took a step towards her and stood with his hands at his sides as though waiting for her to make the next move. His closeness tortured her. She could feel the warmth of him and smell his familiar scent. In the silence she could hear him breathing and it was all she could do not to throw herself into his arms. Although she refused to look at him she sensed that he knew it. Then, just when she was wondering how to bear the tension, there came the sudden pounding of a dozen pairs of feet over their heads, accompanied by the piano. The sound reverberated through the house, shaking the floorboards and rattling the window frames; a sound so strikingly evocative that Carol's eyes swept up to meet his and they both dissolved into laughter.

'Those were the days, eh?' Steven chuckled. He reached out his hands and rested them lightly on her shoulders. 'Remember, Carrie? Carefree days when everything was so simple. I wonder if you ever realised how grown-up and protective you made me feel when you brought me all your dragons to kill? Such a funny, serious little girl with your freckles and wide blue eyes, weighed down by such insurmountable problems.'

'But you weren't there when the biggest problem of all came along,' she said. 'Why couldn't you understand how I felt, Steven?'

'All I wanted was to have you with me. Was that so wrong? It hurt knowing you didn't want to share in my success; to realise that I didn't come top of your list of priorities.'

'Do you think the choice was easy for me?'

He smiled wryly. 'I enjoyed killing your dragons, Carrie, but I never had any ambitions to *be* one. Still, I'm

461

glad you've made such a success of your job and I hope you feel it was worth it?' He tilted up her face and looked into her eyes. 'Does it make you feel good, knowing you made the right decision?'

'Not particularly.'

The pounding above them, accompanied by Kitty's inexpert rendition of *Who's Sorry Now?* on the piano, grew to a crescendo. Steven winced. 'Can't make yourself heard here. Tell you what, why don't we go out somewhere for a cup of tea. Do you know if the Clipper is still open?'

'I don't know, Steven. I should go home really.'

'Why? Do you have someone to see?'

She shook her head.

'Then let's walk down to the river and sit under a willow tree like we used to in the old days. I could use some fresh air.'

They walked across The Meadow side by side, without touching. It was a sunny afternoon and there were other people – mothers with prams; children playing; dogs chasing after balls; sunbathers taking their ease on the grass – but when they reached the towpath down by the river it was quieter. A colourful narrow boat was moored at the bank with a line of washing fluttering in its bows. Its owner waved to them as they passed. Reaching their old favourite bench they sat down.

'So, what's it like, being the star of a soap opera?' he asked.

Carol shot a swift sidelong glance at him. Was he being patronising? 'I daresay it's a far cry from being the composer of a successful West End and Broadway musical.'

He chuckled and took her hand, holding it firmly in his own. 'Why so prickly? You know, in the old days when you were defensive like that, I always knew you were cross about something.'

'I *am*,' she said. 'At least, I was. I had to find my own success in my own way, Steven. But you wouldn't understand that. You expected me to throw away the job I'd got on my own and take the one you'd engineered for me. All you could see was your own hurt. You couldn't see that I was hurt too.'

'Okay! I've already said you were right. You're a big success.'

'I know.'

He looked at her. 'But I have missed you, Carrie.'

'Have you? You didn't even write; not properly.'

'I never could express myself on paper,' he said. 'At least, not in words. I knew that if I tried to write down how I felt it would sound pathetic. I thought you might laugh and tear it up. Anyway, I told myself you didn't really deserve any love letters.' He looked at her. 'Your letters weren't much to shout about either.'

'I couldn't think of anything to say.'

'Okay then, I guess we should call it quits.'

'I suppose we should.'

She turned to look at him and noticed for the first time how long his hair had grown. It was almost touching his shoulders. He looked tanned and fit but leaner, his jaw and cheekbones were more prominent than before. He was dressed casually in jeans and a polo-necked jumper. She looked down at the hand that still held hers firmly on his knees. The square brown musician's hand that she remembered so well, fingers long and sensitive. She shivered a little, remembering their touch and how much she had longed for it these past months. On his little finger he still wore the heavy gold signet ring that he'd worn ever since she'd known him, but around his wrist he wore a new chunky gold identity bracelet. She wondered with a pang of jealousy if it had been a present from someone – Karen Livesey? As she was looking at it his fingers laced through hers and he lifted her hand to his cheek. The slightly rough sensation of his beard on the back of her hand made her long almost unbearably for his kiss.

'I meant it when I said I'd missed you, Carol,' he said.

'I missed you too,' she whispered. 'How could I not?'

'The time we spent together, before I went away, it was so good. I haven't forgotten – never will.'

'Nor me.'

'Where did you go that night?'

'To Janet's flat. After that I got a bedsit and then the flat in Richmond where I am now.'

'And it worked out, all of it? I mean – you're happy?'

He didn't say, *without me*, but she knew that was what he meant. 'I'm okay,' she said lightly.

'What does that mean?'

'What do you want me to say, Steven?' she said sharply. 'I came to see you off at the airport. It wasn't easy but I tried so hard to make you see how I felt. You've no idea how much I tried. Or how upset I was, seeing you go. You wouldn't give an inch. All you could think of was yourself.'

He frowned. 'I see. So I'm not forgiven?'

'It's not that. It's . . .'

'What?'

'Just – just that it made me wonder if I knew you as well as I thought I did.'

'You're saying I'm a self-centred, thoughtless bastard.'

A denial rose to her lips, then she thought suddenly of the nights she'd cried herself to sleep; of the loneliness and longings she had endured because of him, the sketchy postcards that told her nothing. And she heard herself say, 'All right, Steven, *yes*. Seeing that you've said it yourself, that's *exactly* what I think. But then, I suppose success does that to some people!'

There was a sudden chill in the air as the sun disappeared behind a cloud and a breeze sprang up, ruffling the surface of the water. In the silence that followed Carol watched the narrow boat's owner come out and unpeg the washing, piling it into a wicker basket.

Steven stood up. 'No answer to that really, is there?' he said. 'Better get back, I suppose. It looks a bit like rain.'

Chapter Fourteen

Steven and Carol walked in silence at far as Derngate corner.

'Don't come any further,' she said as they stood at the kerb. 'Kitty will be wondering where you are.'

He looked at her. 'Are you staying long?'

'Till the end of next week.'

'I'll be here till after this weekend.' He raised an inquiring eyebrow at her. 'Do I get to see you again?'

'I don't know. I've got a family crisis on my hands. It depends.'

'Don't make excuses, Carrie,' he said gruffly. 'Surely we can at least be honest with each other, can't we?'

'I *am* being honest. Mum has a problem – a serious one. That's why I'm here.'

He nodded. 'Okay. I'm sorry.' He held out his hand. 'We're still friends, aren't we, Carrie?'

She nodded, her heart heavy with misery. 'Of course we are.'

'You're all set with this *Queen's Square* thing then, are you? I mean, it looks okay for a long run. Obviously you're going to be tied up for ages.'

She hesitated. No doubt Kitty would mention their conversation so she may as well tell him. 'As a matter of fact, I've been thinking of getting out,' she said. 'I've been in it for a year. My contract is coming up for renewal soon and I've got doubts about staying with it.'

'I think you're wise,' he said. 'Getting type-cast at this

stage in your career wouldn't be a good move.' He smiled at her. 'I suppose you've got something in mind?'

'Nothing definite.'

'But something tentative?'

'Sort of.'

'I see.' He looked at her. 'I'll go then. No hard feelings?'

'No hard feelings.'

'As I said, I'll be around until Sunday evening if you want to see me again.' He shrugged, grinning wryly. 'Vain hope, eh?'

As he turned to walk away she called after him. 'Steven . . .'

'Yes?'

'I'm sorry – for all of it.'

He nodded. 'Me too.' He shrugged. 'One of those things, eh? People change – grow apart.'

Carol let herself into the flat, took off her coat and tied on one of Eve's aprons. Then she set to work preparing vegetables for the evening meal, determined to occupy herself. His last words had cut her to the heart and she didn't want to give herself time to think about their conversation too deeply. Seeing Steven again so un-expectedly had been such a wonderful surprise and then she'd had to go and spoil it. She hadn't meant to speak her mind so bluntly, but there was something about his air of always expecting to be forgiven that irked her. She felt tears gathering at the corners of her eyes. Why, oh *why*, was it that they seemed destined to hurt one another?

She opened the fridge and took out some chops. She found a bottle of wine in the door rack and took that out too. Rummaging at the back of the sideboard cupboard she fished out Eve's cherished candelabra and set the table with her best cloth and flowers, determined to make the meal special.

Mike had promised her that his letter would silence Eddie once and for all. She hoped he was right but couldn't imagine Eddie being silenced forever, not even by a solicitor's letter. She wondered how long it would be before he thought up some new, devilishly ingenious plan with which to persecute them. She hated the thought of Eve's being so alone and isolated and wondered what she could do about it. She could ask her to sell the business and come to live in London, but she knew Eve would never agree to that. If only she and Aunt Rose would bury the hatchet!

Suddenly making up her mind, Carol put down the vegetable knife, dried her hands and went into the hall to dial her grandmother's number.

It was Freda herself who answered. 'Hello, Carol. You're home then. When are we going to see you?'

'Soon, I hope. Look, Gran, can't we do something about this feud between Mum and Aunt Rose?'

'I wish we could, love. What I'd really like would be to arrange a family reunion while you're at home, but the two of them are so stubborn. If either of them got wind of what we were trying to do, wild horses wouldn't drag them here.'

'Well, we'll just have to make sure they don't hear about it then,' Carol said. 'I think a family reunion would be lovely, even if it has to be a surprise one. Could we have it this Sunday?'

'The day after tomorrow? It's a bit short notice, love. And I happen to know that Elizabeth and Harold are taking the twins over to his mother's at Moulton this Sunday. It's her birthday.'

'I'll be gone the weekend after, though. Couldn't you persuade them to at least drop in?'

Freda sounded doubtful. 'Well, I suppose I could try.'

'I won't let you do all the work, Gran,' Carol promised.

'I'll come round and help you tomorrow. And I'll think up a sure way to get Mum there, don't worry about that.'

'Well, all right then.'

'I'll be round tomorrow morning as soon as Mum's gone to the shop. We can go shopping together. Then in the afternoon we can do some baking.'

Freda's voice brightened. 'That sounds like fun. It's a long time since I had you helping me in the kitchen. You used to love it when you were little. All right then, dear. See you in the morning. I'll ring round this evening and let everyone know.'

Eve looked tired when she came home, but brightened when she saw the attractively-laid table and smelt the appetising aroma of the meal cooking. Carol insisted that her mother went off to relax in a hot bath while she put the finishing touches to it.

When they had reached the coffee stage she said, 'Gran wants us both to go over for tea on Sunday.' Forestalling Eve's doubtful look, she added quickly, 'It might be the only chance I get to see her and Granddad. I don't want to go on my own. You will come with me, won't you?'

Eve sighed. 'I suppose so. I just hope she doesn't start on at me again to make it up with our Rose.'

'Mum – there's something else. I think you should confide in someone else, preferably Gran, about what you told me last night.'

'No!' Eve laid down her knife and fork. 'I couldn't.'

'But, Mum, you need their support.' Carol leaned towards her mother. 'You can't carry this alone any longer. You have to get it out of your head that you committed murder. What happened was an accident.'

'*But I caused it!*'

'That doesn't make it murder. Listen – a series of things caused Sally's death: the weather, the air raid that night; the fact that she was running away. Even – no, *especially*

469

– the fact that she'd had me! Don't you see, Mum? Any one of those things is equally to blame for what happened. I could just as easily say it was my fault! You mustn't take it all on yourself.'

Eve sighed. 'I can't get it out of my mind. All these years I've lived with it.'

'That's why you should have told someone,' Carol said. 'Why didn't you, Mum?'

'I wanted to forget, to put it behind me. Pretend it hadn't happened if you like. You were always *my* child, Carol, even before you were born. I wanted you so much. Sally carried you so miserably; so unwillingly. It was me who looked forward and planned and longed for you. Me who made all your little clothes and got everything ready. It was all arranged long before you were born that Jack and I should adopt you. I can't tell you how happy I was that night when you were born.'

Eve sighed and lifted her hands helplessly. 'Then it all went wrong. Sally changed her mind. I never knew why. She'd never been particularly interested in you. It was me who did everything for you. It tore my heart out when she said she wanted to keep you after all. Then, when it came out that her husband was alive after all, I had fresh hope. I thought she wouldn't want him to know she'd had another man's child. Then suddenly there was a change in her. She grew sly and secretive – said she was going to ask him to forgive her – let her keep you. Once we were good friends, but in the end I think I truly hated her. And all the time she was lying to me, Carol. Lying through her teeth – planning to run off with Eddie Wilson and take you with her.' Eve looked up at her daughter. 'Now can you see why I felt as I did? Maybe I did feel murderous towards her right at that moment. Maybe I *did* want her dead!'

Carol got up and gathered her mother close. 'That's

470

probably true. But you didn't *do* it, Mum,' she said gently. 'That's what you have to hang on to. You didn't do it. Listen, I've got a confession to make now. I've been to see Mike today. I told him what you told me.' As Eve's eyes widened fearfully, she held up her hand. 'No! It's all right. Mike's a solicitor. He won't breathe a word to a soul. That's the cardinal rule of his profession: confidentiality. He thinks just as I do, that it was a tragic accident. He's sending Eddie a formal letter tonight. Eddie has already committed the crime of blackmail more than once so he hasn't really a leg to stand on. Mike says you won't be hearing from him again.' Carol clasped Eve's hands tightly. 'Isn't that good news, Mum?'

'I suppose so.' For the first time she smiled. 'Yes. Yes, it is.'

'So, you see, you did right in telling me. And now I think you should talk to Gran and Granddad about it.'

'We'll see.'

Carol and Freda worked hard all day on Saturday preparing for the party. In spite of prior arrangements and the fact that it was short notice, Freda assured Carol that everyone would be there. Rose and Ted would be coming with Elizabeth, Harold and the twins, after looking in briefly on Harold's mother.

On Sunday at breakfast Eve announced that she had a headache.

'I don't think I'll go with you to your Gran's,' she said. 'I don't want it to turn into a migraine. Got to be fit for work tomorrow.'

Carol's heart sank. 'You'll be all right, Mum. Just take some Phensic. You know they always put you right.'

Eve shook her head. 'I really don't feel well. You'll be fine without me. Just tell Gran . . .'

'*Mum!* You're ducking out, aren't you?' Carol got up

from the table and fetched the bottle of Phensic tablets from the bathroom cabinet. Shaking two out on to the tablecloth, she poured her mother a fresh cup of tea. 'Now – take those and go back to bed for an hour. You'll be fine, Mum. And you *are* going with me.'

After a light lunch Eve was protestingly chivvied into her best frock and bundled into Carol's car. At Freda's, when Eve had gone upstairs to take off her coat, Carol looked at her grandmother.

'Thought I'd never get her here,' she whispered conspiratorially.

'Just keep her away from the kitchen,' Freda whispered back. 'I've got the tea laid out in there. If she sees all that food, she'll guess.'

'Right. When are the others coming?'

'Later, when they get back from Moulton,' Freda said. 'Though Michael's already here.' She raised her eyes to the ceiling. 'It wasn't easy persuading them to come to tea, I can tell you.'

When Eve came downstairs again they all joined Mike and Albert in the front room. For a few minutes they exchanged small talk, then Carol glanced at her mother and said, 'Mum has something she'd like to tell you about, haven't you, Mum?'

Eve flushed scarlet and looked as though she might faint. Freda looked anxiously from one to the other.

'Whatever's the matter? Not bad news, is it?'

Michael cleared his throat and took charge of the situation. 'I think I know what it is,' he said. 'Carol did consult me on the matter and if I can be of any further help . . .'

'It's all right, I'll tell them.' Eve's voice was strong and she looked composed now. Straightening her back, she looked at the anxious faces of her mother and father. 'It's to do with something that happened a long time ago – to

472

Sally, Carol's real mother.' She cleared her throat and went on: 'The night she left, the night she was killed on the old railway bridge, she wasn't alone. I went after her. She took the baby – took Carol with her, you see . . .' She glanced at Carol who reached out and took her hand.

'Go on, Mum,' she whispered. 'Take your time, you're doing fine.'

Eve cleared her throat. 'I couldn't let her take Carol out in the cold. She was so poorly. And then when the siren went . . .' She swallowed and her voice wavered as she said, 'She was my baby really. We always said she'd be my baby.'

'So you followed her to make sure Carol was safe?' Freda put in.

Eve shook her head. 'No, I meant to get her back. I caught up with her on the bridge. I asked Sally to come back with me at first, because of the raid, but she wouldn't. We argued. She said I was like a jealous old maid – that she wasn't letting me have Carol. But she didn't really care about her. She just wanted to hurt me. She squeezed her so tight that she hurt her and that was when I lost my temper and – and hit her.' Eve closed her eyes and the colour left her face, leaving it chalk white.

Freda moved to where she sat and put an arm around her. 'Oh, love,' she whispered. 'My poor Evie.'

Opening her eyes, Eve looked at her mother. 'That was when she fell over the parapet,' she whispered.

'And you blamed yourself? Oh, my dear Lord.' Freda pulled her daughter to her and held her close, cradling her head against her shoulder. 'All these years and you've never said a word? What you must have been through.' She rocked her daughter as though she were a child again, smoothing her hair from her brow. 'Why didn't you tell us, Evie?' she said. 'Why didn't you say anything when I came round next morning? You must have realised then

473

that it was the bomb that killed her. It was nothing to do with you.'

Eve shook her head. 'If it hadn't been for me catching her up she would have been gone from there by the time the bomb fell. I've looked at it every way possible. Even if it wasn't just me who made her fall, I'm still responsible.'

'You must put it all behind you,' Albert said, clearing his throat noisily. 'It was a sad accident, but there's nothing to be gained by dwelling on it. You've been a wonderful mother to Carol and you were a good wife to Jack. You've always been a kind and generous daughter to us too. You've nothing to reproach yourself with, lass.'

'The trouble is that there was one witness that night,' Carol said. 'A man who was waiting for Sally on the far side of the bridge. He's been blackmailing Mum. That's why she was having to sell the flat and move in with you.'

Freda gasped with horror and Albert was on his feet at once. 'Who's this then?' he demanded angrily. 'Tell me the man's name and I'll . . .'

'It's all right, Granddad.' Michael held up his hand. 'I've already dealt with him. I don't think we'll be hearing from him again. Not only that, Aunt Eve, but I'm pretty sure he couldn't have seen anything that night. Not from where he claims to have been waiting. It's my belief he heard your raised voices and guessed at the rest.'

Eve looked up, her eyes hopeful. 'You really think so?'

'I'm ninety percent sure of it.'

She drew a deep sigh. 'It's such a relief to have it out in the open. Maybe now I'll get some peace at last.' She stood up, still trembling a little. 'I think I'll just go upstairs and wash my face, freshen up.'

'Shall I come with you?' Freda asked. Eve shook her head.

'I'd like to be on my own for a few minutes.'

She walked to the door and opened it. Then drew in her

breath sharply as she revealed a white-faced Rose standing in the hall. For a moment the two sisters stared at each other, then Rose found her voice.

'Eve! Oh, *Eve*, why ever didn't you tell us before?'

'You *heard*?'

'I didn't mean to listen. But now I'm glad I did,' her sister said stoutly.

'But why are you here?' Freda asked, on her feet behind Eve. 'And where's Ted?'

'He went with the others to Harold's mother's,' Rose told her. 'I've never liked that woman since the things she said at Elizabeth's wedding, so I decided to come on by myself, on the bus.' She put her arms round Eve. 'Oh, you daft thing,' she said, eyes full of tears. 'How could you keep a thing like that to yourself all these years? How could you shut us – your family – out? Did you think we wouldn't be behind you?'

Freda quietly closed the door on the reunited sisters as they wept together in the hall. When she turned to the others her eyes too were moist. 'Well, that's that,' she said briskly. 'I think we could all do with a nice cup of tea now, don't you?'

Ted, Elizabeth and Harold arrived half an hour later along with the twins, now an engaging pair of toddlers, and the family reunion was complete. The rest of the afternoon was spent in noisy celebration, the twins lightening the atmosphere as they demanded centre stage. All the food Carol had helped her grandmother prepare disappeared as if by magic and the atmosphere was relaxed and festive.

It was after ten o'clock when Carol drove her mother home. As the front door of the flat closed behind them, Eve looked at her.

'You were responsible for all that, weren't you?'

Carol held up her hands. 'Guilty. Except for Aunt Rose arriving early. That was a piece of pure fate.'

Eve chuckled. 'Ironic to think that it wouldn't have happened if she hadn't fallen out with Harold's mother! Still, I'll admit that it's good to have made up our quarrel. And it was lovely, all being together again.' She hugged Carol. 'You've taken such a load off my shoulders. I'm so grateful.'

'I just wish I could have done it years ago, Mum. Now, I'm going to come and help you in the shop tomorrow.'

Eve looked scandalised. 'You'll do no such thing! The star of *Queen's Square* serving in a newsagent's shop!'

'No one will recognise me,' Carol said. 'I'll do my hair differently and wear glasses. And if they do know it's me, what does it matter? It'll be good for business, won't it? I want to be with you as much as I can while I'm here.'

Although Carol stayed on until the following Sunday afternoon she didn't see Steven again. As she drove back to Richmond she remembered their meeting and wondered bleakly if she would. She'd thought a lot about the renewal of her contract during the time she'd been at home. Turning down the offer of steady work was a desperately difficult decision to make. Zelda was bound to be against it. Suppose she was already type-cast and couldn't find other work? After all, she'd been appearing twice a week in *Queen's Square* for more than a year now.

On Monday during a break from rehearsals she decided to confide in Madge. The older actress had been in the business for many years and they'd become good friends. She knew that Madge would be honest with her.

Carol invited her to share some sandwiches in a pub close to the studios, and when they were settled on stools at a quiet end of the bar, she put her question.

Madge sighed and took a long drink of her gin and tonic before answering. 'Well, I can't pretend I wouldn't miss you if you went. It'd probably mean the end of my

476

character, too, which would be a shame. Still, you never know. I'm the old bat they love to hate and that always goes down well. They might still find a place for me.'

'I hadn't thought of that,' Carol said in dismay. 'I'd hate to think I was putting you out of work.'

Madge shook her head and smiled good-naturedly. 'One piece of advice ducky. You've got to put yourself first in this business. No one else will. It's sink or swim. You're just a kid yet and you've got a good career in front of you if you play your cards right. *Queen's* looks set to go on for years, but you never can tell. Now that there's competition from other commercial companies, some similar programme to *Queen's* could pop up any day and cut our ratings in half. Then it'd be . . .' She drew one finger across her throat and made a choking sound. 'Are they going to think about your loyalty then? Not on your nelly! Out on your bum like the rest of us, star or no star! And stuck with a label round your neck that could choke you.' She drained her glass. 'But I don't want to influence you one way or the other. It's your life, love. You do what you think best.' She lifted an inquiring eyebrow. 'Got anything buzzing, have you?'

Carol shrugged noncommittally. 'Only vaguely.'

'Well, for what it's worth, I'd think hard before committing yourself to twelve whole months more of your working life if I were you.'

As Madge hailed the barman and ordered them another drink each, Carol suddenly remembered Kitty's greeting and passed it on. Madge smiled reminiscently.

'Kitty Manson! And you say she was your teacher? Well, I never, what a small world it is! She was Kitty Gray when I knew her. Drop dead *gorgeous*, she was. Put all the rest of us in the shade with those green eyes of hers and that red hair. And talk about talent!' Madge raised her eyes to the ceiling. 'Danced like a devil and sang like an

477

angel. She could act too. Real star quality, she had. We all thought she was on a one-way ticket to Hollywood. Then she had to go and marry that no-hoper Al Manson.' She sighed and shook her head. 'Love really buggers you up, you know. No doubt about that. You'll stay away from it, ducky, if you take my advice.' She grinned. 'Not that you will!' She frowned. 'Hang on a minute. Is Steven Manson the composer any relation to Kitty?'

'Her son.'

'Well, blow me! That's the bloke you were seeing before he went to America. I read that he and his partner have a new show in the offing. Why don't you ask him if there's a part in it for you?'

Carol felt her face colouring. 'I don't want any favours.'

Madge threw back her head and laughed. 'Wash your mouth out with soap, child! That's what this business is all about, Carol, my love – giving each other a helping hand up the ladder.'

'All the same, I'd rather get there on my own,' she said stubbornly.

Madge paid for the drinks and winked at the barman. 'Well, why not? You can still afford pride at your age, I suppose. Just wait till you're a washed-up old has-been like me.'

'You're not!' Carol said indignantly. 'You're still a wonderful actress. I've learned so much from you since we've been working together.'

Madge wriggled down from her stool. 'Get away with you! I'm ready for the knacker's-yard, me! Come on. We'll be late for rehearsal if we're not careful.'

Carol went to see Zelda to talk about leaving *Queen's Square*. She went on an afternoon when she wasn't needed for rehearsal. It was some time since she'd visited

478

the Old Bond Street office but she found the stairs as steep as ever, the brown paint just as dingy and in need of renewal. But Zelda and Marty's welcome was as warm and effusive as always. Over coffee they told her their news. They'd got several rising stars on their books now and the agency seemed to be going from strength to strength.

'I think you'll agree that we do work hard for our clients,' Zelda said.

Carol cleared her throat. The moment had come to drop her bombshell. 'I wanted to talk to you about something,' she began.

Marty chuckled. 'No! And there we were thinking you'd come all the way Up West just to look at our wrinkled old mugs.'

Zelda bridled. 'Speak for yourself, Marty Waring. Go on, Carol. What's on your mind?'

'It's almost time for renewing my contract and I . . .'

'Want more money? Of course you do, darling. And you shall have it. We'll see to that.'

'No. Actually I want out.'

There was a stunned silence as the Warings stared at her and then at each other.

'*Out?*' they said in unison.

'Surely not, darling? You've got it made with *Queen's Square*,' Zelda said.

'But there are other things I can do – *want* to do,' Carol said. 'I don't want to get stuck in a rut.'

Zelda looked dubious. 'A lot of young actresses would give their eye teeth for the kind of rut you've got,' she said. 'The prospect of steady work isn't to be sneezed at, you know.'

'I'd like a pound for all the youngsters I've known who've thought the world was their oyster after one success, only to belly-flop,' Marty put in.

'All the same, I'd like to try,' Carol said.

'Well – what have you in mind?' Zelda asked, picking up a pen and rolling it between her fingers. 'I mean, you must have visualised something you want to do?'

'Not really.' Carol paused. Obviously the Warings expected her to have something in view. They would think her foolish to be giving up steady work without. 'Gareth Dean did mention a new project he was interested in,' she said. 'Have you heard anything about that – on the grapevine?'

'Has Gareth been dangling goodies under your nose?' Zelda asked, her eyes glinting. 'Because there's only one reason a man of his age makes offers like that to young, inexperienced actresses, you know. He's simply trying to get you into bed, darling.'

'No, he isn't! And he hasn't offered me anything,' Carol told her hotly. 'It's just something I heard, that's all. I wondered if you had too?'

'No, we haven't. Maybe we're plugged into the wrong grapevine,' Zelda said tetchily, her pen tapping an irritable tattoo on the desk. 'Well, if you've made up your mind, so be it. But I do think you're being remarkably foolish, passing up a golden opportunity as though it was nothing!'

'I'll be happy to start again at the bottom – take anything you can get for me,' Carol said humbly.

'Might mean going back to the fluffy chickens again,' Marty said, eyes twinkling wickedly.

But Zelda wasn't seeing the funny side of it. 'I must say, darling, that apart from anything else, I do rather feel you're letting us down. But there, you're employing *us*, not the other way round, so I suppose we shall just have to grin and bear it.'

Carol stood up. 'I didn't want to remind you, Zelda, but I got the part in *Queen's Square* myself. I daresay I can do it again if I put my mind to it.'

'And *I* could remind *you* – if I wanted to be bitchy – that it was me who negotiated the best terms possible for your contract. *And*, if it hadn't been for us you wouldn't have met Gareth Dean in the first place,' Zelda said sharply. 'It was us who got you the audition for the Carl Gibson play – remember?' She rose to face Carol. 'As Marty's just said, we've seen this so many times in the past. Girls who get big-headed after one success. Well, you'll learn, darling. And I promise you, the lesson will be even more painful without friends to support you!'

Dismayed, Carol said, 'Zelda! I don't want to fall out with you and Marty. I know you've been good to me in the past. I haven't forgotten that. It's just that I want to widen my horizons.'

Zelda's anger dissolved as quickly as it had flared. Her face relaxed. 'I'm sorry, darling. Of course you do. We'd hate to lose you, wouldn't we, Marty? But we do like our clients to be guided by us, you know. We do have years of experience between us.' She opened a drawer and riffled through a card index. 'I can't see anything suitable here at the moment. Anyway, you've got a few weeks to run yet, haven't you? There's sure to be something coming up. I'll ring you.'

Carol retired, shaken, to a coffee bar and sat in a corner table with a cup of coffee and a Danish pastry. She had been thoroughly dismayed by the encounter with Zelda and Marty. She'd had no idea that Zelda would take her decision so badly. It seemed she was losing all her friends lately. It was all very well making your own decisions and thinking of yourself, but if it left you isolated, was it worth it?

Passing a toy shop, her attention was taken by a pretty doll sitting in the centre of the window. She thought of Clarissa's baby and her unfulfilled promise to visit – their recent coolness. Making up her mind on impulse, she rummaged in her handbag for her address book and hailed a taxi.

When Clarissa opened the door, her mouth fell open in surprise.

'Carol!'

'I thought it was time I came to see you,' she said, and held out the gift-wrapped box. 'I've brought a present for your daughter.'

'Oh, you shouldn't. There was no need for that.' Clarissa held the door wide. 'Come in. Freddie has taken Fiona to the park. They've only just gone so they won't be back for a while. You must stay and see them. Tea?'

In spite of the recent cup of coffee, Carol nodded. 'That would be lovely.'

The new flat was airy and spacious, but the sleek, sophisticated woman whom Clarissa had once been had been replaced by a softer, more domestic version. Instead of the immaculate clothes and flawless make-up that had been her trademark she wore a cotton skirt and teeshirt, her bare feet were thrust into sandals and her red hair tumbled loose about her shoulders. She looked radiant and seemed totally fulfilled as a mother, perfectly content to be at home with her small daughter all day.

'I'll probably go back to work when she starts school,' she said. 'But for now I have to confess that I couldn't be happier.'

'Confess? I think you should be proud,' Carol said.

'I am. I didn't really expect to have any children and I don't suppose I'll have any more at my age, so I intend to make the most of Fiona's childhood.' Clarissa glanced speculatively at Carol as she offered a plate of biscuits. 'Have you seen Steven since he's been back?'

'Yes. I ran into him by accident on a visit home when I went to see Kitty.' Carol looked at her. 'Didn't he tell you?'

'Well, yes, he did actually,' Clarissa conceded. 'I was being tactful – didn't know whether you'd want to talk about it or not.'

Carol sighed. 'He will have told you that we quarrelled – again?'

'What is it with you two?' Clarissa asked. 'I really thought you had everything going for you after the opening of SS. I have to admit I was annoyed with you for walking out on him.'

'I gathered that,' Carol said wryly.

'Before I had Fiona I might have seen your point of view,' Clarissa said. 'But I see things from a different angle these days.' She looked closely at Carol as she poured the tea. 'I've always felt that I had a stake in your relationship. I gave Steven up for you, Carol. Oh, I always knew he didn't love me – not as I wanted to be loved. As I *am* loved by Freddie. I told him what he was too blind to see at the time: that there'd never be anyone for him but you.' She shrugged. 'I worked really hard to get the two of you together. Then you had to go and throw it all away.'

'I didn't intend to throw it away,' Carol told her. 'It was Steven. He's so selfish. He can't see that I want to make my own way; my own career.'

'If you ask me, you're as bad as each other.' Clarissa passed her a plate of home-made buns. 'Stubborn as mules, the pair of you.' She looked at Carol across the table. 'By the way, I don't suppose he told you that the new show was written with you in mind?'

Carol stared at her, her cup halfway to her lips. '*Me?*'

'Yes, you! It was meant to be a surprise, but now I don't think wild horses would make him tell you. He says you'll just think it's some kind of favour. I can assure you it isn't, Carol. It was done purely and simply out of love.'

Carol stared at her.

'It's a musical version of *Vanity Fair*,' Clarissa went on. 'And it's going to be brilliant. It's to be called *Eve's Daughter*.'

'*Eve's Daughter?*'

'Yes. Do you need any more proof than that?'

'But – he's always known my singing voice isn't great.'

'All your attributes have been taken into consideration, believe me,' Clarissa said with a smile. 'And Steven always said that with coaching he was sure your singing voice would develop.' She refilled both cups, glancing at Carol as she did so. 'Still, I daresay he'll find someone else now that you're tied up elsewhere. We're great fans of *Queen's Square*, by the way.'

Carol was still stunned by what she'd just heard. '*Queen's*? Oh, but I'm out of it soon,' she said abstractedly. 'I'm not renewing my contract. I've just had a bit of a battle with Zelda about it.'

Clarissa looked up sharply. 'So you'd actually be free to do it – if it were offered?'

Carol shrugged. 'I would have been, I suppose.'

The front door slammed at that moment and the sound of a child's voice could be heard babbling excitedly. Freddie came into the room, carrying his daughter on his shoulders.

'Carol! Well, what a nice surprise.' He swung the child to the ground. 'Look, Fiona, this is your Auntie Carol. Say hello.' He put the toddler down, but she popped her thumb into her mouth and turned her face into her father's trouser leg shyly.

Carol went to kneel on the floor beside her. 'Look, Fiona, I've brought you a present. Shall we open it and see what's inside?'

It was two days later that Carol received an unexpected visitor. It was almost nine o'clock and she'd just parked the car on the forecourt of the flats when she saw the sleek black Ferrari waiting at the kerb. The car was unfamiliar to her and she watched warily as a tall figure emerged from it and began to walk towards her through the evening dusk.

'Hi!'

Her heart gave a lurch. '*Steven!* Have you been waiting long?'

'About an hour.'

'This is the night the show goes out. I'm always late on Tuesdays and Thursdays.'

'Of course. I should have known.'

'If you'd rung I'd have told you.'

'And you could have told me not to come.'

She turned aside to fumble in her bag for her keys. 'Well, now you're here, are you going to come up?'

He followed her up the stairs and waited for her to unlock the door. In the flat he looked around appreciatively. 'This is nice.'

'I like it. Coffee? Or would you like something stronger?' Carol took off her coat and put the briefcase containing her script on the desk.

'Nothing, thanks. I'm here to talk, Carrie.'

'You might as well have something after your long wait. It's no trouble. I can put the kettle on and then . . .'

'Carrie!' He crossed the room and reached out to grasp her shoulders. 'Just stop babbling for a minute and listen. Rissa told me you'd been to see her.'

'Yes, I wanted to give the baby a present. I . . .'

'That wasn't what it was about really, was it?'

'I don't know what you mean.'

'Yes, you do. You wanted to talk to her – about me.'

'About *you*? Really, Steven! How conceited can you get?'

He shook her gently. 'It's true though, isn't it?'

485

'If you must know, I went to see Clarissa because I wanted to be friends with her again. She's been very cool with me since you and I split up.'

'Oh, *yes*?'

'*Yes!* I'd just had an uncomfortable session with Zelda and Marty. I seem to have been upsetting people lately. I'm advised by more experienced colleagues to put myself first. Not to think too much about others. But I don't care for the way it loses you your friends.'

'You can't be popular with everyone.'

'So I've noticed. With some people it couldn't matter less, but as far as Clarissa was concerned, I cared about it. I wanted to redress the balance.'

'And me? The cause of it all. Do you care about *our* relationship?'

She turned away. 'Of course I do.'

He dropped his hands to his sides. 'You said you wanted to find out who you really are, Carrie. You wanted to make it on your own, without any help from me or anyone else. Well, you've had plenty of time to do that now and you must have realised that there are two sides to that particular coin. You can have all the talent in the world but it's no use to you unless someone recognises it. Right?'

'Yes, all right.'

'Rissa tells me she told you about the new show. Although I swore her to secrecy it seems she told you I wrote it with you in mind.'

'Yes, she did.'

He looked at her. 'And . . . ?'

'It sounds wonderful, Steven.'

'So – would you do it?'

She bit her lip, her stomach suddenly turning to water. 'Surely you'd want an established star?'

He grinned. 'Isn't that what you are?'

'You know what I mean. West End, Broadway. I'm not in that league.'

'Neither were a lot of big stars until they had their first hit.'

'I don't know. What would Graham Lang feel about it?'

'I've already told him it was written for you. He's met you, of course. And he's seen you working in *Queen's*. He likes you and he's willing to trust my judgement.' He put his hands on her shoulders again and looked into her eyes. 'This is no favour, Carrie. Surely you don't think I'm doing it out of some kind of misplaced charity? Do you really think I'd risk seeing my show flop? I'd never do that. Not even for you!'

'No.' Her mouth had dried and she couldn't trust herself to look at him. His hands tightened on her shoulders and he drew her towards him.

'So how about it, Carrie? You can read the script and hear the songs before you decide of course.'

'Well, yes, I'd like to do that.'

'And – all things being equal . . . ?'

She looked up at him, her eyes wide with apprehension. 'Oh, Steven, it's such a terrifying thought. I'm not sure I could do it.'

'*Do it?* Damn it, I've known your work since you were eight years old. I wrote the bloody thing for you! Of *course* you can do it!'

She was trembling. 'Do you think we could work together, Steven?'

He sighed and rubbed his chin. 'Well, there could be a problem with that, of course. There is one way I think we could, though. Not that you'd ever agree to it so it's hardly worth mentioning.'

'So mention it.'

'It's just that – if we were married, I could always beat you into submission.'

487

For a moment she stared at him, then she laughed shakily. 'You're mad!'

'I know. And getting madder by the minute.' He drew her towards him. 'So – will you? Marry me and take the part of Becky in *Eve's Daughter* – in that order?'

'Are you serious?'

'God!' He threw his hands in the air. 'What do I have to do to convince you?' Without waiting for her reply, he pulled her into his arms and kissed her hard until she found herself struggling for breath.

'I'm going to go on doing that until you say yes,' he murmured, holding her close. 'Call me a selfish bastard if you want to, but I don't intend to let you out of my sight again, whether you like it or not.'

'Steven . . .' She reached up to touch his face. 'Steven, please don't rush me like this. I need time.'

'Okay. How much time? A day? A week?'

Taking his hand, she sat down on the settee and drew him down beside her. 'I'd love to take the part you've written for me. I'm so flattered, and so proud. But I think we should take it one step at a time, don't you?'

He slipped an arm around her. 'I had an idea you'd say that.'

'It makes sense though, doesn't it? There's my notice to give in here at Riverside TV. I'll have to work for however long it takes to wind the character down. Then there'll be lines to learn, music, lyrics. I haven't done any of that for ages. It will all be so new, and so *important*. I think I should concentrate on that first, don't you?'

He grinned. 'I've an idea this is what they call being "hoist with your own petard".' He kissed her. 'Okay then. As long as we can be together. You'll move back into the flat with me?'

'I'd love that – once I've finished with *Queen's*.'

'Not till then?'

'Not till then,' she said firmly. 'This is close and convenient for the studios. But we can see each other as often as you like, when work allows.'

He cupped her chin. 'You really have found yourself, haven't you, Carrie?'

'Perhaps. You might have to get to know me all over again. For all you know, you might not even like the new Carol Kenning.'

'Not a chance!' He looked at her with narrowed eyes. 'Are you suggesting that I set out to court you, Miss Kenning?'

'Well, why not?' She laughed. 'After all, you never have, have you?' She wound her arms around his neck. 'There's just one thing I'd like you to do for me, Steven.'

'Anything. What is it?'

'Contact Zelda and ask her to make the offer. Don't tell her you've already told me. And let her draw up the contract. It'll make up for the disagreement we had.'

'If you like.'

'Oh, and something else.'

'Go on.'

'When we do get married, don't let's make it a big showbiz splash. Can we have a quiet family wedding at home with just my family and Kitty to share in it? I really feel I owe Mum that.'

Steven held her close. 'If that's what you want, darling, I wouldn't have it any other way.'

The weeks that followed were a whirlwind of activity. All Carol's spare moments were occupied in reading the script of *Eve's Daughter* and going over the songs with Steven. He'd also taped the music for her so that she could listen to it at home. The part of Becky was a dream for any young actress and she was so excited about it she could scarcely sleep.

Gareth had shown no surprise when Carol told him she wanted to leave the show. She told him about the part Steven had written for her and he was delighted for her.

'When you're a big international star, I'll be able to say that I gave you your first chance,' he told her. 'When I'm old and feeble I'll still be able to dine out on that.'

As soon as it became known that she was to leave the show there were script conferences: discussions as to whether to kill off the character of Harriet Jameson or contrive an open-ended plot so as to leave the option open for her possible return. Gareth was all for a strong storyline with her going out with a flourish, insisting that it wouldn't be practical for Carol to appear as Harriet again once she had been on the West End stage.

'But we must make sure the press doesn't get hold of the ending,' he said, swearing everyone in the room to strict silence. 'We'll get the viewers on the edge of their seats with this one. We'll have the ratings going through the roof! Then we'll have to dream up a good follow up. Possibly with a strong storyline for Madge.'

But in spite of all the precautions Gareth took, somehow the press did get wind of the fact that the popular character of Harriet was to leave *Queen's Square*. And, in spite of the strict secrecy employed by everyone on the team, they also managed to unearth the fact that her reason for leaving was that she was to take the starring part in the new Manson and Manners musical, *Eve's Daughter*.

Journalists pestered her, both at Riverside Studios and at home, until at last both Steven and Gareth agreed that she should give an interview, giving away as little as possible, just to keep them out of her hair.

The syndicated article appeared in the popular daily tabloids along with photographs and a rehash of the biographical story that had appeared earlier. Everyone gave a sigh of relief. So far no one had uncovered the dramatic ending of the final storyline, now in rehearsal. They could concentrate on the job in hand and breathe once more.

The storyline that was to take Harriet out of the show concerned a suicide attempt by her mother. Harriet was to try to save her when she jumped from a cliff on a daytrip to the seaside – to be filmed on location and video-taped. In doing so she was to be badly injured herself. Her life would hang in the balance for several episodes but finally she was to die in an emotional hospital sequence, leaving her mother a remorseful, reformed character.

On Wednesday evening, the week before Carol was to make her final appearance, she arrived home to find the caretaker of the flats waiting for her in the entrance hall. The man looked anxious.

'Miss Kenning, you've got a visitor,' he said. 'I suggested she should wait in my office till you got home but she insisted that she'd come a long way and needed to rest. So I let her in with my pass key. I hope I did right?'

Carol paused, about to step into the lift. '*She?* Who is it? Did she give you her name?'

'Well, of course when she said she was your mother, I agreed at once,' he said. 'It's a strict rule as you know not to use the pass key except in an emergency, but under the circumstances . . .'

'*Mum!*' Carol's face brightened. 'Why didn't you say so? That's all right, Mr Timson, don't worry about it.'

It was only while she was going up in the lift that Carol had time to wonder why her mother was here. Was something wrong? It wasn't like her simply to get on a train and arrive without warning. Why hadn't she telephoned? By the time she reached her floor and put her key into the lock she had convinced herself that something must have happened.

Opening the door, she called, 'Mum! I'm home. Why didn't you . . . ?'

She stopped abruptly as a woman appeared in the doorway of the living room. She was a well-built woman of about fifty, with heavily applied make-up and brassily bleached hair. She wore a black suit with shiny red plastic shoes and handbag. As far as Carol knew, she had never set eyes on her before.

'Who are you?' she asked. 'And what are you doing in my flat?'

The woman smiled. 'Like I told the bloke downstairs, love, I'm your mother,' she said calmly. 'The name's Sally Tyler.'

Chapter Fifteen

For what seemed like an eternity Carol stood staring at the woman.

'You – can't be,' she said at last. 'Sally Tyler is dead. She was killed in an air raid more than twenty years ago.'

The woman chuckled. 'That's funny,' she said. 'I don't feel dead!'

Very carefully Carol removed her key and closed the front door behind her, using the time to try and assess the situation. The woman had to be an imposter. It was some kind of trick. Did she have an accomplice? Was he hiding in the flat somewhere, waiting to attack and rob her? Should she call the caretaker?

Sensing her rising fear, the woman said, 'It's all right, there's no need to be afraid, dear. I can prove who I am. Why don't you come in and sit down? You look quite shocked. You can make me a cup of tea if you like. I've travelled a long way today – just to see you.'

Glad of the opportunity to sort out her thoughts, Carol went into the kitchen and put the kettle on. She was still finding it impossible to take in what the woman was telling her. It was too bizarre. Hadn't Eve confessed to causing this woman's death – insisting that she'd seen her topple over the parapet of the bridge that night in the raid? Hadn't Grandad identified the broken body under the bridge as Sally's?' Her first impulse was to blurt all this out, but as she went about the mundane task of spooning tea into the pot and setting out cups something told her to be cautious; let the woman tell her story first.

Better to hear what she had to say without giving too much away.

She carried the tray into the living room and set it down on the coffee table. The woman who called herself Sally Tyler had made herself at home on the settee, where she sat with her feet up, the cheap red shoes discarded on the carpet.

'Hope you don't mind, dear,' she said. 'Only I'm not strong. I have to be careful not to get too tired, and as I said, I've travelled all the way down from Manchester today.' She tapped her chest. 'Heart, you know.' She pointed to the cups. 'Milk and two sugars if you don't mind, dear, and not too strong.'

Carol poured the tea, wondering at the woman's unruffled manner. Surely one should be a little nervous, meeting for the first time the child one had given away more then twenty years ago?

'Perhaps you'd like to tell me why you've waited all this time to make yourself known to me?' she said, passing the cup.

The woman smiled. 'I didn't feel entitled, dear. You were adopted after all, weren't you?'

Carol paused. Everyone knew that she was adopted by now after the magazine and newspaper articles. 'But you feel entitled now?'

The woman smiled. 'You're a grown woman now, aren't you? When you get to know me, you can make up your own mind.'

'You said you could prove your identity,' Carol said. 'I'm sure you'll forgive me for asking, but . . .'

'Of course.' The woman reached for her handbag. 'It's only natural.' Rummaging in the red plastic bag she produced a dog-eared envelope and drew out a handful of snapshots. Swinging her legs to the floor, she passed them one by one to Carol. 'That's me holding you as a baby,'

494

she said. 'I know I've changed.' She laughed. 'Well, haven't we all? The date's on the back.'

Carol turned the snapshot over. Scrawled on the reverse side in pencil were the words, *Me and Carol Louise. Brook's Lane. October 1942.* She bit her lip. The snapshot was blurred and faded. The fairhaired girl holding the baby might have been anyone. And the writing on the back could have been added at any time.

As though reading her thoughts, the woman handed her the next one. 'This is you on your first Christmas at Eve's mum's house. And here's one of you with Eve herself.'

Carol stared at the photograph, which was unmistakably of Eve. There was an identical one in the album at home. She looked up at the woman, dazed. 'I don't understand. What happened?' she asked. 'Everyone thought you'd been killed.'

The woman drank the last of her tea and passed her cup to Carol. 'It's a long story, dear. Any more tea in the pot? My mouth's as dry as dust – that's part of the condition, you know.' Again she tapped her chest. She watched as Carol poured the tea.

'Tell you the truth, that night's still a bit of a blur. I seem to remember I was going somewhere though I can't remember where. There was a raid going on. All I remember is the loud bang and then, much later, finding myself lying under a heap of rubble. Somehow I dragged myself out and managed to crawl a little way. Then I must have passed out and the next thing I knew I was in the hospital. Trouble was, when they asked me who I was I couldn't remember a thing. Didn't even know my own name. I didn't have a handbag or anything on me that could identify me. All I had were these few snaps in the pocket of my skirt.' She shook her head. 'It wasn't unusual. There were a lot like me during the war, dear, people who lost everything and had to start again.'

'You must have found it hard,' Carol said.

'I did. I had a bad head wound among other injuries so they transferred me to a hospital in Manchester. And when I was better I stayed on there and got a job as a ward maid at the hospital. They'd given me a new name by then – Mary Smith. That's what I've been called ever since.'

'So when did your memory come back?' Carol asked.

'It took years. It happened gradually, bit by bit. To start with I kept getting flashes and then it would be gone again. I remembered a little house and a factory, then I worked out that the house was in Brook's Lane and knew I'd lived there when that snap was taken. I remembered someone called Eve and recognised her from another of the photos. Then I remembered that you were my baby and how I'd left you behind that night. That was a terrible memory, dear. Cried myself to sleep that night, I can tell you, knowing I'd left a baby behind somewhere.'

Carol looked at the woman's simpering face and tried hard to feel something for her. Surely if she was her birth mother there should be some kind of affinity – an emotional pull? There was none. She felt nothing. 'But you didn't come back to find out what had happened to me,' she said.

The woman shrugged. 'Didn't know where to come. Brook's Lane could have been anywhere. I couldn't remember the name of the town. Then one day it came back to me that I'd had a husband – but that you weren't his child. That was when I knew I'd given you away and the rest came back quite quickly after that. I remembered Eve saying she'd adopt you. Kept on and on about it, she did, and I realised that by that time you would have been going to school. You'd have been settled in with the couple who had adopted you – with Eve and Jack

Kenning, because I knew Eve would never have let anyone else have you. It didn't seem right or fair to try and find you again then.'

'Did you look for your husband?' Carol asked. 'Or the man who – the man who was my father?'

The woman shook her head. 'No. Maybe I was wrong, but I felt it would only cause more pain to look for my Dave. By that time he might well have married again. As for the other bloke, I only remembered him vaguely and I had an idea at the back of my mind that he was married already when I knew him. So it stands to reason he wouldn't have been too pleased to see me again after all those years, would he?'

'When did you remember your real name?' Carol asked.

'Not for a long time. But even when I did, I never told anyone. After all, I've been Mary Smith for more years than I was Sally Tyler.'

'Didn't you have a family somewhere?'

The woman nodded. 'In Portsmouth. I did inquire about them. All dead, wiped out in a raid in '43. So . . . you're my only living relative in all the world, Carol. I can't tell you how thrilled and proud I was when I read all about you in that magazine. And now I'm here. That's all that matters, isn't it? Back with my girl again.'

The prickling of suspicion was as tangible to Carol as insects crawling on her skin. There was something repellent about this woman who claimed to be her mother. She badly wanted her to be an imposter, yet she knew so much that only Sally Tyler could know. 'Why are you here now, after all these years?' she asked.

'I just wanted to see you before it was too late, dear, that's all. I know I can't take any credit for what you've made of yourself, but you're still my daughter; my own flesh and blood. When you've been through what I've been through and you're all alone in the world, that counts for a lot. Maybe you'll understand one of these days, dear. You start thinking about the past a lot when you're getting on a bit and your health starts failing.' She hauled herself to her feet. 'Well, better be going now. Wouldn't do to outstay my welcome.' She reached down to retrieve her shoes, forcing her feet into them with difficulty. 'That's another symptom of my condition,' she said, looking up at Carol. 'Angina makes your feet swell up something horrible.'

It was with relief that Carol went with her into the corridor and pressed the lift button. Looking at the woman's swollen feet bulging out of the cheap red shoes she felt a sudden pang of guilt. 'It's a bit of a walk to the station,' she said. 'Would you like me to drive you there?'

'No, it's all right. I've taken a room quite near here as a matter of fact. Bit expensive, but what does money matter when it's for your own flesh and blood?' As the lift purred to a halt and the doors opened she turned to look at Carol's surprised face. 'Well, there was nothing to keep me in Manchester and I suddenly thought, why don't I go and live near my Carol Louise for a bit? After all, I'm getting on now. If I don't see something of her soon it might be too late, what with my poor old ticker being what it is.'

For a long time after the lift doors closed on Mary Smith, Carol stood staring at them, stunned by the bizarre events of the past hour. It was like a dream, her true mother suddenly arriving out of the blue after all these years. How had she survived the fall from the bridge? And – more to the point – was her real motive for coming here now just, as she had said, one of nostalgia?

When the lift stopped and the doors opened again she jumped violently, and when Steven stepped out of the lift she threw herself into his arms.

'Steven! Oh, thank goodness!'

He smiled down, arms going around her. 'Well, this is a nice welcome! What can I have done to deserve this?'

Taking his hand, she drew him into the flat and closed the door. 'Steven, something has happened,' she told him. 'Something really weird.'

Carefully she recounted the visit from the woman who claimed to be her mother, and her extraordinary story.

'Are you doubtful about her?' he asked.

Carol nodded slowly. 'Somehow I can't bring myself to believe that this woman *is* Sally Tyler,' she said. 'Even though she seems to know so much about what happened.'

'What reason did she give for coming to meet you after all this time?'

'Just that she's older now and in poor health. She said she wanted to meet me before it was too late.' Carol shivered and Steven slipped an arm around her.

'What is it?'

'I don't know,' she said. 'It's just that there's something about her . . . I don't like her, Steven.'

'Nothing says you have to like her, Carrie, even if she is your real mother.'

'It's not just that, though. There's something about her that gives me the creeps.' She looked up at him. 'She's moved into a room near here. She obviously intends to come back. I don't know how to deal with it. What should I do, Steven?'

'Tell her she isn't welcome,' he said simply. 'If what she says is true, she deserted you years ago so she has no claims on you now. If she's lying and you're convinced of it you could even threaten her with the police.' He looked at her doubtful face. 'You don't have to see her again if you don't want to either, Carrie. She had no right to come here without warning in the first place.'

She was silent, fearing that there were deeper implications in all this. Maybe some that she had yet to discover. Steven knew nothing about Eve's confession, for instance, the guilt she had nursed all these years. She looked at him. 'Can you stay tonight? I don't want to be here alone.'

'That woman has really spooked you, hasn't she?' He laughed. 'Of course I'll stay, darling. And you know you can move into the flat any time you want to get away from here. There's nothing I want more than to have you with me all the time.'

He'd brought a tape of a new arrangement of one of the big numbers from the show and they went through it together, working until after midnight. Carol was still sitting with the manuscript on her knees, going over the words, when Steven took it from her and put a mug of hot chocolate into her hands.

'Time you wound down, my love,' he said. 'After next week, when you've finished at Riverside, we have a busy schedule for you.'

Carol knew that already the dancers were rehearsing at one venue, the singers at another, whilst the principal actors were busy learning lines and rehearsing songs. In two weeks' time they would be ready to move into the theatre and begin putting the show together.

When she'd finished the drink he took the mug from her, lifted her into his arms and carried her to the bedroom. Undressing her tenderly, he drew back the covers and pushed her gently into bed, pulling the covers up around her.

'You know, I still can't believe all this is really happening,' he told her a few minutes later as he joined her and gathered her into his arms. 'I've loved you almost since I can remember, but I'd got used to believing we were destined never to be together.'

'Oh, Steven.' She shivered with delight at the intimate

thrill of his skin against hers, returning his kisses and allowing her own desire full rein as their excitement gave way to passion. Every time they made love he seemed to take her to new heights and just for a while the feeling of foreboding Mary Smith's visit had instilled in her was forgotten. But later, as Steven slept and she lay with her head on his chest, his steady heartbeat matching her own, the ominous feeling she had felt in Mary Smith's presence crept back. Going over the visit again, she felt her heartbeat quicken and, with a sensation of urgency, made up her mind that after next week she would pack and move up to Steven's Mayfair flat. She would give her forwarding address only where it was absolutely necessary and she would ask the caretaker of the flats not to disclose it to anyone. It seemed deceitful and unkind if the woman really were her natural mother to turn her back on her, but she couldn't help it. The idea of seeing Mary Smith again made her shudder.

They wakened at first light and made love again and it was only as they lay, limbs entwined, languorously waiting for their heartbeats to slow, that Steven raised himself on one elbow to look down at her.

'Darling, I'm afraid I have to go away for a couple of weeks,' he said.

She opened her eyes and looked up at him. 'Oh, Steven, no! Where? And when?'

He lifted a strand of her hair and wound it between his fingers. 'Today. I'm sorry, darling,' he said regretfully. 'I'm booked on a flight this evening. I was going to tell you last night, but I couldn't when you were so upset.'

'Where are you going? And why, so near to rehearsals starting properly?'

'Lang has someone he wants me to meet in the States. It could mean a big recording contract. I've done as much as I can on the music for the time being so it seemed like a good opportunity. Before we start rehearsing in earnest. They want me to go down to California to this chap's home so I could be away for about ten days. No more.' He hugged her close. 'I hate the idea of leaving you behind, darling, especially just now when this problem has cropped up. If it hadn't been that this was your last week with *Queen's* you could have come with me.'

'Oh, Steven!' She buried her face in the hollow of his shoulder. 'Do you really have to go? Couldn't it wait until the week after?'

'Afraid not, love. Lang is off to Australia the week after.' He kissed her. 'I promise I'll get back as soon as I can and I'll write every day. Proper letters this time, not scrappy postcards.'

'You know you won't,' she said. 'You won't have time by the sound of it.'

'I will, I promise. Look, I'll leave you the keys and you can move into the flat whenever you like. Or why not go and stay with Rissa and Fred? I know they'd love to have you.'

The week that followed was so busy that Carol scarcely had time to worry about Steven's absence, or to think about Mary Smith's visit. Rehearsals for the finale of her big storyline had been intensive. Gareth wanted as much tension and emotion as possible and almost every character in the show was involved. After her final episode of *Queen's* went out on Thursday evening the atmosphere was euphoric. Carol had invited all of the cast and crew to a farewell party at the flat. It was a tight squeeze as they all gathered, and although there was a feeling of relief and a job well done, the atmosphere also held a tinge of sadness.

By the time the last straggler had left, with fond farewells and promises to keep in touch, Carol felt drained. Madge stayed behind to help her clear up the used glasses, plates and overflowing ashtrays.

'I'm going to miss you,' she said as they washed up together. 'And I have an idea that Gareth will miss you too.' She glanced at Carol out of the corner of her eye. 'Correct me if I'm wrong but I've always had the impression that he had a bit of a thing for you.'

Carol shrugged noncommittally. 'He's been a good friend to me, but there's never been anything deeper between us.'

Madge smiled. 'Poor Gareth. I've known him for years and he's never had any luck with his love life.'

As Carol came down to see her into a taxi later, Madge said, 'You're doing the right thing, love. I can't wait to see you in the new show. I just know you're going to be a big success.'

Carol hugged her. 'I'll make sure you get some tickets as soon as they're available,' she promised.

She was waving the taxi out of sight when a figure suddenly emerged from the shadows, making her start.

'Who's that?'

'It's all right, dear. It's only me.'

Carol was dismayed to see Mary Smith step forward. 'How long have you been there?'

'About two hours. I came up once, but I could see you had some kind of a do going on and I didn't want to intrude.' She shivered. 'None too warm out here at this time of night. Could I come up, dear? Just for a warm before I start walking back.'

Carol hesitated. Her practical side urged her to refuse, after all, the woman was here uninvited. But her conscience would not allow her to turn away an elderly person with a heart complaint, especially one who claimed to be her mother. 'All right,' she said reluctantly. 'Just for a few minutes. I'll make you a drink. Only I am rather tired.'

As they went up in the lift Mary prattled on about *Queen's Square*.

'I saw the last show tonight. So sad and beautiful,' she said. 'The way you died! So realistic. It brought a lump to my throat, honestly.'

'I'm glad you enjoyed it,' Carol said crisply.

In the flat she put the kettle on and made the woman a cup of drinking chocolate. 'I'll run you home when you've had that,' she said as she handed it to her.

Mary Smith regarded her over the rim of the mug as she sipped her chocolate. 'Will you be staying on here now that you've left the telly?'

'I may move nearer the West End,' Carol said guardedly. 'I'll have to see.'

' 'Cause I wouldn't like us to lose touch now that we've found each other.' The woman sipped her drink thoughtfully. 'That would never do, would it?' She paused. 'There was another reason I came to London, apart from seeing you.'

'Was there?'

'Yes. I told you about my heart trouble, didn't I, dear?'

'Yes, you did.'

'Well – I don't want you to worry, but my doctor told me a month ago that if things go on the way they are, I don't have long to live.' The woman paused again, glancing at Carol to assess, her reaction to this piece of news. 'No more than a year at the most,' she went on. 'That is, unless I have this operation. It's called a heart by-pass and there's this fantastic heart surgeon in Harley Street who would do it for me right away.' She drained the last of her chocolate and handed the mug back to Carol, looking her straight in the eye. 'If I had the money to pay for it, of course.'

'I see.'

Mary Smith took a handkerchief out of her handbag

and dabbed at her mouth. 'I thought if I came down to London, I could get a job – cleaning, bar work, anything – so's to save up enough to pay for the operation. Only as far as I can see there's nothing I could do that would pay enough. Rents are too high, never mind food and everything. I can see now that it'd take me years to save enough money.' When Carol made no reply she snuffled dejectedly into her handkerchief. 'So – seems like I'll have to go home again and just – just make the most of the time I've got left.'

'Have you seen this heart specialist?' Carol asked.

The woman shook her head. 'I've been up and seen where his consulting rooms are,' she said. 'But even the fee for a consultation is more than I've got. I made inquiries.'

Suddenly the reason Mary Smith – or Sally Tyler – had come looking for her was very clear and Carol knew in that moment that everything depended on her next words. She stood up, steeling herself.

'I'm sorry, but if you've come to ask me to help, the answer has to be no.'

'You mean, you'd see your own mother die for the want of a few pounds?' The woman was suddenly on her feet. 'Earning all you must be earning too!'

'You're not my mother,' Carol said firmly. 'I've never set eyes on you before. My mother is Eve Kenning.'

'*Oh?*' The whining voice was suddenly strident. 'Well, we'll see about that. Maybe I should go and see Eve myself.' Her eyes glittered dangerously as she stood up. 'Maybe *she* can persuade you where your duty lies.' She took a step towards Carol. 'Eve made up her mind to get you off me, you know, even before you were born. I tried hard to keep you but I was only a young war widow and she was too strong for me.' Her eyes bored into Carol's. 'Oh, yes, there's a lot I could tell about Eve Kenning if I'd

505

a mind to. I could tell a powerful story if I was forced. One that would shock a few people. I don't doubt that the newspapers would be interested in it,' specially with you being so popular and well known. I daresay *they'd* pay me enough money to have the op. Not that I want to go to those lengths, of course,' she added slyly. 'Put your career in danger that would, wouldn't it? Still, if you won't give me a helping hand, I'd have no choice. I mean, it's my *life* that's at stake here.'

Carols blood had turned to ice. God alone knew what a visit from this woman would do to Eve. The shock would kill her. Whatever it took she would not put her through any more trauma. She'd keep it from her at all costs. The woman was watching her through shrewd eyes as though she could see right inside her head to her thoughts.

'What about that feller of yours?' she said suddenly. 'Steven Manson, the swanky composer? I daresay he'd let you have the money for your poor mum's operation if you was to ask him.' She leered at Carol. 'You know how to get what you want from a bloke, don't you? Besides, he wouldn't want the papers full of unpleasant stories about his leading lady, would he? Not when he . . .'

'*Get out!*' Carol interrupted. 'I don't believe you're who you claim to be. How dare you come here blackmailing me like this? Get out before I call the police!'

'Blackmail's not a nice word,' the woman snapped, eyes flashing dangerously. 'All I'm asking is a little compassion for the woman who gave you birth. I just want enough money to give me back my health again. Any human being would do that for another, surely? Somehow I don't think the public would be very sympathetic to you for refusing me that.'

'I don't care. I want to you leave – now!'

'*No!*' Mary Smith stood her ground. No longer the wheedling, pathetic figure she had been half an hour previously, she was now strong and menacing. 'Call the police if you want to. Make me prove I'm Sally Tyler, your real mother. But only do it if you want to involve Eve Kenning, because she's at the bottom of this. She's got a lot to answer for.' She narrowed her eyes at Carol. 'Make sure you know what you're starting before you go out on that particular limb, my lady. If you open that can of worms, you might live to regret it.'

It was very clear to Carol that the woman meant business. For a long moment she stared at her, at a loss, then she said, 'How much do you want?'

'That's more like it.' The woman's eyes glittered. 'Twenty thousand should do it.'

Carol gasped. '*Twenty thousand!* I haven't got that kind of money. Anyway, surely even a Harley Street surgeon doesn't cost that much?'

The woman shrugged. 'They do. You can check if you like. If you haven't got it you can pay me half now and half later.'

'I haven't said I'll pay you anything,' Carol said. 'Anyway, I need time to think about all this.'

The woman picked up her handbag. 'You can have until this time tomorrow. After that I go to Eve.' She walked to the door and then turned. 'I'm sure you're a sensible girl, Carol. You don't want to see your family plastered all over the papers, do you? 'Cause I've got a whale of a story to tell once I do start, believe me!'

Michael was in bed and fast asleep when the telephone wakened him. Pulling on his dressing gown, he lurched out into the hall to answer it.

'Hello, Michael Robson?'

'*Mike!* Thank God. I thought you'd never answer. It's Carol.'

'Never answer?' He was squinting at his watch. 'You do

know it's almost three o'clock in the morning, don't you?'

'Is it? I'm sorry, Mike. I wouldn't have bothered you at this time but I need your help. Something really awful has happened. Listen, I'm driving up there tomorrow morning but I don't want Mum to know. At least, not until I've had time to talk to you.'

'What is it, Carol? What's happened?'

'I can't tell you over the phone. Can I meet you somewhere for lunch?'

'You'd better come straight to the flat. We'll have more privacy here. I'll leave the key for you at the tobacconist's shop next door and come back from the office at about one o'clock and meet you. Okay?'

'Okay, Mike. And thanks. You're a real friend.'

It was almost twelve when Carol arrived at Michael's flat the following morning. She collected the key from the tobacconist's shop and let herself in. The flat was neat and tidy as always and as she stood in the living room memories flooded back. The last time she had been here was the dreadful morning when Rose had barged in and accused her of seducing her son. Carol would never forget that morning. It was the worst humiliation she had ever suffered and although she was happy that Eve and her sister were reconciled, it would be a long time before she could forgive her aunt for the things she had said.

Looking at her watch, she saw that there was still almost an hour before she could expect Michael. She decided to go out and shop for the makings of lunch. She would have a meal ready for him when he arrived. It was the least she could do and it would be something with which to occupy herself.

At a newly opened supermarket nearby she bought steak and salad vegetables, fruit and cheese, and hurried back to the flat with her purchases.

As promised, Mike arrived at one o'clock and sniffed as he closed the front door behind him. Putting his head round the kitchen door he grinned at Carol, nodding appreciatively to see the table laid with a gingham cloth.

'That looks nice. I didn't expect this.'

'It helped pass the time for me,' she told him. 'I needed something to do to keep my mind off things.'

'That bad, eh?'

'I'm afraid so.'

As they ate Carol unfolded the story of her encounter with the woman claiming to be Sally Tyler.

'And you think she's an imposter?'

'I *want* to think she is,' Carol told him. 'But how does she know so much about what happened all those years ago?'

Michael nodded, pulling a notebook out of his pocket. 'You say her name is now Mary Smith and she's from Manchester?'

'Yes. And she had photographs of me as a baby. Mum too. One of them even had the address of the house where I was born scribbled on the back.'

'Right.' Michael took out a pencil. 'Tell me everything she told you. As much detail as you can remember. I've got a friend in the CID. I'm sure he'll do a discreet check for me if I ask him.'

Carol looked at him in alarm. 'The police! I don't know . . .'

'It'll be off the record.'

'But *Smith*, Mike. Mary Smith. There must be dozens of them.'

'Not ones with amnesia who had a head injury treated and stayed on as a domestic worker at the hospital.' He completed his notes and closed the notebook. Looking up at her with a smile he said, 'Try not to worry about it too much.'

'But I do worry about it. If I don't give her the money

509

and she goes to the papers . . .' She bit her lip in anguish. 'Maybe I should just give up my part in the show and disappear before Steven gets back?'

'Now you're panicking. You're not even to think of doing anything like that.' He smiled gently at her. 'You'd really do it, wouldn't you? You'd actually make a sacrifice like that – for him.'

She nodded. 'Yes, Mike. I couldn't let anything like this ruin his chance of success.'

He sighed wistfully. 'I wonder if he has any idea what a lucky chap he is? But nothing anywhere near as drastic as that is going to happen. I'm sure of it. So . . .' He slipped the notebook into his pocket. 'What are you going to do now?'

She shrugged. 'I don't know. If I stay here I'll have to see Mum. And I don't know how I'll keep all this from her. She always knows when I'm worried about something. If I go back to Richmond that woman will be back again. She said she'd give me until tonight to make up my mind.'

'I think you should have the support of your family,' Michael said decisively. 'It isn't right that you should bear this alone. I'll come and pick you up at your mother's later and we'll go and see Gran and Granddad.'

She tried to argue but he wouldn't listen and at two o'clock they walked back into the town centre together.

Michael had already telephoned his grandparents and told them to expect Eve and Carol that evening. He had also outlined the reason for their visit, so when they arrived at about seven that evening they were prepared. The news of Sally Tyler's apparent reappearance had come as a shock to Eve. She sat white-faced on the settee in Freda's front room, clutching Carol's hand as Michael filled in the details for his grandparents.

'Now here's the good news,' he said, looking round. 'My friend in the CID has been checking with a colleague in Manchester. Between them they've rung all the hospitals in the area and none of them has any record of an amnesia patient, subsequently called Mary Smith, who worked for them as a ward maid at that time. It looks very much as though this woman's story is pure fantasy.'

Freda was shaking her head. 'Things were so confused during the war, Michael. The records could have been lost in the bombing. It doesn't necessarily prove anything.'

Albert was of a different opinion. 'I'd stake my life on it that was Sally's body I identified,' he said. 'I'd seen her in that red coat so many times. It was like her trade mark.' He stroked his chin thoughtfully. 'Of course, the poor girl's injuries did make it almost impossible . . .' He broke off, glancing at Eve as she stifled a sob. Then suddenly he got to his feet.

'My God! Why didn't I think of it before?' Without another word he hurried out of the room. The others looked at each other.

'Now what?' Freda asked no one in particular.

They sat in silence, glancing apprehensively at each other as Albert's footsteps could be heard walking about overhead. Drawers could be heard opening and the thud of cupboard doors. Finally they heard him coming back downstairs and looked expectantly towards the door.

He came into the room holding something in his closed hand, but for the moment he did not disclose it.

'I helped the ambulance man get her on to the stretcher,' he told them. 'They were understaffed that night – short-handed with the raid. I'd already told him I knew the girl and as they were putting her into the ambulance I mentioned that she had a baby and how lucky it was that the child wasn't with her. That was when he gave me this.' He opened his hand and revealed a cheap metal charm bracelet. 'He took it from her wrist and gave it to me – said to give it to the child. I can still remember his words: "*We're not supposed to do this but it'll be all the poor little perisher will have to remember her mum by, by the looks of it.*" ' He looked at Eve. 'I remembered you giving her that bracelet that first Christmas she was with you,' he said. 'She showed it to everyone. That and the silk stockings she'd got from a girl at the factory.'

'Why didn't you ever say anything about it?' Freda asked.

He shook his head. 'It didn't seem right. Eve adopted Carol and we knew, didn't we, that she never told the kiddie she was adopted; not for years. How could I give the child a bracelet that had belonged to her mother? Then when she did know it seemed too late somehow. Anyway . . .' He glanced at Eve. 'I wasn't sure you'd have liked it.' He lifted his shoulders. 'The bracelet wasn't valuable so I just shoved it in a box with a lot of other junk and forgot all about it – till now.'

Michael nodded. 'I think we've got all the proof we need.' He took the bracelet from Albert and stood up. 'I've arranged to have tomorrow off. I'll come back to Richmond with you tomorrow morning, Carol, and we'll face this woman together. I've got my own ideas about who's at the bottom of this.'

When Carol opened the door of her flat the following morning there was a letter from Steven lying on the mat. Her heart lifted as soon as she saw the American stamp. Michael saw it too and smiled at her.

'That should make your day. Shall I go and put the kettle on for coffee while you read it?'

Steven wrote that the recording contract was in the bag and that he would be coming home as soon as he could

512

reasonably get away. He said that the Californian scenery was wonderful but that he loved and missed her. As letters go it was far from eloquent, but Carol didn't care. He'd written as he'd promised her and just holding his letter in her hand made her feel stronger. When Michael came back with two cups of coffee, he found her smiling.

'That's better. First time I've seen you smile in the last two days.' He put the cups down on the table and nodded towards the letter in her hand. 'I take it that's from Steven. Okay, is he?'

'He's fine. No letter writer but at least he's made the effort.' She laughed. 'If he could write me a piece of music I think I'd do better.'

Michael smiled. 'He's done more than that, hasn't he? Written you a whole show!'

When she'd finished her coffee Carol went down to the caretaker's office to see if there were any messages.

'That woman called last night,' he told her. 'The one who made out she was your mother the other day. Cheek! Said she'd be back this morning. I warned her you might not be here but it didn't seem to put her off. She said if you weren't, she'd wait.' He looked at her curiously. 'If you want me to send her packing you've only got to tip me the wink. I'm used to dealing with unwanted callers.'

'No. It's all right, Mr Timson. I've got my cousin with me so I'm not alone. We'll deal with her.'

She was washing the coffee cups at the sink when her doorbell rang. Michael appeared in the doorway, his finger to his lips.

'I'll slip into your bedroom and listen from there, if you don't mind.'

'OK.'

'Right. Don't let her know you're not alone. Just let her talk.'

When Carol opened the door the woman strode past

her into the flat. 'Where the hell have you been?' she demanded. 'I told you I'd give you till last night. Think yourself lucky I haven't already been to the papers.'

'I had an appointment,' Carol told her. 'You didn't give me your address so how could I let you know?'

'Well, you're here now and it's just as well for you that you are!' The woman eyed her up and down. 'So – what have you got to say for yourself? Made up your mind, have you?'

'Yes.' Carol told her. 'And the answer is still no.'

'Right. Then I shall have no option but to go to the newspapers,' the woman said. 'You're going to be sorry when my story hits the headlines, miss. But believe me, Eve Kenning is going to be even more sorry.'

'*Oh, and just why is that?*' Michael walked into the room and faced the woman.

Her jaw dropped and her face reddened. 'Who's he?'

'This is Mr Robson, my solicitor,' Carol told her.

'I've been making a few inquiries, Mrs Smith, or whatever your real name is,' Michael said. 'And I'm not satisfied that you're telling the truth.'

'I *am*!' The woman stood her ground defiantly.

'Then you won't mind answering one or two questions, will you?'

'What questions?' The expression on the woman's face seemed less confident as she looked from one of them to the other. 'What are you saying?'

'It's what you are saying that interests me.' Michael took a step towards her. His hand was in his pocket and suddenly he drew out something small and shiny and held it up in front of her. 'What can you tell me about this?' he asked her.

She stared at the cheap little charm bracelet, tarnished from the years it had lain forgotten in the box of junk. 'I . . .' She swallowed. 'It's a bracelet – isn't it?'

Michael nodded. 'It is indeed. But whose bracelet is it?'

The woman's eyes darted shiftily between Carol and Michael, trying frantically to guess at the answer they required. 'If this is some sort of trick . . .' she said at last. 'If you're trying to make me say something so's you can say I'm lying . . .'

'No tricks,' Michael said calmly. 'All I'm asking is that you tell me the truth, Miss Smith – or whatever your name is. It's very simple to tell the truth. Maybe you should try it.' He held the bracelet out in front of the woman. 'Here, take it. Have a good look. It isn't valuable but I think you'll agree that it's quite distinctive. Just tell me – *whose bracelet is it?*'

The woman withdrew her hand, refusing to touch the bracelet. She was backing away now, her face suddenly pale.

'Very well, I'll tell you, shall I?' Michael said. 'This bracelet belonged to Sally Tyler. It was a present, given to her by her friend, Eve Kenning. And it was removed from her body as she lay dead under the railway bridge on the night she was killed in an air raid. It was given to Eve Kenning's father to pass on to Sally's baby daughter. We have several witnesses to bear this out.' He put the bracelet back into his pocket and looked intently at the woman. 'I think that proves conclusively that you are an imposter, Miss Smith. Do you have any idea of the penalty for impersonating a deceased person? Not to mention blackmail.'

The woman turned and made a dash for the door, but Michael was there before her, barring her way. 'I wouldn't bother trying to run away,' he said. 'I've already sent for the police and they're on their way. And the caretaker of the flats has been alerted to prevent you from leaving the building.'

'I never wanted to do this,' the woman spluttered, eyes

wide with panic. 'I – I *told* him! I said it wouldn't work. If I go down I'm taking him with me! I swear I will.'

'*Him?*' Michael's eyebrows rose. 'Who are we talking about?'

'Eddie Wilson!' The woman spat the name out as though it had a bitter taste. 'I used to work for him before he went bust. All this was his idea. It was him gave me the photos and told me all the stuff about Sally Tyler and the baby she had. *His baby!*' She glanced at Carol. 'He said that he had a good idea Eve Kenning pushed Sally off the bridge too, but I never believed that and I always knew he had no proof.' Her mouth twisted into a bitter sneer. 'Greedy bastard was only going to give me twenty percent of what we got anyway. He said he wanted what he was entitled to, him being *her* father.' She nodded towards Carol. 'I must've been mad – taking all the risk for that. Conniving little rat!'

'If you take my advice, you'll tell everything to the police,' Michael said. 'You might find that if you're honest with them it will go in your favour.' He looked at Carol's white face and stepped forward, taking Mary Smith by the arm. 'I think perhaps we should wait for them downstairs.'

Carol busied herself in the kitchen making a snack meal when they'd gone. She would not let herself think about the scene she had just witnessed. The one thing she was grateful for was that Eve hadn't been subjected to the sordid spectacle. The meal was on the table before she heard the flat door open and close again and knew with relief that Michael was back.

'It's over,' he said, coming into the kitchen. 'They've taken her to the police station. There's a warrant out for Wilson's arrest and I'm afraid you'll have to go to the station and make a statement later.' Seeing her dismayed expression he slipped an arm around her shoulders. 'Don't worry. I'll come with you.'

'Do you think he'll make accusations to the police about Mum?' she asked anxiously.

He shook his head. 'I don't think even Eddie Wilson would be foolhardy enough to add slander to the charges already stacked against him.' He glanced at the chicken salad Carol had prepared. 'This looks good. We'll go along and get it over with after we've eaten, shall we?'

'All right. And thanks, Mike.' She looked at him. 'I'll tell you one thing. You're not driving all the way home again tonight,' she said. 'You must stay here.'

He nodded. 'You're right. It could be quite late by the time the formalities have been gone through. I'll check into an hotel.'

'You will not! I've got a perfectly good guest room. It's the least I can do for you, Mike. I don't know what I'd have done without you tonight.'

He grinned. 'Just glad I was here to help,' he said modestly.

Michael had been asleep for some time when he was wakened by the sound of someone persistently ringing the doorbell. It had been late by the time they returned from the police station. He had helped Carol make up the bed in the guest room for him and had fallen asleep the moment his head had touched the pillow. Knowing how exhausted she had been, he hastily pulled on his trousers. Swearing softly to himself as he padded to the door on bare feet, he reflected it was a good thing he was here. Anyone who came calling at this time of night was surely up to no good. He opened the door and peered out into the dimly lit hallway.

'Carrie?' a man's voice said quietly. 'Sorry to wake you, darling, I forgot my key. My flight was delayed and I couldn't wait till morning to see . . .' He pushed in through the door at the moment that Michael switched on the hall light. The two men stared, each of them as surprised as the other.

Steven found his voice first. 'Robson! What the hell are you doing here – at this time of night?'

Michael held a finger to his lips. 'Shh. Carol's asleep. It's a long story. You'd better come into the kitchen.'

Carol woke at eight o'clock and lay quietly for a few moments as the events of the previous day gradually filtered back to her. The nightmare was over. With Eddie Wilson finally behind bars, Eve could relax. Mike had assured her that all Eddie's devious methods of extracting money over the years would be taken into consideration and he would be punished accordingly. Eve would never recover the money but at least she would be allowed to live in peace from now on.

Suddenly wide awake, Carol remembered that Mike was still here. He had to drive back to Northampton this morning. She must get up and make him some breakfast.

In the kitchen she took eggs and bacon from the fridge and filled the kettle, cutting bread for toast while it boiled. When the tea was made she poured a cup and carried it through to the guest room. Tapping on the door, she opened it and peered in.

'Mike, I've brought you some tea. It's time you were thinking of getting up if you're going to drive . . . *Oh!*' The dark head on the pillow turned, she met a pair of familiar eyes. Not Mike's eyes but Steven's.

'Where's Mike?' she asked, nonplussed.

'You might well ask!' Steven sat up. 'I got in late last night and came straight here. And what do I find? A half-naked man in my fiancee's flat at two o'clock in the morning! A good thing I was brought up to be broad-minded!' He took the cup from her hands and pulled her down beside him. 'Come here, woman. And take that guilty look off your face, or I'll start to believe the worst!'

'Steven!' She threw her arms around him. 'Oh, darling, it's so good to see you. You'll never believe what's been happening . . .'

'I will, Mike told me everything over a stiff whisky when I arrived in the small hours. I can't tell you how terrible I felt, imagining you coping with all that on your own.'

She hugged him close. 'Never mind. It's over now, thank God. And you're home. That's all that really matters.' She looked round. 'Where is Mike, by the way?'

'He left at first light – wanted to get back in time for work.' Steven kissed her. 'So, now that I'm here, how about welcoming me home properly?'

On the opening night of *Eve's Daughter* Carol was at the theatre early. Ridiculously early by some standards. But she had her own special reasons, which she didn't expect anyone else to understand fully. No one could really know what this evening meant to her. Her whole future career hung in the balance. For her, tonight was make or break time.

Steven and Freddie had already had a hit. If *Eve's Daughter* were to fail they could write another show on the strength of their first success, and cast it with a new star. She was known only for playing Harriet Jameson in *Queen's Square*. If the public didn't like her in this, her first major part – if they thought she had grown too ambitious, too big for her boots – it would be back to TV commercials and walk-ons. What Marty teasingly called the 'Fluffy Chicken Syndrome'.

Backstage everything was quiet as she walked through the dusty corridors, with only a buzz of conversation and the occasional laugh from behind the closed doors of the prop room where the stage hands were having a well-deserved tea break. She walked softly past, feeling like the theatre ghost, then up the short staircase to the stage area, avoiding the lighting cables that snaked over the floor.

The stage had already been set and dressed for Act One, a beautiful set designed by a talented young newcomer called Peter Redmond who had also designed the Regency costumes. Carol stood centre stage and tried to imagine herself making her first entrance. Her heart gave a sudden lurch when she realised that in a little over one hour she would be doing just that. She looked out into the darkened auditorium and tried to imagine the rows of empty seats filled with people, all eagerly anticipating an evening's entertainment.

Peering out at what would shortly be a sea of faces she felt a sudden upsurge of panic. Could she really do it? Was she ready? Would she forget her lines or the words of a song at some crucial moment, with all her family and friends watching? Eve and the rest of the family would be there in the front row of the stalls; Zelda and Marty; Kitty – even Janet and Geoff, down from Edinburgh especially for the occasion. Not to mention the whole cast and crew of *Queen's Square*, including Gareth – dear Gareth to whom she owed so much – out there waiting expectantly. All the people who had faith in her. Her dressing-table mirror was bordered with the telegrams of good luck she had received from each and every one of them. She shuddered with sheer terror at the thought of their embarrassment and disappointment if she were to let them down.

The dress rehearsal yesterday had been a nightmare. Some scenes had been repeated again and again before Graham Lang had been even moderately satisfied. Steven too had been tough and exacting, taking her through her solo numbers over and over. She pictured him shaking his head exasperatedly and raking his hand through his hair till it stood on end. But the older members of the cast had seemed unperturbed. 'Bad dress rehearsal – successful first night' was the old maxim. She only hoped they were right on this occasion.

Her mind drifted back over the past weeks. In spite of her promise to move in with Steven she had remained in her flat in Richmond. After a long and arduous day rehearsing they had each needed their own space. Steven often had work to do, and she had felt a need to get right away from the theatre, back to Richmond where she found the river soothing and relaxing. Occasionally at weekends Steven had joined her there, but as the weeks went by there had been a lot of revisions for him to do and additional material for him and Freddie to write, so more often than not he had stayed in town where he had his piano.

She had worried a lot about Eve over the weeks, and the effect the case against Eddie Wilson and his accomplice would have on her. But when he came to trial Eddie had done the decent thing for once in his life and pleaded guilty, saving Eve the trauma of giving evidence in court. Oddly enough, the dramatic appearance of the woman who'd claimed to be Sally Tyler seemed to have laid poor Sally's ghost for Eve once and for all. She was finally convinced she hadn't been solely responsible for the girl's death. And now, with Eddie safely behind bars, the anxiety had gone from her face and she looked ten years younger. Carol had promised herself that if the show were a success she would help Eve to retire and buy a nice little house with a garden again. Maybe there would even be one in Sunnyside Crescent where she and Dad had been so happy.

Carol cleared her throat and tried the first few notes of her opening song, her voice tremulous at first; then, as Steven's beautiful melody took shape like the opening of a lovely flower, her confidence blossomed too and she suddenly knew with blinding certainty that everything would be all right. She *could* do it. With Freddie's brilliant lyrics and Steven's wonderful music to back her up, how could she fail?

Straightening her shoulders she finished the song, and as the last pure note died away she heard the sound of clapping. Spinning round she saw Steven standing in the wings, his face wreathed in smiles.

'Put it over like that tonight and you'll have them eating out of your hand,' he said, coming forward to give her a reassuring hug. 'Now I think you should go and make a start on getting ready.' He kissed her. 'Break a leg, my darling.'

She traced his mouth with one finger. 'Break a leg,' she whispered. She made to walk away but he held on to her hand, drawing her back to him.

'Carrie. We are still all right, aren't we?'

She looked into his eyes and saw the uncertainty there. 'Darling, of course. Why?'

He shrugged. 'It's just – over these past weeks we've both been preoccupied. We've worked so hard and there's been so much to do. Our relationship has been very much on hold. Sometimes I've been – well, tough with you at rehearsals. I wondered . . .'

She reached up to touch his face. 'I love you,' she told him quietly. 'I always have and I always will. No matter what. I couldn't have done any of this without you. I need you like I need the air I breathe. Does that answer your question?'

He kissed her hard and held her close for a long moment. 'It'll do for now,' he said huskily.

As the curtain came down the applause was thunderous. The audience was euphoric. The music had been memorable, the acting superb and the production spectacular. As the curtain rose on the cast, assembled for their final call, the applause mounted to a crescendo.

In her place at centre stage Carol looked piquant and spirited in her high-waisted scarlet gown. Her blonde hair was dressed in an elaborate upswept tumble of ringlets and her eyes shone mischievously as she curtsied to the audience. Her leading man, Martin Whitaker, took her hand and raised her up, leading her towards the footlights in acknowledgement of the applause. But the audience refused to let her go until, at a signal from Steven, the orchestra struck up the introduction to the number which had stopped the show in the last act. Carol and Martin sang their duet, *A Love Like Ours*. Their voices blended perfectly. The tender words and melody touched the hearts of everyone afresh and there were several pairs of unashamedly misty eyes in the front row.

Finally the applause ceased and the curtain came down for the last time. The audience, still chattering animatedly about the success of the evening, began to leave the theatre. After so much tension and anxiety, the opening night was over.

Still centre stage as the rest of the cast filtered away to their dressing rooms, Carol stood as though in a daze, hardly able to believe that the evening was over – that they had actually played their opening night, not only successfully but to acclaim.

'You were wonderful, Carol,' Steven whispered, coming up behind her. 'Just perfect. But then the audience has already told you that. How does it feel to be a star?'

She shivered a little and held up two pairs of crossed fingers. 'I'll wait to see what the critics say before I let myself be drawn on that,' she said cautiously.

Hand in hand they walked back to her dressing room. Once inside Steven closed the door and took her in his arms. 'In a few minutes the place will be thick with well-wishers,' he said. 'Everyone will want to see you and hug you and tell you how wonderful you are. But just for a moment I want you all to myself.'

'Me too.' She held him close, closing her eyes and savouring the moment. 'Oh, Steven, is it really over? Was it really as good as I think?'

'Better! Tonight was – *is* something very special,' he said. 'Something we'll always remember. A night to bore the pants off our grandchildren with in the years to come.' He looked down at her. 'And for that reason I want us to have something else to remember it by.' He took a tiny box from his pocket. 'It seems years ago that I asked you to marry me. Sometimes during rehearsals I wondered if you'd even speak to me again, but earlier tonight you said you still loved me so I took a chance that it just might still be on.'

He opened the box. Inside, nestling against a white satin lining, was the loveliest diamond solitaire ring Carol had ever seen. Her eyes shone as he took it from the box and slipped it on to her finger.

'This is for Eve's daughter,' he said, raising her hand to his lips. 'Soon, if I'm lucky, to be my wife.' As he kissed her there came a pounding on the door and he smiled. 'What did I tell you?' he said. 'They're here, your adoring public.'

'Then they're going to have to wait, aren't they?' she said, drawing his head down for a kiss. 'It's not every day a girl gets engaged.'

'No,' he said, firmly disengaging her arms from his neck. 'Tonight you belong to them. Tonight you're Eve's Daughter, that's only fair. Steven and Carol Manson have the rest of their lives. All the time in the world.'